Stepping Out of Line

Stepping Out of Line

A Workbook on Lesbianism and Feminism

by Nym Hughes, Yvonne Johnson and Yvette Perreault

Press Gang Publishers

Canadian Cataloguing in Publication Data

Hughes, Nym, 1952-
   Stepping out of line
   Bibliography: p.
   ISBN 0-88974-016-X
   1. Lesbianism.   2. Lesbianism - Congresses —
Handbooks, manuals, etc.   3. Feminism.
I. Johnson, Yvonne, 1947-   II. Perreault,
Yvette, 1953-   III. Title.
HQ75.5.H83   306.7'663   C82-091154-2

Cover design by Pat Smith, based on a photograph by Marion Barling
Photo credits: Sarah Davidson pp. 9 & 67, Sarah White p. 147

First impression August 1984

Typeset by Makara Cooperative and Baseline Type & Graphics Cooperative
Printed by the collective labour of Press Gang Printers
Bound in Canada
Published by Press Gang Publishers, 603 Powell St., Vancouver B.C. V6A 1H2

Contents

Acknowledgements

Stepping Out of Line is, in a very real way, the creation of the lesbian and feminist communities of British Columbia. Almost a hundred women, most — but not all — lesbians, have directly contributed stories, artwork, resources and production skills. Many, many more have provided ideas, inspiration and support.

This book exists because of the women who participated in the workshops. For your honesty, courage and challenge, we thank you. The women of the B.C. Federation of Women deserve particular credit for affirming our belief that it possible for women to organize across the miles and the differences that divide us.

Members of the Lesbian Caucus of the B.C.F.W. developed the original workshop and shaped the political analysis and strategies which underlie this book. We are especially indebted to Esther Phillips for nurturing our political vision and assisting with the early workshops.

Another crucial figure in our work is a woman we have never met, Charlotte Bunch. Her writings have been a major source of analytical tools.

The financial generosity of a number of groups and individuals helped make this book possible. Thanks to the B.C.F.W., Ellen and Reg Dixon, Donna Kennerby, the Victoria lesbian community, Vancouver Rape Relief and many others.

The women whose stories, interviews, articles, photographs and drawings make up this book are too numerous to name individually here. We celebrate your clarity and creativity. We do, however, want to list those who have made contributions through work on editing, typing, research, layout or typesetting. Our appreciation to Eve Zaremba, Ottie Lockie, Penny Goldsmith, Mary Schendlinger, Jan Lancaster, Suzanne Perreault, Nicole Kennedy, Jill Kelly, Teresa Reimer, Janie Debo, Oksana Peczeniuk, Esther Shannon, Sarah White, Jean Burgess, Makara , Janet Morgan and Baseline Type & Graphics Cooperative, especially Aryn.

We particularly want to thank Billie Carroll for her work in designing *The Workshop* section, and Dorothy Elias for a splendid job of graphics coordination.

The women of Press Gang, past and present, have been consistent supporters of this book for what seems like endless years. Thanks especially to Barbara Kuhne of the Publishing collective. From the Printing collective, our thanks to Lynn Giraud (the printer), Paula Clancy, Rachel Epstein, Carmen Metcalfe, Marilyn Fuchs, Dorothy Elias, Chantale Laplante, Alex Maas, Helen Krayenhoff and the other women who work to keep the presses going.

Finally, there are two women without whom, as the saying goes. . . Sarah Davidson has been involved with *Stepping Out of Line* for three years. She has contributed the benefits of her extensive experience in printing and book production, her living room for meetings, her editing and design skills, her unerring nose for illogical argument and a calming influence on our wilder flights of fancy. Nancy Pollak was an avid supporter of this book while she worked at Press Gang and has for the past two years devoted her considerable energies and talents to dragging an unfinished manuscript and a perfectionist collective into the light of print. She has done absolutely everything, but most notably editing, research for the resources, the design of *Organizing for Change,* paste-up and general production work. Despite the difficulties of book production and life, it was a joy to work with both Sarah and Nancy. Thanks and congrats!

Our households, friends, lovers, children, co-workers, animals and gardens deserve credit for their patience with our unending obsession with 'the book.' Siobhan, in particular, put up with rowdy meetings in her house every week for three years and entertained us with glimpses of the real world.

To all of you, for your patience and support and belief that this was worthwhile work, our gratitude and our love.

Introduction

The beginnings of this book can be traced to the 1974 founding convention of the British Columbia Federation of Women, an umbrella organization of feminist groups. A number of lesbians in attendance were disturbed that proposed policy made no reference to the discrimination faced by lesbians or, in fact, to the existence of lesbians at all. A week later, 30 lesbians met on a Sunday morning at the Vancouver Ms. Club — a women's bar of that era — and formed a Lesbian Caucus of the B.C.F.W. We were energetic, idealistic and convinced that we had merely to bring this regrettable oversight in policy to the attention of our sisters and the women's movement in B.C. would unite in revolutionary fervour and we would achieve the liberation of all women almost immediately.

It is taking somewhat longer than we anticipated.

That was a rough year for the Caucus. For many of us, the struggle within B.C.F.W. over public support for lesbian rights was our first real confrontation with homophobia. We didn't understand the fear and hostility that faced us. Our Caucus became smaller — and very efficient. Through reading and talking, we came to understand that lesbians are subjected to an extreme level of social harassment and ridicule because we do not conform to the accepted standards of female behaviour. We saw that compulsory (institutionalized) heterosexuality tied women to a sexual division of labour, the nuclear family and emotional and financial dependence on a man — and was *not* in women's best interests. We considered an understanding of lesbianism to be crucial to any feminist theory and we became, through necessity, skillful and articulate proponents of our point of view.

At the second annual B.C.F.W. convention, we introduced explicit and militant policy on lesbian rights. It was passed, and a Rights of Lesbians Subcommittee became a formal part of the organization.

We, however, wanted more than words on a piece of paper. We wanted every women in B.C.F.W. to understand why it was so important for feminists to support lesbianism and we wanted every women's group in B.C. to be prepared to speak out publicly on lesbian rights in their community. So we developed and began offering a consciousness-raising workshop to member groups. We did workshops in big cities and in small northern towns, for 5 women and for 50 women, at conferences and at festivals. Eight of us did over thirty-five workshops.

By 1978 we knew we had a workshop that was extremely effective in encouraging personal and political growth. The three of us listed as authors of *Stepping Out of Line* decided to write up the workshop material and pass it along to other B.C. lesbians. A 30-page gestetnered booklet was what we had in mind. Because we lived far apart and worked full-time, we would meet only one weekend a month to plan and divide up the writing and researching and interviewing, and then to edit and rewrite. After a year, we gave our notes to a friend to type. She brought it back and said, "Why don't you try and get this published? Women outside of B.C. would find it useful too."

Hesitantly, we approached our local feminist press. Yes, they would be interested. We spent another year adding material, then gave the manuscript to friends for editorial comment. They returned it saying, "We think you should leave out the feminism. Just do a straightforward little book on doing a workshop to educate the public about lesbianism."

We went into crisis. We had, by this time, five years of workshop experience. Individually, we had been working openly as lesbians in drop-ins, feminist coalitions, conferences, rape crisis centres and community groups. We had five more years of living in a lesbian community. We saw ourselves as feminists who were doing political work using lesbianism as the focus. We knew the workshop was effective in educating non-lesbians, but it was equally effective in giving *all* women a way of beginning to make sense of their lives, of seeing the connections between individual experiences and the social structures of oppression, of creating a vision of the world-as-we-would-like-it-to-be. We couldn't leave out the feminism. In fact, we decided to make our political perspective even more explicit and enlarge the book to include a wider range of organizing ideas.

So we rewrote again. And every time we did a workshop or went to a conference or resolved a personal crisis there would be new insights that simply *had* to be included.

By 1981 it was clear that we had enough material for a huge book and we had to just *stop*. Yes, the book was incomplete. We didn't have stories from lesbians about the impact of racism and disability and other forms of oppression on their lives. We had no stories from lesbians who lived closeted and isolated. We didn't really know the *best* way to organize, the *perfect* tactics, the *magic* answer. Nevertheless, we gave the manuscript to our editors. It came right back, "Unclear...repetitive...*rewrite.*" We began to wonder how anyone ever got a book finished. We had dreams about swords hanging over our heads and would wonder in our bleaker moments whether, by the time the book was out, it would be of any use to anyone at all.

But here it is. And we do think *Stepping Out of Line* will be useful and, given the present blight of right-wing thought and governments, even timely. It contains the *Workshop Script,* notes on setting up and running workshops and, in *Organizing for Change,* stories, analyses and resources collected from many women on topics ranging from planning a conference to personal relationships.

Stepping Out of Line represents a distillation of the political work of hundreds of B.C. lesbians. It is intended to de-mystify feminism, lesbianism and political activism. We offer this book as a starting point for lesbians wanting to change the condition of our lives and our society, for activists wanting to gain support for lesbian rights within their workplaces, political circles and community groups, for any woman who wants to know how lesbianism and feminism connect.

Use this book. Disagree with us, change what you want to change, find your own materials. Develop your own strategies, set your own goals, organize in ways that make sense where and how you live. Today, more than ever, there is a need for strong lesbian voices, for accessible lesbian communities, for a vigourous lesbian presence within all progressive movements, for alliances, for lesbian organizations to fight those who would force us back into silence and powerlessness.

Every time we say lesbian out-loud we challenge the assumption that heterosexuality is the only option for women. We assert *all* women's right to choice and self-determination.

— Nym Hughes, Yvonne Johnson, Yvette Perreault

The Workshop

What follows is the *Script* for a two-day workshop on lesbianism and feminism. This section has been structured to be useful to workshop facilitators. In the left-hand columns you will find notes: explanations of the purpose of each part, directions for exercises and tips on possible responses. In the right-hand columns is a word-for-word script that could be read aloud by facilitators. These are the words we use; there are lots of blank spaces for you to add your variations and additional materials.

The next section — *Notes to Facilitators* — suggests how to set up a facilitating collective and how to go about organizing and giving workshops.

This workshop has been an extremely powerful consciousness-raising experience for many groups of women. Reading the *Script* on your own certainly can be interesting, but it isn't the same as participating in the workshop. We suggest you and some friends read and experience it together...

Introducing the Workshop

Purpose   To present the purpose of the workshop by outlining the expectations of the facilitators and getting agreement on the agenda; to establish agreements about smoking and break times. To establish an atmosphere of safety and support within the group by reaching agreements about confidentiality, taking risks, staying with the group, giving and receiving emotional support, clearing up disagreements between us and working with our differences.

The women have arrived, everyone is seated in a circle. The agenda is printed up and put up on a wall so women can see what is being proposed for the day or two days. The facilitators are ready to begin. Start with introductions. Each facilitator tells about herself—her name and her background and work so the women can get a sense of her as a woman, not just a "lesbian" or a "group facilitator". Give a brief explanation of the intent of the workshop, the purpose and expectations, such as:

Lesbians have long been silenced. Slowly more and more of us are taking risks and saying out loud *we exist and we have the right to exist without oppression.* We recognize that coming to terms with lesbianism is a process that means emotional conflict for every woman, whether or not she identifies as a lesbian. This workshop is meant for all women. We are going to examine what we have been taught about lesbianism, what it really does mean to love women and act on that love. We will be situating our understanding of lesbianism within a feminist context, a perspective on how the world functions based on our shared experience as women. In order to begin to create a world where freedom exists for all people, the world of our feminist vision, we begin with ourselves. Change occurs when we begin to act on what we know. Going through the process of this workshop means opening ourselves to change, opening ourselves to action.

Go over the proposed agenda for the entire workshop and get agreement on what work will be accomplished in what time frame. This gives women an opportunity to make an informed decision about whether or not the workshop looks like it will meet their needs, and gives them a chance to suggest additions which would better fulfill their expectations.

Ask the group for a quick decision about smoking in the workshop. Suggest a break every hour and a half, or one cigarette at a time.

Once agreement has been reached about the agenda and break times, facilitators encourage each woman to take responsibility for making sure the group sticks to those decisions.

Agreements   Acknowledge that change is a process, that the workshop may be quite emotional and even painful for some women. Make a clear statement about how agreements for working together help establish the safety necessary for women to give and get the support they need to go through a difficult process:

It is useful to have the following agreements written in point form on sheets of paper on the wall. They will serve as a good reminder throughout the workshop of what women have agreed to do to make the workshop as safe, yet as productive and intense as possible. We suggest pausing after each point to make sure you do have agreement.

It should take no more than twenty minutes or so to go through these agreements. If it appears to be taking much longer, or if there is serious disagreement about any of the points, suggest moving on, and coming back to the points of contention after the Round.

Maintaining confidentiality is the first agreement.

Be certain you get agreement from each woman before you go on. We would ask a woman to leave the workshop if she were not prepared to make this commitment.

We have found that the most powerful and productive workshops take place when women have the safety necessary to expose their ideas and emotions and when women have a way to constructively challenge mistakes, ideas, behaviours, and suggest new ones. Women make dramatic changes in their lives when the problems being raised and dealt with are real ones chosen by the women themselves, and when women leave this workshop prepared to take action. But, no one will risk talking openly and honestly about their lives and ideas and feelings if they do not believe that the workshop is a safe place.

Trust and intimacy can be created in a workshop. We are asking you to make some very specific agreements that will help everyone here take responsibility for their own learning and for caring for each other. These are agreements that increase the possibility for each of you to decide to say a little more than you thought you would. We know that this results in a dynamic process of new learning. We want you to be willing to expose contradictions and conflicts and make commitments to individual change and to integrating that understanding into your actions in the world.

We want all of you here to agree not to talk outside of this workshop about specific information you hear about another woman's life. It is necessary for all of us to have a place to talk openly without fear of punishment or reprisal. There are very real consequences for women who are rumoured to be lesbians: loss of jobs, social scorn, custody cases, verbal and physical harassment. There may also be women here who have very painful experiences they believe will be valuable information for all of us to have, yet they do not want their stories to become community gossip, taken out of context. We want to offer each of you an opportunity to discuss these experiences, with the knowledge that it remains in this room.

Expressing emotions. The breaking of silence on lesbianism can be very intense. Facilitators must be prepared to offer the emotional support necessary to take the group from individual emotional reactions into the social and political meanings of our experiences.

We encourage you to *feel* during this workshop. We give you plenty of opportunities for acknowledging your emotions and figuring out what ideas and experiences they are connected to, and then planning how we can together change such painful realities. We want you to come forward and tell us how you are feeling. We ask that you be prepared to work with us as we create new understandings of where those emotions come from. So, it's more than okay to be sad, to be frightened, to be angry. We want you to talk about your feelings as well as your ideas. Sitting on any intense emotions, choking back your tears will only keep you distant and prevent you from fully participating in this process. You will not be left alone with your feelings. We have enough time and resources here to at least begin to clarify emotional responses.

Staying with the group. Women may react with fear once they are informed that the workshop can be intense. Encourage women to ask for what they need in order to stay open and fully present for the workshop. Struggle is a necessary part of growth and change, and as facilitators, we do have some responsibility for providing what women may need in order to go through this process.

We want each of you to make a commitment to stay with the group, not to just get up and leave at some point. We want you to inform the group if you are having trouble, to ask for what you need to continue, or to ask for a short break if you want to get some air or to spend some time alone.

We all have a responsibility to care for each other. There is enough experience with emotional work, and enough genuine caring for the women in this room, enough time and feminist analysis to make it possible for all of us to get what we need.

Taking Risks. For the workshop to be more than an information session, women must make a choice to expose their own emotions and ideas about lesbianism and feminism. By being honest and direct, no woman will be left carrying unvoiced fears, questions, doubts or criticisms which interfere with her participation in the workshop and her willingness to take action once she leaves the workshop.

Each of you knows your own limits. You will actively make choices about how much to tell us. We want to encourage you to push those limits a bit, to express more of your ideas and feelings than you normally would. You will know when you have gone far enough. We believe that our very best growth and movement takes place when we learn something new, not just with our heads, but with our guts and feelings as well. This workshop is not only to get new information about lesbianism, it is to further your own growth and self-discovery, and to create real change in the world. We want you to challenge yourself, to challenge each other, and to challenge us.

It is important that women in the workshop establish how they will deal with conflict and disagreement. Let women know that they can talk openly about their fears and disagreements and ask that the women in the group be prepared to hear and help resolve conflicts raised during the workshop. It is also useful for women who experience a particular or additional form of oppression in the world to have a way to get together and talk in a manner which is safe for them and doesn't disrupt the group. Some formalized ways of accomplishing these goals are to use the Constructive Criticism/ Paranoid Fantasy agreements and to set up caucuses within the workshop group. If you decide to ask women to use these particular forms, now is the time to explain how they work, using hand-outs or wall charts. Women may have different or better ways of working, so be open to suggestions. (The essential point is to provide women with a clear way of approaching difficult and emotional issues in a manner which promotes unity within the group.)

Exercise: A Round   Facilitators are to participate in the Round as well, giving additional information to that presented in the Introduction.

In order for all of us to get a sense of each other and to begin speaking out loud in the group, we're going to have a Round. Each woman speaks in turn, without being interrupted or responded to. In this round each woman tells about herself: her name, her life situation, any past or present political work, her emotional state at the moment, her hopes, expectations and fears about the workshop.

When the Round is over, facilitators may respond to women who have expressed fears or a need for further explanations about the workshop. If specific fears are expressed during the Round, facilitators ask the woman what she needs in order to participate fully in the workshop. If a woman says: *I'm really afraid. I want to start crying and I don't know why,* facilitators can reassure her that the workshop will open up emotional areas: *We do have ways to safely express feelings, to find out a new context which will help make sense of those feelings and give us new ideas about how to act.*

Facilitators also sum up the tone or themes from the Round, e.g. *There are many women here today who are very nervous about talking about lesbianism. We hope we will all understand more about why this is so, and work towards being more confident about what we have to say by the end of the workshop.*

Facilitators point out the stated and apparent differences between the women there, e.g. *Many of us here are lesbians, some women are heterosexual, some of us are mothers, others are not, some of us come from wealthy backgrounds, others are very poor. We are confident that we can be open about these differences, respectful of each other and argue in healthy, productive ways.*

Before proceeding, check with women to see if they are ready to move on. Ask if there are any fears or criticisms which need to be talked about now to enable a woman to be fully present for the next section.

Remembering

Purpose   To encourage women to begin to remember what they have learned about lesbianism; to acknowledge their emotional reactions and to talk about the attitudes toward lesbianism that they have accepted on both conscious and subconscious levels. This section gives a sense of the diversity in the attitudes and realities of the women present.

Facilitators should introduce the section by talking about how all of us in this culture have consciously or unconsciously absorbed ideas about lesbianism. Say that it is important for us to remember what we were taught and how; to acknowledge the emotions we have had and do have.

Exercise   Say that the exercise is private and that women will be asked afterwards to share only as much as they want. One facilitator should read the exercise while the others participate. Ask the women to close their eyes, take deep breaths and sit in a comfortable relaxed position or lie down. Facilitator speaks very slowly, pausing between sections to allow the participants time to remember.

This is a guided memory exercise

lesbian . . . notice the feeling inside you . . .
just feel it

what images come to mind when you hear the word?

lesbian . . . there are no right or wrong pictures —just your experience

think back . . . when was the first time you heard the word lesbian?

how did you learn about lesbianism? . . . what did you learn? . . .

when was the first time you had contact with a lesbian?

what was your reaction? . . . how did you know she was a lesbian?

now . . . what is a lesbian? how can you tell if a woman is a lesbian? . . . what do lesbians look like? . . . how do lesbians live? . . . what jobs do they do? . . . how do they spend their time? . . . how do lesbians make love?

are the images in your mind of old or young women? . . . children? . . . remember these images.

notice the emotions/feelings inside you

now think about or imagine **you** being a lesbian . . . think about your life . . . think about telling your friends you are a lesbian . . . telling your children . . . think about how you would tell your co-workers . . . think about being in public with a woman lover? . . . would your relationship with your friends change?

notice the emotions . . . what do you feel when you think about living as a lesbian? . . . is there anxiety, fear, pleasure?

take a few moments to think and feel and when you are ready open your eyes and we can talk about what happened.

One of the facilitators can start the sharing round; this encourages other women to speak. Often a great deal of emotion is expressed.

Facilitators should make sure that each woman gets a chance to speak if she wishes to and receives whatever support is most useful for her. A woman who is having difficulty speaking out can be encouraged by being asked what she needs in order to participate. Sometimes women ask to be held, or request a short break, or need to have their ideas and past experiences reflected to them in a new context.

Defining

Purpose   To give a working definition of the word lesbian as we use it in the workshop and to introduce the concept of lesbian oppression.

Present a definition of lesbian, such as:

Open discussion for a few minutes to get general agreement on a definition. Because our understanding of lesbianism is based on our lives and experiences, heterosexual women are not in a position to create a definition.

Summarize some of the themes of the *Remembering* round and say that although our conditioning is important we cannot base our actions on lies and myths. Say that the purpose of this section is to explore the reality of living as a lesbian in this culture.

What is a lesbian? What is the reality of lesbianism? **A lesbian is a woman who prefers other women on many levels: sexually, emotionally, intellectually, psychically—and who defines herself as a lesbian.**

Photo/ Billie Carroll

The oppression of lesbians shows itself in many ways. We are invisible and invalidated. History books make no mention of us and we rarely appear in fiction. When we are mentioned in psychology or sociology we are seen as deviant or ill. The media rarely gives us images of ourselves, and never positive images. A young woman growing up has no chance of receiving the information and support she needs in order to see lesbianism as a valid life choice.

Images of lesbianism in both popular myth and "objective" scholarly writings portray us as evil, sick, shameful, corrupting and exclusively sexual. We are presented to ourselves—even from the more "enlightened" viewpoints—as tragically doomed to promiscuity, alcohol, drugs, violence, despair and suicide.

These stereotypical images reinforce negative attitudes about lesbianism and sanction more overt forms of oppression. Lesbians are ridiculed, harassed, verbally abused, shunned. As lesbians we are disowned by our families, evicted from our homes, fired from our jobs. Our children are taken from us. We are sexually assaulted, beaten, raped. We are incarcerated in mental hospitals and psychiatric institutions.

We have no civil rights and consequently no legal recourse. Legally, custody cases must be decided "in the best interests of the child" but lesbian mothers are usually automatically branded as "unfit" regardless of the quality of the mother/child relationship. Choice of sexual orientation is not protected by Human Rights codes (except in Québec) or most union contracts, so there is no protection against discrimination in housing or employment.

For more specifics on oppression, facilitators should use examples from the *Remembering* exercises or from your lives. Refer to *Organizing for Change* too!

Choosing

Purpose   To present a positive image of lesbianism; to introduce the concept of lesbianism as choosing to love women, including ourselves.

Discuss why women would make the choice to love women. Facilitators may speak from their own lives, their own positive experiences, their experiences of loving women, coming-out, working on relationships, growing. Alternately the facilitator may read:

Why then would any woman choose a lifestyle that involved all this? Living as a lesbian means for many of us living an integration between our beliefs and our lives. It means questioning all our concepts of what women **are**, in all areas of our lives. It means that it is all right to be tough and assertive and physically strong and it is also all right to be soft and to be cuddled.

It means that we have a chance to be both nurturing and nurtured, giver and taker, lover and loved. It means feeling part of a great wave of woman energy and woman effort that is creating a better way of relating to each other, our children and the earth. And for many of us it means that we fell in love with a woman and that the strength and joy and the pain and the growing of that loving was the impetus to define ourselves as lesbians.

As lesbians we've always known that each of us is a woman who does not want to depend upon a man, who does not even want to de-

pend upon another woman—upon other women, yes, in a collective sense, for that's part of our dream too, but not upon any other single person; either consciously or unconsciously we've known that we have in us a strong tendency toward self-governance and a desire to give up the habit of governing other people; we've always known that we want our own self-reliance and that of every woman. For sure, very few, if any of us, have gotten "there" yet: that's no surprise in a society where we've been brought up to hate our selfs. Even to begin to love our self, a woman, in a woman-hating society that has tens of thousands of years of history behind its misogyny is quite an accomplishment.

—Sally Miller Gearhart, *Our Right to Love*

Facilitators invite discussion about the material presented. Ask women why they have chosen to be either lesbians or heterosexual. Check how women are doing emotionally, intellectually. See whether a break is needed now.

Myths

Purpose   To examine the social and cultural stereotypes of lesbianism and to explore the reasons for the existence of the myths. Women have a chance to listen to information which will help to make sense of the emotions we have all just shared. The myths section is funny in parts and the laughter is a welcome release.

The myth section should be presented in a dramatized manner emphasizing humour and absurdity. Facilitators can alternate myth/reply. It is important that the myths be presented in such a way that women do not think they are being judged or stupid for believing such things. We have found that facilitators talking about "when we believed that lesbians would attack us in washrooms etc." is useful in allowing women to hear that we all believed these lies and that we have to work hard to stop believing them. If the workshop is with women who identify as lesbians it is even more important for facilitators to stress that all of us—even lesbians!—were taught these myths and that in our daily lives we often act out beliefs that we think we don't have.

This section examines the myths about lesbianism we have all been brought up to believe. These myths are lies and these lies have a purpose.

Myth: An invented story or belief which has no basis in fact and is used to explain phenomena; it reflects the attitudes and values held and passed on by the majority of people in a culture.

All of us who grow up in this culture absorb myths about lesbians; they give us a stereotypical image of what lesbians look like, how lesbians live, what jobs lesbians hold, what lesbians think and feel, how and with whom lesbians make love, etc. We learn that any woman who even partially fits this stereotype must be a lesbian, and conversely that in order to be a lesbian you **must** fit this stereotype. We learn that lesbian behaviour is shameful and that lesbians are to be ridiculed and despised. These myths depict lesbians as "different", "other" or "not women". It is obvious that unacceptable female behaviour constitutes lesbian behaviour. It is harder to realize that with these myths we are also being taught what constitutes **acceptable** female behaviour.

1   The first group of myths has to do with male/female roles:

Lesbians are not real women   This myth is the primary one. It is the underlying myth about lesbians. It is the basis for many of the other myths. What is it really saying? Obviously lesbians are biologically female, but are not seen as "real" women. A "real" woman must therefore be both biologically female **and** be fulfilling the traditional female role.

Lesbians want to be men   If lesbians are not "real" women they must want to be men. After all, what else is there?

Lesbians are male egos trapped in a female body; lesbians are victims of a confused sexual identity.   Who is confused? Lesbians are women who love women.

Lesbians hate children; lesbians are afraid of childbirth.   Since all "real" women love, nurture and want children and since lesbians are not "real" women, lesbians must hate children . . .

Lesbians wear male clothing   What is male clothing? It is sturdy, warm, and comfortable. Female clothing, on the other hand, is usually expensive and flimsy. It is designed to decorate

Facilitators can alternate reading each myth.

us rather than to protect us from the elements or allow us to move freely in it. In fact, a lot of women's clothing is physically restraining and even crippling—girdles, high heels, straight skirts, tight pants, and so on. The major reason to differentiate between male and female clothing is to make the difference between men and women readily apparent. If men and women looked the same how would men know who to treat as inferior? Hire as secretaries? Rape?

Lesbians are all truck drivers   Absurd. There aren't enough trucks for all of us.

2   The second group of myths involves causes and explanations.

> Lesbianism is a phase.
> Lesbianism is a sickness (communicable).
> Lesbianism is a crime against nature.
> Lesbianism is a sin against God.
> Lesbianism is caused by a genetic defect.
> Lesbians are ugly.
> Lesbians are afraid of men.
> Lesbians hate men.
> Lesbians can't get a man.
> Lesbians have had bad experiences with men (what woman hasn't).
> Lesbians just need a good fuck.
> Lesbianism is a way of avoiding the responsibility of a family.
> Lesbianism is caused by a dominant mother/passive father.
> Lesbianism is caused by a dominant father/passive mother.
> Lesbianism is caused by too close an identification with the father.
> Lesbianism is caused by too close an identification with the mother.
> Lesbianism is caused by the lack of a father.
> Lesbianism is caused by the lack of a mother.
> Lesbianism is caused by excessive sibling rivalry/jealousy.
> Lesbianism is caused by too much aloneness/no sibling interaction.
> Lesbianism is caused by . . .
> Seems miraculous that anyone ever grows up heterosexual!

These myths all assume that heterosexuality is the only normal, natural preordained way for mature, responsible human beings to live. Anything else (lesbianism) is unnatural and sick, and must have a cause.

There is no historical, anthropological, sociological, psychological, or biological basis for this "assumption of heterosexuality". In our society, heterosexuality is a cultural institution which forms the foundation for social patterns of marriage, childrearing, division of labour and property inheritance. Heterosexuality ordains the social roles of both men and women.

Thus, homosexuality is not merely a choice of life styles, but a rejection of and a threat to male/female roles.

Homosexuality must, therefore, have a cause so it can be explained away, cured, punished, discouraged . . .

3   The third group of myths has to do with sex.

Lesbians are obsessed with sex.
Lesbians are washroom invaders.
Lesbians are wildly promiscuous.
Lesbians lie in wait for any woman who crosses their path.
Lesbians are child molesters.
Lesbians are insanely jealous and possessive and beat each other up with broken beer bottles.
Lesbians lead romantic sexual lives and do nothing but make love.
Lesbians want the pleasures of sexual activity without paying the price. (Right!)

These myths tell us absolutely nothing about lesbians; in fact, they are out and out lies. They do tell us, however, how our society defines women. Women serve two major functions: as sexual objects for men and to nurture and serve men and children. Since lesbians are not "real" women and so do not exist in order to nurture and serve men and children, lesbians must be primarily and obsessively sexual. These myths reflect a fear of women's sexuality—voracious, all-consuming and destructive unless controlled and defined by a man.

These myths also connect lesbianism with aggression, domination and sexuality linked with violence. In reality, it is men in our culture who commit these acts. It is men who molest, assault and rape. Creating a myth of lesbians as more to be feared than men keeps women from identifying as or with lesbians, keeps women dependent upon male "protection", and keeps women securely confined to their traditional female roles. Finally, these myths devalue lesbianism by defining it as irresponsible, solely pleasure-oriented and trivial.

4 There is a fourth group of myths which has become increasingly popular in recent years. These are myths which are often heard in "enlightened" circles such as the women's movement or other political groups. We have used the example of the women's movement throughout but the myths live in any movement for social change.

Lesbians are infiltrating the movement. It's not fair, lesbians have nothing to do but go to meetings. They do not have responsibilities like families, children, like the rest of us. Lesbians are only a constituency in cities. There are no rural lesbians and lesbians are a small minority.

These statements reinforce the image of lesbians as "not women" or "different than women". They are untrue. We live everywhere, and not only do we have the responsibilities of families, children, and jobs, but like all single mothers and women, we often bear our responsibilities totally alone. Our oppression is a more obvious and extreme form of the oppression faced by all women in our society. The women's movement is our movement and our politics and perspective are valuable. We have a right to visibility, recognition and support by any group committed to social change.

There should be no labels, we are all human beings. Lesbianism is personal, not political. We have already dealt with lesbianism and we are all personally comfortable with lesbians; now it is time to go on to something else. Lesbianism is a red herring.
Some human beings have more power and privilege than other human beings. Labels like: "Woman", "Indian", "Lesbian" reflect real

differences in opportunity and privilege. When all people are equal in privilege and power we can discard labels. Labels are not just names: there is the implicit threat of punishment attached. As long as lesbians can be fired from their jobs, lose their children, lose friends and families, lack the protection of even basic civil rights, then lesbianism is not just a personal matter.

As long as any woman can suffer political and legal harassment for how she chooses to live her life, then every woman faces the same threat.

Rural women, native women, poor women . . . are not ready to talk about or deal with lesbianism.

This myth is prevalent among people who are neither rural, native, nor poor. It reinforces the myth that all lesbians are urban, white and middle class.

This myth also defines lesbianism as an issue of relevance to a privileged class only. It denies the realities of women who do not share that experience of privilege, and who are lesbians. This is condescending and arrogant and ignores the fact that individual women in this culture face many forms of oppression—class, race and age, for example. A lesbian who is non-white and/or working class and/or living outside of the lesbian community of the cities experiences oppression in a different way. The myth relieves us of our responsibility as oppressors.

We will alienate too many women/people if we talk about "that". Yes, lesbianism is a crucial, valid, feminist issue and we are concerned but there is too much at stake right now. We may lose our funding. There is a right wing backlash and we will lose our credibility.
Fear of losing social credibility has operated to keep lesbians in the women's movement invisible and silent, and keeps the women's movement as a whole from "going too far". Lesbians face personal, legal, economic and political discrimination every day and in every area of our lives. Anyone openly supporting lesbian rights is likely to face similar punishment and harassment. When the women's movement incorporates and acts from a les-

bian/feminist analysis, we may well alienate some people, lose credibility, lose funding. Every time we hold a belief that is at all different from that held by the majority we alienate some people. At some point, we have to be prepared to back up our beliefs with action, with a commitment to grow and change, with a commitment to see that the people we come in contact with grow and change. Change is never easy. As feminists we must stand together, we must be strong, and we must refuse to be divided and conquered. It comes down to a choice between being accepted and acceptable and actually living, in our day to day lives, what we profess to believe.

The consequences of being a lesbian in this society are severe. The consequences of associating with or supporting lesbians are also severe. But turning on each other, denying and betraying, blaming and fighting is much more destructive to the women's movement than any amount of bad publicity or lack of funding. Working together to create a society where no woman is oppressed is our process and our goal.

—B.C. Federation of Women,
Rights of Lesbians Subcommittee

You can't be a feminist if you aren't a lesbian. Feminism is a perspective on how the world functions and an analysis of how and why women are oppressed. Being a feminist requires more than identifying as a woman; it requires both an analysis of the oppression of women and a commitment to applying this analysis to all facets of personal and social existence. We believe that a feminist analysis includes an analysis of the oppression of lesbians and the role of the institution of heterosexuality in reinforcing the oppression of all women. We believe that heterosexuality, which traditionally means male domination over women, is expected of us and even forced on us. It is not offered as **one** of many life choices.
As long as this condition exists, women have a responsibility to fight against the institution of compulsory heterosexuality in all areas of our lives, regardless of whom we choose as friends, work associates, or lovers. Being a feminist

does not mean being a lesbian. It does mean working to identify lesbian oppression as a specific part of the oppression of all women and struggling against heterosexism in all areas of one's life.

Lesbianism is easy. Women always understand each other. Lesbians have wonderful sex lives. Lesbians all support each other and no one is ever alone and unloved. Lesbians are all so strong and so free and so brave and so wonderful.

There are some myths about lesbianism which at first glance seem positive.

These myths are just as untrue as the rest. Loving women is many things but not, on the whole, easy. We do not always understand each other. As women we have all been taught to hate ourselves. Our rights to define our own self-image, our personal power, our sexuality, have been taken from us. For some of us the reality of living as lesbians has involved much pain. Part of the pain is because we believed that loving women would be just marvelous and what do we do when the sex is not wonderful and the perfect relationship turns horrible and the women in our lives are confused and anguished? We **can** be clear and brave and strong and unafraid and loving. Many of us **are** learning and growing and feeling positive about ourselves in ways we would never have believed possible. But we are changing through time and work and commitment. It did not—and does not—happen automatically upon falling in love with a woman or naming ourselves lesbian. Rita Mae Brown says it well: *None of this is easy. Becoming a lesbian does not make you instantly pure, perpetually happy and decidedly revolutionary.*

Photo/ Sarah Davidson

The Sick and Depraved Chart is useful as a summary of the myths section. It can be printed on newsprint and put up on a wall. After the myths have been presented initiate a discussion. Ask women for their reactions to the myths. Ask women for examples of "things" they had heard about lesbians or believed about lesbians. Answer questions. Finish the discussion by saying that so far in the workshop we have looked at our own emotional reactions to lesbianism and talked about some of the lies that we have been taught. After a break we will be talking about why we were taught these lies and what we can do to change the reality we experience.

Sick and Depraved Chart

Every woman who loves another woman must in some way come to terms with societal attitudes towards lesbianism; that is, she must:

Internalize negative attitudes
I am a lesbian.
Lesbians are sick and depraved.
Therefore, I am sick and depraved.
or
I love another woman.
Lesbians love other women.
Lesbians are sick and depraved.
I am not sick and depraved.
Therefore, I am not a lesbian.

Disassociate herself from the "others"
I am a lesbian.
Lesbians are sick and depraved.
I am not sick and depraved.
Therefore, I am not like other lesbians.

Refute the stereotype altogether
I am a lesbian.
They say that lesbians are sick and depraved.
I am not sick and depraved.
Other lesbians I know are not sick and
    depraved.
Therefore, they must be wrong—or lying to
    me.

Understanding Why

Purpose   This section of the workshop offers an intellectual framework for the emotions and social myths surrounding lesbianism. The point of this theory section is not to get women to agree to our "line", but to have women recognize that we all live our lives based on some ideology, often without acknowledging what that ideology is. By ideology we mean the set of ideas that underlie economic and political systems or theories. In this society predominant theories about women and about lesbianism are insulting to us and directly reinforce women's subordinate role. Feminist theory, in contrast, is created by us out of our experiences and our perceptions of reality. It is an explanation of why the world is the way it is. Feminist theory is not fixed or rigid, but open to the integration of our experiences as we are able to articulate them. Every woman can contribute to the creation of feminist theory.

One of the purposes of this workshop is to make the connections between lesbianism and feminism. The reality of living as a lesbian in this culture has been discussed and we have learned about the myths we've been taught and the function of those myths. To make the connections between that and feminism we need to explore the reality of living as a woman in this culture, and to begin to examine our differences and similarities.

Exercise   Each woman—including the facilitators—takes a sheet of paper and writes at the top *being a woman in this society means . . .* and then writes for 5 to 10 minutes. After the time is up each woman reads out her sheet—or women pass sheets around and read out loud someone else's paper. Expect emotional reaction.

After the papers have been read, remind women of the process of the workshop up to this point:

We have acknowledged our emotional reactions and conditioned attitudes towards lesbianism. We've presented our perceptions of the reality of living as a woman in this society. The work that remains is to ask **why?** We look for an explanation for our pain, our isolation, our powerlessness, our oppression. Why are lesbians oppressed? Why are women oppressed?

The answers to these questions give us an analysis of the position of women and lesbians in this culture. We have been taught that analysis and theory are the possessions of men, of intellectuals. Most of us believe that it is difficult to formulate theory or that theory is strictly an intellectual exercise that bears no relation to our lives, or that women are too emotional for theory—that theory invalidates or is separate from emotional reality. But each of us has some explanation for why the world is the way it is; we all believe in some theory.

We make posters of different ideas about women and lesbians and hang these posters on the walls. Examples of these posters are included in this section. Read out loud all the posters except for **Feminism**.

Individualism/Capitalism

Everybody has equal opportunity to become rich, famous and powerful.

Being rich, famous and powerful is what everybody wants.Those are the most important things in life.

Success or failure in life depends on individual hard work, talent and luck.

Women don't want to be rich, famous or powerful. Women want to be loved, to be wives and to have children. Women achieve their purpose in life by caring for others. Women like doing these things.

Lesbians are not women because they don't want to be wives and mothers.

Lesbians are "weird", "sick", "unnatural", and scary.

Lesbianism is a sexual pastime.

Lesbians want to be like men—tough, unemotional, violent, sexually aggressive.

Lesbianism has individual causes—unhappy childhood, etc.

Lesbians should not flaunt themselves.

Christianity

Men and women were created by God to serve different purposes.

Men and women should join together in marriage to have children.

Sex is blessed only for purposes of procreation.

The "Holy Family" should be acted out in earthly families.

There is a purpose to our earthly sufferings. We will be rewarded and/or punished after death for our performance in life.

The way the world is was ordained by God and is not for mortals to question.

Lesbianism is a cross to bear in life, a suffering imposed by God's will.

Biology

Men and women are different in bodies, capabilities and souls.

Men need to be aggressive, act out in the world, engage in violence because of their genetic makeup.

Women need to be mothers and nurturers because of their uteruses.

Heterosexuality is natural. We have a drive to perpetuate the species. Competition and aggression are natural.

Lesbianism is unnatural and is caused by hormonal imbalances or genetic defects.

Psychiatry (Freudian and otherwise)

Men and women are psychologically different. (see biology)

A psychologically healthy woman wants to be loved, looked after and dominated, and expresses her creativity by having babies.

Lesbians are women who have not fully matured. They are fixated at an immature stage of psychological development and need to be helped.

Heterosexuality is the pinnacle of mature development for everyone.

Lesbianism is caused by early childhood (usually traumatic) experiences.

Traditional Socialism

Society is divided into classes—the ruling class and the workers.

The ruling class controls the money, resources, decision-making and power. The working class sells its labour.

The working class is oppressed by this arrangement.

Revolution is necessary. Revolution means the workers seizing the means of production.

Women need to support the revolution.

Lesbianism won't exist in a socialist state because it is a reaction to capitalism. Lesbianism is a personal, not political, issue.

The rise of homosexuality marks the decadence of capitalism.

Gay Rights

Homosexuality is an okay way to be.

Homosexuals are just as worthwhile and healthy as straights.

Homosexuals are oppressed because we sleep with people of the same sex.

Homosexuals should have the same privileges as everyone else.

Lesbian Separatist

Men are genetically inferior to women.

There are 2 classes: men and women.

Straight women consort with the enemy.

Lesbians should separate themselves from the enemy and their consorts.

As feminists our analysis of the world is based on our perceptions. We will read one feminist explanation or theory and ask you to listen; to ask yourselves *Does this explanation make sense to me? For me? In terms of my past experiences? In terms of what I have learned here today?* Be prepared to explain afterwards how this explanation does or does not make sense.

Lesbian oppression is not separate and distinct from women's oppression. The purpose served is the same: to keep all women in an exploited position. We are exploited by the roles forced upon us by both the patriarchal society and the capitalist system under which we live. Traditional female roles—economic, psychological, social and emotional—place women in a subservient position to individual men in the nuclear family and to all men in the society at large. This society **needs** women to grow up to fulfill these roles, which are primarily those of service and maintenance.

In practical terms, the unpaid work women do in the nuclear family (cooking, cleaning, child-rearing, emotional nurturance) and the role they play in the economy as a pool of unpaid or poorly paid labour (teachers, nurses, secretaries, volunteers, domestics) is essential to the present economic and cultural system.

The range of acceptable behaviour for women in this society is very narrowly defined. A system of social controls and institutions operates to ensure that women grow up to fulfill the roles the society needs them to fulfill. Women are not only discouraged from deviating too far from these roles, we are discouraged from deviating at all. In fact our conditioning even prevents us from seeing that there are other choices.

When we think and act in ways other than how we "should", we are ridiculed, considered irrelevant, fired, harassed, beaten and abused. Women with careers, women who do not marry, women who have more than one male lover, women who are unmarried mothers, women who are not mothers at all, women who do not conform to society's standards in choice of occupation, appearance, thought, speech or behaviour meet with varying degrees of social disapproval and scorn.

Facilitators ask *Does that make sense? How? What parts? Why?* Discussion may be spirited. Women who have strong disagreements with this particular explanation should be encouraged to formulate their own. Stress that there are no fixed answers, no rigid "party line". Theory comes out of women's lives. We all look for answers and we can all create answers that make sense for us, and give us a framework for fighting for changes which will enable us to be free. At this point it may be useful to go through the **Feminism** poster as a summary of this section. We photocopy and have available handouts of our presentation of feminist theory. We also recommend Lesbian/Feminist theory, by Charlotte Bunch in *Our Right To Love.* This is important information for women to keep after the workshop. For us, this section is the core of the workshop. If the workshop is running for two days, this is a good time to end the first day.

We are "punished" according to our degree and form of deviation. Lesbianism symbolizes the extreme of women's deviation because lesbians are seen as having rejected all of the criteria which determine female identity in this culture. Lesbians are considered "other than women", not "real" women, and receive social punishment. The severity of that punishment is a warning to all women of the consequences of deviation in any form or degree and functions to keep all women "in their place".

The threat of being called a lesbian is a very efficient control over women's behaviour. The word is thrown at many women who have never and may never love another woman. Women who are independent, assertive, articulate, regardless of their actual social and emotional or sexual lives, have probably at some point or other been called lesbians. The term "lesbian" is used against any woman whose attitudes and actions do not reflect the passivity and dependence upon men which is demanded by our society. The myths and fears which have been created about lesbians function to keep us in the position most useful to society — subordinate and powerless. It also encourages us to see lesbians as different from other women, so that we won't find out that lesbian oppression is an extreme form of the oppression all women suffer.

Feminism

The social and economic roles of men and women have been created by our culture. They are maintained in order to perpetuate a male-dominated capitalist economic and social system. Women are as oppressed by all existing economic and cultural systems including socialism as it is practised now. Women are primarily oppressed through our role as reproducers and unpaid and/or cheap marketplace labour.

Social institutions such as heterosexuality, the family, marriage, enforced motherhood, exist in order to reinforce women's and men's economic and social roles.

Lesbianism is an expression of women's love for ourselves and other women. Loving ourselves is discouraged. Lesbians are punished for being lesbians in order to keep all women "in line" i.e. working and nurturing men and children within the nuclear family and society as a whole.

Revolution is necessary. Revolution means a transformation of all power relationships. Revolution begins with the way we live and act NOW. Feminist theory and practice grows and changes to reflect the diverse qualities of our lives, our diverse experiences of oppression due to class, race, age, disability, etc. as well as sex.

Feminist theory and practice stress such values as: cooperation, respect for individuals, integration of personal and political, personal power, equal participation in decision-making, cooperative structures, individual responsibility, collective process . . .

Creating Visions

Purpose   To create a vision of how we would like our lives to be. Split into small groups. This section is often an emotional uplift.

We are now aware on an emotional and intellectual level of the reality of living as women, and we have an explanation, a theory which enables us to understand that condition. Having an idea of why that oppression exists, we now ask: What do we want to be different? How can we make a difference? This section of the workshop begins to deal with the question of how to create change.

We have to know what we are fighting for before we can outline how best to get there. By imagining what kind of world we want to live in, we are taking the first step to making it a reality. What we want to come up with is a vision of a non-oppressive, liberating society.

Exercise   Facilitators have big sheets of newsprint and felt pens. Divide into 4 to 5 small groups. Have the women answer the following questions and record the responses on the sheets. Ask the women to note their emotional responses as they are brainstorming and talking. Groups are encouraged to allow each woman to express emotions and to support each other.

A free world would mean?
In a free world, how would people feel and
    act toward women?
In a free world, how would people feel and
    act toward lesbians?
In a free world what would you be like?
    What would your life be like? (work?
    relationship? environment?) How would
    you be living?

Facilitators have already prepared a sheet stating their "vision" and put this up on the wall. This leaves them free to be available to answer questions and act as a resource for the groups.

A Sample Feminist Vision

A free world would mean a world where everyone would live as a free, fully self-defined human being. People would live by principles of equality, respect for the uniqueness of each individual, personal power, participation in decision-makng process, integration of body, mind, feeling . . .

The experience of living as a woman would be valued—important and powerful.

Lesbians would be respected for their choice to love other women—lesbianism would be seen as a valid, positive life choice.

Life: integrated . . .

After half an hour ask women to put up their sheets on the wall and have someone report briefly on the work and process of each group.

Using sheets on the wall, facilitators point out similarities between responses. Most often the concepts and values reflected by the responses are similar to our **Sample Feminist Vision** (non-oppressive, liberating, powerful). Using the examples of the women's answers, facilitators can demystify feminism:

For us, feminism is a perspective on the way the world functions from the experience of living as a woman—a vision of the world where women would be free, full, self-defined human beings and a commitment to work at making that vision a reality.

If anyone has described a vision which does not incorporate non-oppressive, liberating values, facilitators could ask: *How do those examples mean freedom? How does that mean women and lesbians would be free from oppression?*

Facilitators work toward agreement on as many points as possible. Emphasize that we base strategies for change on our visions.

Our strategies must incorporate our values. If we want to live in a world where people have power over their own lives then we must work for change both on an individual and societal level. The actions we plan must be based on principles of respect, self-determination, equality.

Exercise   To allow each woman an opportunity to examine privately her own life, to acknowledge in herself the places in her life where she is integrated and whole and the places where she knows there are contradictions. This exercise is another guided fantasy. Explain that the reason for doing this exercise is to allow each woman a way of choosing an area of her life that needs to be worked on. It is a way of deciding where to start. Read very, very slowly; use words and concepts from the visions discussion.

Sit or lie comfortably.
Close your eyes and breathe.
Think about the world we've just talked about.
    Think about how you would feel living in
    that world.
Healthy . . . autonomous . . . connected . . .
    integrated . . . useful . . . loved . . .

Think about your life now.
Think about your job.
Your living situation.
Your children.
Your friends.
Your relationships.
Your body.
Your family.
Your sexuality.
Your political work.
Notice the feelings inside you.
Where do you feel connected . . . whole?
Where do you feel split? uncomfortable?
    contradictions?
When you are ready, come back to the
    group.

Leave some silence at the end of the exercise. Invite women to speak. This is an appropriate time for a break.

Changing Our Reality

Purpose   To emphasize our individual and collective responsibility to work for change. It is designed for a small group problem-solving format.

Write and/or adapt standard "problems" during the break. Try to use problems that will be connected to the women present based on what has been learned about their situations so far in the workshop. We have included here some sample problems that we have used successfully. Some are geared towards women who do not identify as lesbians and the emphasis is on their responsibility for confronting their own and other's homophobia. Others are geared towards women who consider themselves part of a lesbian community and the women's liberation movement and focus on individual and collective responsibility within these groupings. Many can be and have been used in any group. Make it clear that the small group can choose to make up different problems, or, best of all, use a current problem out of their own lives.

Exercise   Ask the women to break up into small groups for problem-solving. Hand out cards with problems written on them. Each group has 3 different problems to solve. The groups can use real problems that exist for women in the group or within their communities.

Ask women to consider the following points when coming up with solutions: *How does this solution lead us toward our "vision"? Would you be prepared to do this in your community?* Record your responses for evaluation by the entire group.

Time in small groups should be about 45 minutes. Facilitators can make themselves available to the groups during this time. If women are not able to see solutions, facilitators could suggest role-playing.

Example: A facilitator takes on the role of the woman from the women's centre who is responding to a reporter asking questions about lesbians in the group; one woman from the group plays the reporter. (See *Public Speaking Tips* in *Working in Progressive Movements*.) If the facilitator plays the woman from the centre, the women in the group will develop some ideas about how they could respond.

When we think of oppression, it seems so overwhelming that we are often paralyzed and immobilized by the amount of work to be done. Having an understanding of why oppression exists, how it functions in this society, and keeping in mind our visions, help us develop strategies necessary for changing our condition.

Real change occurs when people begin to **act** on what they know to be true. In this society we are conditioned to believe that real changes are made by someone "out there", by the government, by laws, by powerful people. We are taught that **our actions** cannot and do not affect the world. It is time that we begin to take ourselves seriously enough to believe that our personal changes in attitude, the resulting changes in our behaviour and our joining together to push for changes in **our lives** and in **our communities** is indeed creating change, real change. And if we can change we know that the people around us can too.

The process of change is not steady or fast. We make small steps, evaluate our successes and failures, make new plans, incorporate new pieces of information into our analysis.

The point is to **begin to believe** that how we live our lives, how we relate to others, how we push for changes, how we **act** is a crucial and integral part of our struggle to be free.

Today we will take ourselves seriously enough to begin to do some of that problem-solving and planning. **Together we can change the way things are.**

Each problem-solving group reports back. Women evaluate the proposed solutions using the agreed-upon vision sheet translated into questions.

For example, if our vision list reads: Personal power, equality, non-violence, horizontal structures and process, respect for uniqueness of individuals, self-determination . . . non-racist, we translate these into questions for evaluating solutions. How does this solution increase the woman's sense of personal power? How does this solution encourage self-determination? Does this solution promote cooperation? Does this solution show respect for the people involved? Does this solution lead us towards our vision?

We also use adapted evaluation questions (from *Quest,* vol. 1, #1 and vol. 3, #4):
1   How will this strategy affect women's sense of self and the sense of our own collective power?
2   How will it make women aware of problems beyond questions of identity, and strengthen the bonds between women?
3   How will the strategy work to build organizations which will increase both our strength and competence, and give women the power to weaken the white male capitalist authority over us?
4   Does the strategy contain at least the seeds of its own growth? Or is it a way of forever doing the same things for the same people?

Facilitators should keep discussion spirited and moving and provide summaries after each solution is evaluated. We often have one facilitator responsible for "chairing" the discussion and another facilitator responsible for offering suggestions, comments, ideas about what we know works well in practice. Facilitators should encourage women to actually carry out the strategies they have suggested.

At this point, facilitators ask if the women present are facing any situations in their work, lives, community that they would like to bring up to get ideas, suggestions, concrete assistance and support from the other women present. If the situations have been chosen to reflect real problems in the women's lives some of the solutions may be immediately useful. Quite often the women present begin now to plan ongoing actions or projects. The facilitator could act as a resource person to assist women in discussing plans and making decisions about their strategies. Facilitators can present information about other groups working in similar areas so the women are not left isolated.

Sample Problems

Your 19 year old daughter tells you she's a lesbian, in love with another woman. She wants your approval. How do you respond?

Your best friend or next door neighbour tells you she's in love with you. She is married, defines herself as a heterosexual, has never had a sexual relationship with another woman. How do you respond?

A 17 year old woman who has been hanging around the fringes of your group for some time tells you one day she thinks she is a lesbian and wants to know more. What do you do?

You are on holidays and visiting a small northern town. There you meet a woman who says she's a lesbian. She tells you she is alone, afraid to tell anyone else, and in much emotional pain. What do you do?

You know two women involved in a relationship who are physically violent and abusive to each other. What do you do?

You know that a lesbian in your group drinks too much. Her drinking is affecting her work, her life, her daughter. What do you do?

A woman comes to your group saying she is a lesbian mother and her husband is threatening to take her to court for custody of the children. She asks for help. What do you do?

Renaissance Canada, an anti-homosexual organization, is coming to town. What do you do to organize against it?

You are active in a women's group that doesn't have a position on lesbianism. You want the group to take a stand—publicly. What do you do?

You overhear your children using "queers" and "lezzies" as insults to each other. What do you do?

You and a woman friend are walking down the street carrying your groceries. A group of teenage boys start yelling "dyke" at you. What do you do?

A story appears in your local paper accusing your women's group of being "riddled with lesbians" and that you "preach lesbianism." What do you do?

Closing

Purpose   To give the facilitators an opportunity to review the work of the day; and to give participants a chance to acknowledge their emotional responses, any changes in attitude, and their personal commitments to act:

The workshop was designed to take a topic called "lesbian oppression" and "lesbian feminism" and to create a situation in which we:

examined our learned attitudes about lesbianism;
looked at our experience of being oppressed as women and lesbians;
formulated a theory which explained that oppression;
developed a vision for a free society;
considered strategies which would lead to that vision;

The workshop has been an experience of consciousness-raising and change. We will take a few moments now to quietly explore our responses to these 2 days.

Exercise: Guided fantasy   Read very, very slowly, pausing between the steps of the fantasy to give women time to think.

Sit back, or stretch out on the floor, close your eyes, make your body comfortable, take deep breaths and relax . . .
You are going to do some role-playing with yourself.
Imagine an incident from your life. We all have them . . . remember from the past or now in the present, or a situation in which you are aware of an attitude or a behaviour that was or is oppressive to lesbians . . .
It could be remembering the time you were at work and someone made a disgusting homophobic joke and you said nothing. Or the time when you were reluctant to let your children play with the children across the street because you had seen their mother kissing another woman on their front porch . . . or the time when a kid yelled out "lezzie" at you and you denied it and never wore that flannel shirt again, or the time your collective said *lesbianism—that's just a personal issue.* and you

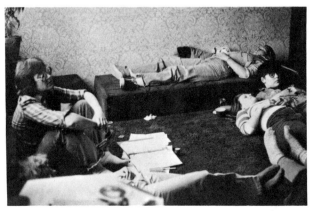

Photo/ Billie Carroll

didn't say you were a lesbian, or the time when your daughter got beaten up for having a "queer" mother and was afraid to tell you, or the time your group didn't want to put the word "lesbian" on a leaflet because they didn't want to "alienate" anyone . . .

Think about one such time.

What are you feeling? Are you angry? Hurt? Embarrassed?

These are the kinds of incidents that we all encounter each week, every day. . .

From the workshop today, we know that change begins with individuals taking personal responsibility to act. We know that change and growth is a long process for all of us. We believe that it is possible to begin now . . .

So fix the incident in your mind and remember the information and ideas from this work shop . . .

Imagine yourself taking the initiative to respond to the situation in a way that makes you feel powerful and in a way that reinforces the reality and positive value of lesbianism. Imagine yourself feeling confident, proud, a little scared, but knowing that what you're saying and doing can and will make a difference.

What would you say?

What would you do?

How are the people around you responding?

How does it feel to have the power to change your reactions and attitudes, daring to take risks and finding a way to begin changing the world?

Stay with those feelings . . .

Slowly open your eyes, and, when you're ready come back to the group for the closing round.

Exercise: Closing Round   This exercise is to put into words the changes in self-image and commitment that we hope have occurred as a result of the workshop. We do a final round where each woman is asked to say one thing that she will do as a result of attending the workshop. This is intended to leave women with the expectation that they will take their actions seriously and receive the encouragement and concrete support for what they plan to do. Women make commitments covering a vast range—taking information on lesbianism back to a group, talking to their children, speaking up at work when someone makes a queer joke, finding a supportive therapist or group to work through emotional conflicts that have surfaced, starting a lesbian drop-in, planning a demonstration . . . fighting for changes within their group to encourage greater participation of lesbians.

Facilitators are to participate in the round and can state their follow-up commitment to the group. Each woman's statement will be listened to with respect, support, and encouragement. Remind women that they do not have to fight all alone, that there are other women working in this area, that there are resources available to them.

Exercise: Appreciations   This exercise is to end the workshop by asking for and giving appreciations to the facilitators and to the participants:

We do not often take time to appreciate ourselves for our work and struggle and commitment. This gives us an opportunity to acknowledge openly what we value about ourselves and each other. Appreciations are most easily heard and most useful when they are direct and specific.

The facilitators can start by giving an appreciation to one of the participants. Here's an example: *I want to appreciate you, Joan, for the risk you took today when you spoke, very emotionally, about your reality as a lesbian who has to live in the closet because you are a grade school teacher. You expressed your fear well, and asked for concrete support from the women in the room who also live in this community. That was important in decreasing your isolation and in letting other women know what it's really like to live as a lesbian in a society that hates us. Now other women will be in a better position to offer concrete support and to help you in changing that reality.*

Hand out evaluation sheets to all participants. Ask the women to fill them out and return them.

Celebration

Purpose   After the workshop is over or on the evening of the first workshop day we like to have a celebration. This is a more relaxed time where we affirm our strength as women and celebrate our connections to each other.

We have included a script for a celebration that we sometimes use but you should develop whatever seems best. We have also used films, a concert, a theatre presentation, a meal, or just wine, music and talking. The purpose is to provide a time to wind down from the emotional and intellectual intensity of the workshop itself and to end the day with warmth, relaxation and a sense of connection with women who have shared the experience of the workshop.

As lesbians, as women, it is important that we find ways of affirming our power and our strength. We are all too isolated from each other. We are often isolated from ourselves. And we are isolated from the strength that can come from feeling part of a tradition of women who fought before us and endured and succeeded. Tonight we are going to share some information about our herstory.

Women's herstory has been ignored and actively repressed for centuries. In the last decade women have seriously begun the work of reclaiming and rediscovering our achievements, our traditions. In doing this we are providing a perspective for the work we do now and a background for our feminist goals. Finding lesbian herstory is an integral part of this total search. We don't know many names, which reflects the biases of the history recorders. We know a little about a few rich, white women who lived openly as lesbians. But of the vast majority of women who have loved women, the pain and joy of their lives, we know nothing.

A logical place to start is with the word "lesbian". The word is derived from the island of Lesbos, where, around 600 B.C. a woman named Sappho presided over a community of young women. She instructed them in the arts of poetry, drama, and graceful living. The women built their lives around love of beauty and love of each other. It is a tribute to her poetic genius that today she is considered one of the greatest poets who ever lived, even though all that remains of her work is a few fragments. The bulk of her work was destroyed during the Middle Ages in a purge against "sensuality".

There is evidence of Amazons and matriarchies but if we discard speculation and mythology, what remains is only a shadow. We know that Amazon tribes existed in Mesopotamia, central Europe, and North Africa. We know that these tribes venerated horses and shunned the sea. We know they reproduced by arrangement with neighbouring tribes, keeping only a few males whom they crippled at birth for slaves. We know they wore star-covered helmets, jerkins, and high leather boots and that the famous Amazon axe, the labrys, was indeed their weapon. As far as we can tell the last of the tribes was destroyed by wars with budding empires.

There is some evidence of a time when a matriarchal culture was predominant. These people worshipped the Mother, the Goddess and a female principle—the life force. But of their daily living arrangements, their social and emotional structures, we know nothing. It is our loss.

From the time of Sappho until the late 19th century a huge void exists in our written herstory broken only by the memory of a few rare individuals.

At the turn of the century Paris became the centre of a renaissance in art and culture that was based upon decadence and innovation. The atmosphere was correspondingly more liberal than the society-at-large and lesbian culture had a rare public decade. Gertrude Stein's famous salon was a guiding light to the literary and artistic community and Natalie Barney headed a movement in poetry, art and theatre, which included a positive celebration of lesbianism. Her circle included Colette, the poet Renee Vivien, the painter Romaine Brooks, the author Radclyffe Hall and many others. Although politically there is much to question from this period, the memories of cucumber sandwiches, Sappho's New School of Poetry, and nymphlike dramas on the lawn evoke a time when lesbianism, at least in a small circle, was accepted as a superior way to live.

Radclyffe Hall's famous novel, *The Well of Loneliness*, was the centre of a bitter censorship controversy. In a herstorical sense the book is important, despite the fact that it reinforces the image of the lesbian as a misfit who is doomed to live a dramatically tragic life. It

Photo/ Sarah Davidson

was the first widely read novel which openly discussed lesbianism. Incidently, Hall fought the censorship of her book in both the United States and England and ultimately won the right to have her book released.

There are other eras and other individuals whose stories are being resurrected as part of our herstory. We have our celebrities—Queen Christina of Sweden for example; the poet Emily Dickinson whose poetry was altered for publication so that the pronoun 'she' would appear as 'he'. Virginia Woolf, too, had lesbian relationships and there are countless others whose names mean nothing today. Their lives and times have been almost irretrievably lost through the brutal alterations effected by the male-dominated recording of history.

We all have a stake in the work of reclamation. We have been scientists, musicians, poets and monarchs. We have been healers, farmers, midwives, and artisans. We have been mothers, factory workers, fighters and dreamers; we have lived rich and interesting lives for thousands of years. Now we begin to remember. We add to our knowledge and reinforce our self image. We claim the strength and pride inherent in our herstory.

We are in the midst of another and more diverse renaissance in lesbian culture. We are redefining ourselves as poets, musicians, artists. We are creating a culture which reflects positive images of women and celebrates our loving each other.

Facilitators could share poems, stories, quotations which are affirmations of women, or use poems, journal excerpts of your own and your friends. Each women could present a story, a poem, a song, a piece from her journal, or a memory of a woman who has been important to her.

Each of us has a story, a herstory. We know our mothers, our grandmothers. We ask women here to tell about a woman in her life, in the past or present who has moved, touched, inspired her. I remember . . .

After everyone who wants to has spoken, facilitators can acknowledge the atmosphere of emotional closeness that has been created. Now is a good time to put on some music and relax.

Follow-Up

The workshop can be an intense experience for women. Personal conflicts can surface; political contradictions can arise. Women need to have ways of dealing with personal changes that may start in the workshop. Facilitators should make sure that women attending the workshop have sources of support afterwards.

1   Make sure women take from the workshop the information they need. This means handing out reprints of portions of workshop information or alternatives; having books, records, pamphlets, papers available to sell and/or lend; having a list of local, regional (by mail) resources such as feminist groups, women's centres, lesbian groups, women's bookstores stocking lesbian/feminist literature, addresses of feminist newspapers and magazines, etc.

2   Make sure the women leaving the workshop have somewhere to go to talk about their worries, reactions, fears, personal responses. Do this by ensuring that women in the group have other women they can talk with afterwards. Suggest they agree to meet as a group in a week to share their responses, evaluate the steps they took and that they continue meeting together to plan further activities. Say that facilitators will be available after the workshop to any women who want to talk. This can be in a relaxed social space—sitting around someone's house, going out for a coffee or a drink.

3   Let the group know that the facilitators would be prepared to do a follow-up workshop in 3 months to continue the process started in this workshop. Leave a contact number so the group can reach the facilitators to ask about setting up the follow-up workshop.

4   Ask whether the women present would like to have names and phone numbers of women to contact for further information or conversation. Facilitators should decide beforehand which of them is willing to commit herself to be available on this basis.

Sample Evaluation Form

1   How did you find out about this workshop?

2   What did you expect of the workshop?

3   Were your expectations met? How? Was this workshop useful to you?

4   Please comment on
physical space: good, adequate, poor? why?

meals and breaks

childcare

resource material

5   Please comment on the workshop: was the information presented clear and useful in defining lesbianism and describing our realities?

developing our analysis of the oppression of lesbians and women?

creating a vision?

developing strategies for change?

encouraging commitment to follow-up?

the presentation by facilitators: were you listened to?

6   What is your opinion about your contributions to the workshop?

7   Are there changes you would like to suggest in the workshop?

8   What kind of follow-up would be helpful?

Notes to Facilitators

Notes To Facilitators is written for women who are looking for ideas about forming a collective, and for those women who are interested in facilitating workshops. The material will also be useful for an already existing feminist group which wants to incorporate this type of educational work into their ongoing activities.

The first section is written specifically for those women who want to form a collective to do workshops or other political work. We describe some of our experiences as a collective, and provide ideas for coming together, working together and staying together as a group.

Notes To Facilitators also provides detailed information about preparing for and setting up a workshop. We cover such topics as researching the group you will be working with, media coverage, childcare, money, physical setting for the workshop, advertising, etc.

We attempt to demystify the role of facilitator by giving information and examples of how we work with women during the workshops. We offer ideas for dealing with emotions, encouraging women to come forward with their disagreements, handling conflicts and creating unity within the group. We include a section on caring for ourselves as facilitators, and suggestions for evaluating a completed workshop.

In the last section, we give brief outlines for workshop variations, with specific suggestions for speaking about lesbianism with a variety of audiences. We offer descriptions of an hour with a high school class, a day long seminar for professionals, an evening with the general public, a series in a community college, and a two day follow-up workshop with a group of lesbians, feminists, or lesbian feminists.

Much of what we have written will make more sense to you after you have some experience within a workshop situation. Process skills, dealing with emotions, resolving conflict, taking care of each other, are not difficult or mysterious.

We emphasize the importance of 'practicing' the workshop many times within the facilitating collective or with friends before starting 'real' workshops. Doing workshops on lesbianism and feminism exposes our own internal conflicts. Be prepared for almost any reaction. And remember that what you are doing is changing the world!

Forming a Group

If you are interested in facilitating workshops, or if you simply want to experience the workshop as we have outlined it, we suggest that you gather together a small group of friends for a weekend and actually go through the workshop. At least two women should share the facilitating role, or each woman could take responsibility for leading a section. Use the workshop script as it is written, and take plenty of time to evaluate your reactions.

This workshop can be quite difficult for women. It is often the most painful for women who have identified as lesbians and feminists for years. Possibly many of us who identify as lesbian feminists don't find it easy to acknowledge the struggles we are going through daily, the contradictions that still exist in our lives, the amount of social conditioning and self-hatred we still carry around. So take note — you will not be in a position to facilitate workshops until you have found effective ways to understand and take care of your own emotions, ideas and contradictions.

If, after going through a test workshop, you decide to continue passing on what you know to others, the next stage is to formally create a facilitating collective. We are offering some ideas for beginning.

An existing group may decide to sponsor these workshops in addition to their ongoing work. We think the ideas and suggestions in this section will be useful both to women who are considering forming a group, and to those women already working in feminist collectives.

Coming Together

We believe that the women in a facilitating collective or in a group giving these workshops should identify as lesbians. We are not 'studying' lesbianism as objective outsiders, or as an interesting topic, when we do these workshops. We are coming together, as lesbians, to speak out from our lives and experiences.

We also strongly believe that women in the facilitating collective must be grounded in feminist theory and practice. Lesbianism is much more than sexual intimacy with another woman. We situate our oppression as lesbians within the context of all women's oppression. Ending our oppression as lesbians necessitates feminist activism. The theory and practice of feminism is constantly changing as we undertake new actions, as we gain new insights which deepen our analysis and give rise to new problems, which require new solutions, which promote new learning... an exciting process of ever-increasing discoveries about possibilities. In order to encourage the participants of the workshops towards political activism, facilitators must be very familiar with feminist analysis and practice. Teaching others to organize without speaking from your own experience makes the workshops hollow and is much like sitting in a lecture. What we pass on to others comes not only from our ideas, but from our experiments at putting those ideas into practice.

We learn by doing and analyzing. But before you actually set out to do, particularly these workshops, a certain amount of ground work is needed!

Who are you?   Take the time to discover who you will be working with. Each woman will bring something special and unique to the group. Make a regular time to meet and go over the following questions. Add others that are of interest to you. Keep track of your responses. Making time to expose your backgrounds and beliefs is also a valuable process for an already existing group and for women who may know each other socially. The stories will be moving and inspiring and thought-provoking. You will be better able to connect with each other as women when you understand the particular context (life experiences) which lead someone to their present political perspective. Too often we are so busy day-to-day that we forget to stop and remember where we came from, how and why we got here, and to value our individual and collective steps toward our own and all women's freedom.

This is a process of revealing yourselves to each other. There are no right or wrong answers. There is no need to come to agreement on any of these points. The more you know of the experiences and beliefs of the members of your group, the more information you will have to begin pulling together commonalities and pinpointing areas of potential conflict.

Some questions for the women in the group:

* What is your race/ethnic background? your class background? how did you grow up because of this?
* How old are you? are you employed? what do you do for money?
* Do you have any children? how does this affect your life?
* How do you live? do you live alone? collectively? with others?
* Talk about your relationships with family, friends, co-workers, women you are sexually intimate with.
* How long have you identified as a lesbian? how did you come to that decision? what does it mean to you to identify and live as a lesbian?
* How did you come to identify as a feminist? Talk about what feminism means to you in terms of analysis, vision and strategies.
* What political work are you doing now? what have you done? what are your experiences of working politically? as a feminist?
* What other groups do you belong to? what are your commitments to these groups?
* What other groups do you see as being part of our struggle for freedom? what other groups do you believe are working for social change in a direction or manner which benefits us as lesbians and as women?

Where are you headed?   Spend time talking about working together as a group, with a specific focus on doing the workshops. Again, rounds of questions are a useful way to begin:

* What is your vision of this work? why do you want to do this work?

* What would be your short and long term goals for the group?

* Do you see this collective providing more than workshops? what?

* What are your limitations?

* Are you prepared to make a commitment to this work and to this group?

* What specific skills do you have to offer the group? (typing, years of facilitating workshops, layout, graphics, etc.)

* Do you have access to resources such as typewriters, photocopiers, money, paper, libraries, media contacts, cars, free telephone lines, time?

Record your responses to these quesions. There will be a variety of ideas, experiences and resources that will begin to shape the purpose of the group, how you will work together, and actions you could undertake.

Ideally, you will have visions of taking on the world. Practically, you now need to take all the ideas and information and work out clear agreements for the group. Establish what you hope to accomplish, and outline several specific projects that will lead you there—this becomes your plan of action, your short and long term goals. Some initial agreements we made as a group were to clearly define lesbian and feminism. We sat down and wrote a paper called *Feminism as Ideology*, which essentially became our basis of unity. This process of clarifying and defining greatly facilitated our process and actual work as it gave us our analytical context and our direction for change.

Forming a collective of lesbian feminists may be your first step in coming together to take on many activities. As a general statement of purpose, your group might want to:

Raise consciousness about lesbianism; put lesbian oppression in a feminist context and encourage actions leading to social change that will end all oppression.

The goals you set from there will be specific actions that make those objectives a reality. Some concrete ways of putting that into practice could be:
to facilitate workshops on lesbianism and feminism for the women's community, for feminist groups, for lesbians and for the general public;
to offer an ongoing lesbian drop-in in your area;
to raise funds for the lesbian mothers' defense fund. Developing measurable goals for each of these projects will provide you with a way to regularly evaluate your work and assess your progress.

You don't need to have all the answers right away. As you work together, new ideas will come forward as you develop new insights.

Working Together

Basis of unity   You have a group of women who share a common understanding of lesbian and feminist. You have agreed on a purpose for working together and you are committed to carrying out several projects, presumably one of them being these workshops! These points, written down, become a basis of unity—what you agree on. This can be referred to when you are figuring out whether or not a proposed action fits into your reason for being. A written basis of unity also becomes a position paper to exchange with other politically active groups, and can be used as a basis for articles, brochures and leaflets.

Collectivity   We believe collective process to be consistent with our feminist principles of organizing. Working collectively means that every woman shares in the work and in the decision-making process. Every woman's opinion matters and is carefully considered. Decisions are made by the group working toward unity or consensus. Each woman is encouraged to dream up new ideas, to make the best use of her skills and experience, and to learn new areas of work. Women share in the responsibilities and the benefits. There are no bosses or secretaries and the tasks that keep a collective functioning efficiently are rotated.

Discuss collectivity: what does it mean to you? How will you work together? How will decisions be made? Who will be responsible for what?

Meetings   It is likely that one decision you will make about working together is to hold regular meetings. Meetings are an opportunity to check in with each other, to discuss new ideas, to evaluate past work, and to plan the next event.

Many of us are very familiar with attending meetings and have definite ideas for how meetings should be organized to be the most effective and efficient. We are including some guidelines here: some of these suggestions have been used by us as a collective, and others come from our experiences with other groups.

* It is useful to discuss the general purpose of meeting together: what do you hope to get out of the meetings? How formal a structure do you want? A set time limit? Where do you want to meet? What about childcare for the meetings?

We have found regular meetings important in maintaining contact with each other. We make time to talk about our personal lives, our emotions, and often use the group as a resource for specific problem-solving. We do not come to meetings cut off from our joys and sorrows, from the successes and problems of our lives. Meetings are a way to get things done, opportunities to learn from each other through clearing disagreements we may have, by increasing our understanding of women's experiences, by examining personal and political contradictions, evaluating past activities, planning new work, and by valuing and appreciating what has been done by individuals and by the group.

* You will want to structure your meeting time effectively, efficiently and productively. An agenda is a useful way of organizing your time. What do you want to accomplish? What kind of time limit for each area? Are there items you want on regularly? Where do new items belong? Who draws up the agenda?

Agendas can be decided on roughly at one meeting and added to at the beginning of the next. As a collective, it is important to have the agenda approved by all women before beginning the meeting.

* In a small group, it often seems unnecessary to have a chair, but we have found that if a group dispenses with that role, either as a conscious decision or oversight, one or two women will, in fact, end up acting as chairs. Since that function has not been clearly agreed on by the group, resentments could build.

Chairing, or facilitating, is a task that can be rotated to give each woman that experience. Chairing means that a woman takes responsibility for starting the meetings, getting approval for the agenda, keeping track of time. She also summarizes discussion when that would be useful to the group, suggests alternate ways of proceeding (rounds, breaks, caucuses) if the group is stuck or if emotions are building to a difficult point, she repeats decisions so that everyone is clear. A good chair is sensitive, flexible and firm.

* How will you record the process and decisions of your meetings? Will that be done on a rotating basis? Will they be typed and distributed after each meeting? Where will the notes be kept? Are they accessible to every member?

Minutes can be as formal as recording every word, or as simple as recording only the actual decisions of the group. Minutes will be invaluable when members of your group are in disagreement about plans and decisions made by the group!

Getting along   There are several techniques which greatly facilitate working together. Some have already been explained in the *Workshop Script,* and they are equally useful in collective process.

* Rounds are great! They give each woman an opportunity to speak, in turn, without being interrupted or answered. We begin each meeting with a round where each woman lets the others know how she's been, her emotional state at the moment and any information she believes is relevant to the meeting.

Rounds are also used during the meeting. At any time when we seem to be disagreeing on a topic, misunderstanding each other or when one or two women are voicing strong opinions and the rest are being quiet, we will use a round to enable each woman to express her thoughts and feelings about the topic under discussion. From there, we go on to make decisions having heard everyone's opinion. It sounds ridiculously simple but it works amazingly well.

* Disagreements can remain unresolved, seriously hampering the effectiveness of the group's work. We see it as absolutely necessary for women working together politically to find, and invent, new and better ways of disagreeing with each other. We need to change our concept of conflict from negative to positive. We need to see disagreements and contradictions as ways of increasing our understanding, and helping us all develop new insights.

Groups have found many ways to structure disagreements between members. In our experience, explicit and formal ways create the room and safety necessary for any woman to bring forward criticism, and check out fears, without causing extra tension and disruption to the group. Some of the structures and agreements we know are useful can be found in these books: *Solving Women's Problems* by Hogie Wykoff (New York: Grove Press, 1977) and *Constructive Criticism* by Gracie Lyons (Berkeley: IRT Publications, 1976).

We suggest that you take these books, read them and discuss the ideas. Talk with other groups who use these and other methods of clearing disagreements, then decide for yourselves.

How do you want to resolve disagreements? Is this a way to promote unity within the group? Does this method reflect the caring you have for each other? Does this reflect your commitment to the development and implementation of feminist theory and principles?

* As well as finding useful ways to argue, finding ways to consistently reinforce, validate and encourage positive work and contributions is essential in maintaining the well-being and growth of any collective.

Is there structured time in your meetings to offer each other emotional and problem solving support? How will you let each other know what you have valued and learned from each other? Is there a regular time at the end of each meeting or work session to give specific appreciations to each other? What about giving self-appreciations regularly?

To sum up, we offer an example of a regular meeting agenda which includes all of the above points. With time and experience, your group will come up with a structure that best suits your purpose and needs.

Agenda
1. Round: checking in with each other
2. Clearing: any unresolved emotional material, or criticisms
3. Information-sharing: anything you've read, heard, thought about that relates to the work of the group
4. Correspondence
5. Budget
6. Major work items: reports from any work groups, evaluation of the last project, planning the next workshops
7. Planning the next meeting: where, when, chair
8. Appreciations

Staying Together

How many women's groups do you know of—ones made up of intense, committed, active women—which did great things, for a while, then disintegrated? Women who left because they were burned-out? Groups falling apart because of unresolved political disagreements? Women leaving simply because they were bored? There are no magical solutions to keeping a group together, but we have learned some things which help us plan to do sustained, long term, serious productive feminist organizing!

There must be a balance. Feminist organizing is basically the integration of several components:
we need to have a place to acknowledge our emotions, to give and get support for our individual struggles;
we need a place to develop theory and analysis, to understand, in a political context and from a feminist perspective, why things are the way they are;
we need to have an effective way of putting our feelings and ideas into practice, to take action.

There have been numerous articles written on the balance of process and product within groups. We now know that women are most likely to be satisfied and stay with a group when there is an ongoing combination of opportunities to feel, think and act. If women express dissatisfaction with the meetings or the work, if women leave meetings groaning and exhausted, frightened or silent, without good-will for each other, if your numbers begin to dwindle—take it seriously. Meetings will often be tiring, but there should be a sense of accomplishment, of "getting somewhere". There should be a feeling of respect and love for each other, of excitement about the work. If this is not true in your group, check to see which of the above elements are missing, then take the time to correct that.

Women stay with a group because it offers a way of having their needs as individual women met, as well

as meeting their wish to organize politically. Don't overlook the needs of individuals in the group. Situations in our lives are relevant to this work. If women are sick, if money is a problem, if childcare isn't working, then it becomes our responsibility, as feminists, as friends, to figure out a solution. If we are not able to do this for each other, our feminist vision remains very far away indeed.

Women of colour in the group, working class women, mothers, disabled women—any grouping of women who experience another dimension of oppression in this society should be given the opportunity to form a caucus within the larger group. This is a place to support each other, to develop the analysis and understanding of how to confront the other women on their oppressive attitudes and actions. The caucus is in a position to ensure that the work of the group reflects their realities.

Disagreements are always difficult. We are just learning to see conflict as beneficial to our organizing. What appear to be political contradictions or very opposite positions on the surface, can often be worked on to create a new perspective and position that will unify and strengthen the entire group. This requires a commitment on the part of the members to go through hard struggles *with* each other—keeping in mind the ideals that brought you together in the first place.

If you are spending more than a third of your meeting time clearing disagreements or working on unresolved emotional or political conflicts, you could consider setting aside a whole day for clearing. Spend the time to really figure out what is going on. You could consider asking an outside woman to facilitate the session if it seems particularly difficult.

Watch for trouble spots within your group if you have been under pressure from external sources. For example, if you are under attack in the media, if you have lost a source of funding, if your last workshop was a disaster, be especially careful with each other. We tend to take out our fear, anger and resentments on ourselves and each other, rather than continuing to see events in the context of our oppression.

Regular evaluation of your work is essential for the group's well-being and continued productivity. Women need a strong sense of accomplishment in order to persist, particularly in the face of a task as huge as "transformation of society." If your goals and objectives were clearly outlined at the beginning of your work together, one idea is to hold an annual meeting where the work is evaluated on the basis of those original aims. Successes and problems are pinpointed, the actual work is reviewed and appreciated or criticized as specifically as possible, and new plans are drawn up for the coming year. It is time to celebrate the 'process and product' of your group and to reaffirm·your commitment to this work.

Pass on what you've learned: breaking silence about lesbianism is revolutionary. Women coming together, working together as feminists, and staying together, is revolutionary. Your successes and failures are relevant to other women who are organizing. Take yourselves seriously—brag about your work! Write articles for lesbian, and feminist and gay papers and journals. Exchange tips on how to organize, or develop analysis with other groups in your area. Set up ongoing dialogue and discussions with other politically active individuals and groups. Organize a joint action, then take the time to evaluate it and be sure to tell the rest of us about it! *What you are doing does matter!*

Photo/ Billie Carroll

Preparing to Do Workshops

You have a working collective. You have agreement on a general feminist analysis and vision. You are united on specific goals and objectives for your group. You are planning a number of activities and are ready to begin offering workshops on lesbianism and feminism. The following are points to consider as you prepare to do the workshops.

It is quite likely that you have begun this work or that you already have done a significant amount of research. You can use these topics as a check-list.

Familiarize Yourselves with Local Materials and Resources

Read everything: this workbook, go through bibliographies, haunt your local bookstores. Find out what groups exist in your area—feminist groups, women's groups, gay liberation groups and others. Make time to meet with them and find out more about who they are and what they actually do. Exchange information. This also gives them an idea of who you are. Find out where lesbians go to meet each other, to socialize, to get information. What are the formal and informal networks in your town or city? How are lesbians integrated into the feminist movement? Into the gay liberation movement? What have women created to provide concrete support, services and resources for

each other? What do social services and community groups offer for lesbians? What do lesbians do to break their isolation? What groups, unions, churches, political parties and organizations have supported lesbian and gay rights? Look around, what is the level of acceptance of lesbians in your community? What about acceptance of homosexual men? Of feminists? Where would a lesbian mother go if she were fighting a custody case? Losing her job? Where would a lesbian call for help if she were in emotional crisis? What would she find?

Keep lists of everything you find. Write down your observations of the various groups and individuals you come into contact with. Use this workbook and add to it. These resources will be invaluable to you in your work.

Select Who You Want to Reach

This step requires taking into consideration several elements:

* What your group plans to do—your overall objectives and your specific goals;

* What exists in your community—the resources, groups as well as the social and political climate.

From there, you begin to figure out what you believe to be the most effective way of creating the kind of change you want to see in your community.

If your goal is to provide people with accurate, positive information about lesbianism and give them opportunities to act on this new information, both individually and collectively, you still need someplace to start. It is useful to select several "target groups" — groups you are most interested in reaching. You may decide to begin by educating a large number of people already active in feminist, gay and left groups. Your intention is to teach them what you know about lesbianism and from there develop a broad base of political support before you reach out to the general public. Or there may be a "hot issue" in your area right now, such as a teacher being fired for lesbianism. This gives you an opportunity to organize concrete support from political groups and individuals within the community. Or you may select a more specific focus:

* women who are already active as feminists, but are not lesbians and/or are not supporting lesbian rights;

* lesbians who are active in the gay liberation movement and who are not supportive of feminist issues;

* lesbians who are in the closet or lesbians who are not politically active, either individually or as part of a group;

* community and church groups;

* teachers, guidance counsellors and social service workers.

No matter what the target group, the important point is for you to have a clear understanding of why you are selecting these particular groups.

Promote the Workshops

You will want to inform various groups that you exist, have something important to say, and are ready to facilitate workshops on Lesbianism and Feminism. Written material is a good way to initiate contact. Having a brochure or pamphlet that describes your group, your perspective and your work is useful because it can easily be handed out or sent to groups. It is material that can be taken to rallies, information tables at community events, left in offices, distributed at resource centres, and used to leaflet any number of activities. Pamphlets contain information that can also be easily adapted for more descriptive articles about your group. You can say something like:

The Workshops are an excellent resource for any group which wants to discuss lesbianism; for any group providing services for women, some of whom are undoubtedly lesbians; or any group which is feminist or is working for social change.

The Workshops are an opportunity to integrate lesbianism and feminism on an emotional and intellectual level, to look closely at our conditioning and to work at problem-solving both on an individual and group level.

It's easy for information about the workshops to unintentionally be withheld from interested women. Making workshops accessible to disabled women — in terms of information, services and location — is essential. Make a point of contacting groups or associations of disabled people to find out how best to reach disabled women (via newsletters, drop-ins, etc). Also, ask groups and individuals what is required in order that the workshop be accessible. Women with sight or hearing impairment and women in wheelchairs should not be excluded from the workshop due to oversights in preparation and promotion.

Having a consistent mailing address or contact telephone number is essential, particularly in the early stages of making your group and your work known. You have to be accessible to people and prompt about replying to requests for information if you expect to be taken seriously. What about designing an advertisement for feminist and gay newspapers? What about letting people know about you through articles in their newsletters? Do you have access to community television and radio? We know from our experience that people *will* be interested and *will* respond to these ads and articles, so be prepared.

Before the Workshop

You have contacted a group, offered them a workshop on Lesbianism and Feminism, and they've said yes; or maybe they have heard about you and agreed to sponsor the workshop for women in the area. Now the planning begins. Often we are so glad to be invited anywhere that we don't prepare thoroughly enough to make maximum use of the contact. We have written a list of questions that we answer before we begin any workshop. Once we can answer all of these questions, we are certain the mechanics of the workshop will function smoothly and unobtrusively, as our purpose will be clear and responsibility will be delegated and communication open.

In order for a one or two day workshop to run smoothly and effectively, a great deal of preparation and organizational work needs to be done. Some of this involves only your group while other areas require assistance from the sponsoring group. Once you have made contact with a group, it is useful to have a consistent contact within that group — usually one individual, possibly a committee. It is usually their responsibility to assist with the arrangements that need to be made before a workshop. They can also provide you with necessary background information.

Research
the Area and the Group

What is the area, that town or city like? What is the population? Who lives there? How do people make money? What do they know about lesbians? How? What exists as part of the women's liberation movement? What resources and activities are available for lesbians? for women? What are the active groups there? What is the history of this group? Who is in the group? What work do they do? Why would they be interested in a workshop on lesbianism and feminism? What are their expectations? Why did they invite your group? What are their hot issues? What has come up about lesbianism? What is happening in their area right now that people know about, are worried or angry about? What is taking place right now that lesbians are a part of? What would this group be prepared to do? to support?

The Workshop Participants

How many women are coming? (We find 10-15 women a good number to work with). What do we know about these women? Are they already feminists? Are they lesbians? Are they politically active? Are they part of groups? What is their community like? Have we had previous contact with any of the women who will be attending? Who is keeping track of registration — us or the sponsoring group? What is the cut-off number and date for registration? Are there plans made for providing information to those who wanted to come to the workshop but couldn't get in?

Concrete Goals
for the Specific Workshop

The kind of information you get from answering the above questions will be very useful as you establish long and short term goals. Here are some additional points to consider in your planning:

Long term goals and objectives   What do you want to achieve in the long run by working with this group? Why? How can the contact be mutually beneficial?

Short term   What do you want to achieve with this particular workshop? How does that fit into the long term goal?

Procedures   How are you going to put your short and long term goals into practice? How will this politicize more people and create change for lesbians?

Evaluation   Each of the goals must be stated in a simple and clear way so you can actually measure your achievement. How will you know if you have succeeded at achieving your short and long term goals?

Often we are reluctant to set really concrete, measurable goals. We are content to simply "educate." Keep in mind when you are establishing objectives that it is absolutely necessary that we ask for, encourage and demand change if anything is ever going to actually change!

While it is necessary to push for changes in attitudes, it is essential to also ask for support in the form of concrete actions and practice. Do you want support for a local women's group which is in danger of losing its funding because they spoke out in favour of lesbian rights? Do you want hundreds of telegrams and letters to go to the government by next week protesting that cutback? Do you want twenty new groups visibly represented at the next planned action? Do you need to raise $5,000 for a lesbian mother's custody case? Do you need rent money to cover costs of the space used for the Lesbian Drop-In? Then these are the things you ask for. By setting specific goals, you make your work of evaluating your successes, mistakes and progress much easier. More important, though, is the fact that you are giving people something concrete they can *do* to act on their new understanding of lesbianism. You are providing people with a way to believe in their own power by helping them understand that creating change in this society is a lengthy process and *each individual and group contribution matters.*

Planning the Workshop

Which woman is taking primary responsibility for which parts of the workshop? How will we take care of each other during the workshop, evaluating our progress as we go? Are we rested? Emotionally and physically okay?

We have done workshops with as few as 2 facilitators and as many as 6. Our preference is for 2 to 3 women to take primary responsibility and occasionally one woman to act as a monitor. Working this intensely and closely with women in the workshops is a tiring experience. We attempt to be rested and emotionally clear and calm beforehand; we also make sure that we have settled any disagreements with each other.

Location

What kind of space will the workshop be in? Is it quiet? Comfortable? Well-ventilated? Is it arranged with chairs and tables in a circle or with cushions on the floor? Is there a washroom nearby? Is there space for coffee, breaks and lunch close? Are there tables for displays? Who is taking responsibility for these arrangements?

Wheelchair accessibility is important. Locations should have appropriate washroom facilities and ramps or elevators (or no stairs). This accessibility should be clearly stated on any advertising for the workshop. We've done workshops in women's homes, in classrooms, in community services buildings, in offices, in women's centres, outdoors at women's festivals. Our preference is for a large enough space so women can get up and move around, where we can be comfortable and uninterrupted by other people coming and going. If the room looks like a classroom or lecture area, we rearrange the furniture so we can be facing each other and be physically close to each other.

Childcare

Is childcare being offered? Who is arranging this? Where? Are hours compatible with the workshop? Is food for children arranged? If childcare is not near workshop is transportation arranged? Is the childcare being paid for? By whom?

We believe that it is crucial to provide childcare. In some of our workshops, group childcare has been organized for the workshop time. At other workshops subsidies are available so women can pay for childcare at home. Some of the most creative and exciting childcare we've seen has been parallel workshops for children. The goal is to provide as stimulating, educational, and non-oppressive an experience for the children as for the adults.

Food

Who is arranging food? What kind? How is food being paid for? Are women in the workshop also responsible for food preparation and clean-up? Are there sign-up sheets or some system for sharing work? Is there provision for vegetarians? For an all-day workshop we need beverages for 3 to 4 breaks and food for lunch and supper. The best kind of food for a workshop like this is food that can sit for half an hour or so without being ruined. It is difficult to break for meals at precise times. Bread, cheese, raw vegetables, fruit, muffins and soup are wonderful for lunch and any leftovers can be put out again at breaks. We have had success with pot-luck suppers and this

arrangement also cuts down on preparation time. Have a clear idea beforehand of what work has to be done to feed women and how women can participate in sharing the work. Have one or two women take responsibility for making certain coffee and hot water are ready for the breaks. In our experience, women in the workshops want time with the facilitators at breaks and meals, so it is a good idea to have women other than the facilitators preparing coffee and snacks. Be sure to inform the group about these decisions.

Time

When will the workshop begin? When will it end? How flexible can the time be? Can the childcare be extended if necessary?

The workshop as outlined in the workbook can be done in one long, hard day from 10 a.m. to 10 p.m. but we strongly recommend taking 2 full days to allow for time to discuss and deal with emotions and plan actions. The material can also be presented over a period of weeks in 2 or 3 hour sessions as an ongoing series in a consciousness raising group or a drop-in or as an ongoing radio series.

We try to start by 10 a.m. and finish for supper by 7 p.m. — and it doesn't always work! We set time for each section of the workshop beforehand and get approval for this time frame from the group. If there are changes in the time, be certain this is approved by the entire group. Encourage everyone to take responsibility for time — everyone will need to make certain the releasing of emotions and the discussions do not take up all the time. A good workshop also includes theory, problem-solving and action planning!

Money

Is there a fee being charged for the workshop? How much? Set by whom? What about women who can't pay? Are food and rental of space and childcare costs being paid out of the registration costs? Does the sponsoring group need money? Is all of the money going to the facilitating collective? Who is paying for the travel costs? Who is paying for the facilitators' travel? billetting? food? childcare? Does the sponsoring group have money? These decisions need to be clear to everyone — write them down.

We want to reinforce again that we do not want this work to contribute to the creation of professional and paid lesbian feminist workshop leaders. We do these workshops as part of our commitment and work as feminists, and the workshops and this workbook are *not* profit-making undertakings; we do not want them to be that for other individuals or groups either.

If the workshop is being sponsored by a group with funds, such as a social service group, a well-off gay group, a college, or association, we ask for a 'fee for service as facilitators' and our travel, food and childcare costs. We establish minimal workshop costs and charge participants on a sliding scale. No woman will be turned away because she cannot pay. Having money from groups who have it makes it possible for us to subsidize workshops for groups with no money and to pay our travel costs to far-away places to reach groups we otherwise would never have contact with. Usually we request that our travel costs be covered and that we be billetted. Most groups collecting money from the women who attend the workshops do so to cover the costs of food and childcare only. If the group can afford it, we ask for donations to cover the costs of future workshops. Recently, we have asked for donations to cover the printing costs of this workbook. Money is also made available to financially support other groups — such as the lesbian mothers' defense fund. We have never, and don't intend to, profit personally from doing these workshops.

So, if you can make enough money to publicize your work, to cover travel costs, food, billetting, childcare, and offer subsidies to other groups and have enough left to contribute to the work of other groups — you will be doing well. Any profits belong to lesbian and feminist groups organizing to end the oppresion of lesbians.

Advertising

Is the workshops being advertised? Where? Which papers? Which groups? How? By whom? What is the wording? Do we have control or the final say about everything that goes out? Do we think the advertising is effective in reaching who we want to reach?

We have advertised the workshops only through the feminist and lesbian media. When we advertise at all, we word the description to attract the women we hope to work with this time. We use several options for advertising. We may work with the sponsoring group to prepare the leaflet, poster, article, newsrelease, or letter to the editor. We also have provided a standard poster of our own with space for their specifics about time, dates, location, contact phone numbers. We always use the words *lesbian* and *feminist* in advertising to be accurate in our description of the workshop so women aren't surprised about the content when they arrive. We say *come prepared to speak openly about your feelings, to share your ideas, bring your problems; come prepared to hear from other women.* Women need to know this is not a lecture!

When the workshop is being given in a small town or rural area or a city we don't have much contact with,

we leave most of the publicity to the sponsoring group. We will supply examples of advertising materials to give the group an idea of what we usually say, but we believe that the women there will know the most effective way of making contact and reaching out to those they want. Often information about the workshop is given only to members of particular groups — through word of mouth or small announcements in a newsletter. Going public about a lesbian workshop in a small town may not be appropriate.

A sample of our wording:

A Two Day Workshop on Lesbianism and Feminism
This workshop for women explores our reactions to lesbianism and makes emotional and intellectual connections between lesbianism and feminism. This is a chance to talk, to learn, to share ideas and information, to begin creating strategies for individual and social change. This is a place for women to examine our diversity and our commonality as we work toward changes in this society that will benefit all women. Come prepared to speak openly about your feelings, to share your ideas, to bring your problems and come prepared to hear from other women.

Fee (if any and why) Childcare and subsidies available — Phone for more info — Sponsored by: Workshop facilitated by:

Resource Materials

For the workshop you will need: pens, papers, large felt pens, big sheets of newsprint or other paper to put up on the walls, masking tape, thumbtacks. Do you have books, records, buttons, papers you want to make available to women? Do you have posters, charts to put up on the wall? Inspirational quotes you want to write up and hang up? Do you have information and listings of lesbian and feminist groups and other resources to hand out? Booklists? Lists of other local resources?

We think it is crucial to leave material with women once the workshop is over — especially in areas where women do not have easy access to women's bookstores and feminist groups. A selection of basic books on lesbianism and feminism available for sale is very useful (see *Organizing for Change* for booklists). Often our women's bookstore has given us boxes of books and records and T-shirts and buttons to sell on consignment. A selection of feminist papers and articles can be duplicated and left. We want to provide women with a sense of the diversity and richness of women's work and culture, as well as concrete information and places to contact for more ideas and support.

Media

Do you want media coverage? Does the sponsoring group? Consider media coverage as a way of reaching out to those who need the information and would not come to a workshop. What about a local radio hotline show? A newspaper interview? Will you do this with the host group? How will you take control of the media coverage? What about contact with the local alternative media — feminist and left newspapers? See *Media* in *Organizing for Change*.

Follow-up

What is the commitment of each woman facilitating the workshop? Are you willing to be available to women after the workshop? What are you prepared to offer to the women and to the host group after the workshop? What local resources and groups can you encourage to offer follow-up? Where can women go for more information? for more involvement and action? What other work are you prepared to do in that area if you are asked?

During the Workshop

Using this Book

Even though we are familiar with the material in the workbook, we still find it essential to have the script in front of us during a workshop. We put the workbook in a three-hole binder so it opens flat for lying on the floor during workshops. That way material can be moved around to wherever it's most appropriate for that particular workshop, and notes, poems, quotes, reminders, resource lists and photocopies can be written in or inserted.

Facilitating

There is nothing magic about facilitating. You don't need years of school or a degree to know how to care for women, how to challenge ideas and suggest behaviour changes. You don't need years of experience watching 'experts' to be able to present a radical feminist understanding of our situation as women in a language that is accessible to 'ordinary' women. Remember how you learned about feminism.

Remember how exciting those new ideas were—ones that explained your reality. Remember how scary it was to stand up for the first time to do something to fight back. Remember how we are taught not to give value to our own experience. Remember that the reality of our lives is often very painful. Remember that we all need loving support and encouragement to take the risk of becoming better, stronger, clearer and more committed in a world that actively works to stop us from doing so. Facilitating is about keeping all of this uppermost in your mind and reaching out to women with your heart.

Emotions Building trust within the workshop occurs when women are assured that there will be room for emotions — that there will undoubtedly be conflict and pain and that we are able to disagree productively.

As facilitators, we recognize that how we treat each other and the other women in the room is as important as what we say. No matter what our words are

Photo/ Sarah Davidson

saying, women will not believe us unless the words are accompanied by a tone of voice, expressions and actions which are consistent with the message of respect, trust and caring. Facilitating a workshop is giving a demonstration of how we live our beliefs.

You will need to explain, and then demonstrate with words and actions that individual experiences will be listened to with respect; and if a woman is having a difficult time expressing emotion, she will be encouraged to take the time to understand where those feelings come from and what she can do about them. Facilitators need to be prepared to spend time with women on a one-to-one basis during lunch and breaks so women will be able to participate fully in the workshop, knowing there will be time later to continue with their emotional responses.

If there are women carrying so much emotion that it is difficult for them to stay in the workshop, you can make a decision to stop what is happening and ask the entire group to assist the woman in releasing emotion and finding out what is going on. Another choice would be to have the woman leave the workshop with one of the facilitators, or another woman, to talk with her and work with her until she is ready to return. We are very direct with women whose questions or emotional responses are disruptive to the workshop.

Sometimes women's pain comes out as hostility and anger toward us as lesbians. We use criticism, suggest a woman leave for a period of time to do "emotional work" then come back and tell us what she learned, and we have stopped the workshop to spend time working through a woman's fears and anger in the group. This gives all the women present an example of how to handle this type of response in their own lives.

Working with Emotions

(adapted from "Making It Happen," *The Canadian Association of Sexual Assault Centres National Newsletter,* March 1981)

Facilitating emotional work is shorthand for the process of:

* noticing the feelings;

* giving yourself or another woman the time and room to express those emotions, either alone or with others depending on what is judged to be a safe place;

* thinking about those emotions, what they are connected to, what ideas are behind them, what is their context from the past, and why they would be present now;

* making a decision about how to act in the situation, both immediately and in the future, which would increase the women's power and decrease the emotion.

The woman who is doing the work is the only one who can say what is useful, and what is not. If she doesn't think something is a good idea, don't do it! Be certain a woman knows that she always has choice and control over what emotional work she does. Ask questions, examine ideas, check out your hunches, challenge assumptions, make suggestions.

Emotional release is useful because it empowers us to *know* what we feel and to express it. Expressing emotion allows us to think more clearly (minus some of the emotional load) and to act. Emotional release and expression is never a replacement for action!

It is essential when doing emotional work not to confuse support for agreement. You may support a woman in her sadness, anger or fear, and be critical of what she decides to do about it.

Reflecting back, or mirroring what you see (body postures, facial expressions, breathing) is always useful information to give to the woman. Her breathing and body posture may be a way of cutting off feelings. With the information about how she is holding herself, she can make the choice to stay in that position, or to change it and see if that changes how she feels and what she wants.

Contexting is making sense of a behaviour or idea in a particular situation. Given the situation and our oppression as women and as lesbians, how the woman felt, thought or behaved may have been the best response or the only choice at the time. Examine it: what did the woman know at the time? Who did she have to call on besides herself? Who had power over her?

Recontexting behaviour is political problem solving. What is different now? How has the situation changed? Does that idea, emotional response or behaviour still make sense? Does it still get her what she wants? If so, actively choose it, and if not, what other choices does she have now? What will get her what she wants now? How will that choice affect other women?

Every time we do emotional work with someone, we are experimenting. You will learn something new everytime!

An example of facilitating emotional work:

Anne asks for some time during the workshop. She says she is angry and she is afraid of the amount of anger she has. She says she really has no right to be so angry—she has a nice apartment, is in school, is relatively financially secure and is very happy with her woman lover. Yet she is angry all the time. She jumps at everyone, and it interferes. We ask her if she wants to express some of that anger. She thinks it would be a good idea, but is afraid that if she starts, she will never stop. We ask her if she is angry now, and if so, to pay attention to how she is holding her body, where she is tense, and what her breathing is like. Her shoulders are hunched and tense, her legs are crossed and she is breathing shallowly, and holding her breath when she talks.

We point out that she is in control of her anger now by holding herself this way. She can choose to stop expressing her anger any time by repeating her posture and breathing — she is in control. We say it makes sense to us that she cannot always choose to yell at the people she is angry at. We remind her that she is not in that situation now, and we are willing to hear that anger.

In order to express her anger, we ask her to consciously change her posture, uncross her legs, pull back her shoulders, breathe into her stomach, sit or better yet, stand up and say out loud what she is angry about. She begins:

I am angry that no one in the world seems to recognize my love for Jane as anything more than friendship.
I am angry that I have to be quiet in school about being a lesbian.
I am angry that my professor teaches history as if women didn't exist . . .

She goes on for 10 minutes, getting louder and fuller in her description of the realities of her life. Near the end of her time, she begins to wind down and relax. Afterwards, Anne says she feels better, her shoulders are no longer tight, her breathing is easier, and the headache she never mentioned is gone. Yes, she is still angry; the realities of her life are still the same, but she can think more clearly, and act more effectively. She also has an experience of being very angry, *and* in control.

We agree to do some problem solving with her about how to tell her family and friends she is a lesbian, and how to confront her professor on his sexism and homophobia.

— *Vancouver Rape Relief*

Differences and Disagreements

Challenging old assumptions about lesbianism and coming to terms with our oppression as women is a difficult process. Women in the workshops will experience a wide range of emotional and intellectual reactions and, occasionally, there are disagreements and conflicts between women in the group or between the participants and the facilitators. We consistently encourage women to challenge assumptions and ideas and to express their fears and disagreements. This is often difficult for women to do. We are trained to behave appropriately and not to disagree with someone we perceive as knowing more than we do, or

someone who is teaching us something. We are taught to ignore our emotional responses and to think that someone else knows better. To break this conditioning requires both a belief that each of us has something valuable to contribute and a willingness to take the risk of speaking out.

In several workshops, we provided women with structured ways of expressing fears and of openly criticizing us and each other. These are agreements about delivering paranoid fantasies and giving and receiving constructive criticisms. (For a detailed description of giving and receiving criticisms, see *Constructive Criticism*; for paranoid fantasies, etc., see *Solving Women's Problems*) If you use these agreements as a regular part of your own group's process, it will be simple for you to explain and then use the same principles in facilitating disagreements in a workshop. It will be very difficult to use these agreements in a workshop if you are not familiar with them from first hand experience. If you want to use Constructive Criticism and paranoid fantasy in a workshop, practise in your own collective first. If you do not use these formal agreements, you will, as a group of women working together, undoubtedly have established other successful methods of disagreeing with each other. It is useful to make these methods explicit and to offer them as guidelines to the women in the workshop.

With your agreements written in point form and either handed out, or put up on the wall, they can then be quickly explained to women at the beginning of the workshop. Women will have the information in front of them if they want to challenge an idea, deliver a criticism or check out a fear that is getting in the way of their full participation in the workshop.

Giving women ways to openly disagree and to deal with their fears empowers them to do just that! So be ready to facilitate conflicts between women and handle criticisms directed to you.

Caucuses   If the group is made up of heterosexual women and lesbians, white women and women of colour, middle and working class lesbians, mothers and non-mothers, there will be obvious differences in experiences and personal perspectives and maybe in analysis. There is a danger of promoting false unity and blurring the lines by saying, "we're all just women here." There is the opposite danger of focussing on the differences and not building the unity (of commonality of experience) which is essential for effective political work. Acknowledge that there *are* very real differences between us as women. Get agreement that, as women, we are all oppressed, and that some of us face an additional oppression. If there are a number of heterosexual women and others who are lesbians, or if there are a number of women of colour, or women

Photo/ Billie Carroll

who define themselves as working class and are struggling over these ideas and experiences, introduce the concept of caucuses early in the workshop.

In this context, a caucus is a grouping of women, within a larger political grouping, who are united by a *specific* oppression. The women who are in the caucus are committed to emotional support of each other. The caucus is a safe place to express emotions. There is also a commitment to developing an analysis and understanding about the connections between the particular oppression that brings the women together as a caucus, and our common oppression as women. The women in the caucus figure out ways to bring that analysis back to the larger group, along with criticisms, or concrete suggestions for change and action designed to bring all of us closer to our goal of liberation.

For example, a lesbian in the workshop may have a problem she wants to discuss first with other lesbians only. Or, there may be several native Indian women in the group who are ready to criticize a racist remark, and they want to prepare it together. Any woman who experiences an additional form of oppression can call for a caucus.

When the caucus is meeting, the women who do not share that specific oppression meet as a group, with one of the facilitators. There may be emotional responses to deal with. The responsibility of the women not part of the caucus is to be prepared to hear, as openly as possible, any criticisms and suggestions for positive change. There may be self-criticisms coming from the women in this group.

After the caucus has met, dialogue then takes place between the two groups. Fears and criticisms and suggestions for change are brought forward.

Facilitators need to carefully ensure that any struggle is productive. Confrontation may be painful, but it can also be incredibly positive if the experience leaves all of the women confident about their ability to disagree *respectfully* in a way that brings the women closer together rather than dividing them.

Caring for Ourselves as Facilitators

Facilitators are sometimes in a contradictory position within the workshop. On the one hand facilitators have to be able to be emotionally open and vulnerable; to truly share the emotions and fears and joys we have experienced in our lives. On the other hand we must remain sufficiently detached from the process of the workshop to offer support to other women and to take the responsibility for making sure the workshop moves ahead. Facilitators very often have to insist on accomplishing the goals of the workshop especially when women seem reluctant to move beyond talking about the personal reality of lesbianism. It is helpful to have one facilitator who is not responsible for presenting any part of the workshop. This woman can participate in exercises, help get discussion started, and monitor the process of the workshop. She can offer evaluations to the other facilitators at break times and can act as a support woman for the other facilitators.

The amount of emotional and physical support needed by the facilitators depends, of course, on how the workshop goes as well as the individual capacities of the facilitators. We need someone to put food in front of us at meal times and make sure we eat. Sometimes we need to be reminded to go outside for a walk. If the workshop is being held in a strange town and we're staying in a hotel, it is really useful to have one woman to take responsibility for travel and time arrangements, meals, etc.

Occasionally workshops have been held with groups who are having strong disagreements about lesbianism. As facilitators we absorb much of the tension and often afterwards are quite wrecked. A woman with the energy to run baths, rub necks, listen sympathetically, pour tea, and remind us why it is crucial to keep on talking about lesbianism is truly a lifesaver!

The workshop may be very powerful for some women. Occasionally a woman who is moved by the workshop will interpret her feelings as a sexual response to a facilitator. This is not surprising given our sexual conditioning. We have received strong cultural messages connecting sexuality and power and are often attracted to persons we see as more powerful than ourselves. The facilitator is in a position of power and influence within the workshop. She is a source of information and emotional support. She "gives permission" for remembering, feeling, imagining and expressing. For a facilitator to interact sexually with a woman participating in the workshop would be an abuse of power and would directly reinforce all of our confusion about vulnerability, power and sexuality. We make commitments as facilitators not to become sexually involved with anyone participating in the workshop.

After the Workshop

Be certain to set aside a time after the workshop to meet and evaluate your work. Check in with each other: are there disagreements between you which need to be cleared? Do you think someone made a mistake? Are there new things you've learned you want to share? Are there changes which need to be made to the workshop?

Go over the goals you originally set before the workshop and assess your effectiveness. What changes did you see in women? What do you expect to happen now? How will you know? Go over your follow-up commitments.

What did you value and appreciate about your own work and the work of others?

Keep notes about each workshop you do. Include the initial contact with the group, your goals, a write-up of the work done with them, what you found out about that group and the information about that area, notes from your evaluation, and any follow-up activities or actions as a result of the workshop. This gives your group a way to evaluate work on a yearly basis.

Workshop Variations

The basic workshop script presented works well for groups of *women:* we have used it for groups of women who are feminists but not lesbians; women who are lesbians but not feminists; women who are neither. We have done workshops for groups of women with a wide range of self-definitions and the script and exercises seem to be inclusive enough to be of use to everyone. Of course, the emphasis of the workshop alters, depending on who is in the group. Different questions are asked, different issues arise out of the memory and writing exercises, different sorts of responses are called for from the facilitators. This section outlines *additional* points to be taken into consideration when giving a talk or workshop with a mixed group, or with professionals. With any workshop, the questions asked in *Before* and *During the Workshop* must be thoroughly responded to before you begin.

Follow-up Workshop

About the group: At the conclusion of a workshop, we inform women that we would be available to do a follow-up workshop if they requested one. Participants would already have gone through one workshop on lesbianism and feminism. We ask women beforehand to clearly define what they want from us and what specific information would be useful in a follow-up workshop.

Purpose   To increase women's understanding of lesbianism and commitment to feminist action. The main purpose of the follow-up workshop is to provide women with an opportunity to examine and evaluate the changes in their attitudes and actions which have occurred as a result of the commitments they made in the first workshop. The intention is to assist them in developing an ongoing group, with a serious action plan, or to encourage them to join existing feminist groups. Often, the workshop is an opportunity to develop and carry out an action as an actual part of the workshop.

Format   A suggestion is to use a format similar to that of a group meeting (see *Forming a Group*). The process and work of the two days would include:

* rounds: how women are, what they've done and learned since the last workshop;

* building unity:
  checking out any fears and disagreements;

* any specific problem solving or emotional work;

* evaluating the work that has been done since the last workshop;

* planning and carrying out new work (this could take a day in itself);

* appreciations.

The focus of the workshop will be to hear from women what their lives have been like and how they have begun to integrate a new understanding of lesbianism and feminism into their thinking and working. Facilitators need to structure time for emotional work, for thorough evaluation of individual and group work done, and for planning future work.

If the workshop runs over a two day period, an action could be planned and actually carried out during that time. For example, if there is a sexist movie in town which is particularly offensive to lesbians, a leaflet could be written and copied and the group could leaflet the audience as they were entering the theatre, requesting that people boycott the film. Another idea is to spend the evening postering the town with *Lesbians are everywhere* posters. Or the group could take a day to conduct a survey of their community, looking for resources available about lesbianism and for lesbians. Women could go to their local library and bookstores looking for information on lesbianism and feminism. They could meet with school counsellors to discuss what information is provided to students about lesbianism and homosexuality. They could set up a meeting with local MLA's and MP's to lobby for inclusion of sexual orientation in provincial and federal human rights codes. Time would be set aside after any action to evaluate and plan for any follow-up that could result, such as media and community response.

The Workshop as a Series

About the group   The material usually presented over one or two days can be successfully adapted to a six or eight week series. This can be done with a group that meets two or three hours every week: a drop-in, a collective, and it can also be used for presentation on a weekly radio show. Remember, as with any group, several of the participants will identify as lesbians or be wondering if they are lesbians.

Purpose   To get out a lot of information over a longer period of time; to allow for emotional reactions and more opportunity for questioning and evaluating the relevance of the information to one's life. The participants have a longer time to focus on specific areas and there is more opportunity for sharing and discussion as well as for planning and carrying out individual or group actions.

Format   We use the basic workshop script in sections:

Week 1   *Introduction* and *Remembering*

Week 2   *Defining, Choosing, Myths*

Week 3   *Understanding Why*

Week 4   *Creating Visions*

Week 5   *Changing Our Reality* (individual problem-solving)

Week 6   *Changing Our Reality* (group problem-solving)

Week 7   *Closing*

Week 8   *Celebration*

Since there is more time to share experiences, ideas and reactions, this format can be used for larger groups than the one to two day long workshops. Bring additional information, films, books, photocopies of articles for distribution and discussion.

The structure is the same each week and is similar to that discussed in *Forming a Group:* open with a round during which every woman talks about her past week and how she is at the moment. Then there is time for clearing disagreements. Women who want to take time for specific problem-solving or 'emotional work' can do so. Facilitators summarize work done to date and present new material. The remainder of the time is used for reactions to the ideas presented, discussion of how to apply the material in our lives. Women are asked to make a commitment to *do* something in the up-coming week: to read, write, talk to other women, check out resources for lesbians — some project of relevance to the area discussed that week. By the time we reach the strategy section, we expect serious commitments such as challenging homophobic remarks, giving money to the lesbian mother's defense fund, actively supporting the two lesbians in the group, or organizing a lesbian rights demonstration.

Expect substantial changes in attitudes and in self-image from the women who participate in the series.

Highschool and College Classes

About the group   This will usually be a one to two hour speaking engagement to a younger mixed audience. There have been difficulties in speaking to adolescents who didn't want to be in the classroom, so, rather than have a captive audience, you could request that only those who *want* to be there stay and the others take a spare. You could also organize the speaking engagement at lunch hour when young people are free to choose whether or not to attend. It's important to remember that several young women in the group will already identify as lesbians.

Purpose   To confront the most obvious stereotypes and myths of lesbians and give young people a way to confront homophobia. To present a positive image of lesbianism. To make connections between lesbianism and the position of all women in this society. To point out the similarities between the myths about lesbianism and the myths about male homosexuals.

Format   When introducing themselves, facilitators should talk briefly about their lives, where they come from, their work, their children, to give a sense of themselves as real women. If possible, at least one woman should be close in age or life situation to the people in the group.

Clearly state the purpose of the speaking engagement: that you are here to present accurate information about a taboo subject, to find out what they know about lesbianism and what they can do to fight back.

A useful way to begin is with the *Defining* section from the workshop. You will get a good idea of how much they know.

Follow with a simplified presentation of the *Myths* section. Present explanations for why people believe these myths and their relation to traditional male and female roles. Stress the importance to this socity of men growing up to be breadwinners and women as wives and mothers. Lesbianism threatens these roles, is therefore a threat to social order and so is ridiculed, discouraged and punished.

Discuss feminism as the belief that all people have a right to make choices in their lives, whether or not to have children, what kind of work and who to love.

One way to initiate discussion is to ask, *How do you know if you're a lesbian?* Use information from your own life and from *Organizing for Change* to answer questions. Ask direct questions about the realities of being a lesbian in school: what are the problems? How can those situations be changed? Hand out resource materials, articles, booklists, leave behind lists of local groups, drop-ins, upcoming actions they can participate in.

If the group is small enough, you can spend time on the realities of their lives. How are *they* not free? How have they been oppressive to other people who are 'different'? What commitments are they prepared to make to change that? Inform the group that you will stay afterwards and be available for anyone who wants to approach you individually.

If dialogue with the group is a problem because no one is speaking or asking questions, you can try this: circulate papers and pens, ask the participants to write down questions, comments or observations they may have from the presentation. They may also have general questions about male homosexuality. Have them drop their papers into a question box during a short break. This gives the facilitators time to go through the questions and select a number of them to respond to during the discussion period.

If a number of questions come up about male homosexuality or if a number of young men appear interested, suggest they invite a speaker from a mixed or gay male group to come in and present additional information.

Professionals, Teachers, Counsellors, Social Workers. . .

About the group   Professionals are trained and paid to maintain the status quo. Their potential for change as professionals within structured institutions is limited but their potential for change as individual women and men is great. Expect that several participants will identify as lesbian, homosexual or gay and remember that these professionals may be paid workers and as such can organize to change situations within their respective services and institutions.

Purpose   To have the women and men examine their own attitudes towards lesbians and towards feminism; to examine how those attitudes are reflected in their work; to present factual information on lesbianism; to assist them in changing oppressive attitudes; to encourage them to organize and create changes in practice or policy within their institutions.

Format   This workshop can take three or four hours, and can be expanded to a day.

Introduction:

Facilitators introduce themselves and make strong statements of purpose such as, *We are here today to examine attitudes towards lesbianism and how those attitudes are reflected in the work you do. We are not here to argue or debate lesbianism; we are here to teach. Lesbians are the experts on lesbianism and you, along with the vast majority of people in this culture, carry a lot of untrue ideas and myths. Too many lesbians have suffered damage because of the wrong ideas and bigoted attitudes of many professionals.*

Our aim today is to change that situation — beginning with the people here in this room. State that if anyone is there for other reasons, or is not interested in doing that work, they are free to leave.

Use beginning section from *Remembering*.

Break the group up into pairs or threes. Each group gets a card saying:
You can tell a woman is a lesbian because. . .
Lesbians mostly have problems because. . .
Lesbians need psychological counselling in order to. . .
Lesbians mostly work at. . .
Lesbian relationships are mostly based on. . .
A woman becomes a lesbian because. . .

Have the group quickly go through each question and say out their answers to each other. Someone can make notes. The intention is to have their beliefs about lesbians exposed to each other.

Come back to the large group and do the *Myths* presentation. Afterwards, ask people to examine their answers to questions and pick out the myths. Emphasize that everyone in culture is taught these lies. We as lesbians have had to examine the myths and understand why they exist. As professionals, how they interact with people will be based on what they believe.

After a break do a presentation of 'realities'. Use material from the workshop script as well as information from our own lives and *Organizing for Change:* for example, if they are counsellors, use the material from *Psychiatry and Therapy;* if teachers, from *Schools,* etc. Stress that there are women and men who are workers in this field who are harassed, closeted and vulnerable because they too are homosexuals. Emphasize how workers in different fields are joining together to get sexual orientation included in contracts, and are forming gay caucuses within unions.

Break into small groups for problem-solving. Each group gets a hypothetical situation. Use the following or make up situations more applicable to the group. Give each group fifteen minutes to figure out the situation, then have the groups come together and share solutions. Or have groups role-play their solutions. Other participants and facilitators can evaluate the solutions based on whether the solutions reflect stereotypical or oppressive attitudes. Some examples:

* A lesbian mother is fighting a custody case and needs 'expert' witnesses. She asks your help.
* A teenage girl comes to you for counselling. She thinks she might be a lesbian.
* One of your co-workers is active in the gay rights movement. She is about to be fired. The excuse is 'incompetence' but everyone knows the supervisor is very traditional and homophobic.

* Two women come to you for therapy because they are having difficulty with their relationship. They are lesbians.
* The parents of a young girl come to you for help for their daughter. They say the daughter says she is a lesbian and they want her cured.

Close with a guided fantasy from the workshop script that has been adapted to the situation of the participants, . . .*remember a situation in your work life when a student came to you and said. . .a co-worker told you. . .a client asked you for help and you said. . .*etc. Finish with a final round with each person stating one thing she or he will do to implement what has been learned today.

Have resource lists and handouts to distribute.

Be certain to leave lists of groups and upcoming activities so they have an opportunity to offer concrete support by donating money and participating in events.

The General Public

About the group   For a general audience of women and men and also for people from a specific group such as a trade union, a church group, a non-feminist social activist group, a community group or an evening at a college or a school. The situation would involve limited time, mixed audiences with little/or no feminist analysis, possibly hostile reactions, fear, sensationalism. Some of the audience will identify as lesbians, homosexuals or gay or be close to a homosexual man or a lesbian. This workshop would be initiated by an invitation from the sponsoring or host group, presumably for specific purposes which would need to be defined. There could be possible difficulties connecting with the women in the audience, because of men being there and because of women's own fear of lesbianism. The audience is there by choice. Different approaches are needed depending on the size of the audience.

Purpose   To seriously challenge the cultural stereotypes of lesbianism and lessen the fear. To make connections between lesbianism and women's liberation, where possible. To leave them with concrete suggestions of what they could do. To get active support for the women's liberation movement and for gay liberation in their area.

Format   Know your audience before the workshop. What do they know about lesbianism? What's been in the paper lately? Any major issues about homosexuality? What about the political climate? Do these people vote conservative? Are there fights about sex education in the schools? Fights about abortion? Is there a feminist presence in the community? What is it? Is there a 'gay' presence?

Be introduced by the host group since this will establish a link with the audience. Then, introduce yourselves: give information about yourselves, your backgrounds, how you came to identify as lesbians and why, what that has meant for you. Explain why you are here to talk to this particular group.

It can be fun to find out who the audience is. Ask people to raise their hands if they've personally known a lesbian or homosexual. Ask them if they've read any good books about lesbianism. Have any of them gone to a march or demonstration in support of gay rights?

If you have a good film or video, show it now. Then present the myths. You can ask, *"What do you know about lesbians? What have you heard?"* Write the responses on the blackboard/large sheets of paper and then refute with factual information about lesbianism and contexting in feminist analysis.

Give a definition of lesbian and present the realities.

Connect again to the audience and say, *"In an audience this size at least a few of you are connected to a lesbian and know the pain of hiding, silence, isolation. Probably most of us are feeling or have felt close to or loved a member of our own sex, if we look deep enough, far enough back...some of you probably felt funny about your feelings and didn't act on them or maybe you did. Maybe some of you in the audience know what we're talking about when we say how we repress our feelings."*

Present the reality of living as a lesbian, working and being politically active and connect this with our feminist analysis. Encourage the audience to relate that information to their own life experiences: how being called a lesbian when that isn't true is a threat to keep us all in line; how oppression and discrimination work in jobs, housing and custody; talk about scape-goating and how in hard times we blame each other; remember the concentration camps and who else was kept in line; provide a historical perspective and the reality now with the KKK, Moral Majority. This repression is in the best interests of whom?

Discuss our vision. *"We want to live in a world where differences between people are respected, where we are not persecuted for what we're doing as individuals, groups, movements."*

Talk about strategies   Reinforce that change is a process that starts with ourselves, and talk about what they can do: talk about lesbianism, read, educate themselves; challenge jokes about lesbianism; talk to others, talk to children. As a group, they can back groups organizing on lesbianism by giving money, by being visible at demonstrations, by writing letters to editors. Ask what else they can offer to do? Perhaps they can endorse a policy statement or a resolution supporting lesbian rights? Have plenty of information available to leave behind: information on lesbianism, a list of groups and resources, books, books to sell, information on rights of women and the women's liberation movement, policy statements from your group, other groups and coalitions supporting lesbian rights, sheets on how to fight back and strategies for change.

First they came for the homosexuals, but I was not a homosexual, so I did nothing. Then they came for the Social Democrats, but I was not a Social Democrat, so I did nothing. Then they arrested the trade unionists, and I did nothing because I was not one. And then they came for the Jews and then the Catholics, but I was neither a Jew nor a Catholic and I did nothing. At last they came and arrested me, and there was no one left to do anything about it.

— Martin Niemoller, a Nazi prison survivor

Photo/ Sarah Davidson

Handling Men

In a workshop or speaking engagement, there may well be a few men, usually a minority. However, anyone who has ever participated in a mixed workshop or speaking engagement on lesbianism, feminism or women's issues will be familiar with the one or two men who end up asking 80 percent of the questions, who always have an opinion and who refuse to be quiet and let women speak because it is 'reverse discrimination'.

This is not a workshop for voyeurs. It is the responsibility of the men to clearly explain, as part of the round, why they have chosen to attend. Let them know that you expect them to be there to learn, and that you want them to be prepared to take actions that address their male privilege, whether or not they are homosexual. If they appear sincere about their desire to learn and change, encourage them to get in touch with a men's group afterwards so they can continue this process.

If a man in the workshop is being obstructive, ask him to simply sit back and *listen* so he can learn and take in the information. Tell him he can ask questions later, after the women have spoken. Put these requests in a context of our lives as women: never being heard, always being encouraged to be silent and let men go first, never believing our opinions mattered. We are now beginning to take our courage in our hands, and taking and demanding the room to tell our truths and learn from each other. This is doubly true for lesbians and any other minority groups. There are so few spaces in the world where we can be open and direct, and we have set up these workshops to give us an opportunity to do just that. As a man, he can take up plenty of room in the world at large. This is a different situation, and we are demanding his respect through his silence.

If there are a number of men in the group, you may want to call a caucus for the women and perhaps a lesbian caucus within that. This facilitates clear confrontation between men and women.

If male participants are being particularly obnoxious, disruptive or abusive, request that they leave the workshop. Supply them with literature to read, with lists of books and groups to refer to. Encourage them to deal with their homophobic, sexist, anti-woman attitudes elsewhere; refer them to a men's group. There is no need to spend valuable time in the workshop arguing with an individual who is not open to listening or refuses to hear criticism and make the appropriate behaviour changes.

If men are looking for information on homosexuality, you can refer them to a gay men's group. Be sure you have lists of reading material men would find useful.

Organizing for Change

Organizing for Change developed from the piles of file folders we took to workshops. Women always asked a wide variety of questions and we felt some responsibility for providing suggestions of what to read or where to go for information.

Our primary response to questions has always been to tell stories from our own lives. We've tried to follow a similar format here: stories, a little bit of analysis of why we experience what we do and some ideas for beginning to change both ourselves and the society we live in.

Many women contributed stories and analytical articles. Since it was easier to write a story ourselves than find someone else to do it, our lives are quite over-represented. It is also important to note that these stories and articles were written over a period of five years from 1978 to 1983. Perspectives and ideas change all the time and many of us would no longer agree with what we wrote five years ago. We've kept the stories because they are valuable illustrations of certain times in our lives.

Organizing for Change has some serious limitations. We are a collective of white women and although we've tried to list resources which speak directly to the differences in women's lives caused by racism, we acknowledge the inadequacy of our efforts. The lesbian voices heard here are those of women who are, on the whole, young, white, living in urban areas of B.C. and connected to a feminist or lesbian community. They cannot and should not be taken as representative of the diversity of lesbian experience.

Organizing for Change consists of four sections, starting with descriptions of our experiences living as lesbians and progressing through ideas for connecting with other lesbians and consciously choosing to work for social change. The final section, *Finding Lesbian Resources,* lists print and other media, bookstores, publishers and contact groups that appear to have an on-going existence. Addresses for publishers of books listed throughout this book may be found here. We hope that readers will send us information about their resources so we can expand the next edition.

Organizing for Change is designed to be used as supplementary information for workshop facilitators and participants. Appropriate text could be used as hand-outs. The overall emphasis of *Organizing for Change* is to encourage women to see their individual situations in political terms and to work with other women to find solutions.

Feminism as Framework

We use the word 'feminism' a lot. We say, "Feminism as an analysis and a strategy for change is the most effective tool for a lesbian trying to make sense of her life and the world." We think that it is important to be clear about what we mean by feminism, what we believe and why.

> While feminist theory begins with the immediate need to end women's oppression, it is also a way of viewing the world. Feminist theory provides a basis for understanding *every* area of our lives...
>
> — Charlotte Bunch
> *Our Right To Love*

Feminism is a political ideology: a perspective on the way the world functions, developed and articulated by women from our experiences. Feminism analyzes power relationships in human society. The goal of feminism in the broadest sense is equalization of power.

We live in a society where a very small percentage of the population controls the wealth, the resources, the sources of information, the decision-making, the power. This small percentage is white and male. The rest of us provide the labour, consume the goods, birth and raise more workers and consumers. This arrangement is maintained by an interlocking system of capitalist, racist and sexist ideology and institutions. Within this society, women as a group are in a subordinate position. The discrimination against lesbians only makes sense when viewed as part of the overall oppression of *all* women. Specifically, capitalism, the nuclear family and institutionalized heterosexuality are underpinnings of our oppression.

A basic aspect of women's oppression is economic. In a capitalist society, there is an assumption that every woman is economically connected to a man. His wage is supposed to buy his labour, plus a woman's labour of child-rearing, housekeeping, and propping up and caring for the man and children, who are future paid and unpaid workers. This model nuclear family, consisting of a waged worker (the man), an unpaid domestic worker (the woman), and children is also the market for consumer goods produced for profit.

Women often *must* be economically self-sufficient, yet face tremendous disadvantages in the waged work force. Most women work in occupations where the vast majority of other workers are also women: a segregated job ghetto.

We are the last hired, and the first fired. Women's wages are 59% of men's, and despite the lip service paid to equality, that wage gap widens every year. It is too expensive to pay us properly. We're much more useful to society quiet, passive and in the home — and/or quiet, passive and working for low wages in offices, factories, hospitals and restaurants.

Women are in a subservient, dependent relationship to individual men in the family and to all men in society as a whole. Men control governments, money and power out of all proportion to their numbers. This male supremacy is seen not only as an unquestionable reality of life, but as 'natural' and 'right'. In Canada, it was not until 1929 that women were legally defined as "persons". Women in Québec didn't have the right to vote until 1949.

Individual women do, of course, sometimes have power in individual relationships with men. But in the relationship between the group that is men and the group that is women, it is men who hold power. It is not only the economic system that upholds this imbalance, but society's institutions. The ideology behind, and impact of the law, religion, medicine and psychiatry are oppressive to women, and their messages are clearly brought to us through the education system and the media.

Institutionalized heterosexuality is reinforced by and in turn reinforces women's unequal position. Heterosexuality in this society is not seen as a sexual/emotional preference but as the 'natural' pattern for life: family life, emotional life, sexual life and economic life. The institutionalization of heterosexuality is created and upheld by myths, media, education, workplace patterns — in fact, by all the structures and systems of society.

Women who do not fulfill their expected role in society — that of wife and mother — are punished according to their degree of deviation from that role. This social and economic punishment operates as a horrible example to all women of what happens if we step out of line. Lesbians are symbols of the rejection of women's traditional role, and the social taboos against lesbianism and the social punishment lesbians experience exist in order to discourage *all* women from rebelling in any way against the conditions of our lives.

Lesbians are punished for refusing to relate to men and to society as a whole in the approved female role, rather than for loving women.

Feminist theory describes and analyzes reality;

it also creates a vision of a different way. Feminism envisions a society in which respect for the uniqueness of each individual and concern for each person's well-being is foremost. In an ideal feminist society, all productive work would have equal value, and service and maintenance tasks would be shared. All people would be responsible for themselves and would be able to share in nurturing others.

Feminism is committed to horizontal rather than vertical decision-making and organizational structures and to the concepts of co-operation, collectivism, demystification of knowledge and a classless society. Not only must our personal lives reflect our political analysis, but our politics should reflect our personal experiences. We work for integration of body and mind, emotions and intellect, thought and action. Consciousness is not a static goal. The struggle for integration demands a high level of personal responsibility and implies a commitment to using that responsibility in a collective manner. The feminist movement attempts to incorporate these values and principles into our lives *now*. We do not wait for some mythical time after the revolution.

> ## Women constitute half the world's population, perform nearly two-thirds of its work hours, receive one-tenth of the world's income and own less than one-hundredth of the world's property.
>
> *United Nations Report, 1980*

The lesbian is most clearly the antithesis of patriarchy — an offense to its basic tenets. It is woman-hating, we are woman-loving. It demands female obedience and docility; we seek strength, assertiveness, and dignity for women. It bases power and defines roles on one's gender and other physical attributes; we operate outside gender-defined roles and seek a *new basis* for defining power and relationships.

— Charlotte Bunch
Our Right To Love

Resources

Lesbianism and the Women's Movement, ed. by Nancy Myron and Charlotte Bunch (Baltimore: Diana Press, 1975) A collection of articles originally appearing in *The Furies* in the early seventies. The first articulation of a specifically lesbian perspective on feminism. Passionate, angry and inspiring.

Amazon Odyssey, Ti-Grace Atkinson (New York: Links Books, 1974) Atkinson is not easy reading but well worth it. One of the women's movement's major theoretical writers, she explores, among other topics, the reasons why the feminist movement must understand and use the symbolic and actual meaning of lesbianism.

Amazon Expedition: A Lesbian Anthology, ed. by Phyllis Birby et al (New York: Times Change Press, 1973) An anthology of articles covering a wide range of issues. Includes a classic article by Ti-Grace Atkinson on lesbian feminism.

Sisterhood is Powerful, ed. by Robin Morgan (New York: Random House, 1970) One of the original anthologies of the latest wave of feminism. A good intro to the range and diversity of the early movement's thinking.

Radical Feminism, ed. by Anne Koedt et al (Quadrangle Books, 1973) Another anthology of articles relating primarily to the development of radical feminist theory. Includes famous article "Woman-Identified-Woman" by Radicalesbians.

Lies, Secrets and Silence, Adrienne Rich (New York: W.W. Norton, 1979) A collection of Rich's articles and essays spanning a decade. Traces her development of a feminist and lesbian identity and analysis. The introduction alone is worth the price of the book.

Lesbians, Women and Society, E.M. Ettore (London: Routledge and Kegan Paul, 1980) Developed from a phD Thesis in Sociology, this book is somewhat convoluted, but useful and interesting nonetheless. Lots of questionnaires and interviews leading to a fairly comprehensive feminist analysis of lesbianism viewed "in relationship to the position of all women in society".

The Dialectic of Sex, Shulamith Firestone (New York: Bantam Books, 1970) The original articulation of a radical feminist perspective.

Women in Sexist Society: Studies in Power and Powerlessness, Vivian Gornick and Barbara Moran (New York: Signet Books, 1971) A collection of writings covering a wide range of systems and institutions affecting women.

This Bridge Called My Back: Writings of Radical Women of Color, ed. by Cherríe Moraga and Gloria Anzaldúa (Watertown: Persephone Press, 1981) "I had nearly forgotten why I was so driven to work on this anthology. I had nearly forgotten that I wanted/needed to deal with racism because I couldn't stand being separated from other women. Because I look my lesbianism that seriously." — Cherríe Moraga (*Preface*). An uncompromising definition of feminism by women of colour in the U.S. An essential book. (Now available from Kitchen Table Press.)

Building Feminist Theory: Essays from Quest, A Feminist Quarterley (New York: Longmans, 1981) Focusses on the process of creating theory out of women's life experiences. Useful.

Still Ain't Satisfied: Canadian Feminism Today, ed. by Maureen FitzGerald et al (Toronto: The Women's Press, 1982)   An anthology surveying contemporary issues in the Canadian women's liberation movement, including lesbianism.

Last Hired, First Fired: Women and the Canadian Work Force, M. Patricia Connelly (Toronto: The Women's Press, 1981)   Socialist-feminist theory, with a clearly written analysis of women's economic place.

"Lesbian Feminist Theory", by Charlotte Bunch from *Our Right To Love: A Lesbian Resource Book,* ed. by Ginny Vida (Englewood Cliffs: Prentice-Hall, 1978)   The clearest explanation of what lesbian feminism is in her customary concise logical style. An article which we re-read regularly and recommend.

"Lesbian Separatism as a Strategy", by Charlotte Bunch from *Lavender Culture,* ed. by Karla Jay and Allen Young (New York: Jove Publications, 1978) Another excellent and useful article by Bunch. Traces the development of lesbian feminism as theory and practice.

Heresies, 225 LaFayette St., New York NY 10012 A feminist publication of art and politics.

Quest: A Feminist Quarterly, P.O. Box 8843, Washington D.C. 20003   A journal of articles on feminist theory, strategy and practice. Always interesting; often brilliant. Some *Quest* articles have been very important to us, especially Charlotte Bunch's "Developing Feminist Theory."

Sinister Wisdom, P.O. Box 660, Amherst MA 01004 A journal specifically meant to "make women visible" and "to see women from a perspective that does not accept the structures of enforced heterosexuality" (Adrienne Rich). There is an emphasis on culture with lots of poetry, stories, lovely graphics, book reviews, as well as thoughtful and visionary theoretical writings.

We have focussed here on a limited selection of those books and periodicals which have been most important to our thinking about the relationship between feminism and lesbianism. A more general selection of feminist theoretical writings would be available through women's and progressive bookstores. The catalogue of the Canadian Women's Educational Press (The Women's Press) is a good resource for Canadian works: The Women's Press, 16 Baldwin St., Toronto Ont. M5T 1L2 (416-598-0082)

To find feminist groups and bookstores in Canada and the U.S., see:

☐ *Finding Lesbian Resources*

See also *Resources* in:

☐ *Work*
☐ *Creating Communities*
☐ *Working in Progressive Movements*

What's It Like to Live as a Lesbian?

Women in workshops always want to know, "What is it like to be a lesbian?" What can we say? We live in the world as individuals with friends, lovers, families and children; jobs, neighbours, grocery shopping, laundry and bills; interests, problems and responsibilities — just like everyone else. But we live as lesbians and that does make a difference.

Lesbians discover the passion and delight of loving women in the midst of a society which denies the validity, often the very existence, of that love.

So I showed up at the Lesbian Drop-In when I was thirteen. I put on my jeans and my plaid shirt and my boots and I just stomped on down and said, "Hi, I'm a dyke!" The women were really quite terrified.

How Do You Know?

During workshops, facilitators are often asked, "How do you know if you are a lesbian?"

Because we are brought up to assume that everyone, including us, is naturally heterosexual, women have to go through a process of *deciding* we are lesbians. This journey is unique for each woman who embarks upon it, yet the similarities between our stories reflect both the overwhelming cultural restrictions against lesbianism and the courage and power of our loving.

*W*henever someone asks me, "How do you know if you're a lesbian?" I remember when I was asking that question of the first real live lesbian I had ever met. It was a hard question for me to ask then, and it is still a hard question to answer. Basically, you don't *know*. There is no magic answer. There isn't even a right answer. You know you're a lesbian when you decide that's a name you're going to call yourself.

We are all brought up to assume that we are heterosexual. For each of us, the realization that there were other options for our lives came at different times and in different ways. Some women say that they knew they were lesbians as young girls or teenagers. Some women say that the possibility of loving women never crossed their minds until they were forty. Some women live women-centered lives, including close, loving emotional and sexual relationships with women

and never call themselves lesbians. Each woman's life is unique. We come to our self-definitions by a variety of paths.

— *Nym*

*I*t wasn't even a question for me! I was simply a normal heterosexual woman who just *happened* to be loving and making love with a woman for what I thought would be a short period of my life. I was 'between good men', and thought I was being rather kinky and liberated, being open enough to enjoy the delight of an intimate connection with this marvellous, incredible woman. I just loved Judi — it had absolutely nothing to do with her being a woman. I loved the *person* that she was. If I found those same qualities in a man, it would be the same thing . . .

She, however, was the lesbian in our relationship. She identified herself publicly as a lesbian and organized politically as a lesbian feminist. She was hurt by my constant denial of my lesbianism. She left books for me to read. We fought continually. I was firm: "No, I am not a lesbian because I have never been a lesbian before and if I was a *real* lesbian I would certainly know it by now!"

Gradually I met other perfectly 'normal' looking, sounding, and acting women who identified as lesbians. I felt safe enough to acknowledge that I was in a 'lesbian relationship'.

I read and read, but always with an observing, detached perspective, out of interest. I listened to the stories of other women who had come to love women when they had never thought it was a possibility. I began to understand why women loving women was so dangerous to this society; why no one ever gave us the option, but instead made certain that we thought lesbianism was dirty, awful and disgusting. I had to confront all the myths I secretly believed because the reality of women loving women and the information I got from my new lesbian friends was vastly different from all that garbage.

I thought I would die when the relationship with Judi ended. Little by little I pieced my life together again. When I was again interested in other sexual and emotional connections, I realized I had a *choice* to make. I could wait and see what happened, I could look for a man because, after all, I had only loved Judi, not all women, or I could make a conscious decision to seek out other women. That would mean choosing to love women. That would mean identifying myself as a lesbian.

That was the first time I had used the word in relation to myself. Then it dawned on me — that was how I would know whether or not I was a lesbian. Choosing to love women and using the word lesbian to describe my love and commitment to struggle with women meant that I was a lesbian. Knowing I was a lesbian was a matter of choice — a process.

— Yvette

I found out about lesbianism when I was twelve. I got into a fight with another girl. It was outside the school building. The principal saw us and I ended up seeing the school psychologist. She said to me:

"Have you ever wanted to be a boy?"

"Naah," I said. "Boys are nothing. Boys are weaklings."

"Let me rephrase that," she said. "Are you attracted to women?"

"Oh well," I said. "I like women if they can hold their own."

"Let me rephrase that," she said. "Have you ever thought you might be a lesbian?"

"What's that? Is it like a faggot?"

"A faggot is a male homosexual. A lesbian is a female homosexual."

I told her I didn't want to talk about it and walked out. I went to the library and looked up homosexuality and psychology. A book shelver saw me and told me not to bother reading all that schlock. She said it was all written by grey-haired old men and gave me a book on gay rights and Kate Millett's *Sexual Politics* and *Flying.*

So I showed up at the Lesbian Drop-In when I was 13. I put on my jeans and my plaid shirt and my boots and I just stomped on down and said, "Hi, I'm a dyke!" The women were really quite terrified. They told me the age of consent was 21 and that you had to be 19 to get into the gay bars. They told me where the gay bars were.

I never went back. When I was 16, I went to the Young Gay People's Association, but between 13 and 16 I didn't talk to anyone. I knew it was something you kept under your hat.

When I first went to YGPA there was a room full of fifteen men and three women. Most of them were street kids and hustlers. As soon as I got there they all starting telling me that I had to dress up properly and sneak into bars. They had a whole thing about being gay. You had to look a certain way and dress a certain way and act a certain way to be gay. I got into a whole group of people through the bars. A real freaky scene. I had never had a sexual encounter and the pressure from my peers was to 'pick up' women. Everybody said that's what you had to do and I was playing the game, but I was real scared.

I joined the army and when I was stationed in Vancouver I would go clubbing. The army messed me up. I found the same sort of women in the army that were in the bars. I thought, "If this is lesbianism, it's not what they write about in books. It really sucks." I got thrown out of the army because the Special Investigation Office had a picture of me kissing a woman outside a gay bar.

I got involved with Co-op Radio. I met a whole lot of really different gay people there. It was a really different trip — I could relate to who these people were because that's who I was underneath all this discoid plastic person. I really changed my head around and I started to get into feminism. I could see gay culture from a different perspective — a more entire perspective. I mean — it's so hard to deal with all the shit. When you're sixteen and you have to deal with 'coming out of the closet' and 'what's mommy going to say?' and then all of the shit from the gay culture about being 'cute' and 'tight-assed' and 'beautiful'. I look at these kids in YPGA — 16 and worried about what to wear and wrinkles.

I think now I want to work with women. I've devoted enough of my energy to trying to educate a group of men who don't want to be educated. The women's community is pretty organized, but isn't accessible to young women.

Lesbianism and feminism seem to complement

Photo/ Wendy L. Davis

each other. But I'm still very green politically and sometimes I feel like I say things that are off the wall.

What is a lesbian? A woman who is thoroughly independent. Even if you have a lover, you don't have to cling. You work together. You're strong emotionally and physically. If you can't do something, you're not afraid to ask your friends. You're aware of yourself and you're not going to put on a mask.

— Wendy

*I*t always seemed to me that some women were heterosexual one day and then lesbian the next. Not me. That process took me three years. Three years from where I was not heterosexual to where I was a lesbian. During this three years, which I now refer to as my 'bisexual days' I had the opportunity to view and feel heterosexual privilege from many different places.

When I first heard the term heterosexual privilege, I had a two year old son, was eight months pregnant and miserable in my marriage, so I had a real hard time seeing any privilege at all in heterosexuality. Over the next few months, I got out of my marriage, had a baby and got involved in numerous relationships with both men and women. (I now refer to this as my 'new feminist, bisexual, non-monogomous phase'). I began noticing that out in the world my relationships with men were *seen* as relationships

(i.e. in restaurants, stores, schools, airports, etc.) and my relationships with women were not *seen* at all (men would walk up and interrupt a conversation because they saw two women alone, not two women together).

Well, I decided that since I knew what was allowed behaviour between men and women in public I could therefore do the same with women. I soon found out that when my relationships with women were noticed, they did not get the same reaction! In retrospect, this lack of validation seriously hurt my relationships with women. I didn't want to know that even I was susceptible to the world's disapproval — I'd always believed that I had outgrown that the year before!

A year later I was living with a man and continuing to be involved in relationships with women and extremely involved in the women's movement. My love and complete commitment to women was very clear to me, but the rest of the world didn't seem to see it. They could choose to see my love for women or my relationship with one man. Guess which?

My existence by now was becoming rather confused. There were days when I could walk around with my arm around a man and get smiles of approval. That same evening, with a woman, we'd get names and much worse hurled at us. As time went on, it became clear to me that my 'bisexuality' was impossible. It implied that I could love a man or I could love a woman and that it was somehow the same. It denied sexism and heterosexism.

I was at a women's dance one night and I ran into a woman I hadn't seen in five years. She said, "Oh are you a lesbian now too?"

What could I say? I was completely committed to women. I was in love with the woman I was at the dance with. Of course I was a lesbian. So I said yes, and immediately felt sick. And I suddenly understood what heterosexual privilege meant. It meant 'passing'. It meant validation. It meant always having a choice. It meant always having that place to hide.

— Ellen

I found a copy of a letter I sent to Shirley, an adult friend I was relatively close to in Powell River. Also, some of my lists, pages of points I grappled with in my struggles before I left my marriage.

September, 1974

Dear Shirley,
    If you had been home and if Wally would have

agreed to it, I would have talked to you before I left. I knew you would be concerned and anxious for all of us, and I value your friendship too much to leave without any explanation.

Wally and I have had the usual problems in marriage and have been able to handle most of them through maturity, compromise, acceptance and letting each other go his or her own way at times. There have been some ongoing difficulties though — lack of communication, few common interests other than the children, difference in life goals and sexual incompatibility. Four years ago I asked Wally to go with me to a marriage counsellor. His answer was, "No — I don't think there's anything wrong with our marriage."

Typical Wally — what he doesn't see doesn't exist. You know how quiet he is — well, socially he is really chatty but when we're home he has never ever initiated a conversation unless he's been drinking quite a bit.

Mind you — he doesn't think this is a problem. So I accepted it and found outlets elsewhere — church, night school, dancing lessons, and recently school and wanting to go back to teaching. But mostly my outlet was my girlfriends who I enjoyed being with. No guys, because I didn't want any sexual entanglements and I figured that if I grew to love a guy the way I cared about some of my women friends, sex would be inevitable.

Lack of common interests you know about. Sexual incompatibility — the big one! I went through all the standard frigid periods, did the personal analysis, read the magazines and books, tried thinking less and feeling more, tried loving more, did the personal appearance bit to improve my self-image as a woman — everything I could think of. All this while Wally was apparently ignorant that what was so damned important to him was neither important nor fun for me. Also, about eight years ago I fell in love with a woman and was sexually attracted to her. After that, and after a near-complete emotional collapse the following six months that near-sighted Wally didn't even realize was happening, I tried even harder to adjust sexually in my marriage. With effort, time and patience, things improved to a state of tolerable and often pleasant sex. No orgasms to speak of — but I had read that often women just didn't, so why worry.

Well, I've fallen in love with two other women since the first, and I know now that I'm a homosexual. Shirley, I can't pretend any more. I fell in love, headlong, with another woman last year. I've found in loving a woman that I am complete, sexual, orgiastic, warm, receiving, giving . . . the whole thing that love and sex is all about. Except that for me it's only with someone that I love deeply, and with whom I have a total relationship. Deb and I communicate, we share common interests, we have the same ideas and goals, we laugh together a lot, we complement each other's weaknesses and strengths and I want to live with her.

I started seeing a counsellor last spring. I knew I had to make a choice. At that time I had no idea it would mean losing Lynn and Bobby. My counselling was mostly to keep my head from splitting in two — or three — and splintering. Mostly I wanted to find out what was best for the kids. By then I knew I would leave Wally eventually. I wanted to find out, though, if there was a 'best time' or a 'best way' for the kids to handle it.

We talked to the kids in May and said we were considering a divorce and the summer would be a trial separation while I went to summer school in Victoria. I went home one weekend during the summer because I missed the kids so much. When I didn't come up to Wally's demands sexually he went out, got drunk, came home and found me on the phone to my girlfriend. He got mad and beat me up, then fell into my arms crying and sobbing. One hell of a night.

But in talking the whole thing out, we saw that we just couldn't drag it on any longer. Too much hurting has happened already. So after summer school I came home to pack up my things and return to Victoria. I almost reconsidered. For two days — when Wally finally stayed home long enough for me to talk to him — I wondered all over again if we could stay together for the kids' sake. But it would mean little or meaningless sex, I would lose the most beautiful love gift I had ever received, the kids would be leaving home in seven years and so much damage was irreparable. I was in tears most of the time. I tried to get myself put in hospital.

I miss the kids. I never realized how much I loved them until this summer. I grieve for them often, especially Lynn, as Wally isn't going to hire a housekeeper and no 12 year old should have to be the woman of the house.

Wally told me last spring that he would never let the kids live with me if I went to live with Deb. He would fight for custody in a divorce case and he would win, I'm sure. My lawyer did some research and said that some British Columbia courts had awarded custody to the mother in similar cases, but since Wally is known to be a 'good father', I would lose them. So I've given the kids to Wally to finish raising. In a way, my action is selfish and irresponsible. I have some very heavy guilt feelings about leaving the kids. After all, mothers don't do that. I know I'll be criticized sharply by others but they aren't in my shoes and they don't know the whole story.

So I've come back to Victoria. I'll be able to get work here, and I'm starting over. I believe that time will prove this to be the right decision. I hope the kids will be living with me in one or two years time. I hate losing so much of their lives. I'm not sorry I married Wally but I am sorry we never developed our marriage into a total one. I'm discovering now what a total relationship is and I'm no longer lonely.

You mustn't worry about me. After the past ten months I can handle anything.

Peace and love to you.

Sharon

June 1974

I guess what it really boils down to is:

If I stay married to Wally:

PROS
1. keep reputation semi-intact
2. keep steady contact with kids
3. help Wally raise or live with kids
4. financial security guaranteed
5. work part-time as sub or maybe full-time as teacher
6. family acceptance
7. Wally really does love me
8. the kids love me
9. compromise is realistic

CONS
1. no sex - or for Wally's benefit only
2. tension and distrust
3. superficial relationship in family and socially
4. guilt of betraying Debbie
5. much damage irreparable
6. loneliness of my deeper parts
7. could never see Deb again
8. would have to be very careful of who I had as friends
9. I could have a complete emotional breakdown
10. I would be staying out of duty, out of obligation - not from wanting to - it would be a choice made in deep sorrow

If I leave and live with Debbie:

PROS
1. happiness internally
2. a sure sense of direction in my life - a sense of home
3. adventure and excitement - new challenge in making my way economically
4. more education - get a degree?
5. a creative, fired-up lifestyle
6. Debbie loves me and I love her

CONS
1. I would lose the kids - only occasional contact
2. I could have a complete emotional breakdown
3. guilt feelings from leaving the kids could be pretty bad
4. I would lose most of my friends and not see them again
5. I can't ever tell my parents and likely not my brothers and sisters
6. I am betraying the moral values of the church I love and letting down a lot of people who believe in me

OTHER CONSIDERATIONS

1. Wally is finally starting to think about himself and do some growing up
2. I've gone through fads before - will this love with Debbie be a passing thing?
3. I wonder if I have a right even to choose Debbie
4. Wally and I don't have mutual goals

1. Debbie is mature, growing and stimulating
2. We share the same desires, the same goals
3. I'm in love with Deb and happier than I've ever been
4. In time the kids would understand and accept the situation
5. I will tell my brothers and sisters and they will likely accept the situation very well
6. I'm not God - I make mistakes, I'm an ordinary person

Somewhere to Start

☐ Only you can decide. No one but you can possibly know whether identifying as a lesbian makes sense. Don't listen to people who tell you you *must* come-out. And don't listen to people who say you couldn't possibly be a lesbian.

The process of identifying as a lesbian is different for every woman. There isn't a correct way to do it. Some of us feel that our coming-out to ourselves took 15 minutes, and others feel it took 15 years. Remember too that there are all kinds of different lesbians and a multitude of ways that lesbians live. There is no *one* way or *right* way to be a lesbian.

☐ Find out as much as you can about lesbianism in general. Read books, subscribe to newspapers and magazines (see *Resources* and *Finding Lesbian Resources*).

☐ Try to find lesbians to talk with. Most large cities have lesbian or gay phone lines, drop-ins or coming-out groups. You can find out about these resources at women's or progressive bookstores, ads in lesbian, feminist or gay publications or local newspapers, and sometimes through community centres and social service agencies (see *Finding Lesbian Resources*). These groups are glad to talk with women who have not decided whether or not they're lesbians and just want information and contact.

In small towns and rural areas, it is much harder to find other lesbians. Alot of women who can't find lesbians nearby go to a large city for a while — a holiday, six months, a year — to gather information and talk to women. We wish this wasn't necessary. With every passing year, there are more visible lesbians and gay groups in small communities; but for finding large numbers of lesbians relatively easily and quickly, you have to go to a city.

☐ Coming-out is usually a very highly-charged time. Most of us experienced lots of emotional upheaval in the process of identifying as lesbians. Confusion and anxiety sometimes went along with excitement, joy and often an upsurge of emotional, sexual, intellectual and creative energy.

Lesbians who have been out for a long time look back on their coming-out months or years as having been a really special time, sometimes a really crazy time, certainly an intense time.

Even if you have started a passionately happy and healthy relationship, we still strongly recommend that you try to connect with other lesbians. The stresses on any relationship are intensified by isolation, and it's really important to have someone other than your lover to talk to.

☐ Given information, contact with lesbians who are out and an atmosphere of support, women come out. Lesbian organizers need to remember that one of the side effects of any kind of visible lesbian presence will be women taking the step of identifying as lesbians. Giving these women support is an on-going task for organizers.

In cities, set up structured coming-out groups. These could be weekly facilitated meetings that run for eight or ten weeks. Much of the *Stepping Out of Line* workshop material could be used here. The group would also give women a chance to talk about their concerns and fears, find out what service, social, cultural and political events and organizations are happening, and meet other lesbians.

Outside cities, try to establish a network of contact lesbians in towns and regions. Phone numbers could be publicized in regional or national publications that women seeking such information might consult.

☐ If you aren't a lesbian and someone you know is in the process of coming-out, you need to check out your own attitudes. Most people have an emotional reaction to lesbianism, and close women friends especially can feel upset, scared, angry and generally strange. Some of the responses that non-lesbian women can have to their friend's or even aquaintenance's lesbianism can include: feelings of anxiety, nervousness, anger, betrayal, curiousity, sexual attraction, jealousy. These are all emotional manifestations of homophobia and can be worked through. You'll want to read lots of books (see *Resources* in this section and in *Families, Friends and Children*). Attend a *Stepping Out of Line* workshop if it's offered in your area; it provides a safe place for you to explore the complexity of your emotions around lesbianism.

Acknowledge that your emotions *are* involved and try not to dump them on your friend — she has her own! It would be useful for you to be patient and to listen non-judgementally to her. Give her books to read, and encourage her to connect with other lesbians. And let her know really clearly that you will continue to care for her if she chooses to call herself a lesbian.

Resources

Print

Our Right To Love: A Lesbian Resource Book, ed. by Ginny Vida (Englewood Cliffs: Prentice-Hall, 1978)

Lesbian/Woman, Del Martin and Phyllis Lyon (San Francisco: Glide Publications, 1972)

The Coming Out Stories, ed. by Julia P. Stanley and Susan J. Wolfe (Watertown: Persephone Press, 1980)

The Lesbian Path, ed. by Margaret Cruikshank (Monterey: Angel Press, 1980) Another collection of coming-out stories.

Sappho Was A Right-On Woman, Sidney Abbott and Barbara Love (New York: Stein and Day, 1973)

Woman Plus Woman: Attitudes Towards Lesbianism, Dolores Kliach (New York: Wm. Morrow, 1974)

We're Here: Conversations with Lesbian Women, Angela Stewart-Park and Jules Cassidy (London: Quartet Books, 1979)

From the Closets to the Courts, Ruth Simpson (New York: Viking Press, 1978)

The New Lesbians: Interviews with Women across the U.S. and Canada, Laurel Galana and Gina Covina (Berkeley: Moon Books, 1977)

After You're Out, Karla Jay and Allen Young (New York: Pyramid Books, 1975)

Out of the Closets: Voices of Gay Liberation, Karla Jay and Allen Young (New York: Jove/Harcourt Brace Jovanovitch, 1972)

Word is Out: Stories of Some of Our Lives, Nancy Adair and Casey Adair (San Francisco: New Glide Publications, 1978)   Based on the documentary film about 26 gay men and lesbians.

Positively Gay: New Approaches in Gay Life, ed. by Betty Berzon and Robert Leighton (Millbrae: Celestial Arts, 1979)   Anthology on a range of subjects concerning lesbians and gay men.

Lesbians Crossroads: Personal Stories of Lesbian Struggles and Triumphs, Ruth Baetz (New York: Wm. Morrow, 1980)

The Lesbian Reader, Gina Covina and Laurel Galana (Berkeley: The Amazon Press, 1975).

The Lesbian Primer, Liz Diamond (Somerville: Women's Educational Media, 1979)   Written in question-and-answer format, this is a light, accessible educational tool for family and friends. Available from 47 Cherry St., Somerville MA 02144.

Youth

One Teenager in Ten: Writings By Gay and Lesbian Youth, ed. by Ann Heron (Boston: Alyson, 1983) Coming-out stories, for the most part.

Young, Gay and Proud! For Adolescents Wondering If They Are Gay, ed. by Sasha Alyson (Boston: Alyson, 1980)   Very accessible. Information about parents, coming-out, myths, school, health, etc.

Changing Bodies, Changing Lives: A Book for Teens on Sex and Relationships, Ruth Bell et al (New York: Random House, 1980)   Non-sexist in approach, with information on lesbianism.

Growing Up Gay, ed. by Al Autin and Keith Hefner (Youth Liberation Press)   Available from 2007 Washtenaw Ave., Ann Arbor, MI 48104

Film

The Word is Out, by The Mariposa Film Collective (1978)   A feature film consisting of 'portraits' of numerous lesbians and gay men. Distributed in Canada by New Cinema, Unit One, 75 Horner Ave., Toronto Ont. M8Z 4X5. In the U.S., New Yorker Films, 16 W. 61st, New York NY 10023

Groups

To find lesbian/gay groups, phone-lines, drop-ins or coming-out groups, see:

☐ *Finding Lesbian Resources*

See also Resources:

☐ *Families, Friends and Children*

Cartoon/ Melissa Mathis

I asked my 10 year old son, "What's the difference about me being a lesbian mother?" After a long pause he said, "Uh...not much. Women sleep over."

Families, Friends and Children

My sister and I had both been lesbians for five years. The other six kids in the family knew, but we were not out to our parents. It was getting harder and harder to be real with them when we went home, and I was very tired of hiding my life from two people I loved so much. So, one day when the family had come to visit, my sister and I decided that this was to be the night. We took Mom and Dad out for dinner so we could get some time alone with them.

I finally said to Mom and Dad (we'd been talking all night and it was 4:30 a.m. at this point), "There's something I've wanted to tell you for a long time and I guess this is the time. My entire life is women-identified. Everything I do, I do with women. I work on a radio show called the *Lesbian Show*." I showed Mom the article about the *Lesbian Show* in the paper and her face turned to stone. She said, "Is this what the women's movement is all about? Why do you have to go around with a label on your forehead saying lesbian? I'd be so ashamed if anyone found out you were a lesbian!"

I tried to explain how 'lesbian' is something that people are going to have to start changing their attitude about. "I'm proud of who I am. I'm happier with women." Mom talked about how unnatural and sick it was. She was disgusted and disappointed and said she felt weird about ever touching me again or having me touch her. She said "Why not call yourselves women or feminists and not sleep with women?"

Dad began quoting the Bible about the sinful life I was leading and how I would be miserable. He said the devil was taking over and instead of giving in I had to fight and resist him. Mom and Dad both cried.

I was overcome with guilt and sorrow for putting two people through such pain. But what balanced that feeling was a wonderful underlying sense of relief. I could stop playing the hypocrite and expect their love honestly because now they knew who I really was. It was the hardest thing I have ever done.

Four years later, I realize how much that step paid off. Mom and Dad have both read and talked about homosexuality and lesbianism with us. They've tried hard to make sense of the fact that they have two lesbian daughters, but they have very few places to go to talk and get more information. They are pretty isolated in a small francophone catholic community.

But it's made such a difference in my relationship with them. I can be honest about my life, my love for women, my work. They can see that I am relaxed, happy and confident, and although they still don't like my lesbianism, they seem to respect me and admire my courage to live in a way that's obviously good for me.

— Gisele

The family is the institution in this society where we supposedly receive – unconditionally – love, nurturance and support. For many lesbians, coming-out to families taxes this illusion of unconditional acceptance to the breaking point. Some families completely reject lesbian daughters or sisters or mothers; often, the relationships become strained. Many lesbians never openly discuss their lives with their families.

Being a lesbian can set up considerable conflict, especially when our families are important sources of our personal and cultural identity. We want, need, love and respect our families – and want to be loved and respected back. The fear of losing the approval and support of people who are important to us is the major reason lesbians chose to 'not tell'. There are the horror stories: families who say never darken my doorstep again, tears, traumas, arguments and pain. And the all too common stories of lesbians who are under legal age and are sent, against their will, to psychiatrists, committed to institutions, thrown out on the streets.

But for many of us who have chosen to be direct with our families, the rewards are immense. Homophobia *is* a curable disease – and even families respond, over time, to information, patience and emotional honesty.

I am the eldest of three children and the only daughter of an upper class New England family. My parents abide by the Protestant work ethic and, like most people of their class, have the privilege of perceiving the world with a fairly limited view. They are rigid in their thinking. I was brought up with strong ideas about what constituted a proper way to do things and what was clearly unacceptable. I was taught above all to be polite, and we were encouraged not to bring up the more controversial topics of sex, religion or politics in conversation. There was very little expression of strong emotion between us.

I haven't had a 'real' relationship with my parents since I was an adolescent. It was crazy-making to visit them as there was no way for me to talk about anything that mattered to me. So at 37, I finally decided to be 'real' with them; I would give them an opportunity to have a relationship with who I really was, and that meant coming-out as a lesbian.

I decided to write the following letter and take it home so I could read it to them. I chose this strategy because I was doing this alone and was terrified that if I just started to talk, they might yell – and I would freeze. I wanted to be clear. I also wanted them to have the letter to keep afterwards, so once they got over the shock they would have it to refer to.

Dear Mom and Dad,

I think I'll say the hardest things first, then go back and explain the background with a bit of history. The words I use to define myself at this point in time are: lesbian, feminist and radical. Lesbian, because I prefer other women on all levels in my life: intellectual, emotional and sexual. Feminist, because I believe that in the context of this culture at this time, we cannot create a world where all of us have an equal chance in all areas of our lives until we correct the relative imbalance of power between men and women. Radical, because I believe that fundamental (root) changes are needed in the values, structure and economics of this society.

I have known for at least 30 of my 37 years that I was attracted sexually to both women and men. I was aware of it during my adolescence but no one talked to me about sexuality, never mind about homosexuality, so I pretty well suppressed and 'forgot' about those feelings when I got married. I have known some admittedly bisexual men most of my life, but I never knew any lesbians or bisexual women, or so I thought. So I never told anyone, never talked with anyone, and what few things I managed to find in the library weren't very useful. They reinforced the idea that I was somehow 'sick', and that lesbians were ugly, perverted rejects who all wore black leather jackets. When I was about 30 years old, I allowed myself to start thinking about this again. I'm not sure why. In any case, I decided that I could accept this part of myself, because we were all born bisexual anyway and that I would never be in a position to act on my attraction for women since I was monogamously married. I rested there for a number of years, with this knowledge of myself.

At the same time in my life I was aware of another current in myself, one which seemed unconnected. All my life, I have known that I didn't want a traditional life, that I hated restrictions put on me as a woman in this culture. I hated and still hate the fact that many things were impossible, and most much harder, simply because I am a woman. I spent most of my life thinking on some level that I was second best, not surprising since status, money, power and privilege are consigned to men as a group in this culture, especially white men. I learned this early

Photo/ Holly Devor

and I've resented it for as long as I can remember. But I never talked about this either. Who was there to talk to, my husband? He thought I should hold down a full time job, do all the housework and be 'liberated' too. The media had depicted feminists as bra-burning hysterical idiots.

So I continued fighting, alone; fighting hard to be true to myself, fighting the lack of personal confidence, fighting to find out who and what I was, fighting to develop skills and interests that were mine, fighting with Bob who would never actually admit he had faults and who never chose to be emotionally responsive or physically affectionate. His conditioning as a man in this culture taught him well, too.

All this time I was unhappy, thought I was crazy, went to psychiatrists (male, of course) who indeed confirmed I was 'neurotic' and that I needed to accept my female role. They did nothing to support me, they gave me pills which I never took and they certainly didn't encourage me to be independent or think for myself. The only decent thing they did was let me talk, so at least I didn't have to lock *everything* up inside of my head.

Then I met a new friend, and eventually she told me she was bisexual. Not long after that, we made love. And the phrase that kept coming to my mind was not 'coming-out', but 'coming home'. I had forgotten what it was like to have someone touch me with tenderness, look at me with passion, think I was beautiful, want to hear what I had to say. I had never been so intensely 'in love' in my life. It didn't last long. I was too hungry; I had been starving too long. But I'll always thank her; she helped me open doors to

myself that had been closed, and started me on a journey not only of discovering myself, but of creating myself. I told Bob. He couldn't take it seriously. I told him I wanted a year off our marriage, to explore, to learn, but that I would be back, and 'though changes were needed, I was commited to him. He soon told me to make it a permanent vacation. I also told my friends, all but one of whom were pleased and very supportive of my choice to love women.

I've learned to be honest. With myself and with others. I've learned to reveal my feelings, my anger, my passions, my joys, my sadness. I've learned to be responsible for my feelings; that I choose to allow them and no one either makes me feel something or is responsible for fixing it if I am unhappy. I've learned to love others in ways that respect them. I've learned that I'm hungry for equal relationships, and not to give away power to others. I've learned to like myself and to care for myself, my mind, my body and my heart. I've learned to be constructively critical of behaviour without damning the person. I've learned that there's a lot I didn't know and that the process of finding out will last the rest of my life.

I've also learned that there are some things I will not tolerate. I've learned that this society is damaging to those who are not white, male, middle class and heterosexual.

I've learned that 2% of the population controls 80% of the money and therefore the power. I've learned that I'm angry and there are things I will not stand by and put up with. It's not okay with me that friends of mine have been beaten for holding hands with another woman. It's not okay with me that men and women have lost homes and jobs for being homosexual. It's not okay that Native Indian people have virtually no rights in this country. It's not okay that large corporations are poisoning our land, our rivers, our sky. It's not okay that one out of four women is raped at some time in her life. It's not okay that I am in danger because I am a woman, because I am a lesbian. It's not okay that marriage gives a man a legal right to use my body and the product of my work as he sees fit. It's not okay that people are taught they are inferior if they are women, if they are non-white, if they are poor, if they are uneducated.

And I've learned to work hard to change this mess, and I know I can't do it alone. And no, I don't hate men, although I certainly hate some male behaviour. And yes, there are men in my life, not many, but a few.

I want you to accept me for who I am. And I want you to think about these changes in my life, about the contents of this letter, and I want you, too, to make commitments to help change the mess this society is in. I want you to verbally disapprove of every racist remark, sexist comment, or anti-homosexual joke you hear. I want you to support women's rights legislation, gay rights legislation, environmental legislation and anti-discrimination legislation. I want you to give some of the time and money you have to make a concrete difference in the lives of people who are less fortunate than you are. And I want you to be proud of me.

Your daughter, Bet

My parents' response was disappointing. They sat through the letter quietly. My father said afterward that he was in a state of shock and needed to think before he could say anything. He later told me that he had done the best he could. My mother was furious that I had "invaded their privacy by telling other people, particularly my cousins." She still — a year later — has not said anything directly to me about my letter or lesbianism. They both refused to make contact with friends of the family who have two gay children. They persuaded me not to tell my other brother, saying they didn't want me to ruin his first married Christmas. They have seen a minister to discuss it, but I was never informed of the results. One interesting effect: my father immediately stopped carrying my suitcases, which has been a contentious point between us for over 20 years. He now talks to me about cars and carpentry!

My coming-out has so far not produced the real relationship I wanted, and I think now that I was quite naive about what I expected to happen. But I do feel much better about myself. I don't pretend very much anymore. I have come to realize that they will take in as much information as they want and are ready for.

— Bet

*I*am the mother of a lesbian, trying to come to terms with what this means. To me, there is no difference between being a mother of a lesbian and being a mother of a daughter. Fear would be the motivation for any other perspective.

When my daughter came out, I panicked. I saw that life, which is always difficult for any woman, would be even more difficult for one who accepted the label of lesbian. Perhaps what helped me over the initial hurdle was the memory of my own mother who tried to tell me when I joined an extreme left-wing group as a 20 year old, that she feared for my future if I took on a communist label. This was during the great depression years of the '30s, when the only voices in the political arena that made any sense to me were those advocating the revolution of the proletariat.

My mother did not initially understand my political cause, but she respected my right to make choices in my own life even if she saw that I would pay the price for them. We could talk about politics. The respect and affection we held for one another lasted through the 97 years of her life, and it is her influence on me that permitted me to accept without prejudice the choices of my daughter.

When I try to delve into my heritage, I perceive an essence of strong women. This inheritance, coupled with a conviction that did not perceive the world as it now exists to be the best possible of all worlds, encouraged me to listen to and learn from my daughter and her feminist friends. In this process I have shed skins of ignorance, unawareness and misinformation. I have been able to accept that to be a lesbian means to love women. And I have loved women all my life. The strengths of my life derived from women. The rest is politics.

And I could scarcely criticize any young woman for engaging in the feminist revolution since I believe that change is not only necessary but can be achieved, if one is willing to pay the price of non-conformity and struggle. I was able to make my choices and live with them. I extend the same privilege to my daughter.

— Ruth

*A*lthough I had never defined myself as a separatist, my life as a lesbian feminist activist had meant that I chose no intimate contact or connection with a man, or with men as a group. My family lived at a safe distance and there were no males in my day-to-day personal life. As a result, I did not take men into account in my political analysis and practice, except to define them as 'other' or 'oppressor'. Nor did I incorporate other women's attachment to men into my analysis and practice.

Then my younger brother found himself in serious emotional and mental trouble and he badly needed help — the kind of help I could offer. He had been diagnosed as a 'schizophrenic' and I believed my intervention could help keep him off drugs and out of the mental hospital. I made a decision to act on my love and commitment to this young male and to use my political understanding of institutions to his benefit.

So I agreed to work with him and asked for help from groups of women and groups of men who knew about feminist and radical therapy and the integration of emotional support, analysis, and political action to keep us 'sane'.

After seven years of no intimate contact with men, my sudden acknowledgement of the strong emotional connection I had for my brother amazed me. I was then in the uncomfortable position of having to answer some difficult questions for myself during my work with him:

* Did I believe that my preference for women meant not liking or relating to men at all?

* Was this recognition of my deep caring for a male a threat to my lesbianism? Was lesbianism simply a rejection of men?

* What was my view of long term change anyway, if I had not taken my brother into consideration in any of my visions? Were males even *in* my idea of a free society? What did this short-sighted thinking mean, concretely, for the women I worked with who were attached to males who were husbands, lovers, sons, friends?

* What was I to make of the hostile responses of some members of the lesbian community to my visibly befriending and supporting this young man and the men who had agreed to work with him?

As the work of the group formed to help my brother continued, I struggled to clarify some of these questions, and came to some new understandings.

A feminist analysis of the oppression of lesbians and women means that I believe that men are also conditioned, but conditioned to be oppressors. From my own process of change and from being a part of the amazing changes in women close to me, I know it is possible to change that conditioning.

It is possible to love a man and be aware and critical of his sexist attitudes and behaviour. This doesn't mean being there to nuture him and see him through hard emotional times — other men can and should do that for each other.

It is essential for us to have separate time and space to be in contact with other lesbians and women. We need to work, to love and to support each other — to talk, to dream, to analyze, to create and to strategize together, without men.

I reinforced my commitment to develop analysis with other feminists and to put it into practice. Only when we are united as women and operating from a position of clarity and strength can we effectively work with men. There is no room for sloppy thinking, for fighting with each other in front of men.

Actively loving my brother has meant that I have increased my understanding of the reality of other women's lives, and I have carried that understanding into my political work. The majority of women in this society are heterosexual and do love men. Our politics, analysis and strategies must take that into account if our goal is to create social change that will include all women.

My relationship with my brother has taught me to believe that he is capable of changing. He can understand how this society has taught him to be oppressive as a male. Watching him has increased my belief in the possibility of fundamental change in this society, and I begin to think that real changes may occur in my lifetime.

— Yvette

*S*o many different experiences. In my family we weren't orthodox Jews, we were cultural Jews. We didn't keep kosher but it was kosher style. We always kept the holidays and unless you had something really important, you were home for dinner on Friday nights. We had Shabbat, lit the candles. . .

When I was younger my family was my primary source of community, love and acceptance, much more so than my peer group.

My father and I always had a specially warm and loving relationship. I think we're alike in a lot of ways. Some of my best memories are around celebrating Jewish holidays, especially Passover. It was everybody's favourite, probably because it was a home-centered holiday and was focussed around a meal — a *big* ritual meal.

I grew up doing all the things a nice Jewish girl should do. I got good marks in school, I became a teacher and I married a nice Jewish boy, a social worker. I realized I was a lesbian way before I came out. However, I was freaked out at the thought of being so far from the mainstream and of telling my parents, because of their disappointment and all. Those fears kept me from claiming my lesbianism for a long time.

Coming-out to my parents seemed to me to be the hardest task I would ever face. My father's reaction of rage and horror was most painful. My parent's are now trying to understand and accept my choices. We have a strong foundation of loving and caring about each other and that gets us through the hard times.

My family and my traditional Jewish community brought me much joy and a place to belong, but as I got older I felt my role was very limited there. Neither the women nor the men take the strengths of women seriously. Women's concerns are viewed with derision and their capabilities are taken for granted (I'm sure these ideas would be vehemently denied by all involved!). So many of the women of my youth were and still are strong and vibrant, yet few of them know it. I have a lot of anger and sadness about that.

In my family I learned to stifle my feelings and reactions to many things. I've had to be with women in order to find others who see the world as I do, to start to feel comfortable with who I am and to have a place to express myself in ways that feel good to me.

For the past three years I've celebrated Passover with other lesbians. I've sat in 'my father's place' and led a feminist seder. In a way, I feel as if I have come full circle.

— *Baylah*

Friends

For most women in this society, friendships with other women are reliable and life-long sources of emotional sustenance. Women are allowed to be close to their girlfriends, although these relationships are seldom acknowledged as important or meaningful. In fact, the range of relationships amongst women is a spectrum of complex shadings.

*I*t was an incredibly painful experience. I had shared three years of my life with this woman. We were student nurses together and roomed in the residence across the hall from each other. We studied together and planned to share evenings. And we often arranged double dates since it always felt safer going out together, especially with men we didn't know well. We would compare notes after each adventure. She remained my close friend throughout my pregnancy even when I was forced to take a leave of absence from nursing. Unwed mothers weren't viewed positively by a hospital administration which prided itself on the good moral character of its nurses.

Donna was my best friend. We kept few secrets from each other. We remained in constant contact after I had left nursing and moved across the country. So, a few years later, when I fell in love with a woman and finally figured out it had something to do with being a lesbian, I couldn't wait to tell Donna. I travelled to Winnipeg to visit her.

We went to a bar to talk. I heard about her new job, her new home, the new man in her life. I told her about my new job, my new home, and excitedly began to tell her about the new woman in my life. I leaned across the table, touching her arm as I had always done in moments of intimate conversation.

"And Donna, I'm so happy being a lesbian. It's truly the best thing that's ever happened to me. My life is whole, I am understanding and liking myself more than I ever thought possible . . ." I knew I was beaming with pride as I spoke.

But I couldn't figure out what the tight, closed expression on her face meant, no smile, no acknowledgment, no shared joy . . . Her body stiffened. I was puzzled. She pulled her arm back sharply and then stood up. I was now totally confused.

"I think that's disgusting", she sputtered. "I think it's sick. I think you've become very weird. I don't want you to *ever* touch me again. If you're going to be into that sort of thing, I don't want to hear about it, and I don't want to be around it." She turned and literally *ran* out of the bar.

I sat in stunned silence — hurt and very upset by my friend's rejection. I was still the same woman she had known for years. She had listened to hours of conversations about my life. Only this time the information was about my loving a woman and being happier than I had ever been. Why was something so good for me and so right for me suddenly making her see me through totally different eyes? Why would she run from me? I had no political context to put any of this in — no feminist analysis to help me understand homophobia and our own deep fear of women. All I knew was the pit in my stomach that was left after my best friend walked out of my life because I loved another woman, and was finally beginning to love myself.

— Yvette

*T*he first time I saw Ellen was at a Fraser Valley Women's Coalition meeting. I was a British Columbia Federation of Women regional representative and was involved with the struggle within BCFW to change women's attitudes about lesbianism. I was meeting all these women for the first time and I was scared. I knew that I was going to have to come-out to all of them, go through the explanations and fights and hard times, and feared I would be the only lesbian there.

I walked into the room to find a woman wearing cowboy boots, a heavy plaid flannel shirt and a big felt hat. I was entranced — and hopeful that my problems of isolation were over. We talked farming, trucks, dogs and feminism and I was delighted to have found such a kindred spirit. But she wasn't a lesbian, I discovered, as she mentioned a partnership with a man. I visited her farm and liked Reg too. Immensely. They were both potters and gardeners and farmers and artists and wonderful, warm people. The two of them listened to me and fed me and looked after me when I was sick.

Ellen and I saw each other often, worked together and talked a lot. We talked about lesbianism — me trying to explain and her trying to integrate a political perspective with her emotions and experiences. I basked in her affection and caring for me, but I was always a little nervous. Could I be friends with a woman who wasn't a lesbian — *really* be friends? Could she really understand my life? Could she really not either feel threatened by me or fall in love

Photo/Baylah Greenspoon

with me? Sometimes she would hug me and I would stiffen.

Two years into the relationship, I was talking with her on the phone. She had just been to the doctor and was being evasive about telling me why. I pressed for an answer and she said, "I'm pregnant and I didn't want to tell you because I thought you wouldn't want to be friends any more."

I was devastated and angry. We went through another round of conversations about lesbianism and the myths about childhating, about feminism meaning choices and my choices being different from hers and friendship and trust and on and on . . .

Valerie Sage was born and now there were four of us sitting around the kitchen table. Valerie is three now and Ellen and I are still having conversations about lesbianism and feminism and women and friendship.

Finally, about a year ago, we started saying to each other, "This friendship is important to me." And I hug her back now.

— Nym

*S*hirley is a high-school counsellor. She and I are quite good friends, and had team-taught a fitness program together for three years. She was really shaken up when I left Wally and the kids to live with Debbie and she did a lot of thinking and growing because of me.

Within two years, she was including homosexuality on the agenda topics in the life skills/sexuality part of the high school program that she taught, and she was presenting it as a viable alternative. She tried to get speakers for the guidance classes. The parents of some of the kids got wind of it and complained to the school board. They almost caused her forced resignation. But they couldn't because she had an excellent reputation there after 15 years. She did have to retract her plans for the guidance classes. She was accused then and afterwards of being a lesbian. She always faced things head-on. A fine woman.

— Sharon

*N*ina *was killed this afternoon. She was riding her bike and* was hit by a bus. Absolutely nothing prepares you for the shock. She was 22, she played bass and was struggling to make enough money at a waitressing job to finish music school. She had moved across the country to live beside a new ocean and to be as far away as she could from her parents and her sister so she could find a women's community and live openly as a lesbian. She was one of us, a part of our circle, with her friends, lovers and a newly developing consciousness. She was a woman you'd expect to be around, to see at the bar, to be coming to a demonstration, to be whizzing by on her hard-earned Italian racing bicycle, stopping to have coffee.

Death is so far away for most of us. It belongs with our older relatives, maybe our parents. It is something that happens after a long illness.

My first reaction was to go to my friends, to the women who had lived with Nina, to the women she played with, the women she called friends. I was surprised by the variety of responses — shock, tears, hurt, disbelief, anger. Women were not prepared, not familiar with their intense emotional and intellectual reactions, and I was worried for many of them. It is a serious lack that we have not yet created rituals for death, out of our needs as lesbians, as feminists. We have no 'rites of passage', no ways to grieve and celebrate our deaths, no ways to comfort each other, no ways of grasping the significance, the finality, of death.

Four of us stayed particularly close after Nina's death, telling others, caring for ourselves and quite quickly having to be practical. We knew the police had contacted the family in Newfoundland. What else had to be done? So began the stark, ugly reality of dealing with the system — with institutions that take our deaths and make them statistics; that make them pretty bodies turning a profit before being put into the ground, robbing us of our right to experience death and to know someone in death.

We dealt with police, hospitals, coroner and the funeral director — as Nina's 'friends'. I realized with desperation that this whole society has little comprehension of constructed families, and *no* recognition of families made up of women, of lesbians. We had nothing to say that would convey our anguish at the loss of a lesbian sister to those who control the procedures after death. We were not her 'real' family; why were we making this our business?

We were determined to be part of Nina's death and not have her taken from us because society and her family wouldn't recognize a connection as strong and as real as blood. We decided to contact the family directly and offer them a ride from the airport, a place to stay, company and transportation to and from the numerous places they would be going to clear up all the final details.

"Nina's roommate and friends", we said in identifying ourselves. Did they know she was a lesbian? We thought her mother might. Should we tell them explicitly? How? What do we say to indicate that we are the women Nina *loved?* To let them know that Nina was different, that she saw the world differently? That her 'tom-boy' phase had blossomed into outlaw status. That she had made a life-choice of lesbianism? How to give them a context for our hurt and loss — one that would be so easily understood had we been husbands or male lovers? How to gently tell them about the Nina we knew — a Nina they had never wanted to know? She would have wanted them to be happy for her because her choices were good for her. Would all this simply be more hurtful for them?

We were nervous that the family would march in, saying, "Thank-you very much, get lost now", and leave us without information or any decision-making power about the funeral arrangements. We decided to let them know that we were prepared to offer what we could, to talk about Nina when they were ready to hear, but that we would not back away out of respect for them as family. We had been Nina's family too.

There was definite tension when they first arrived. They just didn't understand who we were. Her father commented later in the week that we were, "Alright for women who didn't wear bras." Initially, her mother was very firm about the funeral. They would do it their way with a service in a suburb of the city, inaccessible to women without cars. "We don't want any more of Nina's friends there. You can always do something when we're gone. We know Nina one way. You know her another. We want to say goodbye to *our* Nina." Understandable, but hard to swallow.

Like most of us, Nina had not thought her own death to be imminent. She left no will, no written or verbal indication of what she wanted done with her things in case something should happen. Oh Nina, you left us stuck with some pretty difficult decisions! Legally, everything belonged to her family: her music, her bicycle, her clothes, her sketch book, her money, her journals — everything. And it just didn't make sense. They would not understand her drawings, not cherish her necklace, not appreciate her dykey vest and shirts. What about her photo albums and the pictures of the women she'd loved? Momentos of events she'd been to? What about the intimate letters and cards from friends and lovers? Her writings? What would she want her family to even see?

Before the family came over, her roomate and I went through all of Nina's things, cleaning up and making decisions about what to keep aside. The criteria was simple: would this item be of particular significance to anyone? We kept some clothes, the passionate love letters and writings about and from women to be returned to them, her journals to stay with us, maybe to be given to her sister at some point. We packed up all the remaining clothes and items. We were sad that her parents would be getting her music, her instruments and her money — it made such sense to us that these should go to another young lesbian struggling to be a successful musician.

The funeral arrangements were finally made, her family had sorted through her belongings, taking some and asking that the rest be destroyed. At last there was time to walk along the beach and talk about Nina. There were soft, gentle conversations with her mother and sister about Nina having been a woman who loved women, not as a phase, but as a serious, positive life-choice. Neither of them wanted her father to know. Nothing makes the telling easy. They really didn't understand lesbianism, and didn't want to be close to it, or have to incorporate that reality into their existing knowledge of Nina. It was uncomfortable for them and for us. There are a thousand questions they were afraid to ask.

We are confident that our decision to be open about Nina's lesbianism was appropriate. It means that at least two more people in the world have a connection with lesbianism, that they will have to look differently at their conditioned negative attitudes about homosexuality because they are seeing it through their love for Nina. And in a world where lesbians are feared, hated and persecuted, and in a society where our reality is invisible, that matters.

The family left for home, with Nina's ashes in an urn, to someday go back to the Norway she loved. And here we are, with a hole in our lives, a woman gone from our community, and our sadness that one of us never lived to touch her potential, her passion, never saw her lesbianism, her music, her politics, as making a real difference in this world. We have taken the time to cry, to talk, to be together, telling Nina stories, talking about meeting her, knowing her, describing what she gave to us, saying out loud now all the things we never said — it helped ease the loss of her. It was a way to reaffirm the love and the tenderness between us, acknowledging that living through hard times like this, together, means we are building the bonds that will make us family to each other too.

— Yvette

I'm lying by the pond on a hot summer day with some friends. As we often do, we're talking about our lives and our lesbianism and our connections. How did we meet each other? How did each of us come-out? How did we get involved with the women's movement? Who do we know and how did we come to know them? We talk and laugh and play in the water and the sunshine — four women, four friends.

The afternoon wears on, and we cover the major political and personal histories of the Vancouver and Toronto lesbian communities and are well on our way to commitments to an oral history project for the next lesbian conference. It comes to me that I'm having a splendid time. I would rather talk about our lives and lesbianism that almost anything else. This is my home, this — as one of the woman has been heard to remark — "somewhat dumpy" patch of totally useless but gorgeous B.C. forest, and I'm glad to be sharing it with my friends.

Sunshine. Conversation. Food. Laughter. We have shared a house in the city, the four of us. We share an interest in feminist politics, in writing, in books. I think of the many women who have swum in this pond, the many conversations held in the cabin, and the web of connections that gradually formed amongst us. Women who have been lovers, co-workers, housemates, lovers of friends, friends of lovers, friends. I think of these four women, and imagine the work we may yet do together and the years we will share and the circles *we* will form.

It's been ten years for me now. Ten years of locating myself in this strange uncharted place called 'living as a lesbian'. There will be more times together, more conversations, more shared homes and work, more joy and struggle. On this day, in this sunshine, with these women, I begin to trust in the nurturing, in helping each other with our individual work, in working together, in acceptance and rest. In traditions, rituals, and memories. I begin to believe in lifetimes.

— Nym

Children

*A*bout three years ago I went to Seattle to visit some friends. In the women's bookstore I found some nice T-shirts with a picture of a woman and a child and the words "Women loving women loving children". I bought three — one for me, age 31; one for my daughter Jo, age six; and one for my son Jesse, age eight. The kids loved the T-shirts. I took Jo and Jesse to a local Italian resturant for supper and as we waited for our spaghetti, Jo said, "I'm gonna wear my T-shirt to school tomorrow."

I tried hard to hide my mild panic. It was perfectly clear to me that it was not a great idea for this little kid to arrive at school with a T-shirt announcing that her mother was indeed a lesbian and shameless about it. It was perfectly clear to Jesse that it wasn't a good idea to wear the T-shirt to school. He had always asked lots of questions and knew that in some circles being a lesbian was, to say the least, frowned upon.

None of this was clear to Jo. She had grown up in the women's movement. From her birth she'd been around women loving women in a community where that was the norm. Her mother loved women. All the women she knew loved women. Even the heterosexual women she knew loved women since, for Jo, loving had little to do with sexuality.

Jo had managed to grow up to six years old assuming that all women loved women. So we looked at each other, and I said, "Jo, maybe it's not such a good idea to wear your T-shirt to school."

She of course asked why. I tried to explain that there were some people who didn't think it was ok for women to be lesbians because there were certain roles that people thought women should fit into and being a lesbian didn't fit into those roles. She said, "Why?" I carried on trying to explain that it was like other prejudices and bigotry, like how some people didn't like blacks or Jews. She understood a little since we're Jewish and have talked about Jewish history and persecution. So she thought another minute and looked at me and looked at her brother and said, "But if women can't love other women, how are we supposed to love ourselves?' I could only smile at her and say, "Yes Jo — I know."

Two years later the T-shirts still fit. Jesse resolved the T-shirt question by wearing his inside out. One day he came home from school (his second day in grade five) wearing his — but right side out! I said to him, "Hey Jess — were you wearing your T-shirt like that all day?" He looked up and said, "Yeah, they don't understand what it means anyway and if they do, I don't care." I laughed and said, "Yeah — me neither".

One of the joys of motherhood is when your kids can nonchalantly say, "Yeah, I know you're a lesbian and I know people don't like it — but I think it's just fine."

— Ellen

Photo/ Ingrid Yuille

Many lesbians are mothers. Like all mothers, we had children for various reasons. Like all mothers, we at various times love, resent and are ambivalent towards our children. Like most single mothers, we deal with low incomes, childcare, schools, transportation, feeding, cleaning and nurturing — usually alone. Unlike most mothers, however, many of us live with a continual fear of losing our children.

The question of how to come-out to our children can be difficult, especially given the potential of a child custody case. However, the experiences of lesbian mothers have shown the importance of being open and emotionally honest with our children. Living a lie in the intimacy of our day-to-day lives is not healthy for children or grown-ups.

---

*I*n this culture, we distinctly separate people by age —
adolescents, over 21, over 30, senior citizens. We separate children from adults to the extent that most people, unless they personally bear children, take little responsibility for rearing them. The media is full of the new two-income childless family. Some people resent their tax money going to education, daycare and other programs for children. I believe that it is irresponsible not to integrate our lives with children. If we want a better world and are fighting for it, we must include in the struggle those who will inherit what we create.

Besides all that, I like kids a lot. I like their perspective on the world. They teach me ways of seeing that I have forgotten. I like being in an environment of joy at learning and questioning and trying to figure out how the world works. I like the affecton without strings. I like the playfulness.

I have a few children in my life, but one in particular whom I live with on weekends. We both think our relationship is very important and quite wonderful. I'm the person in her life who has time to spend just walking or talking or teaching things I know. I can be this because I don't have 24 hours a day, 7 days a week responsibility for her care.

My being a lesbian hasn't been an issue until recently. For a time our interaction seemed threatened because of her parents' concern about her fascination with sex. She was getting more information from me than she was getting from them and she was talking in front of them about women loving. Her parents were scandalized. We all talked about it, and it seems ok now, but

sometimes I don't want her to go home or I get scared that something will happen and I won't get to see her anymore.

— Johanna

*W*hen I came out as a lesbian my husband refused me
custody of our four year old son. He said "I would rather see my son in an institution than living your kind of life". He was quite prepared to battle it out in the courts using all of the tools — slander, expert witnesses, social attitudes — at his command.

Well, I couldn't stay so I left. He agreed to my having Aaron every other weekend and for longer periods in the summer. As time went on it was bearable. The women I lived with and I learned to live with being 'weekend parents' and we all fell into a kind of routine. This went on for four years. Then suddenly this spring I called one day to finalize arrangements for picking up Aaron for the weekend, as usual. I asked for Aaron and was told that Aaron and his Dad had moved to Alberta and left no forwarding address.

I was devastated. We all were. We had somehow fallen into the assumption that this couldn't happen to us. We were feminists! We had given workshops about lesbian mothers! We knew all about oppression and were somehow therefore immune to it! No lesbian mother is ever immune.

I was lucky. I had a well-paying job and could afford to try and track Aaron down. I had a community and support from the women I lived and worked with, support from my parents and family and a good feminist lawyer. It was still hell. I didn't know if I would ever see Aaron again. I knew that his father would tell Aaron that I wasn't phoning or coming to get him because I was 'too busy" or I "didn't care". And I knew that even if I could locate them there was no guarantee that I could ever see Aaron again. In the eyes of the world I was an unfit mother — I had given up my child. Obviously I didn't care about him.

After about three months the woman my husband had been living with gave me his new address. And Aaron did come for a visit this summer. And maybe again this Christmas. Maybe, if his father doesn't change his mind or move again or something. And I won't know for certain until I meet the plane and Aaron is on it — or he isn't. And I will never again believe that this can't happen to me.

— Yvonne

Somewhere to Start

☐ Only you can decide whether or not to come-out to your family. There are no blanket rules or all-purpose strategies: just your own sense of readiness, what you already know about your family dynamics — and what the experience of other lesbians has taught us.

Most lesbians who are out to their families are glad they are. Some encountered few difficulties. Others found that despite the tears and trauma and sometimes years of strain, the chance of an honest relationship was worth the price. Some discovered that the reward of telling was a real and supportive relationship.

Many lesbians choosing not to come-out to their families are certain that the outcome would be outright disapproval and rejection. It seems best, emotionally and otherwise, not to take the risk.

☐ It is important to think seriously about the possible repercussions of telling. Is it safe? If you are 17, financially dependant on your family and they have the legal power to have you committed to an institution, you are in a far different position than a self-supporting 26 year old. Do you have children who may be involved in a custody case? Is there a history of violence in your family? If coming-out will put you at risk, you'll have to carefully consider how and *whether* to do it.

☐ If you have decided to come-out to your family, there are various approaches and preparations you can make. It's a good idea to talk with other lesbians about their experiences and to let them know what you're doing: you'll want their support and friendly ears. Some women come out first to a sister or brother with whom they're especially close; then that sibling can be there when they tell the others. Taking one parent aside can also be effective. Writing a letter or a series of letters is one way of easing the tension and giving everyone reaction time and space.

It is not uncommon for parents to 'go into shock' upon learning you're a lesbian; it's equally common for them to fall hook, line and sinker for all the tacky myths about lesbians and the 'causes' of lesbianism — despite what they've known for years about you and themselves. For both your sakes, it's valuable for them to have outside resources to consult. Arm yourself with a few good books to give them (see *Resources* this section and *Religion*). If a Parents of Gays group exists in your area, contact them beforehand or give your parents their number. If they are religious, try to put them in touch with a sympathetic minister, rabbi, etc.

☐ Don't expect everything to go terribly — or wonderfully — at first. Most people need a fair amount of time to come to terms with their feelings and prejudices about lesbianism. Some parents will pretend your conversation/letter never occurred; others will invite self-pity. Things usually settle down after awhile, so be patient.

☐ Being open about your lesbianism with friends is very important. In our opinion, it is impossible to construct healthy, enriching friendships while concealing such a significant dimension of your life. It's not just a matter of coming-out, but of ensuring that your life experiences as a lesbian are part of the give-and-take of the friendship. To be closeted or unable to talk about being a lesbian would be crazy-making for you — and quite possibly bewildering for your friends.

☐ Some friends will have no trouble with your news and others will have an immediate emotional response, and then come round. Supplying them with useful books and the time to work through their feelings is beneficial for both of you. If a friend's response is cold or negative, don't stay around for any abuse. You will need to strike a balance between protecting yourself and being patient with them (see *Somewhere to Start* in *How Do You Know?*).

Inviting your straight women friends to attend lesbian cultural and social events is one way of keeping your life integrated (as well as exposing them to the marvel of masses of women-identified-women!).

☐ The children in your life need to know that you are a lesbian. Living in a family where there is concealment and deceit is unhealthy for both kids and grown-ups. On the other hand, don't expect your children to always be open with their friends about your lesbianism: it is up to them to decide when they feel safe and comfortable enough to do so.

☐ If you might be facing a custody battle and being out to your children could have serious repercussions, you will want to proceed with caution (see the *Law* section for information and resources relating to child custody).

☐ You and your children will benefit from contact with other lesbian moms and their kids. The chance to talk with women facing similar issues and questions is invaluable. The experiences of children raised in lesbian households will differ radically from most other kids. Making connections with the children of other lesbians, feminists and gay men will let them see that they're not alone, that there are indeed other families made up of varying combinations of adults and kids.

☐ Children will need lots of positive, accurate information about lesbianism and their kind of family. Most of what they pick up in the world just reinforces the concept that the nuclear family and heterosexuality is the only acceptable way for people to live. Queer jokes and name-calling start at a really early age. Talk to them about your life and encourage them to come to you with their questions.

There are non-sexist and non-homophobic kids' books available at women's bookstores, as well as some good books for teens. You could ask your local library to stock them. Try to find out what kind of information on lesbianism and homosexuality is being presented in the schools.

Photo/ Dorothy Elias

☐ When planning social, cultural and political events in your lesbian and women's communities, take children into account. Besides having decent childcare, provide the kids with a real programme: workshops, entertainment and opportunities for them to talk about their realities and problems.

Resources

Print

Check out your local or regional library: sometimes they have compiled a list of progressive books on homosexuality for young people or can refer you to another published bibliography. Regardless of where you learn about a book, *never* give one to family, friends or children which you haven't read and found appropriate.

Families and Friends

A Family Matter: A Parent's Guide to Homosexuality, Charles Silverstein (New York: McGraw-Hill, 1977)

Homosexuality: Time to Tell the Truth to Young People, Their Families and Friends, Leonard Barnett (London: Victor Gollancz, 1975)

Now That You Know: What Every Parent Should Know about Homosexuality, Betty Fairchild and Nancy Hayward (New York: Harcourt Brace Jovanovitch, 1979)   Written by two mothers of gays.

Coming-Out to Parents: A Two-Way Survival Guide for Lesbians and Gay Men and Their Parents, Mary V. Borhek (New York: Pilgrim Press, 1983)   Written by a mother active in *Parents of Gays* groups. Includes a chapter about religion.

Parents of the Homosexual, David K. Switzer (Philadelphia: Westminster Press, 1980)   Offers a Christian perspective.

Children and Teenagers

The following books deal with sex and relationships, or are novels with homosexual characters or books by and about gay teenagers.

Young, Gay and Proud! ed. by Sasha Alyson (Boston: Alyson Publications, 1980)   A very good basic book directed at gay teenagers, some of it written by gay teenagers. A clear, feminist perspective. Try giving it to your children, gay or straight. And try to get it into libraries, especially school libraries.

Changing Bodies, Changing Lives: A Book for Teens on Sex and Relationships, Ruth Bell et al (New York: Random House, 1980)   A very good book which mentions homosexuality throughout, discussing it with quotes from teens. Has a specific section on homosexuality.

Girls Are Powerful: Young Women's Writings from Spare Rib, ed. by Susan Hemmings (London: Sheba Feminist Publishers, 1982)   *Spare Rib* is an English feminist magazine. This is a good book.

One Teenager in Ten: Writings by Gay and Lesbian Youth, ed. by Ann Heron (Boston: Alyson Publications, 1983)

A Way of Love, A Way of Life: A Young Person's Introduction to What It Means to Be Gay, Frances Hanckel and John Cunningham (New York: Lothrop, Lee and Shepard Books, 1979)   Useful, but not perfect.

Make It Happy: What Sex is All About, Jane Cousins (London: Virago, 1978)   Excellent book on sex and sexuality for teenagers, with some information on lesbianism and homosexuality. Lists English resources.

Growing Up Gay, ed. by Al Autin and Keith Hefner Youth Liberation Press, 2007 Washtenaw Ave., Ann Arbor   MI 48104

Playbook for Children About Sex, Joanni Blank (Down There Press) A workbook for kids to fill in and keep private. Includes bits on homosexuality. Intended for little kids, but fourteen-year-olds have been known to walk off with it. Available from P.O. Box 2086, Burlingame   CA 94010

When Megan Went Away, Jean Severance (Chapel Hill, N.C.: Lollipop Power, 1979)   A picture book about a mother and child coming to grips with the fact that the mother's lover has moved out.

The following is mainly fiction for teenagers.

Rubyfruit Jungle, Rita Mae Brown (New York: Bantam, 1977)

The Shattered Chain, Marion Zimmer Bradley (New York: DAW Books, 1976)   Science fiction about a world in which some women are chained and some are "Free Amazons." Some violence.

Patience and Sarah, Isabel Miller (New York: Fawcet Books, 1976)   A romantic, historical lesbian novel. Adventurous, too.

Lesbian Lives, ed. by Barbara Grier and Coletta Reid (Oakland: Diana Press, 1976)   Short biographies of famous lesbians.

Breaking Up, Norma Klein (New York: Avon Books, 1981)   An ordinary, positively portrayed lesbian mother in it. Your children may be comforted to know that you are this mainstream.

The Journey, Anne Cameron (New York: Avon Books, 1982)   Dedicatd to "all the little girls who always wanted to and never could grow up to be cowboys." A great book. A number of parts are quite violent, including some rape scenes.

Annie on My Mind, Nancy Gardner (New York: Farrar, Straus & Giroux, 1982)   Another 'young adult' novel. Positive portrayal of two young lesbians. (15 years and over)

Happy Endings are All Alike, Sandra Scoppetone (New York: Harper Row, 1978)   A novel about two teenage women who are lovers. One gets raped and beaten by a boy she knows who then threatens her with exposure if she reports him.

The following are books about living with children.

Rocking the Cradle: Lesbian Mothers, A Challenge in Family Living, Gillian E. Hanscombe and Jackie Fraser (Boston: Alyson Publications, 1982)   A British book with an oddly defensive tone — perhaps meant for straight people. Full of stories by lesbians and some by their children. This is *not* a 'how-to-deal-with-your-children' book.

The Lesbian: A Celebration of Difference, Bernice Goodman (Brooklyn: Out and Out Books, 1977) Speaks to the fears of lesbian mothers leaving marriages — you *can* have fine, healthy children.

Ourselves and Our Children: A Book By and For Parents, Boston Women's Health Book Collective (New York: Random House, 1978)   Has some information on lesbian mothers in a chapter called "Parents Who Are Gay", but the rest of the book seems to neglect our perspective. Overall, a useful book about living with children.

Whose Child Cries: Children of Gay Parents Talk about Their Lives, Joe Gantz, (Rolling Hills Estate. CA: Jalmar Press, 1983)   Interesting for the comments of gay parents and their children; the author's approach, however, is highly suspect.

"Being a Lesbian Mother" by Diane Abbott and Bobbie Bennett from *Positively Gay: New Appraoches in Gay Life,* ed. by Betty Berzon and Robert Leighton (Millbrae: Celestial Arts, 1979)

Growing Up Free: Raising Your Child in the 80's, Letty Cottin Pogrebin (New York: Bantam Books, 1981)   Has a good, extensive chapter on homosexuality and how not to be homophobic and accept that your child might be a homosexual. No mention that the mother may be a lesbian. This book is about non-sexist child-rearing.

Children and Feminism, Lesbian and Feminist Mothers Political Action Group (Vancouver: 1982)   Has a great deal to say about non-oppressive child-rearing, and integrating children and parenting into our feminist and lesbian communities. Available from P.O. Box 65804, Stn. F, Vancouver, B.C.

Bulletin of The Council on Interracial Books for Children, 1841 Broadway, New York, NY 10023 Their *Bulletin* evaluates children's materials, trade and text, for their messages about racism, sexism and classism. Lists resource groups and alternative materials.

Gay Parent Support Packet, National Gay Task Force, Rm. 506, 80 5th Ave., New York, NY 10011

Film

In the Best Interests of the Children, by Iris Films (1977) A film about lesbian mothers and their children, it presents a wonderful array of lesbian lives. Available in Canada from DEC Films, 427 Bloor St. W., Toronto, Ont. M5S 1X7. In the U.S. from Iris Films, P.O. Box 5353, Berkeley CA 94705. There is also a discussion guide for the film, available from Community Relations Division, American Friends Service Committee, 1501 Cherry St., Philadelphia PA

Groups

In some areas, you can find *Parents of Gays* groups through lesbian/gay groups, social service agencies, church groups or progressive health clinics. A number of groups throughout Canada and Québec are listed in *The Body Politic*, P.O. Box 7289, Stn. A, Toronto, Ont. M5W 1X9. To find U.S. resources, consult *Our Right To Love*, ed. by Ginny Vida (Englewood Cliffs: Prentice-Hall, 1978)

See also Resources in:

☐ *The Law*   ☐ *How Do You Know*
☐ *Schools*   ☐ *Religion*

Lovers and Sexuality

For many women, being a lesbian is very closely linked with being in an intense emotional/sexual relationship with one other woman. Many of us define ourselves as lesbians because we are in such a relationship. Relationships with lovers are often primary in our lives. They are sources of intimacy, support and self-definition.

When we were doing the final edit of the book we discovered an interesting phenomenon. Most of the material in this book assumes and speaks to the commonalities between all women. But this section on lesbian relationships and sexuality very definitely speaks to lesbians. Loving another woman cannot be adequately described or understood intellectually: only experienced.

Ah, the myth of romantic love! I, of course, knew all about the trade-offs I was expected to make in heterosexual romantic love. I would give myself, completely and forever, to some fine man and, in return, I would find true love, passion and lasting fulfillment through becoming *his* (his property, his wife, the mother of his children . . .) Eventually, I would get lost in the trappings of wedded bliss and family.

But, try as I did — and I certainly did try — I could never find the man who could move the heavens for me. I wasn't interested in being submissive and subservient without a lot of rewards. So gradually I rejected that standard way of defining myself as a 'real' woman. But — my developing feminist analysis did not

prepare me for the serious mistake of falling into the same trap with a woman . . .

Although it all seemed so right at the time, 'falling in love' proved to be a very unhealthy experience for me. I could tell I was 'in love' with her immediately. The feelings of excitement. The rushes of sexual tension. We did the whole thing. We ran off together, professed our undying love and devotion to each other until the distinctions between her and me blurred and we became 'one'. We spoke without words, wrote poems about how magic, how special, how perfect this connection was, how well we fit together, how we were just made for each other, how we would never need anyone else. It was so easy to be with her. We were secure in our new love.

It was so different with a woman: the heavens did move and I did see stars when we made love. This was really revolutionary! We would never be bound by men's rules. We were free to love and create our lives together as we chose. But I never realized how much we had internalized those male rules and how they would continue to be in operation even though there were no men around.

What happened? To begin with, I had never stopped to analyze those feelings of 'in love'. I had never learned that being 'in love' was much more an indication of my own state of vulnerability than it was about seeing someone else as a real woman, liking her, *then* choosing to build a relationship on solid friendship with shared understanding of the world, and common work. Those 'feelings' meant that I was ready and willing to take risks, to expose myself, to be open, all without really knowing *why* I was behaving that way, or thinking I was in control.

Sexuality became an expression of the intimacy and a symbol of the vulnerability and submission — "I'm yours." I thought she *made* me feel that way; that she opened me up — "I never felt this way before — you are magic." Because of this, my sense of well-being and wholeness became more and more dependent on her presence and constant reassurance of loving me — "But I just can't live without you." Eventually, all the unrealistic expectations that go with believing two individuals are only halves of a whole came down on us and insecurity became the overriding theme of our day-to-day lives. We were trapped in an unorthodox, undefined, but very real, marriage.

I could hardly believe my own emotional responses. Sexual jealousy, possessiveness, fear — just like the movies about the passionate, heterosexual romances, except that there was to be no happy ending here. We often behaved like classic hysterical females — we fought with each other and hurt each other, sometimes even physically.

I recognize now that my inability to deal with all the pain and to put my hurt into an intellectual, political framework was in part due to the lack of emotional support from other lesbian feminists. We weren't working together to create healthier ways to relate intimately and sexually with another woman and other women.

At that time there was an immense contradiction between my political work and my personal life. In my theory development collective, we carefully studied and examined the position of women in this society and developed a feminist analysis of our oppression as lesbians. We looked at the nuclear family, marriage, enforced heterosexuality and violence. Yet I struggled in isolation with the intense emotional pain caused by not understanding how these institutions were not simply about men holding down women 'out there'. They were also ideas and beliefs that I had absorbed, and they were affecting me in a very direct way.

— *Yvette*

I like getting older. I know so much more now. When I first came out I loved Chris with all my heart and soul, and when she left me it was so painful I was sure I would die right then and there. Women would say to me, "There, there — first relationships are always a disaster." It was not comforting at all. I gave up on love. I almost gave up on sex. I certainly gave up on trusting or being vulnerable or really caring about another woman.

Now I have been a lesbian for a few years and I find myself saying to women who are crying on my shoulder, "There, there — first relationships are always hard."

I am very tactful, but it's true. First relationships are always hard and second relationships are often reactions to the first relationship and have their own problems; but after a few, you do learn.

You learn first of all that there is nothing in the world that will ever hurt as bad as the first time. You do survive. With any luck, and some work, your old lovers after a few strained months or years become friends and as time goes by, the worth of a few good friends becomes apparent.

Of course it does get confusing with lovers becoming friends and friends becoming lovers and where the boundaries are between women, if indeed there are any. Perhaps that's what I'll learn in the next ten years. And of course, there is still pain, but on the whole, it is much better than 'love of my life, I will do anything for you', which is how I was ten years ago.

I always want to warn women. I want to wear a sign saying, "Beware — loving women can hurt!" I never have though: solidarity and keeping up a good front and not crying in public and all that. I now think that it is high time we start talking — at least among ourselves — about what happens to us in sexual relationships and intimate relationships and friendships. We have to talk about what we have learned.

— *Nym*

After years of barely surviving the pain of 'on-again, off- again' sexual relationships, I decided to take a serious look at my belief about being, and having a lover.

My pattern with both men and women had been a series of initially intense, relatively monogamous, primary relationships which eventually lost their lustre and became filled with tense, serious arguments. The result was dissatisfaction and both of us would seek out new lovers to ease the frustration, all the while claiming commitment to the sexual relationship with each other. But in practice, we drifted little by little out of the intimate circles of each other's lives. 'Serial monogamy', I heard it called. So much investment for so little return.

I wanted to do it differently and better,

Photo/ Jacqeline Frewin

especially when I began to identify as a lesbian feminist, as a woman who loved women and who had an analysis of how women are oppressed by the traditional forms of sexual relationships. So I worked to figure out what I wanted from sexual relationships with women. I was primarily looking for integration — for an end to the rigid distinction between friends and lovers. I wanted intimate friends who would share my commitment to our relationship in all its changing forms, which could include sexuality at various points. I wanted women who would be a solid part of my life for a long, long while.

I wanted to *understand* my relationships: I wanted both of us to have a realistic appraisal of the other so we would know *why* we were attracted to each other and *why* we were deciding to act on that in one way or another. No more powerlessness when faced by strong emotions. No more, "It just happened, we fell in love." My choice of who and when to love would be based on what I saw, what I knew of the other woman, what we did together and what I felt — not on magic or karma, not because the moon was right.

Making those concepts of clarity and choice a reality was and is no small feat. Like most women, I come attached to a long history of loving in old patterns, of equating sexuality with romanticism, power, powerlessness, pain, dependence, jealousy and insecurity. It was, and it still is, long hard work to learn to love in healthier ways. Society doesn't supply us with any role models to help us build equal relationships —

especially not with other women — so we have to experiment and invent.

And I am finding much joy in recreating sexual relationships. I am learning that equality is indeed possible. I seek out women who share my understanding of the world and the condition of women. I look for opportunities to share political work. A crucial step for me was learning that I am in control of my emotions and actions — that I can give of myself without giving myself away. My choice to love then comes from a position of strength and autonomy.

I am learning to be honest and to take more responsibility for myself, my feelings and my behaviour. I am respectful of myself: no one owns me, no one 'makes' me feel anything. I value my sexuality more and more, taking responsibility for this expression of my vulnerability free of insecurity and possessiveness, and learning to enjoy sexual experiences simply for the physical pleasure.

A major success for me is learning to end the isolation caused by 'loving packaged in couples,' learning to deprivatize the personal. How I treat the women in my life, how I conduct my sexual relationships, how we disagree with each other, how we make love, how we work together and play together all come up for discussion and analysis in my conversations with friends and co-workers.

Integration means that I expect my political theory and practice to be reflected in every area of my life, and I expect to be challenged and supported by the women around me about how I conduct every relationship.

I look forward to constructing new families: ones made up of the women I am emotionally, intellectually and sexually linked with and the children in our lives.

— *Yvette*

*S*he captured my heart, my spirit and my mind immediately, this bright, generous, bold warm woman who came to work as part of my collective. We connected on so many levels: feminism, lesbianism, a love of poetry, of putting ideas into action. We became friends — best friends — quickly, and I was delighted! It was inevitable that the desire for exploring the sexual potential would surface sooner or later. And did it ever! Suddenly, our positive, non-sexual, dynamic friendship became difficult and confusing for me.

Casual gestures of affection were loaded with sexual overtones. The other women we were sexually involved with were threatened by our closeness and freaked out. It became difficult for me to concentrate on working together in the office with all that sexual tension in the air. We were awkward with each other. We started to censor touch and words. The sparkle of spontaneity in the friendship seemed lost in the tense, heavy times.

For both of us, our friendship meant that we had a commitment to work through the hard times with each other. So we talked a lot, and little by little reaffirmed our choice to continue creating a powerful, full connection that wasn't based on the traditional bonds of sexual intimacy. We confronted our ideas that sexual attraction is a force which *must* be acted on. We learned that sexual attraction does not exist in a vacuum, that sexual attraction is based on the love and respect and genuine liking we had for each other. We learned that it really is a choice whether or not to *act* on sexual desire. For reasons that had to do with work and time, we had decided to acknowledge our sexual attraction but not to make love on an ongoing basis, and not to change the definition of the relationship from friend to lover.

The attraction, of course, still remains. We do act on the sensuality and attempt to do that creatively. We exchange cards, share books and poetry and flowers. We are openly physically affectionate. We give each other back rubs, make dates and take the time to cherish and consciously build the friendship.

There are the struggles caused by both of us still giving priority and more intimacy to our lovers but we are challenging the practice of valuing lovers more than friends in our daily lives. We are beginning to blur those distinctions by creating something vibrant, alive and special between us — a relationship that defies categories and inspires us to learn varied and better ways to love on all levels. We are understanding that loving, too, is an evolving process and practice.

— *Yvette*

Sexuality is a complicated and sometimes frightening subject for us to talk about. We don't have a feminist analysis of lesbian sexuality, and most of us have varying degrees of discomfort when we talk or write openly about our personal experiences, conflicts, compromises and questions. We are only beginning to work through this discomfort.

Why is it so hard for us to talk about sexuality? Why haven't we used the process of sharing our personal experiences, discovering commonalities, creating a theory and working out strategies? We have been able to use this process to come to a feminist perspective on other areas of our lives. Is sexuality 'too personal'? Too painful?

In this culture women are defined almost exclusively in sexual terms. All of us grew up tending to define much of our self-worth in terms of our sexual self-worth. Our success in relationships was very important to our success in life; in fact, synonymous with it. Our emotional sexual life was supposed to be our major preoccupation. Love would make us happy, fulfill us, allow us to find ourselves as women. Although many of us rejected this blueprint for our lives when the object of our love and fulfillment was a man, have we transferred many of these same expectations into our lives with women?

If all women share the conditioned importance of sexual and emotional fulfillment, then all women share the fear and insecurity and agony of 'failing' in this area. In the lesbian community where we are, if nothing else, all women, are these expectations and fears strengthened?

Lesbianism is culturally synonymous with rampant, perverse sexuality. Although we reject the cultural definition, how many of us carry some of those sexual myths inside? Do we cling to beliefs that lesbian sex is always easy, blissful, orgasmic, overwhelming? And that there's something wrong with us if that is not our experience? Or do we, in rejecting society's definition of lesbianism, ignore the real interplay of sexuality and passion in our own life? Where does a woman go when she has questions about her experiences of sexuality? What can she read? Who can she talk with?

I was fascinated by sex from the ages of ten to twenty. I read everything I could get my hands on from *The Sensuous Woman* to pornography. I experimented with anyone who crossed my path who was remotely interested. After I was about 14 I confined my physical encounters to males, although my fantasies developed into a very precise pattern of a sexual encounter with a faceless, nameless woman. When I first met lesbians at the age of 19 and started to read feminist articles about lesbianism, I began to believe that my nameless, faceless woman might someday actually appear. Shortly afterwards, I leapt into bed with the first woman who asked me, and we fell in love.

I thought I had finally found the truth, the way and the light. Who needed fantasies when reality was so good? I had read the articles about lesbian sex being non-genital, exploratory, free from preoccupation with orgasm . . . so I was completely unprepared for the power of the desire that I felt. Sure, we spent weeks in bed cuddling and kissing and stroking and talking and playing – and I loved it. But sometimes she would walk into the room and just look at me and my body would melt with wanting her. I wanted her all the time – any time, anywhere, under any circumstances. After years of having an orgasm only after a long hard struggle with the time just right, I was having orgasms from kissing her. I would have orgasms when I made love to her; I would have orgasms when she made love to me. I had no idea sex could be like that.

Somewhat unfortunately, the rest of the relationship was not quite so trouble-free. She left me 14 times in two years. She believed in non-monogamy. That was fine with me except that it seemed as though that meant she slept with me for a month or so, then she slept with someone else for a month or two, then she came back to me. I tried sleeping with other women too. Fair's fair and all that. But it just wasn't the same. So even though I was in emotional pain all the time, when she smiled at me, my body tightened up and I welcomed her back with open arms all 14 times.

Finally she went back to England and I started to reconstruct my life. I decided that sexuality was too much trouble, made me powerless and should be abolished from the world. I carefully chose relationships that would be sexually and emotionally non-demanding and non-intense. I figured that I had had my sexual period, as it were, and now I had to get through life with as little trauma as possible until I died. I didn't want to think about sex or talk about sex or acknowledge I had any needs or desires. Lesbianism meant work and struggle and oppression and politics. Nothing to do with sex.

That was seven years ago. I am still uncomfortable with sexuality – my own or anyone else's. I have started to read about it again. I talk about sexuality now with my lover and a little with a couple of friends. We're having interesting conversations about why we link sexuality with powerlessness, how come sometimes we have orgasms with some women and always with other women and not at all with others. We're talking about how we believe that someone else *gives* us sexual experiences, how sexuality 'just happens' and is 'magic' and if all that isn't true, then what is?

And sometimes my lover walks into the room and smiles at me and my body tightens up and sometimes I even admit that it's happening.

– Nym

Celibacy is not the same as being asexual. I have gone through times of being asexual and know what it feels like. Celibacy for me is wanting to have my sexuality for myself; not wanting to share it with anyone. Celibacy means not being lovers with anyone but myself.

I chose celibacy because I was feeling really raw from a relationship that ended. I realized that I wasn't very happy with my life and who I was. I wanted time and space to help myself and to work on becoming who I wanted to be.

I tend to get very emotionally close to people I am being sexual with, and it was hard for me to keep any sense of myself as having power in a relationship. So I decided on celibacy as a protection for myself. After a few months, I started to see celibacy as a valuable choice. It freed a lot of emotional energy. I didn't have one core person to nurture all the time or to depend on for my nurturance. I was able to look at all sorts of different ways relationships could be, and because I have been sexual with other people since I was 15, choosing this period of celibacy was my first real chance to explore what *my* sexuality was like.

What I really missed was the cuddling, having my feet rubbed and my back scratched: little things that are really rare when you don't have a lover. I started asking my friends for what I needed. I learned how to tell when it was safe, and I certainly got to know people better. My friendships deepened.

Other women's reactions were a problem. A lot of women had a hard time taking my celibacy seriously. They would make jokes and assume that I must be looking for a lover — that there must be something missing from my life. There are a lot more women who are celibate than admit it or define themselves as such. It's something that is ignored and not viewed as valid.

I think I really blossomed. I put all the energy I would have put into a lover into myself. I developed more strong new friendships in the two years I was celibate than I ever had before in my life. Celibacy has also given me time to figure out under what circumstances I would be lovers with someone else. I looked critically at the socially acceptable kinds of relationships and thought about what would be growing relationships for me.

When I first consciously decided to be celibate, women asked me if that meant I wasn't a lesbian any more. I never doubted that I was a lesbian. Being a lesbian for me has given me control of my life and becoming celibate has been an extension of that control.

We were all brought up to believe we would find the perfect partner, the happily-ever-after marriage. Even though we are lesbians, we still cling to those ideas and often find ourselves devastated by the changes that shake up a sexual relationship. It is so important that we believe in ourselves, that we see ourselves as strong, competent survivors, as women who can stand on our own, who enjoy our own company, who don't see ourselves as only 'halves of a whole', unfulfilled unless we find that perfect soul-mate. We need to know that we are already whole beings — and from that position build relationships.

My whole life is, as much as possible, women-centered and defined. I like and love women. Sexuality is important to me, but I know that being a lesbian doesn't just mean being sexual with women.

— Johanna

*F*rom 1975 to 1979 I was part of a lesbian feminist theory collective that talked about absolutely everything — except sex. I had no idea what anyone else in the group actually did while they were making love, having sex or masturbating. Because we didn't talk about sex, I had no way to make sense of my own or other women's experiences.

The things that shaped my ideas of lesbian sexuality were sexual experiences with lovers, what I could get my hands on to read, and some conversations. These conversations were mainly with heterosexual women who were beginning to discuss lesbianism, or women who were coming-out lesbians after finding the feminist movement. Lesbian sexuality was discussed in the context of emotional commitment and love for women. Sex was pleasurable, soft and tender; the focus was not on orgasm. If you had good sex with a woman, it meant you loved her.

There was minimal erotic material by lesbians about lesbian sexuality. The existing material tended to be 'soft', with terms I didn't find at all erotic. Things like, "Then she kissed my rosebud and I heard the sounds of the sea and became engulfed by the passion of the waves . . ." just didn't turn me on.

I was not prepared when the newest element of lesbian sexual expression began to hit the women's bookstores and newspapers: S/M, often written by lesbian feminists who defined themselves as sado-masochists. Along with other women, I read the material, shocked and worried about women assuming such male postures, and playing with domination and control, pain and humiliation. Why would women want to take on something so oppressive?

What I didn't say out loud at the time was that I liked how these women explicitly described their sexual experiences. They were clear about what constituted an erotic charge for them, they knew how to claim sexuality, they knew how to build sexual tension. Sexuality was an element of themselves they were willing to focus on, to explore and to push. I liked the confidence, the directness. And I was totally freaked out by the conflict and contradictions it presented for me. If

I could relate to what they said, and if I liked the powerful descriptions, what did it mean about me? I was horrified that perhaps I wasn't a good (politically correct) feminist lesbian in my sexuality, as I worked so hard to be in all other areas of my life.

I knew that sexuality was an important element in my life. I have long been sexually active with a number of women. I masturbate often and creatively, I enjoy fantasizing and am always ready to learn new things. I love being sensual: I like the feel of satin shirts, my body moving on a dance floor, walking in the sunshine. I can spend hours stroking and touching a women's body, playing with the different sensations and textures of skin, hair and muscle. I eagerly learn what excites and satisfies another woman because I want to consistently please her — and offer her an opportunity to learn new ways of taking and giving pleasure. I know I am a sensitive and inquisitive sex partner and lover.

So far, so good — I know all that to be acceptable. There's more. I especially like to be touched hard, all over. I like to be vigorously penetrated. I like to pull and really feel another woman's body against mine. I sometimes like to have my nipples and my neck bit. I like anal sex. I use vibrators. I have acted out sexual fantasies. I love being playful, teasing, coy, aggressive and pushy. I have experimented with being tied down and with tying women up. I enjoy orgasms and can easily have a dozen orgasms in a love-making session. I like sex that leaves me hot and sweaty and breathless and moved.

There's not a variety of sexual expression I wouldn't try if the idea excited me and made sense to me. And I began to worry about all of that, listening to the reaction of feminists to lesbian S/M. S/M was clearly a disgusting phenomenon: at best these women were to be pitied as poor, depraved sickies; at worst, they should be forbidden entry to our groups, our bookstores, our newspapers and our communities. With all the discussions about violence against women, internalized misogyny and S/M, anything that bordered on 'rough' sex seemed unacceptable. I didn't dare open my mouth about my own sexual practice now! So I kept my sex life and my fears private. I was agonizing — asking questions and answering them all alone, deliberately separating my activities in bed from my politics.

There were other damaging effects. Because I didn't talk about my fears and doubts with my peers, I backed away from all the things that might confuse me sexually. I stopped pushing myself. I carefully selected sex partners and lovers who were outside of my political circles. I slept with women who wouldn't challenge or threaten me sexually. I stopped reading about sexuality. I came out publicly denouncing lesbian feminists who were into S/M. It left me uncomfortable so I wanted it out of my way. The whole topic of sexuality became off-limits.

Then I became sexually intimate with Deb. She is a strong woman, a lesbian feminist with a long history of being a bar dyke and a jock. Her primary commitment is to women, and political activism is an integral part of her life. We share a deep identification as 'dyke' and our life histories are similar with our working class backgrounds and francophone heritage. We became friends quickly. We both enjoy sex for its own sake, and do not confuse sexual passion with loving, although the integration of the two has proved to be incredibly intense for both of us.

The first time we had sex she talked to me, telling me she liked how I fucked her and that she loved my cunt. I freaked. Those were words men had used to hurt me, to objectify me. I was scared. But I also noticed, and quickly pushed away, the uncomfortable realization that her raw-edged, hard language had given me a rush of sexual excitement.

I ended up writing Deb a lengthy criticism about her use of language, drawing the comparison between men's use of 'broad' and 'chick' and her use of 'fuck' and 'cunt'. I argued that language reflected how we saw women, and I wanted her to stop using those words.

She agreed that, as lesbians and as feminists, we desperately needed new ways of perceiving and conceptualizing the world, and a new language to express that. In the meantime, it was important for her to make use of what we did have, to reclaim and redefine it, similarly to what lesbians had done with the word 'dyke'.

She needed me to understand that this was a new context for that language. She was a woman who loved women, who had committed herself emotionally, politically, sexually, socially to other women for her lifetime. There was no hurtful objectification here. Use of that language was her way of building sexual tension, to make love with that edge of excitement. She agreed to not use those words with me, and I agreed to drop it. I could go back to being safe again.

But I couldn't relax. I was worried that our lovemaking would now be sterile, dull and silent. Since I wanted to keep playing sexually, I decided to read out loud to her one night. I

Sculpture/
Persimmon Blackbridge

chose a safe book of lesbian erotica and was very surprised to come across words like "tits, cunt, fuck" — and even more surprised when they flowed easily off my tongue.

Deb, of course, didn't miss it. As we made love, she took a calculated risk and pushed it. In a moment of extreme tenderness and warmth, she looked up at me and said, "I love your cunt, Yvette." I began to shake: the candlelight on her face, this moment of loving, the strength in our passionate woman's sexuality. I cried and cried — years of hurt, of fear, of denial, contradictions not dealt with. I sobbed with release and immense relief. This is what context was about. I began to believe it was possible to face my unvoiced sexual goblins.

As the months passed, I kept choosing to talk with Deb about other areas of my sexuality. We wanted to figure out the grey areas, the apparent contradictions between feminist analysis and our sexual practice. We wanted to increase our awareness of our sexuality, and find more possibilities and more language for pleasure. And, as lesbian feminists, we needed to discover ways to share those experiences with other lesbians so together we could construct a better understanding and an analysis of our sexuality.

But it's scary! It's one thing talking about sexuality with a lover in the intimacy of a bedroom, and it's quite another having open political forums about something so intensely private and personal! But it is absolutely crucial that I do it, and that we *all* do it.

As lesbians we desperately need an under-standing of ourselves as women constructing sexual practices in relation to ourselves and each other. We need to first *talk* about sexuality, to let down our guard, keep our defenses and shyness out of the way, voice the fears, choke back some of the judgements — and talk. Forget the scale: soft, romanticized, gentle, non-orgasmic sensuality on one end, and rough, hard sex on the other. What is *your* sexuality like? How would you like it to be?

The exploration of women's sexuality and of a healthy lesbian sexual practise may be complex and difficult. But there must be room for us to create a comprehensive framework that makes sense of *all* our realities and provides an analysis for continued sexual exploration that is positive and reaffirming.

I long for the day when intimate conversations about sexuality are as everyday and ordinary as dinner table converstions about organizing childcare for the next weekend; when we discuss our sexuality out loud, with care and consideration; when we grow and learn as we claim our bodies and our pleasure; when each of us come joyfully to a sexual practice that is satisfying and exhilarating.

— *Yvette*

*L*ike many women in our society *I* experienced my sexuality only in terms of men. Fortunately my experiences were, by and large ok — no wierdos, no violence. I managed a couple of long-term relationships — one in a marriage of six years and several short-term ones and even a couple of one-night stands.

All this with fairly ordinary men, some good sexually, most ordinary. I never had too much difficulty having orgasms. It seemed to me, given my age and background, about what could be expected, and that this was likely to be all there was to look forward to in the future.

When I first fell in love with and experienced sexual feeling towards another woman I was astounded by its intensity. I still am occasionally. My feelings covered a much wider range than I was used to. Tenderness was there, wonder, sensuality, the sheer pleasure of looking at and touching a woman. Even the desire was different — more diffuse.

As for the first time we made love — along with all of the power and wonder and tenderness and wanting, there was a sense of coming home. I was, for the first time in my life, where I belonged.

That's not to say it's always wonderful with women. There have been women with whom the sex doesn't work well. And times when it doesn't work even with long-time lovers. And pain and anger and frustration and guilt and all of the emotions we carry with us. All of the ways we punish ourselves and each other for not being perfect all of the time.

But still, with all of the pain and frustraton and struggle, for me, when I lie alongside a woman I love, I have come home.

— Yvonne

*What is sexuality between women? Where does sexual-*ity start? End? Is it hugging? Kissing? Stroking? Orgasms? When I hold you when you cry, is that sexuality? When I meet your eyes across the rooms and the years of the 16 hour meetings and the work becomes visible — what bond is this? When I hold you steady on the ladder as you pound the fenceposts and your body is warm and strong in my arms and the sunlight and the laughter surround us — is this lovemaking too? When I dance in the circle of a 100 women and the music and the energy transports me — are you all my lovers? And the curve of a woman's face. And your breast cupped in my hand. And the always-new, always-shattering smoothness and warmness and wetness of your body. Of my body. Of all our bodies.

— Nym

Somewhere to Start

☐ Clear communication and healthy conflict resolution don't just 'happen' between women. We have to learn how to listen, how to tell someone what we feel, how to disagree without being destructive. You could read books on communication and expressing emotions; since most of those kinds of books are thoroughly heterosexually-based, read critically. Ask other lesbians how they conduct their relationships, how they resolve conflicts.

We all have deep and sometimes not very useful patterns regarding intimacy, loving and sex. It's just not true that we find the right woman and live happily ever after. As lesbians, we are isolated and invisible in the world. We bear the brunt of that stress as well as all the usual difficulties of being self-supporting women. Our intimate relationships are often the place where all that stress gets acted out.

Give serious thought to what your expectations of a lover relationship are. What constitutes the perfect relationship for you? Look at the differences between what you believe and what you've experienced. Find out what your lover's beliefs are, and share ideas and insights. Talk about potential problems — money, class, politics, sexual styles, children, how and why to break-up, other lovers — at the beginning of your relationship, while you're getting along really well. Establish agreements. You can always change them later.

Remember that there are many different kinds of lesbian relationships; only you can figure out what works best for you.

☐ Sometimes we get totally involved in the shared excitement of our lover relationship. To avoid isolation and too much dependency, make efforts to maintain your individual friendships, interests and sources of satisfaction.

☐ If your relationship is causing you unhappiness and conflict, reach out to other lesbians for contact and support. Most of us have had relationships that were painful and difficult at times. A friend acting as a mediator can be helpful. In large cities, social service agencies may offer counselling for lesbian and gay couples.

☐ Ending a relationship almost always hurts. Experienced break-up survivors say that it is useful to see lots of your friends, to think up new and exciting things to do and do them, to tell yourself all the benefits of breakup up — more time for yourself and friends, no more irresolvable conflicts, no-one to be accountable to...

If you don't know other lesbians, talk to sympathetic non-lesbian friends. If possible, try to find other lesbians (see *Finding Lesbian Resources*).

☐ Sexuality is a very emotionally charged area in this society. Our conditioning and experiences as children probably contained generous amounts of fear, guilt, shame and ignorance. We all have some kind of anxiety about sex.

It is important to remember that it is a myth that lesbians *always* have wonderful blissful sex. Often, yes; but not inevitably. There is incredible diversity amongst us: our bodies, what we find erotic, how we like to make love.

We need to talk with our lovers/sex partners about what pleases us. Conversations about sex are hard to initiate the first few times, but it gets easier. And it is helpful, not just as a problem-solving technique, but as a way of enriching our erotic communication.

Talking about sex with lesbians other than lovers is even harder, but equally useful. We carry so many 'shoulds' about sex: "I should like this, I shouldn't think that, I should do that." Listening to what other lesbians like and don't like can relieve us of the all-too-common belief that "I must be the only lesbian who likes..." Reading books is also helpful.

☐ Support groups or workshops for lesbians that focus on sexuality are very useful. In our experience, such opportunities to talk about lesbian sex are exciting, fun and very anxiety-relieving. They can also open up lots of emotion, so we must be gentle with each other (see *Notes To Facilitators* and *Fighting Internalized Oppression* for general information about facilitating and/or participating).

☐ Our loving is not all pain and gloom. Sexual and emotional intimacy with a woman you love has got to be one of life's greatest pleasures. *Have fun!*

Resources

Sapphistry: The Book of Lesbian Sexuality, Pat Califia (Tallahassee: Naiad, 1980)   Excellent, practical and non-judgemental. The most trustworthy resource so far.

Our Right To Love: A Lesbian Resource Book ed. by Ginny Vida (Englewood Cliffs: Prentice-Hall, 1978) The "Sexuality" section is short, but reassuring.

The Joy of Lesbian Sex, Dr. Emily Sisley and Bertha Harris. (New York: Crown Publishers, 1977) Pleasant reading, but somewhat romanticized.

"Sex Issue," *Heresies, #12*   Explorations of the complexities of women's sexuality. Available from: Box 766, Canal St. Station, New York NY 10013.

Loving Women, The Nomadic Sisters (P.O. Box 793, Sonora, CA 95370)   Simple, positive "how-to" book.

The Hite Report, Shere Hite (New York: MacMillan, 1976)   Masses of first-hand information on the sexuality of American women. Some specific lesbian material. Interesting.

Women's Sexuality: Myth and Reality, Kass Demeter (E. Palo Alto: Up Press, 1977)   "The book for women and lovers of women", it does not presume a heterosexual audience. A guide to sex and love-making.

The Gay Report: Lesbians and Gay Men Speak Out about Sexual Experiences and Lifestyles, ed. by Karla Jay and Allen Young (New York: Summit Books, 1977)   A survey of 5000 people.

Make It Happy: What Sex is All About, Jane Cousins (London: Virago, 1978)   A resource for teenagers that has some information on lesbianism.

Changing Bodies, Changing Lives: A Book for Teens on Sex and Relationships, Ruth Bell et al. (New York: Random House, 1980)   Some information on lesbianism.

"Mothers vs. Amazons", *The Body Politic,* (#67, Oct. 1980)   An insightful article exploring common dynamics within lesbian relationships.

"Lesbian Couples: Special Issues" by Nancy Toder, from *Positively Gay: New Approaches in Gay Life,* ed. by Betty Berzon and Robert Leighton (Millbrae: Celestial Arts, 1979)

See also *Resource* listings under:

☐ *How Do You Know?*
☐ *Fighting Internalized Oppression*

What Are We Up Against?

As lesbians, we often face both subtle and overt discrimination in our dealings with the systems and institutions which shape the functioning of our society. Lesbians are invisible. Our realities are not reflected; our very existence is denied or ignored. If we make ourselves known as lesbians we may experience more direct acts of social punishment.

Our ability to survive and flourish speaks of both our individual strengths and of the sustenance we find in each other. Increasingly, we are not stopping at survival. We are joining together to fight for change within existing structures *and* to create women-controlled and lesbian-positive alternatives.

Judges do not have to find out what the average Canadian's view on gross indecency is. They can substitute their personal opinion for that of anyone who might testify on behalf of the person accused...

The Law

The *Body Politic,* a gay liberation newspaper, has its subscription list and material confiscated by the Toronto authorities.

The *Vancouver Sun,* a daily paper, is able to legally discriminate against homosexual and lesbian groups by refusing to print advertisements for the Gay Alliance Towards Equality and the Lesbian Information Line.

A teacher in Saskatoon is fired from his teaching position because someone complained that he was gay. *(Body Politic,* July '79)

Two lesbians from Edmonton are sentenced to life in prison for killing a man who had sexually assaulted one of the women (Women in Prison, Vancouver)

There is a visible and threatening police presence during the 1979 National Lesbian Conference in Toronto. Police later charge an organizer of the conference with violation of the liquor license. (*Body Politic,* July '79)

A lesbian mother who had been awarded custody of her two children has them taken away by a judge because she went to live with her lover. (Canadian — *Bizaire* vs *Bizaire*)

Stink bombs are thrown into a meeting in Vancouver called to protest violence against gays. Two men threaten the participants with 2x4's.

The Progressive Conservatives effectively kill a bill to amend the Canadian Human Rights Act to ban discrimination against homosexuals. (*Globe & Mail,* May '83)

Criminal Law

The law is a collection of rules made and administered by men to protect property and control social behaviour. Laws are made by municipal councils, provincial legislatures and the federal parliament, and interpreted by the courts.

There are very few women in any of these places. Police, lawyers, judges — the enforcers of the legal system — bring to their interpretations of the law their personal and cultural values and beliefs. Women are not visible as important, powerful members of society. Lesbians are not visible at all. The 'maleness' of both the historical legal tradition and the present system is a major reason why it is rare that lesbianism is directly mentioned in legal writings.

Actual 'lesbian acts' are covered under the Criminal Code of Canada, a long and important statute passed by the federal parliament. The Code was copied almost exactly from English criminal law and expresses Victorian values. The sections on sexual offenses in the Criminal Code were amended first by the Trudeau government in 1969 (so that not quite so many Canadians would be committing criminal sexual acts), and again in 1982. The section of the Code under which people are charged for the commission of homosexual acts is entitled gross indecency. Originally the section only covered acts committed by a man with another man. Now, it reads: "Section 157: Every one who commits an act of gross indecency with another person is guilty of an indictable offense and is liable to imprisonment for five years."

Since 1969, homosexual activity is not gross indecency if the acts are committed in private between any two persons, each of whom is 21 years of age or more and both of whom consent to the commission of the act. "In private" means "not in a public place" and with "not more than two persons present." "Consent" will not be considered to exist if obtained "by force, threats, fear of bodily harm or is obtained by false or fraudulent misrepresentations as to the nature and quality of the acts" or if one of the parties to the act is "feeble-minded, insane or an idiot or imbecile."

So, that's the Criminal Code. Case Law is the interpretation that judges make of the meanings of undefined words — such as "gross indecency." In a 1981 Ontario case, the judge said, "Section 157 is directed at acts of oral sex between males or sexual acts between females where one of the participants is under 21 years of age." (Just what do lesbians do in bed, anyhow?) This same judge goes on to say that the average Canadian disapproves of homosexual activity. In 1979, the highest court in Ontario — the Court of Appeal — said that gross indecency "represents a very marked departure from the decent conduct expected of the average Canadian."

Judges do not have to find out what the average Canadian's view on gross indecency is. They can substitute their personal opinion for that of anyone who might testify on behalf of the person accused, such as a psychologist or sociologist. At the same time, the judges say that the test of what constitutes gross indecency is objective rather than subjective. That is, it doesn't matter that the people "committing the act" thought what they were doing wasn't grossly indecent, but that someone else — the average Canadian judge — thinks it was.

The gross indecency section is much more often applied against gay men than lesbians. The only Canadian case we could find involving lesbianism took place in Newfoundland in 1981. To use the language of the case note, a woman over the age of 21 took a 17 year old woman

home with her one night, slept with her in the nude and made love with her. This behaviour was found to merit a criminal conviction of the woman over 21 for gross indecency pursuant to Section 157. There is no record of what sentence she received.

What all this has to do with how lesbians live our lives is quite remote. We are unlikely to be charged with gross indecency, but . . . the way the statute law is worded and the way it has been interpreted to date means that it *is* possible for the type of low-level sexual activity which goes on at dances or bars — hugging and kissing — to be considered gross indecency since it is not "in private."

Making love with a woman under 21 is, legally, grossly indecent. Now, police officers don't as a rule spend the majority of their duty hours looking for lesbians to charge with gross indecency (although they do spend an inordinate amount of time trying to catch gay men in compromising situations). It is more likely that lesbians will run up against the Criminal Code in other ways, and that is where things get murky. Police officers often have the discretion to arrest or not. For instance, on a routine check of a bar, a policeman finds a woman with a joint. Possession of marijuana is illegal, but common. If the officer can enjoy a brief flirtation with the woman, enjoy his masculine 'magnanimity' and her submissive 'femininity', he could very well let it go at that. If it's a lesbian bar and he just knows she's a man-hating pervert, he's more likely to arrest her.

Lesbians often get arrested for breaking the law in relatively minor ways and/or get heavy sentences. Lesbian bars (and gay bars) are often harassed for liquor law violations. Charges for assault or drug offenses against lesbians are much more likely to be pushed through to conviction. If an open lesbian gets arrested and ends up in court, will her lawyer work as hard for her as a client he can 'relate' to? Will the judge be likely to believe her story on the witness stand? When lesbians go to court, it is our 'respectability' that is somehow on trial. We ain't got much of it. We are taught as children that the law is a system of justice and fairness for all, but they lie, they lie.

Family Law

Lesbians who have been married and/or have children are more likely to encounter the area of family law. Just as in criminal law lesbians are seen as threatening and dangerous, so in family law, lesbians are seen as clearly rejecting traditional family roles.

An act of homosexuality is considered a ground for immediate divorce, without a three year waiting period. In order for a man to prove grounds based on his wife's homosexuality he need only have seen her in the act of hugging or fondling another woman in a sexual manner. In

Photo/ Dorrie Brannock

2. Community attitudes towards a lesbian mother. The children might suffer from societal disapproval of their mother's lifestyle.

3. The position of the child among her/his peer group.

In cases where the child has been allowed to stay with the homosexual parent there has been testimony from an expert witness, a social worker or psychiatrist, as to the effect of the homosexuality on parent and child. One psychologist told the court that "homosexual women are no more neurotic than female heterosexuals . . . (and) that the manner in which one fulfills one's sexual needs does not relate to the abilities of being a good parent."

Another factor influencing the courts in favour of the homosexual parent has been the testimony of the homosexual partner who resides with the parent. In the first reported lesbian custody case in Canada, the lover did not appear as a witness in the case. The judge said that it was important for him to be able to judge her because she would have a great deal to do with the care and welfare of the children. The mother in that case lost custody. The winning cases since then have given the judges an opportunity to examine lovers on the witness stand.

The other factors all indicate the judges' concern with societal values. While they may be willing to grant homosexual mothers custody of their children, they do not want to encourage the 'spread' of homosexuality by the mother's example to her child.

One lesbian, who was granted custody on condition that she establish a stable home, permit liberal access to the father and, because of past lesbian relationships, not live with another person without the court's permission, lost her children to the father after she broke all three conditions. While denying her custody, the court reaffirmed that homosexuality is not a negative factor in itself.

In all types of custody cases, the courts make their decisions based on the "best interests" of the child. The parents' qualities, abilities and conduct are supposedly assessed only in relation to their effect on the child. But it is the judge who decides what is "best." Lesbians should make every effort to stay out of the courts. The court is a male forum dedicated to upholding present societal values and anyone who goes to it for justice should remember that what they will get is the justice of older, well-to-do, generally white, men. Men who want to maintain the nuclear family and the traditional roles of wife

the words of one judge, "The test must be: Was the act homosexual? In some cases perhaps, a friendly caress of the bosom by one female of another may not be homosexual, but in the present case it was."

There are not many reported cases where lesbianism is the ground for divorce, probably because most women would not contest such a divorce. (Note: At time of writing, Canadian divorce laws are being revised.)

Women do, however, contest custody. There have been several reported lesbian custody cases in Canada. Some recent ones have awarded custody to the lesbian parent so long as she is not militant and keeps a low profile. One judge said in the course of his decision that "there has been a certain amount of liberalization of the public attitude about homosexuality." As a result, homosexuality is a factor to be considered but is not a bar in and of itself.

The cases have set out certain questions which the courts must take into account when reaching their decision about the effect of the mother's homosexuality on the child. These factors are:

1. The danger of the child becoming homosexual if raised by a homosexual parent.

and mother are not going to be easily persuaded to give custody of children to lesbians.

If it becomes absolutely necessary to go to court (for example, when the husband will not negotiate), lesbians should ensure that they have a sympathetic lawyer, that their case is thoroughly researched and prepared, and that they themselves are clear on what to expect in court. Because negotiating before actually deciding to go to court is hard, and trial preparation is even more difficult, lesbian mothers would be well-advised to seek the support of their community and, in particular, a Lesbian Mothers' Defense Fund. The Fund can draw on its collective experience and knowledge from custody battles throughout North America to provide practical support as well as help to finance the costs of a court case.

Note: Any person can apply for custody of a child. There have been a few cases of lesbians who were not a child's biological mother being awarded custody when the mother is unable to care for the child. If you wish your lover to be your child's guardian if you die, make a will and say so. It's not a guarantee, but it helps.

The above material thanks to Alison Sawyer.

Somewhere to Start

☐ If at all possible, avoid the police and the courts. You could start by getting to know your basic civil rights. Pamphlets are available from civil liberties associations, community legal education services and many lesbian, gay and progressive groups.

☐ When organizing lesbian events, prepare for the possibility of harassment by law enforcers. Dances and other social events may be visited by police looking for liquor law violations. At least a couple of women in the organizing group should be familiar with the provincial laws and be prepared to talk to the cops on the group's behalf. Everyone working at the dance should be informed who these police liaison women are.

For demonstrations or rallies, it's a good idea to have a sympathetic lawyer who is ready to spring into action on our behalf at the ring of the phone (see *Violence* section for information on *Organizing for Public Safety).*

☐ Large cities sometimes have a Gay Liaison on the police force and/or a Police/Gay Committee. In Vancouver, the Gay Liaison Officer has been quite useful to lesbians organizing events by expediting liquor license applications.

☐ Lesbian groups can work towards legal changes that would benefit lesbians, such as inclusion of protection for gay people in human rights laws. Battles for law reform often get lots of media coverage which can be useful in getting people to think about the issues.

Making sure that community-based and feminist legal clinics are both knowledgeable and sympathetic about lesbians and the law is another area of work. You can supply these clinics with written materials, offer to do workshops, insist that they provide and advertise legal services for lesbians, and monitor the experiences that lesbians have.

☐ If you are a lesbian mother, try to avoid a legal custody dispute. If one seems inevitable, you will need to thoroughly inform yourself about the issues and precedents. The best way to do this is to contact, either by mail or in person, any of the existing Lesbian Mothers' Defense Funds. Reading up on the subject is also essential (see *Resources* for addresses and books).

☐ Fighting for the rights of lesbian mothers to our children is a major focus of lesbian organizing. Lesbian Mothers' Defense Funds and similar groups deserve to be vigorously supported. If no such group exists in your area, consider starting one.

☐ Any lesbian group can work to change attitudes towards lesbian mothers. You could distribute positive information on lesbianism and lesbian mothers to local libraries, social service organizations, counsellors, family court workers, legal clinics and lawyers. You could compile a listing of non-homophobic and supportive professionals based on interviews with lawyers, psychologists and social workers. This list could then be distributed to appropriate locations. Make a point of getting accurate information about lesbian mothers into the local media, and respond to homophobic and sensationalist coverage. And finally, you can do fund-raising to cover the legal costs of custody cases.

☐ Lesbians are incarcerated in prisons out of proportion to our numbers in the population. Lesbians on the outside can organize support for imprisoned lesbians by forming or joining existing groups working for the improvement of conditions for women in jails. These groups can take programmes inside, do advocacy work on behalf of individuals, educate the public about women in prisons, and work for the abolition of prisons. You could also support and work with community-based rehabilitation programmes for women.

"...every individual should have an equal opportunity with other individuals to make for himself or herself the life that he or she is able and wishes to have, consistent with his or her duties and obligations as a member of society, without being hindered in or prevented from doing so by discriminatory practices based on race, national or ethnic origin, colour, religion, age, sex *or sexual orientation* **or marital status, or conviction for an offence for which a pardon has been granted or by discriminatory employment practices based on physical handicap."**

An excerpt from the Canadian Human Rights Act, *1977. The* Act *applies to all federal government departments, crown corporations, and business and industry under federal jurisdiction, such as airlines, railways and banks. It applies both to their employment policies and dealings with the public.*

Provincial human rights laws are responsible for areas not under federal jurisdiction, like housing, education and employment. So far, only Québec prohibits discrimination on the basis of sexual orientation. In 1984, British Columbia's Social Credit government is as busy tearing down human rights protection as the forest companies are despoiling the forests.

Resources

Print
General

Femina cum Feminism: A Look at Lesbianism in Law and Society, Ruth Taylor (Vancouver, 1978) This is a very good and useful thesis, available from the law library at the University of British Columbia (in the reserve section) or from Vancouver Status of Women (for cost of copying). Their address is:V.S.W. 400A W. 5th Ave., Vancouver, B.C. V5Y 1J8

"Lesbians and the Law", from *Our Right To Love: A Lesbian Resource Book* ed. by Ginny Vida (Englewood Cliffs: Prentice Hall, 1978) A useful overview, with information relevant to the U.S. only.

A Legal Guide for Gay and Lesbian Couples, F. Hayden Curry and Denis Clifford (Reading: Addison-Wesley, 1980) Practical information on child custody, foster and adopted children, relating to former spouses, property matters, living-together agreements, planning for death, etc. American.

Gay Rights Protection in U.S. and Canada, National Gay Task Force List of law changes, revised quarterly. Available from 80 5th Ave., New York NY 10011

Lesbian Rights Handbook, Lesbian Rights Project (San Francisco: 1980) Gives American information on a range of subjects. See address in *Groups.*

The Rights of Gay People: An American Civil Liberties Union Handbook, E. Carrington Boggan et al (New York: Bantam Books, 1983) An American reference book.

Gay Rights Skills Seminar Manual: What Every Progressive Lawyer and Legal Worker Should Know About the Everyday Problems of Gay People, Gay Rights Task Force and The National Lawyers Guild, 1979 An American resource. Available from 558 Capp St., San Francisco CA 94110

*From the Closets to the Courts: The Lesbian
Transition,* Ruth Simpson (New York: The Viking
Press, 1978)   A fascinating account by a pioneer
lesbian activist in the U.S.

Custody/Canada

Motherhood, Lesbianism and Child Custody, Francie
Wyland (London: Falling Wall Press, 1977)
Political analysis by a member of Wages for
Housework.

Children and Feminism, Lesbian and Feminist Mothers
Political Action Group (Vancouver, 1982) Contains
practical technical information for Canadian mothers
fighting custody cases. Provides details of every
known Canadian case in which "lesbian mothers or
gay fathers sought or are seeking custody or access to
children." See address in *Groups.*

*Grapevine: Newsletter of the Lesbian Mothers
Defense Fund*   Includes reports on activities of
Canadian L.M.D.F. groups, Canadian and international legal disputes involving lesbian mothers,
movement news. Publishes twice a year, available
from local L.M.D.F. groups. See addresses below.

*Gay Fathers: Some of Their Stories, Experiences and
Advice,* Gay Fathers of Toronto, 1981   Written
primarily for gay fathers, about their experiences with
children, lovers and wives. Available from P.O. Box
187, Station F, Toronto Ont. M4Y 2L5

"Custody, Adoption and the Homosexual Parent"
Christine Boyle, *Reports on Family Law* 23
(1976):129   Analyzes the application in Canada of
the "best interest of the child" principle to custody
disputes involving homosexual parents.

"The Homosexual Parent in Custody Disputes",
Harvey Brownstone, *Queen's Law Journal* 5
(1980): 199-239   Compares the legal treatment of
adulterous or promiscuous heterosexual parents with
the treatment of homosexual parents in custody
disputes in Canada and the U.S.

"Best Interests of the Child in Protection Hearings: A
Move Away from Parental Rights?" Jennifer
MacKinnon, *Reports on Family Law* 14 (1980):119
Discusses the tension between parental rights and the
best interests of the child.

"Re: Moores and Feildstein — A Case Comment and
Discussion of Custody Principles," Karen Weiler and
Graham Berman, *Reports on Family Law* (1974):294
Discusses a precedent set in Canada in 1974, that a
child's best interests take precedence over the
"natural" right of biological parents to retain custody.

"The Lesbian Issue", *Resources for Feminist Research,*
Vol. 12, #1 (1983)   Contains an annotated bibliography on child custody and the lesbian mother,
citing both Canadian and U.S. legal articles, case law,
and additional resources. Available from O.I.S.E.,
252 Bloor St. W., Toronto Ont. M5S 1V6

*Taking the Law Into Your Own Hands: A Guide to
Legal Research,* Tim Roberts, (Vancouver: 1981)
Very useful introduction to doing legal research in
Canada. Available from the Legal Services Society of
B.C., P.O. Box 12120, 555 W. Hastings St.,
Vancouver B.C. V6B 4N6

by Mairi

Custody/U.S.:

*By Her Own Admission: A Lesbian Mother's Fight To
Keep Her Son,* Gifford G. Gibson with Mary Jo
Risher (New York: Doubleday, 1977)   A sympathetic
account.

A Legal Guide for Gay and Lesbian Couples,
F. Hayden Curry and Denis Clifford (Reading:
Addison-Wesley, 1980)   Lots of information on child
custody.

Gay Parents Support Package, National Gay Task
Force   A compilation of articles, newspaper
clippings, case summeries, bibliographies, resources
and letters of support from sociologists and
psychologists. Costs less than five dollars. Available
from 80 5th Ave., New York NY 10011

A Gay Parent's Legal Guide to Child Custody, Anti-
Sexism Committee of the San Francisco-Bay Area
National Lawyer's Guild, 1980   Although American,
the information here is general enough to be useful to
any gay parent in a custody dispute. Discusses
alternatives to going to court, how to find a suitable
lawyer, and the issues that arise in custody cases.
Includes a resource list. Available from 558 Capp St.,
San Francisco CA 94110

*Lesbian Mothers and Their Children: An Annotated
Bibliography of Legal and Psychological Materials,*
Lesbian Rights Project, 1980   Describes major U.S.
lesbian custody cases, and where to find them. Also,
recent psychological studies that show lesbians and
their children have no special psychological problems
are listed and described. Seventeen relevant law
review articles are listed. An essential resource. See
address in *Groups.*

Mom's Apple Pie, Lesbian Mother's National Defense
Fund (Seattle)   This newsletter is an important
source of up-to-date information on American lesbian
custody cases. See address in *Groups.*

"The Lesbian Issue", *Resources for Feminist Research,*
Vol. 12, #1 (1983) See above under Canada.

"The Avowed Lesbian Mother and Her Right to Child
Custody: A Constitutional Challenge That Can No
Longer Be Denied," Marilyn Riley, *San Diego Law
Review* 12 (1975):799.

"Representing the Lesbian Mother," Rosalie C. Davies, *Family Advocate* 21 (Winter 1979) Gives a useful brief overview of American cases between 1967 and 1979, and offers a succinct summary of legal strategy for lawyers representing lesbian mothers in custody cases.

"Custody Rights of Lesbian Mothers: Legal Theory and Litigation Strategy," Nan D. Hunter, Nancy D. Polikoff, *Buffalo Law Review* 25 (1976) This very useful article is available in pamphlet form. Hunter and Polikoff summarize current statutory and case law in the United States as it applies to lesbian mothers. They suggest legal strategies and tactics for attorneys representing lesbian mothers.

Prisons

"Love between Women in Prison" by Karlene Faith, from *Lesbian Studies*. ed. by Margaret Cruikshank (Old Westbury: The Feminist Press, 1982) A sympathetic look at some of the dynamics between women in prison.

Women in Prison, Kathryn Watterson Burkhart (New York: Doubleday, 1973)

Instead of Prison: A Handbook for Abolitionists Prison Research Education Action Project Available from 3049 E. Genesee St., Syracuse NY 13224

Cruel and Unusual, Sharon Vance and Gerald McNeill (Ottawa: Deneaut and Greenberg, 1978) An exposé of the Canadian prison system.

Kind and Usual Punishment: The Prison Business, Jessica Mitford (New York: Vintage Books, 1974) A very readable exposé of American prisons.

Women Behind Bars: An Organizing Tool, Resources for Community Change Resource material for people doing prison work. Available from P.O. Box 21006, Washington D.C. 20009.

Groups

Canada:

Lesbian and Feminist Mothers Political Action Group, P.O. Box 65804, Station F, Vancouver B.C. (604-251-6090) Produced the book *Children and Feminism* (see above) and other activities.

Vancouver Lesbian Mothers Defense Fund, P.O. Box 65804, Station F, Vancouver B.C. This is a very small group, affiliated with Toronto and Calgary Lesbian Mothers Defense Fund. They have a collection of much of the material mentioned in this reading list. They also have a list of sympathetic lawyers and 'experts' for mothers facing custody battles. They hold a pot luck supper for lesbian mothers once a month.

Alberta Lesbian Mothers' Defense Fund, #124 - 320 5th Ave. S.E., Calgary Alta. T2G 0E5 (403-264-6328) This group has regular monthly meetings and hopes to be able to help lesbian mothers fighting custody cases in western Canada.

Lesbian Mothers' Defense Fund, P.O. Box 38, Stn. E., Toronto Ont. M6H 4E1 (416-465-6822) This large active group publishes an excellent small newsletter, *Grapevine,* several times a year. They have been able to help several lesbian mothers with custody disputes. They have helped the lesbian community in Toronto become aware of the special problems of the mothers among them, as well as serving as a contact point and support system for lesbian mothers themselves. Through the *Grapevine,* they are helping lesbian mothers across Canada begin to network and organize to fight for change.

Tightwire Collective, Kingston Prison forWomen, P.O. Box 515, Kingston Ont. These women prisoners publish the newsletter *Tightwire.*

Women Against Prisons, P.O. Box 46571, Stn. G, Vancouver B.C.

Prisoners' Rights Groups, 3965 Pandora St., Burnaby B.C.

Prisoner Solidarity Collective, P.O. Box 5052, Stn. A, Toronto Ont. M5W 1W4 They publish *Bulldozer: The Only Vehicle for Prison Reform* (free to prisoners).

Quaker Committee on Jails and Justice 60 Lowther Ave., Toronto Ont. M5R 1C7

U.S.:

Lesbian Mothers' National Defense Fund, P.O. Box 21567, Seattle WA 98111 (206-325-2643) The L.M.N.D.F. serves as an American national clearing house for information and resources about lesbian mother custody cases. They have copies of transcripts and court decisions from lesbian mother custody cases litigated across the United States, as well as other resource materials. A list of the materials they have is available upon request. These materials are free to lesbian mothers. They publish the American lesbian mothers' newsletter, *Mom's Apple Pie.*

Lesbian Rights Project, 1370 Mission Street, San Francisco, CA 94103 (415-621-0675) L.R.P. is a non-profit public interest law firm established in 1977 to address legal problems confronted by lesbians.

Women Free Women in Prison, P.O. Box 90, Brooklyn NY 11215 They publish *No More Cages,* a bi-monthly women's prison newsletter, free to prisoners.

Sisters of Inner-Connections, 3617 Hamilton St., Philadelphia PA 19104 They publish *Writing for Rights/Voices Behind Prison Walls,* a newsletter by prisoners, free to prisoners.

Through the Looking Glass, P.O. Box 22061, Seattle WA 98122 A women's and children's prison newsletter, free to prisoners.

Washington Coalition Against Prisons, P.O. Box 22272, Seattle WA 98122

The prison resources thanks to Jill Bend.

Many of the custody resources are from Children and Feminism, by Lee MacKay, and are reprinted with permission and thanks.

Many lesbian and gay groups make referrals to non-homophobic lawyers and legal clinics, or themselves offer legal advice. See:

☐ *Finding Lesbian Resources*

I saw just how far the union would fight for me if it came down to a management attempt to fire me for my sexual orientation...

Work

*O*n July 1st, 1978, I was fired *from my job as a variety store* clerk. The only reason I was given by my employer was that he did not want homosexuals working in his store. Earlier in the day, my employer's wife had initiated a discussion on sexuality, during which I had told her that I was a lesbian. Even though I was well aware of the consequences of coming-out on the job, I was really shaken by my on-the-spot dismissal.

By the next day, however, all I felt was *rage!* I phoned the Human Rights Commission, who said that while they supported me in theory, they could do nothing practical, as discrimination on the basis of sexual orientation/preference is not covered by the Code.

A group of friends and I quickly gestetnered and distributed leaflets around the store area to inform the public of my firing. Within two days, we held a legal picket line, holding placards which denounced the store owner's policy, and asking people to boycott the store. The reactions to the picket ranged from people boycotting and/or phoning the store and denouncing the owner, to others who were verbally aggressive and tried to intimidate us.

The media coverage was extensive and unusually objective, although with each successive interview, the store owner began to invent stories of my incompetence.

For several weeks after the picket, I was verbally harassed on the street, young boys threw stones at me, and my landlord threatened, unsuccessfully, to have me evicted.

I did not get my job back, nor did I find another for almost two months. However, in fighting back, those of us involved felt a new sense of self-respect. I always have been and will continue to be an open lesbian feminist in all areas of my life, including my place of work.

— Lynn

*T*he issue of feminism in trade *unions clearly cannot be* dealt with effectively without also dealing with the issue of lesbianism. That these issues are inextricably linked is evidenced by the fact that whenever any group or individual woman within a union raises the issue of feminism they will have to withstand the barrage of charges of being lesbians.

If you are working in a unionized job as a lesbian and a feminist, the first thing is to start forming networks of support. Talk with other women about the necessity of having a women's caucus within the union. Start talking about issues. It's important to establish that you recognize the importance of all issues that relate to all women's lives. Maternity and paternity leave is a good one because it starts women talking about their lives, about whether husbands share responsibility for childcare, about whether women can really participate in union meetings with no childcare provided.

A good strategy is to set up alliances. Alliances will be very important later when you start raising issues crucial to you as a lesbian feminist. Most union constitutions do not allow for the formation of caucuses or interest groups based on gender. In one such attempt, we had to get people elected to the by-laws committee and then do a very careful investigation of how to word a constitutional clause which would allow such a grouping.

We found very few men who were supportive of women's caucuses. Many saw it as contrary to basic trade union principles and they were also frightened of our potential lobbying power. This seems to be especially true in unions where the grass-roots membership is female and the executive level is male-dominated.

Once we got the by-laws changed we had to start lobbying with male members. We did gain a certain amount of support depending on how we worded things. We talked a lot about paternity leave, the importance of maternity leave, better UIC benefits for women on maternity leave — all issues that men saw as non-threatening. There was a fair amount of support on these issues. We also met with women from other unions who were trying to organize caucuses, to share our experiences and problems.

Once we got the by-laws changed to allow the formation of special interest groups, we had to fight about whether men could attend meetings. In our local, an attempt to set up a women's caucus had been made several years before. Men had come to those meetings and had consistently re-directed conversations and finally the women just gave up. Because we knew that history we were better prepared. We never said that men couldn't come. We just emphasized the need for a safe place for women to talk. We said we would not discourage women from talking about personal experience and emphasized that at union meetings women didn't speak or participate much.

I think we came along at a good time. The union was negotiating a contract and the executive was feeling a little threatened about what they perceived as lack of support for the union amongst women members. The union saw that management had been hiring vast numbers of young women to work at mechanized jobs. These women had never been part of a union and

had no tradition of union consciousness. We posed the women's caucus as a way to integrate women more effectively into the union structure.

Once the women's caucus was established and had a certain amount of credibility, we wrote a lot of articles about the relationship between feminism and trade unionism, pointing out that they were not mutually exclusive or opposed to each other. We could then start talking about other issues like sexual orientation and sexual harassment.

We talked with women about problems they encountered and what kind of contract clauses they would want. All of this was good public relations for us, and got more women involved with the union. Our proposal for sexual orientation and sexual harassment clauses came out of the women's caucus. When we brought our package of demands to the general union body, there ensued a great, long, heated homophobic debate.

That is how the whole issue of sexual orientation got raised within the union setting. Our work raised consciousness within the union as a whole. That process clarified for me, as a lesbian, who my allies were. I saw where my support lay. I saw just how far the union would fight for me if it came down to a management attempt to fire me for my sexual orientation. And that's important information to know!

If I were doing it again, I would be clearer about seeing our struggles on a national as well as a local level. We fell down by not making enough connections with and not providing support for women in other locals. If we could have encouraged women to form women's caucuses in many many locals from all across Canada we would have gone to the National Convention with a much better chance of actually getting both the sexual harassment clause and the sexual orientation clause included in the contract.

— *Jesse*

Work and money are generally quite important areas in lesbians' lives. We usually support ourselves life-long, and we find work in every conceivable job and profession. Like most women, lesbians are concentrated in low-paying, low-status fields where most workplaces are not unionized. Motivated by necessity and perhaps less controlled by the myths of women's 'proper' work, lesbians are also found wherever women have broken into non-traditional fields. Being a lesbian at work has never been free of difficulty.

Historically, the issue of lesbianism was raised long before feminism was an issue in the workplace. Management charges of lesbianism have been used against female workers in order to cull those who do not 'fit' physically, politically or for other reasons. In most cases, these charges were not overtly spelled out but circulated as rumours, forcing the women to either quit or become totally compliant to management demands.

Lesbians working in jobs related to children or young people (teaching, child care, counselling) have been particularly vulnerable, because of the myth that lesbians are child molesters — even though 97% of sexual abuse of children is perpetrated by heterosexual men.

All of us who have worked, and chosen to — or had to — remain closeted, know the effects of even the possibility of exposure. Even at jobs where there is a union and the possibility of being arbitrarily fired is decreased, ostracization by co-workers and the denial of credibility within the union is a reality that constantly threatens.

Until very recently, it was a rare and unusual lesbian who was out at work. Most of us led divided lives. We kept our straight job persona — competent, but probably very quiet on details of personal life — quite separate from our social, emotional, sexual and policital life with women. This can be crazy-making. Creating ways to allow us to be open, visible, strong, proud — and still employed — is a major organizing challenge. We need more and better public educational material on lesbianism, more caucuses within unions, more support networks, more alliances with gay men, more cases of discrimination being made public, more victories.

There's lots to do. Gay and lesbian caucuses do exist within some unions. Several networks exist for lesbians working in various professions. Groups like Women in Trades are beginning to fight publicly for the protection on the jobsite of their lesbian members. And more and more individual lesbians are taking a deep breath, smiling across the lunch table and saying, "No, I'm not married. I'm a lesbian and I'd be very happy to tell you about my life . . ."

Much of the above material thanks to Jesse Gossen.

Women's Work . . . Women's Poverty

16% of Canadian women are poor

62% of women working for pay are in **clerical, sales** or **service** jobs. Only 5% of employed women are in **managerial** or **administrative** positions.

Women workers are concentrated where the wages are lowest:

74% of the employees in the garment industry are women; the average weekly wage is **$173.**

6% of employees in pulp and paper manufacturing are women; the average weekly wage is **$395** (1979).

Average Income by Education and Sex: All Workers, Canada 1980

Education Level	Male	Female
0-8 years	13,334	5,942
Some High School and No Post Secondary	15,652	7,691
Some Post Secondary	15,819	8,196
Post Secondary Certificate	19,132	10,762
University Degree	27,074	14,249

Source: Statistics Canada, Income Distribution by Size in Canada, Catalogue 13-207.

64% of single parent families led by women under 35 are poor

Nearly **50%** of all adult women are in the labour force; less than **20%** of these women are in a union (1978).

Sources: *Statistics Canada* and *Women and Poverty* (National Advisory Council *(NAC)* on the Status of Women). Our thanks to *NAC* for use of their material.

34% of women who never married are poor

Average # of Years Working Outside the Home, 1978

Married women w/ children	34 yrs.
Married women w/o children	38 yrs.
Single women	48 yrs.

Average Earnings by Occupation of Full-Year Workers, Canada 1980

	Male	Female	Female Rate as % of Male
Managerial	28,668	15,680	54.7
Professional	25,475	16,073	63.1
Clerical	17,580	11,305	64.3
Sales	18,750	9,516	50.8
Service	15,755	7,926	50.3
Processing and Machinery Occupations	20,354	10,985	54.0
Product Fabricating	18,146	10,354	57.1
Transportation and Related Occupations	18,950	10,720	56.6
All Occupations	20,198	11,873	58.8

*Workers (either full-time or part-time) who worked 50-52 weeks during the year.)

Source: Statistics Canada, Income Distribution by size in Canada, Ottawa, Catalogue 13-207.

Somewhere to Start

☐ Many of us spend most of our waking hours on the job. Any act that increases our ability to feel like and act like real human beings is a step in the right direction. Being out at work, even if it's only to a couple of other people, can make a tremendous difference. The easiest way seems to be to develop some level of friendship with a co-worker and come out to them on a personal or one-to-one basis, over lunch or coffee.

☐ Accurate information will make people more open about accepting lesbians, so it's important to keep your co-workers well-informed. You could put an article in the newsletter, leave pamphlets in the lunchroom, or pin up newspaper clippings. Pass on appropriate books and records to colleagues.

☐ The sexist environment of a workplace or union office can be countered by introducing positive, women-centred images and words. Feminist cartoons on bulletin boards, poems, lyrics, posters, calendars and notices of up-coming women's events all contribute to building our power and validating our opinions. You'll need to be strategic about these moves. For example, if you want to post a feminist cartoon in your office, you'll first want to win the support of your women co-workers. Teaming with other clerical workers is the best way to avoid isolation and attacks. Men often insist that we laugh at their sexist jokes and boost their egos as a condition of the job. Be aware of this type of subtle coercion and threat to job-security.

☐ Encouraging your co-workers to commemorate women's historical events, such as International Women's Day on March 8, is a positive way of creating enthusiasm for women's and lesbian issues. Your celebration could be as simple as sharing a cake at lunch, as inspiring as screening a rousing women's film at work, or as militant as walking off the job to join thousands of other women marching in the street!

☐ Whenever and however possible, confront homophobic and sexist remarks and jokes on the job and in union meetings. These jokes objectify and dehumanize us and lead to more direct and harmful expressions of hostility. They also contribute to our feelings of self-hate and fear.

☐ Try to establish contact with other lesbian or gay co-workers. If you don't know any others, you could run an ad in your local gay or feminist newspaper, or in your union newsletter. If you're unionized or in a professional association, why not form a gay and/or lesbian caucus in your local? Such caucuses can give support to workers coming-out on the job or participating in union meetings. They can also coordinate political activity within the local and give power and credibility to anti-discrimination struggles.

Consider forming or joining a 'Lesbians and Work' discussion/support group in your community. It could enable you to exchange solutions to common problems and build collective strategies for protecting your rights on the job.

☐ Organizing and fighting for lesbian protection measures within your union and union contract is very important. Your union's support must be garnered before they will bargain with management for your protection. An initial step could be to work for a no discrimination against gays clause in the union constitution. In the union contract, first aim to have "sexual orientation" included in an anti-discriminatory human rights clause. Then, contract clauses relating to benefits such as maternity or bereavement leave, dental and insurance plans, etc. should be worded so that they will acknowledge lesbian lives. Bargaining for International Women's Day as a holiday can set a precedent for recognition of feminist/trade union issues.

☐ Building contacts among unions is also vital. Structures such as a committee of gay and/or lesbian activists from various unions could coordinate the distribution of information and solicit support for any issues concerning homosexuality within their locals.

☐ If you're in a non-union job, getting together with your co-workers to unionize is your best hope for effecting long-term changes in the work environment (see *Resources* for practical advice on unionizing). When investigating which union to join, bear in mind that some are more progressive and democratic than others. Talk with a potential union directly about their stand on women's and gay issues, and about the extent to which *you'll* be able to control your bargaining terms.

☐ Lesbian groups can pressure the Human Rights Branch of their region to act on complaints of women fired or not hired because of employer discrimination against lesbians. You may have to investigage these complaints yourself before approaching the Branch since discrimination against lesbians is often a hidden matter, taking the form of rumours. Document these rumours and try to get to the source. Be prepared to offer real support to the lesbian who has been discriminated against since the process of filing a complaint can be very painful and tedious. Our suspicions of discrimination need to be confirmed by our sisters because you can bet that the employer will deny it.

☐ If you know of stores and businesses where lesbians have been harassed, not hired or fired, then protest! Leaflet, picket and boycott — let the employer and the public know long and loud why you're there. Employers must be taught that discrimination against lesbians will not be swept under the carpet. There is always somewhere to start to fight back!

SORWUC

service, office, & retail workers union of canada

Dear Sisters,   January, 1984

We received your request for information about lesbian rights in our union. We are lesbians who work in the finance industry in clerical jobs, and are members of the Bank and Finance Workers local 4 of SORWUC. Our lesbian caucus has functioned as a support group within our union. We are starting to identify our special trade union needs.

We have been surveying union contract language and found that no SORWUC contract uses the words 'lesbian, gay, dyke or homosexual.' The only phrase which indirectly acknowledges our existence is 'sexual preference' or 'sexual orientation.' These words are used in Human Rights or No Discrimination clauses which prohibit the employer from discriminating against us in hiring, lay-offs, firings, wage rates, training, promotion, etc. Sexual orientation is included in a long list of other groups who often face discrimination on the basis of sex, race, creed, colour and others.

We did find other contract wording which gives us a foot in the door to lesbian rights. But only occasionally in negotiations with management did union members refer to 'lesbian rights' as an explanation for demanding certain contract wordings. Thus the clauses that might protect us are open to different interpretations and our rights are not established.

The contract clauses that seemed vaguely relevant to lesbian lives were ones on Compassionate or Bereavement Leave which could be interpreted to recognize lesbian lovers or partners; Parental Leave clauses which could apply to lesbian parents; and a Personal Rights clause which contained wording on clothing which struck us as relevant to some lesbians. Also relevant was contract wording which replaces 'spouse' with 'partner.'

Here are some excerpts from SORWUC contracts. We underlined wording pertinant to lesbians:

BOBOLINK DAYCARE CENTRE/ Compassionate Leave: For the case of bereavement in the immediate family and close friends and relatives, an Employee shall be entitled to a special leave at their regular pay ... for five working days.

VANCOUVER-NEW WESTMINSTER NEWSPAPER GUILD/Special Leave: In the case of bereavement in the immediate family, the employee shall be entitled to special leave ... Immediate family is defined as ... any relative or any other person with whom the employee resides...In the event of the death of ... any other person with whom the employee has a close personal relationship, the employee shall be entitled to special leave...

BOBOLINK DAYCARE CENTRE/ Maternity and Paternity Leave: Upon the birth or adoption of her baby, the Employee is entitled to two weeks leave of absence with pay.

GRANDVIEW TERRACE DAYCARE SOCIETY/ Personal Rights: The Employer specifically agrees that there shall be no arbitrary rules regarding dress.

The SORWUC contract with Red Door Rental Agency specifies a special four day leave of absence for personal reasons. We call this the 'falling in love' leave, or alternatively, the 'personal crisis' leave!

So that's about it so far with SORWUC contracts. We also phoned a few other unions to see to what extent they have acknowledged lesbian rights. We contacted CUPE (Canadian Union of Public Employees), CUPW (Canadian Union of Postal Workers) and AUCE (Association of University and College Employees).In these union, contracts with No Discrimination clauses recently added 'sexual preference' to their list of no discrimination groups. In the case of AUCE local 2, under the Compassionate Leave clause leave of five days may be granted at the discretion of the supervisor for the death or serious illness of a close friend. However, lesbian relationships were not mentioned at the bargaining table when the phrase 'close friend' was being argued for.

In our opinion, these unions seem to be making some headway in establishing rights for lesbian workers, but as yet have not fully acknowledged our existence and our special needs for protection in the workplace. As a lesbian caucus within SORWUC, we ourselves are just becoming more aware of our workplace needs and how trade unions can help meet them.

In solidarity, Jean Burgess
Lee Rick
Linda Willis

Photo/Amelia Productions

We want workplaces that are safe for lesbian workers. We also want workplaces that are non-exploitative of workers. Equal pay, worker control, safe working conditions, benefits that improve the quality of our lives, respect on the job or radically changing the whole economic structure may be part of our aspirations for a better society.

Regardless of our political differences on how we view work and the economy, we all (in the here and now) need to work in order to live. In our jobs we can better fight for worker rights if we are not living in fear of being found out as lesbian. We want to turn that fear into pride. Safety for ourselves as lesbians at work empowers us to act along side our co-workers on whatever issues we identify — be it the right to a coffee break, confronting racism on the job, becoming more skilled and competent at our work, or seeking a radical alternative to a capitalist economy.

Whatever our aspirations are for the work we do in our lifetimes, whatever our politics are, as a beginning we want to insist on our right to live our lives openly as lesbians — with pride and safety.

— Jean

Resources

Print

There are very few resources relating directly to lesbians and work. We are also listing materials of interest to women wishing to organize their workplace and improve their working conditions.

"Lesbians and Gays in the Union Movement" by Susan Genge, from *Union Sisters,* ed. by Linda Briskin and Linda Yanz (Toronto: The Women's Press, 1983)   One of many interesting articles in this comprehensive anthology about women and Canadian trade unions.

"Lesbian Ignite" by Anny Brackx, from *Spare Rib Reader: 100 Issues of Women's Liberation,* ed. by Marsha Rowe (London: Penguin, 1982)   An account by a woman who lost her job when she came out as a lesbian — and fought back. This anthology contains other articles on lesbianism.

Getting Organized: Building A Union, Mary Cornish & Laurell Ritchie (Toronto: The Women's Press, 1980)   A practical and readable "how to do it" book on unionizing that goes through all the steps of choosing a union, signing up co-workers, confronting an employers' anti-union actions and negotiating a

first contract. Note: This book is based on Ontario law, but you will find it relatively easy to substitute your own province's Labour Code.

"Women and Trade Unions Issue," *Resources for Feminist Research,* Vol. 10,#2 (July 1981) The collection of articles that became the basis for *Union Sisters* (see above). Available from O.I.S.E., 252 Bloor St. W., Toronto Ont. M5S 1V6

A Working Majority: What Women Must Do For Pay, Pat Armstrong and Hugh Armstrong (Ottawa: Canadian Advisory Council on the Status of Women, 1983)   An excellent contemporary source book — where we work, where we are unemployed, what our benefits are (and aren't), womens' unions, job conditions, etc. Quotable statistics and revealing personal stories about our daily life on the job.

Still Ain't Satisfied: Canadian Feminism Today, ed. by Maureen FitzGerald et al (Toronto: Women's Press, 1982)   A number of articles on women, work and unions.

Never Done: Three Centuries of Women's Work in Canada, The Corrective Collective (Toronto:

Women's Press, 1974)   A large print picture and
story album of womens' paid and unpaid labour. Well
illustrated with cartoons and graphics.

*Women's Work: A Collection of Articles by Working
Women,* The Working Women's Association
(Vancouver: Press Gang, 1976)   A group of women
who wanted to tell it like it was. They wrote it down,
got some great graphics, copied it, stapled it together
and sold it for 50¢.

*An Account to Settle: The Story of the United Bank
Workers (SORWUC),* The Bank Book Collective
(Vancouver: Press Gang, 1979)   Bank workers in
B.C. and Saskatchewan tell the story of how they
tried to organize their workplaces into an independent
feminist union. A readable, exciting and inspiring
book.

*The Eaton Drive: The Campaign to Organize Canada's
Largest Department Store 1948-1952,* Eileen Sufrin
(Don Mills: Fitzhenry and Whiteside, 1982)   An
exciting and absorbing play-by-play account of the
largest union drive in the Canadian retail industry.

Bargaining for Equality, The Womens' Labour Project
of the National Lawyers Guild (San Francisco:
Inkworks Press, 1980)   A useful guide to trade union
contract language on womens' issues that explains and
translates contract terms into non-legalistic, everyday
language.

*Pink Collar Workers — Inside the World of Womens'
Work,* Louise Kapp Howe (New York: Avon Books,
1977)   Beauticians, salesworkers, waitresses, office
workers and homemakerks share the joy, pain, pride,
humour and frustrations of working in the female job
ghettos.

*All the Livelong Day: The Meaning and Demeaning of
Routine Work,* Barbara Garson (Markham: Penguin
Books, 1972)   This book reveals what it's really like
to work in assembly line jobs, whether it's a fish
plant, a lipstick factory or a clerical factory in an
urban centre. These are stories of the degradation of
routinized work and the creative ways people have
fought to maintain their dignity.

*Not Servants, Not Machines: Office Workers Speak
Out,* Jean Tepperman (Boston: Beacon Press, 1976)
A collection of interviews with American women
office workers which reveal the day-to-day issues of
their lives and how they organized collectively to
improve their conditions.

Canada's Unions, Robert Laxer (Toronto: James
Lorimer & Co., 1976)   A historical look at Canadian
unions in the '70's reveals the structure, leaders and
goals of the trade union movement. The book traces
the growth of independence in the Canadian union
movement and exposes the bitter conflicts between
Canadian and American unions.

Office Workers' Survival Handbook, (Nottingham:
Russell Press, 1981)   A British book which details
health hazards in the office: the ones we know about,
those we don't and those we suspect. A guide to
fighting back, unionizing and direct action. Available
from Trade Union Book Service, 265 Seven Sisters
Rd., London N4, England.

Women's Work, Women's Health: Myths and Realities,
Jeanne Mager Stellman (New York: Pantheon, 1977)

Looks at the oftimes neglected health hazards, both
physical and psychic, that women are exposed to in
their various workplaces: offices, homes, factories.
Also examines the sexist biases in research on
occupational health.

Work is Dangerous to Your Health, Jeanne M.
Stellman and Susan M. Daum (New York: Vintage,
1973)   Subtitled "A Handbook of Health Hazards in
Workplace and What You Can Do About Them." A
practical, informative what-to-do book.

Film & Video
There are many good and inspiring films and videos on
women and workplace struggles, like *Union Maids*
(organizing in Chicago in the '30s) and *Operation
Finger Pinky* (a contemporary organizing drive by
office workers). In Canada, many of these films are
available from the National Film Board (see your
phone book for regional offices) or from DEC Films,
427 Bloor St. W., Toronto Ont. M5S 1X7
(416-964-6901). To find feminist producers and
distributors in Canada and the U.S., see:

☐ *Finding Lesbian Resources*

"Women and Work – A Cineography" by Dinah
Forbes in "Women and Trade Unions Issue,"
Resources for Feminist Research, Vol. 10, #2 (July
1981)   An extensive and annotated film and video
list, with addresses of distributors. See address above
in *Print.*

Groups
The following are unions, or groups of women
organized around women and workplace issues.
Excepting the first entry, they are not, as far as we
know, dealing with specifically lesbian concerns — but
the potential is there.

*Lesbian Caucus, Bank and Finance Workers Local 4;
Service, Office, Retail Workers Union of Canada
(SORWUC),* #206 - 402 W. Pender St., Vancouver
B.C. (604-684-2834)   A small discussion / support
group which occasionally holds workshop /
discussions on issues related to lesbians in their
workplace; i.e. dress codes, sexual harassment, 'in' or
'out' at work, subtleties of discrimination, lesbian
rights contract language.

*Service, Office, Retail Workers Union of Canada
(SORWUC)* (see address above).   This small
independent feminist union has successfully
negotiated sexual orientation clauses in some of its
contracts. They could be contacted for information.

*Association of University and College Employees
(AUCE),* 6383 Memorial Rd., Vancouver B.C. (604-
224-2308   Like SORWUC, AUCE could be
contacted for information on sexual orientation
clauses.

Union Sisters, Vancouver B.C.   An informal group of
union and non-union, working and unemployed
women who meet monthly over dinner and network
on work and women's issues. They could be contacted
via SORWUC (above).

Women in Trades, 400A W. 5th Ave., Vancouver B.C.
(604-876-0922)   For women in non-traditional jobs,
this group provides support and contact with other

women in your trade. They could put you in touch with a Women in Trades group in your region.

Ontario Working Women, c/o Ontario Federation of Labour, 15 Jervis Dr., Don Mills, Ont. M3C 1Y8 An association of union women focussing on working women's issues.

Saskatchewan Working Women, Box 7981, Saskatoon, Sask. or Box 4154, Regina, Sask.   A group of union and non-union working women with locals in Prince Albert, Swift Current, Regina and Saskatoon. They are organizing for changes in working conditions, daycare and equal pay.

Action-Travail des Femmes, 2515 Delisle, Montreal, Québec H3J 1K8   A group of trade union women prepared to make womens' workplace issues a priority.

Working Womens' Education Committee, 2708 Gottingen St., Halifax, Nova Scotia B3K 3C7 This is an ad hoc group of women from both union and non-union workplaces who organize weekend conferences on issues such as sexual harassment, microtechnology, occupational safety, women and the economic crisis. Rumour has it that they are becoming aware of lesbian issues in the workplace.

Professional Gay Caucuses List,   Prepared and updated by the National Gay Task Force, with over 50 entries. Available from 80 5th Ave., New York NY 10011

The above Resources thanks to Jean Burgess and Niamh Hennessy.

A paper entitled "Gays and the Trade Union Movement" provided ideas for this section. Thanks to the authors: Wendy Butt, Walter Davis, Susan Genge, Robert Laycock and Robert Powers.

See also Resources in

☐ *Schools*
☐ *Working in Progressive Movements*

Photo/ Teresa Reimer

Graphic/Jeannie Kamins

Schools

When I look back on my school career and the teachers who influenced me, it was always the single, strong and intelligent women that I respected and admired most. These women were dedicated and courageous and later, when I was a teacher myself — trying to create a quality of education that these women had shown me could be created — I came to fully realize just how much strength they had.

I wondered, as I developed high school crushes on some of my teachers, whether they got crushes on other women they liked, admired and respected. As I struggled privately with my own ever-growing awareness of my lesbianism and wondered why it was so wrong, I also wondered if these women were like myself, hiding and wondering why. When I was teaching I was aware of those girls in my classes who had crushes on me, and I tried to give them grinning approval to let them know that they were not sick or wrong. I wonder now if they got my silent message, and I wonder how much longer that message will have to be silent.

— Jeannette

The education system is a major institution of socialization. Its purpose is to ensure that children grow up into proper citizens — believing the right things and behaving the right way. In this society, proper means obedient, docile, unthinking, hard-working and heterosexual. The education system plays a crucial part in maintaining and passing on the values of the society. It is extremely effective in accomplishing this task and it is extremely resistant to change.

The school system also plays a crucial part in conditioning young girls into passivity and acceptance of the appropriate feminine role. Information about lesbianism is not made available to young women in school, not even in schools where feminist demands have resulted in some women's studies courses. This is a particularly difficult front on which to organize due to the controversy surrounding sex education and the vulnerability of teachers and counsellors to personal attack and loss of jobs should they attempt to work for change. However, the difficulties facing a young women in the intensified heterosexual game-playing of school with no lesbian role models, no access to positive books or articles, no context to make sense of her feelings, do make the education system a crucial area to influence.

After I became the co-parent of two children, I watched sadly as the children came home from school feeling completely isolated and depressed because their teachers were promoting values completely different from their parents'. Their parents are feminists and lesbians and nowhere in the school system is that going to be recognized and promoted, nor are the children going to get positive reinforcement for being the people they are.

Teachers have always had to remain beyond reproach in the eyes of the public since the mental and moral growth of a society is placed in their hands.

Women who wished to remain in the teaching profession had to be regarded as 'of high moral character' and totally selfless in their dedication to their job. To a very large extent, this attitude still prevails. In a sexist society strong controls are placed on women, especially single women who have no male proprietor to establish such control. In schools today, single heterosexual women must watch who they are seen with and where they are seen. Single women who become pregnant are not allowed to continue to teach in most areas of the country unless they either terminate the pregnancy or gain 'respectability' through marriage. Lesbians are considered intolerable under any circumstance and must remain invisible.

Both school administrators and parents know how much of an influence teachers can be since children spend most of their waking hours in school. Administrators will not allow students to be influenced by a known lesbian. Such a woman is a threat to the society she has been entrusted to recreate. While the sacred and guarded site of the school represses even overt heterosexuality, lesbian teachers must repress their identity to the point of non-existence, or live with the fear of being found out and then dealing with the resulting economic and social repercussions.

The above material thanks to Jeanette Lush.

Somewhere to Start

☐ Whenever and however you can, work to get lesbian-positive material into the schools. Teachers, students, parents, librarians or outside lesbian activists can all try to make this information available (see *Resources*).

☐ As teachers, lesbian or otherwise, do not contribute to the censoring of any mention of homosexuality. Where appropriate, include information and discussion of lesbianism and gay men. Arrange for speakers from gay and lesbian groups to address the class; try to get the school library to carry a selection of accurate books on being gay.

At the elementary level, remember that probably some students do not live in traditional heterosexual families. Encourage attitudes which acknowledge the validity of many different kinds of families, and include gay parents among the variations discussed.

By high school, many students will be wondering if they are lesbian or gay. Making available information about the resources for young gay people which exist outside the school is probably the most effective thing to do. If no such resources exist — a young gay people's group, a lesbian coming-out group — suggest to local gay and lesbian groups that they start something.

Expose your students to feminist ideas. If young women want to get together to talk about their lives, use your position in the school to get them meeting facilities or whatever is necessary. Then leave them alone to figure out what they want to do.

Discourage name-calling and anti-lesbian and gay jokes amongst students. Those kinds of jokes are dehumanizing in the same way racist jokes are. Often young children really don't know what "faggot" or "lezzie" even mean, and are receptive to an explanation.

☐ Lesbians can face real repercussions, like losing their job, if they are out at work, and the conflict this can cause must be respected. Having the teacher's union pass a policy prohibiting discrimination on the basis of sexual orientation would provide some legal grounds for fighting an unfair dismissal. A gay and lesbian caucus, or a women's caucus or committee within the union could offer support to individuals and organize more effectively to have such a policy passed. Part of your strategy could be to have a lesbian group sponsor an educational workshop on lesbianism for your colleagues.

☐ A lesbian schoolworkers group can offer a place to talk about problems and successes with other lesbians who know what you're going through. To form such a group, put a notice in your local feminist or gay newspaper. Ask interested women to write you c/o the newspaper if printing your phone number seems too risky. As a group you can figure out your goals: just having a place to talk may be all you need, or maybe you have ideas for changes in the schools that would benefit you and your students. Having a group means you can write letters or attend public meetings in the group's name, thereby reducing personal risk. If there are other lesbians who would be willing to fight publicly for changes and who can better afford the exposure, consider forming a Committee of Concerned Citizens...

☐ If you're a lesbian in highschool, try to make contact with other lesbian students. If a young gay people's group exists in town, check it out. If not, contact the nearest lesbian group you can find and ask them to sponsor a drop-in for young lesbians (see *Finding Lesbian Resources*). If you think any of your teachers are lesbians, remember that they may be very concerned about losing their jobs if they're out, and be sensitive to that.

☐ At universities, lesbians can form a group and often get money and space from the student council. A lesbian group can work to provide support for lesbian students, agitate to get lesbian studies courses, make sure that women's studies courses have lesbian content, and do general consciousness-raising on lesbianism. This could include making sure that libraries, especially the Women's Centre library if one exists, have a good selection of lesbian books.

Guidelines for the Evaluation of Treatment of Gay Themes and Characters in Literature for Children and Young Adults

Excerpted from "Young, Gay and the Problem of Self Identity: An Annotated Bibliography" by Stephen MacDonald. Reprinted with permission and thanks from *Emergency Librarian,* 1980.

Central Characters

Young gay women and men can and should be portrayed as simply as their nongay counterparts, with no special emphasis on the sexual component of their identities. If, however, "gayness" itself is a major part of the plot, several points must be considered.

What is the result of a child's discovery that an important person in his or her life is gay? The positive acceptance of a parent, teacher or best friend should be shown happening without destructive repercussions. If the book does contain stereotypic responses, the librarian can point out to the reader that positive acceptance often occurs, too.

The orientation of gay characters need not be "explained" by grotesque family situations or by the pseudo-medical observations of an adult in the story. If one of these "explanations" exists the librarian can point out that no such effort is ever deemed necessary to account for straight characters.

Does the book serve primarily to reassure insecure nongay kids that one can have a gay experience and still turn out "normal"? If so, this may be a legitimate subject, but it is certainly not relevant to young lesbians and gay men. Librarians should be aware of the need for portrayals of growth and development of gay identity as a valid life choice.

Gay adolescents will, realistically, encounter social pressures but they should be shown as coping adequately with them. A wide framework of support is, in fact, available to such young people. If it

is not described, librarians can make readers aware of the non-fiction books and periodicals now in many libraries. They can also mention that gay communities are now quite visible, with such resources as counselling services, coffee hours, and churches and synagogues available.

Minor Roles

In many types of stories, there can be incidental characters — friends, relatives, or neighbours — who are gay. They should be included as a natural part of all kinds of situations, not themselves being the "situation". A few novels of this sort exist today with no explicit identification of the gay character. Librarians should be aware of this kind of book and be able to refer readers to such stories.

Illustrations

Certainly it is impossible to draw a gay person. Yet it is very easy to picture same-sex couples. In books for children there should be illustrations of gay couples as parents, as older sisters and brothers dating kids of the same sex, and just as ordinary people. No books like this are currently available. In this area, as in all areas covered by these guidelines, librarians have a clear obligation to their readers to make publishers aware that such books are desperately needed and will be used when available.

Degree of Explicitness

Librarians know that in contemporary YA fiction, nongay relationships are hardly shrouded in a veil of mystery. Comparably there ought to be more gay relationships

in such novels, with more realistic portrayals of affection and falling in love. It is important to show, with an appropriate amount of physical detail, how gay women and men find each other and how they allow the expression of their emotions to develop.

Impact on Readers

In terms of orientation, there are three kinds of young readers — the straight, the gay and the famous "in-between, teetering-on-the-fence." Before selecting any book with a gay theme, librarians should evaluate each book's effect on all three: Does it give an accurate, sympathetic picture of gays for nongays, so that they can learn to appreciate and not fear differences in sexual and affectional preference; does it give young gays a clear view of the decisions facing them and show that these can be made successfully?

The entire culture rather frantically reinforces the choice of a heterosexual lifestyle. Surely, if those on-the-fence adolescents exist, they have the right to see an up-front picture of gay life, not just the old caricatures.

Author's Attitudes

In our homophobic society any work dealing with a gay theme is prone to include cliches and preconceptions of "gay character". It would be excellent to have a reviewer who is proudly self-identified as gay examine relevant books to point out negative sterotypic attitudes when they occur and to make suggestions as to how the librarian can best counteract such stereotypes.

*T*he Status of Women Committee of the B.C.

Teachers' Federation reports that a policy resolution was proposed at the 1980 B.C.T.F. Convention which would prohibit discrimination on the basis of sexual orientation. This resolution was passed by the B.C.T.F. and was taken to and passed by the Canadian Teachers' Federation as well. A Status of Women Committee spokesperson said that the Committee saw this not only as a positive step in providing protection for teachers who were gay but also in allowing much more information and support to be made available to students making choices about their self-definitions. The passing of this resolution was a result of years of consciousness-raising and organizing work and is a significant victory.

Resources

Print

"The Lesbian Issue", *Resources for Feminist Research,* Vol. 12, #1 (1983)   Discusses issues for research and activism, the lesbian experience in Canada, has lists of international periodicals, lesbian organizations, film, video and slide shows, and annotated bibliographies. Availabe from O.I.S.E., 252 Bloor St. W., Toronto Ont. M5S 1V6

Lesbian Studies: Present and Future, ed. by Margaret Cruikshank (Old Westbury: The Feminist Press, 1982) An extensive collection of writings: autobiography of lesbians in education, the denial of lesbian history, homophobia in the classroom, Third World lesbian perspectives, lesbian perspectives on women's studies, lesbians in science and sports, sample syllabi from courses on lesbianism, etc.

"Lesbian as Teacher, Teacher as Lesbian", by Meryl C. Friedman from *"Our Right To Love",* ed. by Ginny Vida (Englewood Cliffs: Prentice-Hall, 1978) By an activist teacher, this article recounts her work with the Gay Teachers Association, the teacher's union and the Parents/Teachers Association.

Gay Teachers Support Packet, National Gay Task Force, 80 5th Ave., New York, NY 10011 Statements on rights of gay teachers, from professional groups, school boards, etc.

"Women's Studies, Black Women's Studies and Lesbian Studies", *Radical Teacher,* Issue 17 (1981) Available from P.O. Box 102 Kendall Sq., Cambridge MA 02124

The Gay Academic, ed. by Louie Crew (Palm Springs: ETC Publications, 1977)   An anthology exploring gay issues in history, linguistics, literature, philosophy, psychology, science, sociology and political science.

Matrices: A Lesbian-Feminist Research Newsletter, Available from the Dept. of English, University of Nebraska, Lincoln, NE 68588

Lesbian-Feminist Study Clearinghouse, Publicizes research on lesbian experience from feminist perspective. Available from the Women's Studies Program 1012CL, University of Pittsburgh, PA 15260

Lesbian and Gay History Researchers Network, Lesbian Heritage, 1519 P. St. NW, Washington D.C. 20005 An occasional newsletter for those researching or interested in lesbian history.

All the Women Are White, All the Blacks Are Men, But Some of Us Are Brave: Black Women's Studies, ed. by Gloria T. Hull et al (Old Westbury: The Feminist Press, 1982)   An extensive anthology, including sections on Black feminism, confronting racism in education, Black women and social sciences, literature. Has materials on Black women and lesbianism, and bibliographies.

Lesbian Fiction: An Anthology, ed. by Elly Bulkin (Watertown: Persephone Press, 1981)   Includes the essay "Teaching Lesbian Fiction".

Lesbian Poetry: An Anthology, ed. by Elly Bulkin, Joan Larkin (Watertown: Persephone Press, 1981) Includes the essay "Teaching Lesbian Poetry".

"Lesbian History Issue", *Frontiers: A Journal of Women's Studies,* Vol. 4, #3 (1979)   Available from the Women's Studies Program, University of Colorado, Boulder, CO 80309

Sex Variant Women in Literature, Jeannette Foster (Baltimore: Diana Press, 1975)   The first edition of this classic was published by Vantage Press in 1956. Unfortunately, both editions are presently out of print. May be available in libraries.

Lesbian Images, Jane Rule (Trumansburg: The Crossing Press, 1982)   A selective literary and cultural history of lesbians.

Lesbiana, Barbara Grier (Tallahassee: Naiad, 1975) Her book reviews from *The Ladder.*

Surpassing the Love of Men: Romantic Friendship and Love Between Women from the Renaissance to the Present, Lillian Faderman (New York: Wm. Morrow, 1981)

"Homophobia and Education" *Interracial Books for Children Bulletin,* Vol 14, #3/4   This special issue addresses homophobia in children's literature, connections between sexism, racism and homophobia, and gives good ideas for fighting it in the schools. Recommended. The *Bulletin* is published eight times a year and evaluates children's trade and text books for their messages about racism, classism and sexism. It lists resource groups and alternative materials. Available from 1841 Broadway, New York, NY 10023

Gay/Lesbian Almanac: A New Documentary, Jonathan Katz (New York: Harper and Row, 1983)

Gay American History: Lesbians and Gay Men in the U.S.A., Jonathan Katz (New York: Avon, 1978) An extensive documentary history with a huge bibliography.

Canadian Woman Studies/Les Cahiers de la Femme, York University, 4700 Keele St. Downsview Ont. M3J 1P3 A quarterly periodical that sometimes carries lesbian material.

Learning to Lose: Sexism and Education, ed. by Dale Spender, Elizabeth Sarah (London: The Women's Press, 1980) An anthology from English perspective. Not much information relating to lesbians or hetero-sexism, but it has an extensive bibliography on sexism in education and resources for women's studies.

Emergency Librarian, P.O. Box 4696, Stn. O, London Ont. N5W 5L7 A Canadian review publication that is a good source of critical information on children's and other books. Progressive.

Tabs: Aids for Ending Sexism in Schools, This journal reports on materials that would be useful to feminist teachers grades K to 12. Reviews, lesson plans, awareness exercises, news, posters. Available from 744 Carroll St., Brooklyn NY 11215.

Sexism in Children's Books: Facts, Figures and Guidelines, Children's Rights Workshop (London: Writers and Readers Publishing Cooperative) Has nothing about homophobia or heterosexism.

Bibliographies

A Brief Preliminary Guide to Recommended Reading Matter on Homosexuality and *Out on the Shelves: Gay and Lesbian Fiction List,* The Gay Interest Group of the Canadian Library Association These are annotated publications, covering English and French titles. Available from Canadian Library Assoc., 151 Sparks St., Ottawa Ont. K1P 5E3

Homosexuality in Canada: A Bibliography, Alex Spence (Toronto: Pink Triangle Press, 1979)

A Gay Bibliography, Gay Task Force of the American Library Association Annotated, and frequently updated. Includes audio-visual resources, books, bibliographies and contact groups. A valuable resource. Available from P.O. Box 2383, Philadelphia PA 19103

The Lesbian in Literature, Barbara Grier (Gene Damon) (Tallahassee: Naiad Press, 1981)

Black Lesbians: An Annotated Bibliography, J.R. Roberts (Tallahassee: Naiad Press, 1981)

Women Loving Women: A Select and Annotated Bibliography of Women Loving Women in Literature, ed. by Marie Kuda (Chicago: Woman Press, 1974)

Feminist Resources for Schools and Colleges: A Guide to Curricular Materials, Merle Froschl, Jane Williamson (Old Westbury: The Feminist Press, 1976) Annotated bibliography of non-sexist print materials for teachers and students, pre-school to college. Lists of periodicals, organizations and publishers, and guidelines and analysis of text and trade books.

Film

What About McBride? Tom Lazarus (1974) Two teenage boys discuss whether to invite a third on a rafting trip, though he is rumoured to be gay. Intended to be a discussion starter. (14 mins.) Available from CRM/McGraw-Hill Films, 110–15th St., Del Mar, CA 92014

A Woman's Place is In The House: A Portrait of Elaine Noble, Nancy Porter and Mickey Lemle (1975) An award-winning film about the first openly lesbian state legislator. Originally appeared on PBS television. (29 mins.) Available from Texture Films, 1600 Broadway, New York NY 10019

A Comedy in Six Unnatural Acts, Jan Oxenberg (Iris Films, 1975) Spoofs of lesbian stereotypes. 25 mins.

Home Movie, Jan Oxenberg (Iris Films, 1973) A young lesbian narrates her growing up through her parents' home movies. 12 mins.

Groups

Over 20 universities and colleges in Canada and Québec have lesbian/gay student associations listed in the *Body Politic,* P.O. Box 7289, Stn. A, Toronto Ont. M5W 1X9

To find U.S. lesbian/gay student associations, consult *Our Right To Love: A Lesbian Resource Book,* ed. by Ginny Vida (Englewood Cliffs: Prentice-Hall, 1978)

Gay Teachers Association, P.O. Box 435, Van Brunt Stn. Brooklyn, NY 11215 They publish a list of Gay Teachers Organizations in the U.S.

I started dressing more feminine and one day...some guys on the street whistled at me. I told the doctor about it and he asked me if I liked it. "I guess so," I said. I knew he figured I was cured.

Psychiatry and Therapy

Do you have any idea how bizarre it is to be a psychiatric nursing student complete with a white uniform and a set of keys attached to your belt, policing the 'crazy' women locked up in a ward of the large red brick mental hospital in the middle of the Prairies? Too many patients . . . too many anti-psychotic drugs . . . no alternatives anywhere . . .

I was 18 years old and in training, which meant half days in the classroom studying 'mental disorders' and half days on the wards working with that particular disorder. The patients never had names. I remember the chapter on *Abnormal Behaviour: Deviant Sexuality.* This is what we all absorbed, believed and practiced:

> Very little is known about the causes of sociopathic sexual behaviour deviations; deviant sexual behaviour is considered a surface symptom of a more profound personality disorder. These people have been arrested in their psycho-sexual development at some earlier level of emotional growth. The sex impulse has failed to mature for various reasons or has undergone a deviation in the course of its normal development. Normal psychic aspects of sex are not harmoniously integrated into the total personality.
> *Homosexuality:* caused by a failure of the person to identify with the parent of the same sex, or as a result of seduction of the child at an early age by a member of the same sex.
> *Prognosis:* poor
> *Treatment:* intensive, long-term psychotherapy
> — Manfreda, *Psychiatric Nursing*

I remember spending six weeks on the ward with these 'deviants', among them women and men whose abnormality was being attracted to persons of the same sex. Doctors, psychiatrists, families had them locked up hoping they could be 'cured'.

There was Linda. Her case file said "admitted homosexual tendencies." She had tried to commit suicide. Having never before seen a female homosexual — lesbian, I learned, was the term — I was curious. I chose Linda as my case study and we spent time together each afternoon. I practiced my 'active listening' skills and wrote daily reports for her chart.

She was a shy woman and I was struck by how much she looked like any other woman. Little by little, I learned that she had always loved women, always fantasized about women sexually and that she was tormented by these 'unnatural desires'. Her marriage hadn't helped. Neither had the babies. She had fallen in love with her neighbour and went through months of incredible agony over her mixed-up feelings. She couldn't make them go away. All she knew was that she was horrible, sick, perverted and that she would ruin her husband and children if she ever told anyone. So she kept quiet and, with no outlet and no help, she tried to kill herself.

There was some relief now, being in the mental hospital. Her secret was finally out and she desperately hoped the psychiatrist would cure her of this affliction. The pills helped some, she said.

The ideas didn't come as often. But the pills made her so sleepy . . . she had heard they used shock treatment sometimes . . .

I remember the funny sensations in my chest when she would talk like this. I didn't understand why I was so uncomfortable when the nurses would make remarks about "the queer one" when we discussed the patients. I was told to work on maintaining the proper nurse/patient relationship — empathetic but objective. Nor did I know why I was so relieved to leave Linda when my rotation took me to another ward. I pushed her out of my mind, never asked about her or visited her. I don't know what happened to her.

Years later, when I began to love women and came out as a lesbian with the strong support of the women's movement, I remembered her. And I was very sad.

— Yvette

It is only in the last century that the whole concept of 'curing' people of their 'mental illnesses' has become prevalent. This corresponds to a general cultural shift in attitude towards homosexuality, from a sin against God and Nature to a mental abnormality.

Psychological theories have become so influential as to provide a major ideological direction in our society. How we see ourselves and our world is to a large extent based upon psychological theories and beliefs. Many words we use in everyday conversatons — well-adjusted, neurotic, paranoid, conscious/unconscious — are Freudian concepts. It is completely impossible for any of us to have escaped being affected by popularized versions of Sigmund Freud's theories.

Freudian thought has become the most influential on the societal scale, possibly because Freud's theories fit in nicely with a capitalist, male-supremacist culture. According to this school of thought, people's problems in life are caused by early childhood traumas. We are at the mercy of our repressed, suppressed libidinal urges. Men are motivated by their sex drives and death wishes. Women are motivated by the terrible trauma of being born penis-less and spend the rest of our lives attempting to get one, either unhealthily through 'being like a man' or healthily through giving birth to one. Long years of psychotherapy can help individuals adjust better to life. Lesbians are fixated at an immature stage of development.

*W*hen I was 20 I fell in love with a nun. She used to come and sit in my dormitory room and hold my hand. All my life I had strong feelings about women but I never knew what it meant. She put the name on it one day by asking, "Do you know the difference between loving someone and being in love with someone?" I had never really thought about it before. I had only thought about being 'in love' as related to boys and sexual feelings and I had never had those feelings.

"I'm in love with you," I said. I realized then what my feelings meant. For the first time I thought, "I'm a lesbian."

The shock was so great I started hallucinating. I couldn't cope. The cracks in the wall seemed to open up. I thought I should see a psychiatrist. I walked in and said, "I'm here and I'm sick because I'm in love with another woman." He nodded and put me in another little room to take the Minnesota Multiphasic Test. It's a test to see how crazy you are. It asks questions like, "Are you afraid of spiders? Do you think people are deliberately trying to hurt you?"

I guess I flunked because he looked at it and said, "Well, we're going to put you in the hospital." I was glad because I thought I was crazy. I stayed in for a week and a half. He saw me for half an hour a day. The rest of the time I sat around smoking and drinking coffee. My friend the nun called to see how I was. The psychiatrist said she should leave me alone. Finally, after I passed the test of making brownies in the hospital, they let me out!

I kept seeing the psychiatrist and eventually I got involved with a guy. The doctor was thrilled. I started dressing more feminine and one day on the way to his office, some guys on the street whistled at me. I told the doctor about it and he asked me if I liked it. "I guess so," I said. I knew he figured I was cured.

I thought that if I went on acting normal I would be ok. I got married and had two children. After five years my marriage broke up. Then I got involved with a woman who wanted a relationship with me but who thought it was weird and sick. She said "No one must know." I couldn't talk to anyone. People even asked me and I lied. I went crazy with the lying and the secrets. I got addicted to valium and I was drinking. I put myself in the hospital. I don't remember this period very well.

I didn't get better until I could tell the truth about how I felt about everything. I told my parents I was a lesbian. My father said it wasn't normal but he loved me anyway.

Unladylike Behaviour

Photo / Paula Levine

On the behaviour mod ward they had this system where they gave us tokens for doing what they wanted, and took them away for being bad. You had to pay tokens for anything you wanted to do, even taking a bath. I remember I had this green plaid skirt and matching sweater I used to get tokens for wearing 'cause they were trying to change me into their idea of a proper woman. So this one morning I decided to put on my exalted outfit and net a few tokens. I appeared at breakfast all tarted up and this nurse said "Oh! you look very nice!" in this really phony voice she always used for the patients. Then she told me I'd look better if I shaved my legs. I remember feeling all embarassed and stupid, even though I'd decided long before that shaved legs were silly. After breakfast I signed out the razor and went off to the bath. I think at that point I was going to shave my fucking legs.

I remember the rush of blood as I slashed as hard as I could sort of not looking and then looking, seeing the skin all white and puffy like, splitting, and then the blood welled up and I sat there and let it run in the bath. After a while someone knocked on the door to use the bath so I got up. I went out to the desk and slapped the razor down in front of the nurse with my bloody hand and said, "I'm finished with the razor." She looked at me real angry like and said, "You'll be sorry for that." They stitched me up without anesthetic and I remember it hurt like hell but I pretended it didn't.

Sculpture/Text by Persimmon Blackbridge and Sheila Gilhooly

I had no lovers for two or three years, and during this time I developed a good sense of myself. The next relationship I had was with a woman who knew she was a lesbian and had no qualms about it.

— *Josie*

Today we have hundreds of different kinds of therapy and as many theories on why people are the way they are and how they can be helped. Behaviourist theory, humanistic psychology, reichian, jungian, gestalt, transactional analysis — these are only a few. Virtually all of these theories and therapies consider difficulties with life as being individual problems that can be corrected with individual solutions. Virtually all therapies have been used to maintain the status quo. People who do not fit into proper roles, or who display 'anti-social' behaviour are locked up in mental hospitals.

Women are hospitalized at a far higher rate than men, although men are imprisoned at a higher rate than women. Such ostensibly therapeutic techniques as behaviour modification, anti-depressant drugs, brain surgery and shock treatment are all control weapons used by the state to reinforce the inequalities that exist in society.

Women who are depressed, angry, scared, ovewhelmed, and who display emotion too clearly — especially if the emotions are interfering with the adequate performance of her duties in the family — are drugged and/or locked up. Many, many women have been locked up for saying out-loud that they loved a woman, or for acting on that love. 'Lesbian tendencies' has been used as a diagnosis for many women trying to assert themselves or expressing anger towards men and society.

The sixties and seventies saw the proliferation of therapy 'alternatives': gestalt, primal therapy, rebirthing, encounter weekends, communication skill training and assertiveness training, to name a few. Although women did not as a rule get locked up and drugged at encounter weekends and the sex-role stereo-typing eased up a little, the 'personal growth' movement as a whole did women little service. These therapy models reinforced the concept that each and every person, regardless of sex, age, race, class or anything else could and should transform themselves into the whole, centred, balanced, dynamic creative human beings they potentially were. As well as ignoring the difficulties of exploring one's human potential with six kids and a battering husband, these therapies promoted the ideas that personal unhappiness can be cured by the right therapy, individual solutions are possible, there's nothing wrong with the world, it's just you . . .

Women just needed to learn how to be more assertive, quit being so dependent, maybe have a few affairs. Lesbianism was ok — a purely personal preference, although a truly balanced whole human being would be open to whatever or whoever came along. Coming to terms with the masculine and the feminine inside each of us. . .

A more realistic and coincidentally less popularized synthesis between politics and psychiatry began to be articulated in the late sixties and early seventies under the name of radical therapy. It advocated that personal emotional pain was a rational response to an inhumane society and that it was impossible to cure people's problems without also curing the society that produced them.

Feminist therapy grew out of critiques of traditional therapy, specifically its goal of making women 'adjust' to limited and destructive roles. Feminist therapy rejected the idea that women were automatically fulfilled through being wives and mothers, and provided a supportive environment for women to strengthen their self-image and to make choices about their lives.

However, just because therapy is called 'radical' or 'feminist' doesn't necessarily mean its practitioners are avoiding the individual solution trap. It is a fine line between finding ways of easing our individual pain and learning to endure and fight back, and getting sucked into the 'my problems, my life, my pain, my solution' syndrome. Although most radical and feminist therapists are supportive of lesbianism as an individual life-choice, few have a political analysis of lesbianism which allows them to place a woman's life choices into an overall political context.

Therapy has been and is being put to some very horrible uses. It is a prime mechanism for social control through controlling individual emotions and behaviour. It has been extremely destructive to women and has persecuted and destroyed countless lesbians. Even the most enlightened therapies are unable to avoid a hierarchical model of expert/client, and all too often a fascination with internal motivations obscures the necessity for outward directed work.

It would be easy to reject therapy out-of-hand, considering everything. And yet, faced with the realities of the pain we experience as women and as lesbians, we cannot deny the power of being in touch with emotions, of being able to speak clearly of what we feel, think and want, of personal change. We cannot afford to throw away anything which teaches us ways of hating ourselves a little bit less. What choice do we have but to use what works for us out of various therapy techniques, knowing clearly that still today, women are being strapped down on tables while electricity is pumped through their brains.

We must use and create ways of changing ourselves and our ways of acting. We must find and use ways of staying sane and healthy, *and* keep on fighting. And we cannot stop until every mental hospital is torn down, until valium and shock treatment are obscene words, until no woman is battered, until helping doesn't mean controlling, until all of us are truly sane and human and free.

Somewhere to Start

☐ Unless you have good reason to believe a psychiatrist or therapist is non-homophobic and pro-women, *stay away*. Psychiatrists can be especially dangerous. They can and all too often do prescribe mood-altering drugs, and they have the authority to commit people to institutions.

☐ Don't assume you need a shrink just because you're feeling crazy and depressed. You might very well need any or all of friends, a well-paying and interesting job, childcare, to get away from a destructive relationship. . .Before deciding *you're* crazy, look at the material conditions of your life as the source of and reason for your feelings. Many women have found feminism more useful than therapy.

☐ Self-help support groups and peer counselling are both useful approaches to understanding and changing emotional patterns that are painful to us. These practices are under our control, relatively safe and free (see *Fighting Internalized Oppression* for full descriptions).

☐ If you've decided to see a therapist, it's a good idea to first familiarize yourself with feminist and progressive critiques of the subject. Guidelines for choosing the right therapist can be found in some books (see *Resources* in this section and *Fighting Internalized Oppression*).

☐ Choose a therapist who has been recommended by other lesbians or feminists. Some women's health collectives or lesbian groups have compiled lists of progressive professionals, based on interviews and women's personal experiences. Drop-ins, phone lines, gay community centres etc. often can make referrals and/or offer facilitated groups. In large cities, some counsellors and therapists are openly lesbian or gay and may advertise in gay and feminist newspapers.

☐ Lesbian activist groups can attempt to raise the consciousness of mental health professionals by: supplying them with lesbian-positive materials, giving workshops, conducting surveys and interviews and by various actions at professional gatherings or conferences, such as speeches, confrontations, pickets, etc.

☐ Professional associations of therapists, such as the Canadian Psychologists Association, sometimes have gay caucuses or committees, or some mechanism for bringing together gays and lesbians within the organization for mutual support and for developing pro-gay policy and practices.

☐ There is a strong grass-roots anti-psychiatry movement in North America fighting for the rights of present and former psychiatric patients, an end to forced drugging and electro-shock — an end, in fact, to the whole 'mental illness system' as it exists. Since all of us are affected by the ideology of the psychiatric establishment, and many of us quite directly — as 'clients', patients, activists, workers — educating ourselves about the anti-psychiatry movement is a good idea (see *Resources*).

Mary Barnes wrote of her experience with 'schizophrenia' in Mary Barnes: Two Accounts of a Journey through Madness. *Woodcut by K. Portland Frank from her* Anti-Psychiatry Bibliography.

*T*he aim of the Women's Self-help Counselling Collective is to provide an alternative to traditional therapy. Traditional therapy tends to view emotional difficulties in a personal context, to persuade women to adjust rather than to change the conditions of their oppression and to lay the blame for emotional problems on the individual. In contrast, the Women's Self-Help Counselling Collective views people's problems in a societal context. We are feminist in perspective. We take into consideration that we live in a dehumanizing society where racism, sexism, poverty and discrimination against gay people are constant realities in our daily lives.

We seek to change the power relationships that are reinforced in traditional therapy. We want to provide an alternative to individual therapy (which is often expensive, isolating and usually unavailable) from a feminist perspective. For those reasons, our services will be free and will be available to all women, although we are particularly commited to working with women from lower socio-economic backgrounds whose options are usually very limited. It is our goal to create a centre that will encourage equality and mutual support where women can grow and make changes both within themselves and society.

— *The Vancouver Women's Self-Help Counselling Collective*

Resources

Print

The Anti-Psychiatry Bibliography and Resource Guide, K. Portland Frank (Vancouver: Press Gang, 1979) "With over 1000 annotations of books, periodicals and audio-visual materials...numerous essays and a resource directory for North America and Europe." An entire section on Psychiatry and Women, with sub-sections on Lesbians, Self-Help, and Self-Defence. Comprehensive, feminist, fascinating, beautiful.

Our Bodies, Our Selves, The Boston Women's Health Book Collective (New York: Simon and Shuster, 1971) Includes a Boston Gay collective's advice to lesbians on psychiatric treatment.

Women and Madness, Phyllis Chesler (New York: Avon Books, 1972) A classic, "exposes the violence that psychiatry perpetuates against all women." (K. Portland Frank)

Women Look At Psychiatry, ed. by Dorothy Smith and Sara David (Vancouver: Press Gang, 1975) An anthology written by women involved with psychiatry as patients, professionals or both. Feminist, but lacks specific material for lesbians.

Love, Therapy and Politics: Issues in Radical Therapy — The First Year, ed. by Hogie Wyckoff (New York: Grove Press, 1976) Reprints of the newspaper's articles, with material relevant to women.

Phoenix Rising, Box 7251 Station A, Toronto Ont. M5W 1X9 A progressive publication on the anti-psychiatry movement, published by an ex-mental patients' collective, On Our Own. Lists current resources.

Madness Network News, Rm. 405, 2054 University Ave., Berkeley CA 94704 A longstanding anti-psychiatry newspaper. Good source of current groups and other resources.

Groups

Women's Counselling, Referral and Education Centre (WREC), 348 College St., Toronto Ont. M5T 1S4 A feminist collective that does non-sexist mental health referrals, among other things. They maintain a directory of lesbian and pro-lesbian therapists, and are generally supportive of lesbian issues.

Gay Counselling Centre, 3008 Dewdney Ave., Regina Sask. (306-522-4522) A self-help group that offers counselling to lesbians and gay men by gay counsellors.

Lesbian/Gay Community Service Group, P.O. Box 7002, Windsor Ont. N9C 3Y6 They do referrals and facilitate peer support groups for gay people.

The Anti-Psychiatry Bibliography and Resource Guide, Phoenix Rising and *Madness Network News* are all good sources of mental patients/anti-psychiatry groups, some of which are specifically for women. See above.

Many lesbian or gay groups in Canada and the U.S. make referrals to non-homophobic therapists. See:

☐ *Finding Lesbian Resources*

See also *Resources* listings under:

☐ *Fighting Internalized Oppression*
☐ *The Medical System*

Did 'relations' refer to heterosexual sexual intercourse or did they mean no fooling around, no good old lesbian sex, no nothing? It was my job to find out.

The Medical System

"My doctor wanted to give me hormone shots to cure my lesbianism."

"After I knew for sure that I was a lesbian, I went to a doctor to get my IUD taken out. The doctor told me I was just going through a phase and refused to take it out."

"When I told the doctor I was gay — because he was asking me about birth control — he got really upset and said he was sending me to a psychiatrist."

"My doctor said that I couldn't have Pelvic Inflammatory Disease because I didn't sleep with men."

All women have been and continue to be victimized by the medical profession. Lesbians often receive additional harassment and a lowered standard of care if we come out to our doctors. Lesbians working in the health profession are obliged to be extremely closeted.

For centuries health information was passed from woman to woman, one generation to another. As the medical profession gradually took over the area of health, this information became more and more their property. Women have a right to accurate, readable information on health, but today it is hard to find. If we are to reclaim control of our own health care we need to begin collecting good information and sharing it with each other.

At the Health Collective we know why it has been so hard to find good information on health, why our doctors didn't tell us, or why we didn't learn useful health information in school. It's in the interest of the 'health' industry to keep us ignorant. It's more profitable to treat sickness through expensive drugs and surgery than it is to teach and help people to stay healthy . . . There's little profit in health.
— *Vancouver Women's Health Collective*

At the age of 21, I was living in France with a woman who was my lover. I got sick: a constant lower back ache, discharge, occasional sharp pains. A name was plucked from the phone book, and off I went to a female gynecologist.

She treated me with absolute contempt. Convinced that I was simply pregnant, this was the only question she asked — and she asked it half a dozen times. I told her the first three times that pregnancy was an impossibility, and the last three that I hadn't had 'relations'. I wasn't about to tell her I was a lesbian; my language problems were considerable, it didn't seem relevant to my condition and I didn't go around telling utter strangers, especially hostile professionals in white coats, about this aspect of my personal make-up.

A few days later I was in hospital having an ovarian cyst "the size of an orange" removed. I stayed for almost three weeks, recovering from the operation and an ensuing infection.

The woman with whom I shared a room had had a D & C, and her doctor told her to refrain from 'relations' for two months. My lover became concerned that I would be given similar instructions. Did relations refer to heterosexual sexual intercourse, or did they mean no fooling around, no good old lesbian sex, no nothing? It was my job to find out.

The day before being discharged I was taken to the examination room where my final internal was attended by the entire ward staff and a crop of medical students. My case was discussed and then the doctor gave me final instructions: no this, no that, and no relations for two months. I had decided that the best way to get the desired information was to ask if it was ok to masturbate (you know, that's all lesbians really do, masturbate together) so I popped the big question, "Même avec moi-même?" (even with myself?).

One of the nurses let loose with a shriek of laughter. I turned to her and, with the kind of fierceness born of extreme indignation and embarrassment, said, "It's a *real* question!"

To my amazement, my doctor nodded his head wisely and said to her, "Yes, it's a real question." To me he said, "No, not even with yourself."

A month later I returned to his office for my final check-up. After the examination he asked what kind of birth control I used.

"None," I replied.

"Well then, you must go on the pill." He wrote out a prescription.

I was at a bit of a loss: were the pills for birth control purposes only, or were they part of an hormonal treatment relating to the operation?

"What for?" I asked.

"For birth control," he said.

"I don't want them."

"Yes, you *must*."

"No."

"Yes."

"I'm a homosexual," I said.

He said something that roughly translates as righty-ho and tore up the prescription, and that was that. I left his office, hoping I'd made the old pill-pusher's day.

— Nancy

Somewhere to Start

□ As health care consumers, we can all learn to be more knowledgeable and assertive, to find out more about our bodies and how to care for ourselves and each other. It would be useful to read about women's health, patients' rights and some critical analyses of the existing health care system.

Make use of feminist health resources such as women's health collectives and clinics (see *Resources*). They are much more likely to incorporate a pro-lesbian perspective, or at least be open to change. The same is true of community-based clinics.

□ Find out if a list of non-homophobic and women-positive professionals exists in your area; women's health groups would be a likely source. A listing could be compiled by maintaining a reference file where women can record their personal experiences with professionals — both good and bad. A survey or interviews with health care workers in your area would also be useful and may prove educational for the professionals.

□ The medical professions are woefully ignorant of lesbian health issues. Not much research is done and many false assumptions are made. It is absolutely necessary to challenge the

Graphic/ Lynn Roberson

assumption that all women are relating to men sexually. We must insist that doctors and health research take into account our reality as lesbians.

You don't have to be a lesbian or out as a lesbian to do this. Whatever your connection to the health care system — consumer, worker, activist — keep reminding people that a substantial percentage of the adult female population is lesbian and another substantial percentage is celibate. Medical research and practice which ignore that reality are inaccurate and biased.

☐ If you decide to be out to your doctor, you could be an important educational resource for her/him. Be prepared to supply written materials and suggestions for non-heterosexist care.

☐ Try not to encourage or support self-destructive behaviour in yourself or your friends (see *Fighting Internalized Oppression*).

☐ Medical people are quite often seen as sources of information by lesbians who are coming-out, or by their families. For this reason alone, it is important for lesbian activists to work to educate the medical professions. Attempting to get positive curriculum materials into medical and nursing schools, making written materials available to clinics and doing workshops for health care professionals are all strategies.

Lesbian and gay health care workers are often isolated and closeted. Some work has been done within nurses' unions around anti-discrimination policies, and informal support groups do exist. As pro-lesbian educational work is directed towards the health care field, workers will be better able to organize.

If you are a health care provider, become knowledgeable about lesbian and gay health care issues. Read the available literature, and ask lesbian and gay groups what services would best meet our needs. Talk to your colleagues about their attitudes.

Photo/ Gayla Reid

*W*e lesbians are growing stronger day-by-day. We are learning to build communities of friends for emotional support, to make ourselves visible whenever possible and to demand equal rights in housing, jobs and child custody. We are developing an ever-greater sense of self-respect and insisting that others learn to respect us as fully as we do ourselves. All this is most necessary, yet never easy, in a society which oppresses us, calls us sick and unstable, subjects us to verbal and physical violence and generally lies about who we are. The psychological, emotional and spiritual abuse sinks in and the economic and political conditions that we live under are not supportive of healthy lives and relationships. We are affected; thus it is important that we put conscious energy into taking care of ourselves. Our health is vital to our existence.

— Lesbian Health Matters!

Resources

Print

Lesbian Health Matters!, Mary O'Donnell et al (Santa Cruz Women's Health Collective)   Covers gynecological health, alternative fertilization, menopause, alcoholism, therapy — with a clear feminist perspective, factual information, resources and what you can do. Highly recommended. Available from 250 Locust St., Santa Cruz CA 95060

Lesbian Health Care: Issues and Literature, Mary O'Donnell   An essay and bibliography. Available from the Vancouver Women's Health Collective for cost. See address in *Groups.*

Our Bodies, Our Selves, The Boston Women's Health Book Collective (New York: Simon and Shuster, 1971) Excellent all-purpose resource. Has a chapter entitled "In Amerika They Call Us Dykes."

A New View of a Women's Body: A Fully Illustrated Guide, The Federation of Feminist Women's Health Centers (New York: Simon and Shuster, 1981)   Has information relevant to lesbians.

Changing Bodies, Changing Lives: A Book for Teens on Sex and Relationships, Ruth Bell et al (New York: Random House, 1980)   Non-sexist in approach, with information on lesbianism and homosexuality.

Growing Older, Getting Better: A Handbook for Women in the Second Half of Life, Jane Porcino (Reading: Addison-Wesley, 1983)   Makes some references to lesbianism.

How To Stay Out of the Gynecologist's Office, The Federation of Feminist Women's Health Centers (Culver City: Peace Press, 1981)   Takes a preventative approach to health, suggests alternative treatments and self-defence against professionals.

Healthsharing: A Canadian Women's Health Quarterly, Box 230, Station M, Toronto Ont. M6S 4T3   A periodical with a feminist approach to women's health issues.

Vaginal Politics, Ellen Frankfort (New York: Bantam Books, 1973)   One of the first books to question the status of the medical establishment, the arrogance of doctors and the unquestioning role of women.

Complaints and Disorders: The Sexual Politics of Sickness, Barbara Ehrenreich and Deirdre English (Old Westbury: The Feminist Press, 1973)   Illustrated feminist history of the development of the current medical ideology and system.

For Her Own Good: 150 Years of the Expert's Advice to Women, Barbara Ehrenreich and Deirdre English (New York: Doubleday, 1978)

Seizing Our Bodies, Claudia Dreifus (New York: Random House, 1978)

Groups

These Canadian and Québecoise women's health organizations may or may not offer a progressive service to lesbians, but they are probably your best bet for information, treatment or referrals.

Vancouver Women's Health Collective, 1501 W. Broadway, Vancouver B.C. V6J 1W6 (736-6696)

Women's Health-Action Network, #10805 - 125 St., Edmonton Alta. T5M 0H4 (455-4664)

Health Sharing Inc., Box 734, Regina Sask. S4P 3B1

Saskatoon Women's Health Collective, #124 - 109 St. Saskatoon Sask. S7N 1R2 (477-1193)

Women's Health Clinic Inc., #304 - 414 Graham, Winnipeg Man. (947-1517)

Women's Clinic, 399 Bathurst St., Toronto Ont. M5T 2J8 (369-5934)

Ottawa and Region Women's Health Collective, 539 Gilmour St., Ottawa Ont. K1R 5L5 (995-4927)

Centre de Santé des Femmes du Quartier, 16, bou. St.-Joseph est, Montréal P.Q. H2T 1G8 (842-8903)

Centre de Santé pour les Femmes, 155, bou. Charest est, 2e étage, Québec, P.Q. G1K 3G6 (647-5745)

Women's Health Education Network, P.O. Box 1276, Truro N.S. B2N 5L2 (895-2140)

Women's Health Education Project, P.O. Box 4192, St. John's Nfld. A1C 5Z7

Gay Health Clinic, c/o Montréal Youth Clinic, 3465 Peel St., Montréal H3A 1X1 (514-842-8576)   Call for time and information.

Gay Physicians of Montreal/Les medécins gai(e)s de Montréal, a/s #20, 2151 rue Lincoln, Montréal P.Q. H2H 1J2

Gays in Health Care, Box 7086, Stn. A, Toronto Ont. M5W 1X7 (920-1882)   For lesbians and gay men working or training in the health field.

How to Stay Out of the Gynecologist's Office (see above)   Includes a comprehensive list of U.S. Women's Health Care Centres. Available in bookstores or from Peace Press, 3828 Willat Ave., Culver City CA 90230

The National Gay Health Directory is published annually and lists groups, facilities and individuals who provide a range of health services. Some are gay or lesbian-identified, others are not but do provide services to lesbians. The *Directory* also lists gay caucuses of professional health and social workers' organizations: nurses, doctors, dentists, Black health care workers, psychologists, social workers, etc. Available from The National Gay Health Education Foundation Inc., P.O. Box 834, Linden Hill NY 11354

Other lesbian and gay groups will make referrals to non-homophobic health facilities and professionals. To find these groups in Canada and the U.S., see:

☐ *Finding Lesbian Resources*

See also Resources:

☐ *Fighting Internalized Oppression*

Of course established religion is another way the patriarchy oppresses women; but it is necessary to have a vision of how the world could be in order to continue to struggle against the ugliness that exists now.

Religion

I was 12 at the time, being taught by nuns in a Catholic school. I sang in the church choir and played the organ for mass. I went to confession once a week, and considered myself holy. I listened well when the priest came to our school to preach during religion classes. He would go on and on about the sin of abusing our bodies — what *was* he talking about? He stressed that hand-holding and kissing boys were to be avoided because those acts would certainly lead to greater evils. God would punish us if we were to indulge the pleasures of the flesh permitted only to a man and his wife (what *ever* was he talking about???). Keep going to confession; keep pure; you will be saved.

So I didn't touch boys. But . . . there was my best friend Suzanne. She was my age, loud, boisterous and *fun*. We spent every day after school playing together, examining our changing bodies, giggling over boys. One day we decided to 'practice' kissing and pretend we were each other's favourite boy. After all, the priest hadn't said anything about kissing girls. Soon we went from passionate kissing to exploring each other's bodies in very sexual ways. This was acceptable because we weren't abusing our *own* bodies . . .

I loved her deeply, but I couldn't avoid the uncomfortable contradictions forever. I was a responsible 12 year old and knew that it was the sexual feelings and actions that were sinful, regardless of who you did it with. I also sensed that since nobody ever talked about two girls kissing and touching and feeling like that, it must be *incredibly* evil and sinful. Surely I would be doomed to hell forever if a priest ever found out. I was not telling *all* the truth at confession. How could I continue to receive communion without a clean soul? It was a bind. So Suzanne and I stopped seeing each other with very little said about why. We didn't speak again for years.

I quickly placed my sexual feelings in their proper context and began kissing boys. Every time I did, I would go to confession and confess to twice as many times, hoping that eventually I would do enough penance to make up for my unspeakable sins with Suzanne.

— *Yvette*

Religions are systems of belief which control people through the use of ritual, authority, dogma and fear. Since the power of patriarchal religion is dependent on the powerlessness of its members, structures and mechanisms have been developed which ensure dependence, docility and self-denial. Women in particular are denied the autonomy to control our own bodies, minds and spirits. We are denied our right to love ourselves and each other. The sanctioning of marriage by religions is one example of a mechanism which ensures that women are owned by individual men and, through them, male deities.

I speak from my experiences as an Irish Canadian Catholic and I know that the oppressive experience of any women in any male religious framework differs only in degree from my own. For too many women, this experience has been crippling. All power and authority is vested in 'the other' rather than in 'self'. Women participate in organized religion out of a hopeless but very real longing for connection and community. It is a common experience for a woman to find religious activities her major source of social communion and of time free from family responsibilities.

As lesbians, patriarchal religion offers us nothing. If we are acknowledged at all, we are viewed as disgusting and shameful. This negation provides lesbians with very little reason to remain within these institutions. However, we still need sources of identity, community and belief. In freeing ourselves from false sources, we must at the same time create new ways to meet our needs. We need to build our identity of self — strong, powerful and whole — and with that strength build our communities.

— Paula

*C*an a woman be a feminist, a lesbian and still be a Christian? To answer this question, it is necessary to look at the biblical roots of homophobia. Whether or not we personally are practicing Christians, the bible forms the basis for much of the thinking of our time. And, in the light of contemporary scholarship, it is relevant to re-examine the biblical passages used to justify homophobia.

The Sodom and Gomorrah story in *Genesis 19* is usually cited as an instance of condemnation of homosexual acts. Scholars have shown that the 'sin' referred to here is not the sin of homosexuality, but of inhospitality. It is ironic that no group has been treated less hospitably by the church than lesbians and gay men.

Another area of the bible dealing with homosexuality is the holiness code in *Leviticus 18:22* and *20:13*. The commandments against homosexual acts are put in the same category as not eating meat with blood on it, not wearing garments made of two kinds of yarn, not eating meat and milk products together. If we want to avoid double-think, we should be as aghast at people who are wearing polyester fabrics, or people who eat a Big Mac and a glass of milk, as we would be at people who engage in homosexual acts. Either we take all the items in the holiness code literally, or not.

It should be noted that the question of someone having a permanent homosexual orientation was not even understood in biblical times. As a life choice, and consistent sexual preference, homosexuality is nowhere addressed in the bible. What is referred to are homosexual acts performed by those who are presumed to have a heterosexual orientation. *Romans 1:26* and *Corinthians 6:9-16* should be looked at in this light. Paul speaks of homosexual acts as sins against nature. That this was not addressed to those for whom homosexuality was a natural orientation, but to those whose orientation was considered *naturally* heterosexual is most important. The understanding of homosexuality as a natural orientation for some people is a relatively new phenomena. With this in mind, the passages in Paul are not at all as simple as they appear. For those whose sexual orientation is naturally homosexual, engaging in heterosexual acts may well be a 'crime against nature'.

We should not confuse the patriarchal thinking of the church with the thinking of its founder. And we must remember that the silence of Jesus on homosexuality has been overlooked. As feminists, however, we must confront the patriarchy of the church which has oppressed both heterosexual and gay women. As a lesbian anglican priest has said:

> The church does not listen to women yet, so it is my gay brothers who must speak loudest for our acceptance as gays. I have one fear, though, and it is that when gay men are accepted (because though they are homosexual, their sexuality affirms the virtues of maleness) and when heterosexual women are accepted (after all, they do relate to men closely), lesbians will still be out in the cold because our sexuality is a total and radical affirmation of woman-nature which the church has never allowed.
> — Rev. Ellen Barret
> *The Gay Academic*

I do see a danger, however: that lesbians will not only avoid all contact with the organized church or established religion because of its patriarchal structure, but that we will kill our spiritual dimension. We might come out of the closet in one way, namely as loving women sexually, and go back into the closet in another, namely spiritually.

It is important to distinguish between the outward manifestation of a religion and its spiritual dimension. The term spiritual can be understood as having two references: the deepest, esoteric dimension of a religion, and the deepest exploration into one's selfhood and solitude. As lesbians, we must not avoid taking what has been called the "longest journey, the journey inwards." As May Sarton stated in *Journal of a Solitude,* "That is what is strange — that friends, even passionate lovers, are not my real life unless there is time alone in which to explore."

— Anne

Religions are ideologies — sets of ideas and concepts that shape our sense of self, our sense of the world, our sense of the purpose of our lives. Even if we are not now religious or were not brought up religious, those concepts are widespread in our culture and affect not only our individual outlooks but the shape of society.

In North America, Christianity in varying forms is the predominant religion. Besides providing a major justification for the so-called inferiority and subjection of women — a function shared by other religions — Christian ideology has historically been used to promote and justify anti-semitism, racism and colonialism. Unfortunately, those days are far from over. Although some Christian churches are adopting increasingly liberal positions towards women and are no longer condemning homosexuality per se as a sin, the fundamentalist Christian upsurge in North America views both women's autonomy and gay people with moral horror of the first order. They also consider Jews, trade unionists and progressive and left-wing people in general as repugnant and damned. The links between fundamentalist Christian organizations and right-wing political movements are clear and extensively documented, especially around the battle for women's freedom of choice on abortion and reproductive rights.

Those of us who grew up even nominally Christian need to examine and eradicate the legacies of fear and bigotry we carry. Anti-semitism in particular is alive and all-too-well within many of us. Those of us who grew up outside the majority culture need to talk together about our experiences and perspectives, and demand that our realities be visible and respected within our lesbian communities and movement.

Strategies for social change *have* to take into account the impact of organized religions. We must be prepared to engage in public battles with the fundamentalists who actively promote hatred of us. In any public campaign for lesbian and gay rights, it is extreme right-wing Christian leaders who are the most vociferous opponents of our very existence. It would serve us well to become familiar with their arguments and be prepared, individually and collectively, to refute them. (See *Know Your Enemies* in *Building a Lesbian Movement.*)

---

*O*ne legacy of the patriarchy is a fragmentation of our world view and experiences. In our lives we are constantly split: mind-body, emotion-intellect, personal-political. The one split that has caused the most problems for feminists is the split between politics and spirituality. It is easy for women dealing with the day-to-day realities of violence against women to dismiss spirituality as self-indulgent and airy-fairy and smacking of too much religion. Of course established religion is another way the patriarchy oppresses women; but it is necessary to have a vision of how the world *could* be in order to continue to struggle against the ugliness that exists now.

Spirituality is essentially a vision and an experience of wholeness, of connectedness with each other and all living things. Spirituality offers us tools to heal our splits. We are all healers and must learn the techniques which will help us heal ourselves and each other.

All of us who have loved women, and marched and worked and sung and danced together, have been in spiritual contact with each other whether or not we choose to call it that. But we need more than these occasional bits. We need regular disciplines and techniques — be they meditation, yoga, chanting, visualizations, Tai-chi — to keep us sane and healthy, to prevent burnout and the tendency to addictions. When we are aware and in tune with the senses and abilities we are unaccustomed to using, we can start to employ them as tools for building our communities.

I explored several spiritual disciplines and read and listened to spiritual teachers before coming to feminism. Feminism gave me a cohesive analysis of why the world is such a mess, an analysis that made more sense to me than anything I had heard from the spiritual or political voices of the sixties. Somewhere along the way though, the practice I had learned got lost in the round of meetings and consciousness-raising groups and rallies. But I never lost my vision of the integrity of the world and the potential for beauty and harmony that exists if only we could understand that we are a part of the world around us, not apart from it. In recent years I have felt the power of loving women and working to make the world a better place to live. I have felt the lessening of isolation and the sense

Photo/ Nancy Pollak

of being together for some larger purpose. This has been a kind of spiritual re-awakening.

I know that there is more to political action than marching, organizing, changing legislation, changing attitudes. Reclaiming power is where the spiritual and the political merge. True power is not power 'over' others, but power 'within' and power through others. We can learn this power by learning who we are and what we can do as fully as possible. We may seem isolated by the boundaries of our flesh; through the spirit we can experience our connections and be one.

— Annette

Somewhere to Start

☐ Religious thought and attitudes have affected everyone in this society, even those of us who were not raised in religious homes. Amongst your friends and in the political groups you belong to, explore how religion has shaped our concepts, identities and value systems.

☐ Many people justify their homophobia (and misogyny) on religious grounds. If you're a lesbian with friends and/or family doing this, give them gay-positive books on the subject, and try to refer them to non-homophobic clergy, rabbis, etc.

If you're from a religious background that's haunting *you* with homophobia, you'll want to consult those same resources.

☐ Lesbian groups could interview and compile a list of supportive ministers, rabbis, priests, etc. and make that list available to phone lines and drop-ins. Some denominations and congregations have quite progressive traditions on a variety of social and political issues, and are well worth liaising with. Lesbian groups could do outreach to religious groups by offering to send speakers, doing workshops or putting them on your mailing list. In turn, religious premises can be used for meetings or drop-ins, and sometimes congregations will respond to fund-raising requests.

☐ Lesbians belonging to congregations can work to create progressive attitudes towards homosexuality. Organizing here follows the same pattern as organizing anywhere else. Individual gay people need to connect with each other, form some sort of formal or informal support network, and then begin to do educational and consciousness-raising work with the rest of the congregation.

*How I integrate my Jewishness, my lesbianism and my femi-*nism has changed and keeps on changing. In the past four years since I've been out as a lesbian, I've done different things.

When I was living in Berkeley, I was part of a group of Jewish lesbians who met at the New Moon, the beginning of the Jewish month, to do ritual, to eat and sing and discuss. Rosh Chodesh, as it's called in Hebrew, is traditionally a holiday especially significant for Jewish women.

We celebrated together and we studied. Some of the women were doing research into the matriarchal and pagan origins of Judaism. Look at Hanukah and the holidays of other religions, which are all celebrated using candles or lights around the time of solstice. All Jewish holidays have seasonal as well as historical significance.

After Berkeley I lived on women's land in Oregon. There were about five Jewish women who got together and celebrated holidays, sometimes with the non-Jewish women on the land. That spurred incidents of anti-semitism. We were seen as being exclusive. Some women were angry that we were celebrating what they saw as a patriarchal religion. It was an ugly scene. The land broke up — not just because of that. But it was one of the many walls that divided us.

I have become more private over the years because of experiences like that. It's not safe to openly celebrate being Jewish. I'm choosing to celebrate something that's important in my life, that has shaped a lot of who I am. I don't want to have to explain that to anyone. There is a joy and satisfaction for me in these celebrations. I don't think any organized religion is the perfect thing, especially for women. I look to creating our own rituals and spiritual life: if I had my own way we'd all be celebrating our sameness *and* our differences.

Shortly after coming to Vancouver, I saw in *Kinesis,* the women's newspaper, that some Jewish feminists wanted to meet together. That was over a year ago, and nine out of the ten of us are still meeting. We get together once a month and talk about different issues. We celebrate the holidays together along with our closest friends. It's a safe place to be Jewish.

— Baylah

Resources

Print

Nice Jewish Girls: A Lesbian Anthology, ed. by Evelyn Torton Beck (Watertown: Persephone Press, 1982) Wide-ranging and passionate exploration of being Jewish and lesbian. Examines anti-semitism in the lesbian-feminist community. Essential reading.

Gay Liberation and the Church, Sally Miller Gearheart and William Johnson (San Francisco: Glide Publications, 1981) Explores the issue of gay men and lesbians in the Christian church. Includes an article by Gearheart entitled "The Miracle of Lesbianism".

Is the Homosexual My Neighbour? Letha Scanzoni and Virginia Ramey Mollenkott (New York: Harper and Row, 1980) A very readable book by two journalists that "...offers guidelines and invites Christians to develop a response to homosexuality that expresses Christ's principles...not the prejudices of the world." A good book for heterosexual people.

Christianity, Social Tolerance and Homosexuality, John Boswell (Chicago: University of Chicago Press, 1980) An in-depth, and up-to-date presentation of the issues concerned.

Homosexuality and the Western Christian Tradition, D.S. Bailey (Garden City: Anchor Books, 1975) A pioneer work, one of the first to attack the homophobia in the popular understanding of the Bible. Much of what has been written on the subject since either abbreviates or expands on Bailey's arguments.

The Church and the Homosexual, John McNeill (New York: Pocket Books, 1976) A comprehensive and compassionate analysis of the issues, including such topics as the relation of scripture, moral theology and human sciences to homosexuality, and pastoral ministry to the homosexual community. More readable than Bailey.

But Lord, They're Gay: A Christian Pilgrimage, Rev. Sylvia Pennington (Lambda Christian Fellowship, 1982) Account by a heterosexual woman of her ministry amongst gay people. Available from: P.O. Box 1967, Hawthorne CA

A Gay Bibliography, Gay Task Force of the American Library Association This bibliography has a lengthy list of publications relating to gays and religion. Available from Gay Task Force, P.O. Box 2383, Philadelphia PA 19103

The Church and The Second Sex, Mary Daly (New York: Harper and Row, 1968) Evaluation of the position of women in the Christian church. Feminist.

Beyond God the Father: Towards a Philosophy of Women's Liberation, Mary Daly (Boston: Beacon Press, 1973) A further critique of Christian theology and an examination of the transforming power of women.

Gyn/Ecology: The Metaethics of Radical Feminism, Mary Daly (Boston: Beacon Press, 1978) The formulation of a new way of looking at the world with women at the centre.

Womanspirit Rising: A Feminist Reading in Religion, ed. by Carol P. Christ and Judith Plaskow (New York: Harper and Row, 1979) Contemporary feminist thinking on religion: Jewish, Christian and non-traditional.

Dreaming the Dark, Starhawk (Boston: Beacon Press, 1981) Synthesizing feminism, principles of non-violence and paganism, this book bridges the gap between politics and spirituality. Fascinating and recommended.

The Politics of Women's Spirituality: Essays on the Rise of Spiritual Power within the Feminist Movement, ed. by Charlene Spretnak (Garden City: Anchor Books, 1982) Includes a fairly comprehensive bibliography on feminist spirituality, including works of fiction, history and analysis.

"Lesbian Spirituality", by Denise Nadeau, from *Resources for Feminist Research,* Vol. 12, #1 (1983) Analyzes the origins and significance of lesbian spirituality, focussing on the Vancouver Island experience.

Moon, Moon, Anne Kent Rush (New York: Random House/Moon Books, 1976) A book of women's spirituality.

Many of the above resources thanks to Anne.

Groups

The following are bi-national associations and should be contacted for information about groups throughout Canada and Québec:

Affirm: Gays and Lesbians in the United Church of Canada, P.O. Box 46586, Stn. G, Vancouver B.C. V6R 4G8

Dignity/Canada/Dignite (Gay Catholics), P.O. Box 1912, Winnipeg Man. R3C 3R2 (204-772-4322)

Integrity (Gay Anglicans and Their Friends), c/o #12G, 9820 - 104 St., Edmonton Alta. T5K 0Z1 (403-421-7629) The Toronto group produces a newsletter available from Box 873, Stn. F, Toronto Ont. M4Y 2N9

Over 40 (mainly Christian) lesbian/gay religious groups in Canada and Québec are listed in the *Body Politic,* Box 7289, Stn. A, Toronto Ont. M5W 1X9

To find U.S. religious groups, consult *Our Right To Love: A Lesbian Resource Book,* ed. by Ginny Vida (Englewood Cliffs: Prentice Hall, 1978)

No serious political movement ever relied on the commun-ication systems of its oppressor. Without our own media, we are without a voice.

The Media

In working with the traditional media, my main experience has been with television, radio and newspaper/ magazine reporting and production. I have found that if you are a woman who basically accepts a sexist society's definition of females, you will pose no great threat to the media. You will, however, be treated, however unconsciously by those who work within and control the media, as an appenditure of a man, or you will be easily objectified into one of the two most dominant categories of female stereotypes — that of nurturer or sex object.

If you are a woman who has rejected a patriarchal value system and who has chosen to commit her energies, time and emotions to furthering her own and other women's well-being, you will not only be treated unconsciously in the degrading manner that all women are subjected to, but you will also be seen as a threat to the system that the media props us. As such, you must be discredited.

We must continue to build an alternative lesbian feminist media. This is not to be confused with the so-called alternative media such as we see in the avant-garde art and male left newspapers and magazines. These groups are often as oppressive to women under the catch-all umbrella of 'liberalism', 'freedom of the press' and 'freedom of thought'. Lesbian feminist media must remain by definition women-controlled and women-run. We must continue to learn the ideological and technical skills that are necessary in order for us to tell and show our own life experiences within a feminist framework. The process of gaining this knowledge has been witheld from us and we must continue to fight for the right to define how we see ourselves and to have these images of women accepted as legitimate.

— Marion

The mass media in all its forms — the printed word, the press, films, t.v., photography, graphic arts, comics, radio — plays a dominant part in defining and maintaining stereotypical images of women and their place in society. As are all other ideological institutions that complete the patriarchy, the mass media is controlled and designed by men.

We are spoonfed information about the world and taught not to look analytically at the forces affecting us. Newspapers, t.v. and radio reassure us that our governments have our best interests at heart and are taking care of it all for us. There is nothing more to be understood about the situation — and nothing we can do. As individuals looking at the problems in our lives and in the lives of other lesbians, taking time to consistently and critically examine the social, political and economic conditions of this society as reflected by the media will be extremely beneficial.

There are similarities in the relationship between lesbians and the mass media and that of other oppressed minorities. There are also important differences. As lesbians, we are always an additional threat to a society based on the institutionalization of heterosexuality in all its forms. We are self-defined women taking power away from men and placing it in our own hands. By acknowledging the radical nature of the changes we are demanding we can also understand why the media has a great deal to lose in allowing us to use this effective communication tool.

When we want to use or work in the traditional media, we must be aware that it is a powerful arm of the patriarchy and plays a large part in making and maintaining the oppression of lesbians, feminists and all women. The media works in a variety of ways to trivialize us and our ideas. A naive approach most often results in misrepresentation of the group or individual concerned, as well as damage in the form of personal harassment and loss of self-esteem to the lesbian concerned.

When lesbians wish to 'co-operate' with the traditional media in order to share information with other women in interviews, reports or articles, then we must attempt to implement our own strategies and tactics in order to control the information.

Interviews

Having decided to do television, radio or newspaper interviews, there are ways to prepare that will enable you to communicate your message strongly and intact — and avoid undesirable situations altogether.

First, get to know both the person who will do the interview and the overall interviewing scenario. Ask them *why* they want to do it, *what* they know about the subject, *which* questions you'll be asked and *who* will have control over the final product. Be suspicious of people in a rush, of those who evade or dislike your questions of them, of men reporting on women's issues.

If you get through this first phase still feeling comfortable enough to go ahead, note the following points:

* Know your topic thoroughly. If you are unsure of your analysis or information, don't do the interview. Try and get your friends to practice with you, playing devil's advocate. You might want to start off doing short inter-views, building up to longer ones.

* Figure out the points you wish to make, and then relentlessly direct the conversation to them. Repeat new ideas. They may seem redundant to you, but it takes a long time for feminist and lesbian positive ideas to come across.

* If possible work in twos: someone to back you up is always a good idea. Work out your strategies and politics with your companion *before* — not during or after — the interview.

* Consider in advance who your audience will be and gear what you have to say to them.

* Know exactly what is expected of you and do not hesitate to question changes — or leave.

* Don't necessarily expect much help or support from women who hold traditional media jobs. You can be as much of a threat to them as to the men.

When doing the interview, you will want to speak slowly and deliberately, remaining calm, polite and in control. Interviewers may try to sidetrack you into talking about the opposition's view of your subject. *Your* topic is lesbian oppression (or pride!); you can rely on the rest of the world to say how they feel. Don't volunteer any personal information you are not ready to talk about. Be wary of and don't respond to paternalism: an arm around the back of your chair, or pats on the knee. If you or the interviewer make any mistakes, correct them immediately — and complain loudly if you are misrepresented or abused in any fashion.

Television interviews involve special considerations because of their visual component and the traditonal approaches to filming women:

* If you don't normally wear make-up, don't let anyone make you. It isn't necessary, even under bright lights.

* Wear comfortable clothes. Studio lights, particularly with colour t.v. and video, are *hot*.

* It is best not to wear a skirt or dress unless it's well below your knees. Risers are used to bring your eyes to the level of the camera lens which puts your knees in a vulnerable position when you're seated facing the camera. Similarly, avoid wearing thin materials or low necklines. You can be made to appear seductive by camera-man techniques.

* If it's either necessary or possible, outnumber your opponents. If you expect a problem, have vocal supporters in the audience.

In any interviewing situation, remember to take yourself and your topic *seriously*. See *Working in Progressive Movements* for practical tips on handling homophobia in interviewing/ public speaking situations.

The above material thanks to Marion Barling.

Somewhere to Start

☐ Electronic and print media bring us a particular — and limited — view of the world. Being attuned to the messages that are being served up puts us in a better position to influence the media, individually and collectively.

Watch the news, read the papers, listen to the radio — both the straight and alternate press. What is happening right now around you? What are the 'hot' issues in your town, region, province and country? Who are the people in power?

Whose perspective do you find most commonly reflected in the media?

Take it further — what is being said about *lesbians?* Women? Homosexuals? What are people like your aunt and uncle, parents or straight friends in northern Saskatchewan learning about lesbians, about women's lives?

☐ Letters to the editor are a useful tool and get noticed, especially in smaller papers. They can comment on a homophobic article in the paper or be used to promote a coming lesbian event. Often there will be responses from people who find it shocking that a community paper prints such trash. You can turn that into another good opportunity to reply by letting readers know that lesbians too make up a part of the community and have a right to a voice in the local paper. If you are not in a position to be public, ask that only your initials be used or your name withheld, and explain why you are doing this.

☐ There are effective ways to express your ideas or objections to the media. Did you know, for example, that it takes as little as a dozen protest letters to get an advertiser to withdraw their sponsorship of a radio or t.v. show? For each angry letter they receive, a sponsor calculates that there are thousands who think the same and just don't take the time to write in.

Is there a program that you find particularly offensive to women, or homophobic? Take a few minutes to write out your objections, and send it off to the sponsor (libraries can supply addresses) and to the t.v. or radio station. Encourage your friends to do the same — make an evening of it.

Canada's lesbians celebrate Saturday

Lesbians from cost to coast, from each region of Canada, in small towns, large cities, northern and southern communities, are organizing to tell you about lesbianism.

Representatives attending the recent National Lesbian Conference in Vancouver designated March 27, 1982 as a National Day of Awareness and Action on Lesbian Rights. On this day, women are coming together, endorsed by such organizations as the B.C. Federation of Women and the Canadian Association of Sexual Assault Centres, to break the silence surrounding lesbianism and to publicly speak out against the myths and stereotypes that have long kept lesbians hidden and fears.

This DOES have something to do with you.

Approximately one out of every ten adult women in Canada is a lesbian. This means that a significant proportion of women living in this community identify as lesbians. We are women of every conceivable background, occupation, political and religious belief. We are women who choose to create our intimate and loving relationships with other women. We are women you know; We are your neighbour, your sister, your bankteller, your student, your doctor...

But most of us would never tell you that we are lesbians. We live in fear of being "found out" - and for very good reason.

Lesbianism is cloaked in centuries of fear and prejudice. We have long been a silenced, invisible minority. The punishment for choosing to love another woman is high; We are verbally and physically harassed, ridiculed and beaten. We are told that we are "sick", sent to psychiatrists and incarcerated. We may lose our homes, our jobs, our children. We are alienated from our families, our friends, our co-workers, our churches and our communities. We are forced to stay "in the closet" and lead double lives, keeping our love for women a secret.

Many of us are refusing to keep quiet about lesbianism any longer. We are sick and tired of the myths, the stereotypes, the "queer" jokes, the stories that tell LIES about us.

- It is a LIE that all lesbians are truck drivers that smoke cigars and molest children. The TRUTH is that over 95% of all cases of sexual abuse of children involve heterosexual men and girls.

- It is a LIE that lesbians are poor, tortured creatures who "couldn't get a man" and turned to women as second-best. The TRUTH is that lesbians are women who prefer other women. Our relationships and our lives are rich, full, loving and productive.

- It is a LIE that lesbians are sick and perverted. The TRUTH is that there is something very wrong with a society which fosters such discrimination against us.

Lesbians are standing together to refute these lies. We are demanding an equal place in this society.

We ARE everywhere.
We need you support.
Y. JOHNSON
for Lesbian Action Committee
Box 6, RR. 1
Ruskin, B.C.

As part of a Canada-wide day of action on lesbian rights — March 27, 1982 — press releases were sent to every newspaper in B.C. Many small-town papers printed the press release in full; this version is from the Kamloops News.

On the other hand, if you see a show that is supportive of lesbians, write in and applaud them. If you are part of a group, offer to send it on the group's letterhead. You can be assured that hundreds of Moral Majority (sic) types are sending in their 'appalled and disgusted' letters.

☐ For any event that you are organizing, prepare a press release in advance. It conveys the information *you* think is important and often will be used as the basis of a story, and sometimes is reprinted in full. It's a way to minimize the effect of misquoting and sensationalism that all too often mark reporting on lesbian, feminist and gay events.

Some newspapers will accept news stories written by individuals. Don't send articles to the media unless you have reason to trust your contact person there and they can anticipate their editor's reaction.

☐ A media monitoring group can offer an effective route to improving coverage of our lives. Group members individually check out local newspaper, t.v. and radio stations and send off protest or complimentary letters on the group's letterhead as necessary. The group would also meet regularly to share successes and problems; pick goals and divide up the work.

Projects could include: compiling a directory of supportive media contacts; initiating articles or interviews in the local media; meeting with media personnel to discuss improved coverage of lesbian events; presenting workshops to other lesbian groups on using the media, etc. *Talk Back! A Gay Person's Guide to Media Action* is full of practical ideas and inspiration.

☐ The lesbian, women's and gay movements have given rise to a tremendously energetic communication and cultural environment. We now have bookstores, t.v. and radio shows, music festivals, literary and political journals, media centres, publishers, film and video producers and distributors, coffee-houses, newspapers, record companies and printshops — all controlled and staffed by collectives of lesbians and feminists. It is vital that we help to maintain this media network. Much of it is nonprofit and poor, and is largely sustained by the talents and passion of the women who run it — with our support as consumers, contributors, subscribers, participants, fund-raisers, volunteers.

If you are considering starting up a lesbian newspaper, or radio show, or launching the first lesbian communications satellite (Lavender Channel), there is information available from the voices of experience (see *Resources*).

---

*T*he seven of us in the Lesbian Show collective put on the show because of our political convictions. Lesbianism is not a private subversive activity; it is a political revolutionary identity.

We have difficulty finding a political context for our struggle. When the world is divided into them and us, who does the lesbian feminist align herself with? Are *they* men and *we* women, or are *they* straight and *we* gay? Who stands by our side? This is one of the issues that has brought us together to put on our own programme, instead of trying to share airtime with the gay *Coming-Out* show, although there are lesbians there, or with *Woman-Vision,* although we share many of the same beliefs. Both of these programmes occasionally do material which is of specific interest to lesbians, but we felt that we needed a programme that would be of interest to us all the time.

Which brings us to another reason for putting on our own show. Lesbians are misrepresented in the straight media. When we are mentioned at all — which is rarely — it is in connection with something scandalous. This is not surprising given who controls the media. No serious political movement in history ever relied on the communication of its oppressor. Without our own media, we are without a voice. By putting on the *Lesbian Show,* we are contributing towards a lesbian voice.

The *Lesbian Show* is by lesbians, about lesbians, for lesbians. We have a real need to communicate to each other in a responsible fashion. We have political differences, and the only way to educate ourselves is to air them. Within the collective, we have political differences as a result of having different personalities, different experiences. Rather than trying to merge into a single entity with one voice, we air those different viewpoints. This is part of what we collectively feel is our political responsibility. What we share is political commitment. Every week we share it with our community. The more we talk to each other, work with each other and celebrate together, the stronger we will become.

— The Lesbian Show Collective, 1979

Resources

Print

Talk Back! A Gay Person's Guide to Media Action,
The Lesbian and Gay Media Advocates (Boston:
Alyson Publications)   A very practical how-to
manual.

"Lesbians and the Media", from *Our Right To Love:
A Lesbian Resource Book,* ed. by Ginny Vida
(Englewood Cliffs: Prentice Hall, 1978)   Has an
article on "Lesbian Images in the Media", and a
useful list of U.S. print resources.

The Passionate Perils of Publishing, Celeste West,
Valerie Wheat (San Francisco: Booklegger Press,
1978)   Lots of information on alternative presses,
with a heavy emphasis on the feminist and lesbian
networks. May be dated. Available from 555 29th
St., San Francisco CA 94131

Index/Directory of Women's Media, ed. by Donna
Allen (Washington: Women's Institute for Freedom
of the Press)   Annually produced and up-dated, the
Index/Directory is a comprehensive listing of all
categories of women's media, groups and individuals.
They also publish a periodical, *Media Report to
Women.* Available from 3306 Ross Pl. N.W.,
Washington D.C. 20008

"The Lesbian Issue", *Resources for Feminist Research,*
Vol. 12, #1 (1983)   Includes a bibliography of films,
videos and slide shows, and a list of distributors.
Available from O.I.S.E. 252 Bloor St. W., Toronto
Ont. M5S 1V6

Photo/Wanda Weigers

Guide to Women's Publishing, Polly Joan, Andrea
Chesman (Paradise: Dustbooks, 1980)   Full listings
of women's periodical and book publishers,
writing resources, archives, library collections,
bookstores and distributors. Second edition.
Available from P.O. Box 100, Paradise CA 95969

*The International Directory of Little Magazines and
Small Presses,* ed. by Len Fulton, Ellen Ferber
(Paradise: Dustbooks)   Published annually, this
book gives useful information on subscribing to book
and periodical publishers. Its index lists many
"Lesbian", "Gay" and "Women" publishers. See
above for address.

"Lesbians and Film", *Jump Cut: A Review of
Contemporary Cinema* 24/25 (March 1981)   This
special section is devoted to an examination of lesbian
images in film. Contains an annotated bibliography
and filmography of lesbian works. Available from
P.O. Box 865, Berkeley CA 94701

Words and Women: New Language in New Times,
Casey Miller and Kate Swift (Garden City: Anchor
Books, 1977)   A study and analysis of sex bias in
the English language, with guidelines for non-sexist
usage.

*The Handbook of Non-Sexist Writing: For Writers,
Editors and Speakers,* Casey Miller and Kate Swift
(New York: Barnes and Noble, 1981)   Just what it
sounds like.

Groups

Media Watch, #209 636 W. Broadway, Vancouver
B.C. V5Z 1G2   A feminist organization that
monitors the media in Canada and Québec for sexist
content. They invite input from the public, so contact
them with complaints, suggestions, etc.

To find lesbian/gay radio and t.v. shows, media and
art centres, and film/video producers and distributors,
see:

☐ *Finding Lesbian Resources*

Women have been carefully taught that we are helpless on the street, that there is little we can do to defend ourselves. More and more of us are understanding that these are lies designed to keep us afraid, at home and dependent on the 'protection' of men.

Violence

One Saturday I was walking 'round Vancouver with my woman lover. We had our arms around each other and for the most part we were just getting strange looks. We passed a group of young men who started shouting "lezzie" and "dyke" at us. I was shocked at first. We kept on walking, but I found myself physically pulling away from my lover, and that's when I started getting angry. I didn't understand why I should be harassed when I was just out having a good time enjoying the company of another woman without bothering anyone.

— Kim

A friend named Laura told me this story. She is a lesbian in her early 30's and has lived in a small town in the interior of B.C. for about 10 years. The closest lesbians she knows live several hundred kilometres away. Over the past few years she has developed casual friendships with several women in her community. They sometimes have coffee together, visit and talk.

A couple of months ago, Laura was having coffee at a friend's house when in walked the woman's husband. He was outraged at finding his wife talking to a lesbian. With hardly a spoken word, he hit Laura, knocked her out and then kicked her around. When she came to, she was outside, dizzy, disoriented and in a lot of pain. She managed to get to her car and drive home — passing out again several times on the way. She spent three days in bed before she could move enough to even get to the doctor's.

The tally was a punctured ear drum, several broken teeth, cracked ribs, bruises. What didn't show was the fear. Laura has since been afraid of being home alone, afraid of going out, afraid of seeing any of her friends, afraid of being seen with another woman. She has avoided calling or seeing the women she knew, and she drives an hour to the next town to shop for food. She doesn't know what to do.

— Yvonne

As women, all lesbians are potential victims of male violence — verbal harassment, physical abuse and sexual assault. Men learn to express their anger, frustration and disapproval by using violence. Verbal and physical violence is a common male response to lesbians. Lesbians are breaking the rule that every woman needs a man. We are therefore likely to bear the brunt of male disapproval, which takes the form of ridicule, obscenities hurled at us on the street, being beaten up, being raped, being murdered . . . the fear of physical violence is an ever-present reality in women's lives. For lesbians, even the radical or alternative community is not always a safe place. Many of us have been harassed and threatened by left and gay men.

Organizing for Public Safety

There is no doubt that the visible presence of lesbians at rallies, marches and social or cultural events often provokes threats of violence or actual abuse and assault. We have not hidden all these years without good reason. Homophobia and misogyny are not merely attitudes: they get acted out in dangerous ways. Even if you're a veteran of countless demonstrations, it's still scary to take to the streets as a lesbian. You never know who will be out there, or the response you'll get.

Women have been carefully taught that we are helpless on the street, that there is little we can do to defend ourselves. More and more of us are understanding that these are lies designed to keep us afraid, at home and dependent on the 'protection' of men. We are taking self-defense courses in order to respond with skill and confidence to dangerous situations.

Just as individual women can learn to *act* rather than panic, so can we collectively. For years now we have been organizing public events relying not on police protection or the 'legitimacy' of a march permit, but on our own Safety Committees. Through such Committees, we can not only ensure our security, but increase the self-confidence of all participating women.

The Safety Committee

When organizing an event, put out the call for women with previous marshalling or self-defense experience to form a Safety Committee. Inexperienced women may also join. Initially, the Committee will need to discuss and agree upon fundamental topics:

* What is the Safety Committee's role? It could be: to *plan* in advance for the security of women and children participating in the event; to safely *marshal* the event; to *inform* those attending about safety procedures and their individual responsibilities.

* What is your understanding of and commitment to non-violence? Broadly expressed, non-violence is equal commitments to non-aggression and self-defense. It is an essential part of a good safety strategy.

* What is your previous experience? You'll want to employ safety principles and tactics that are simple enough for women untrained in self-defense to use.

Having agreed on these general principles, you can address the multitude of factors relating to the specifics of your event.

Location   When it's possible to be flexible, choose a location or route that affords some security: avoid isolated, poorly lit areas, or being boxed-in. The needs of women who cannot move quickly or with ease must be considered. Select streets that are wheel-chair accessible, and avoid steep hills.

Traffic   If you're marching without a permit, traffic becomes your responsibility. Will you stay on the sidewalk, or take the street? Will marshals stop and direct traffic, or will you obey signals and have women wait for each other? Supplying each Committee member with a map of the site is useful for planning.

Coordination   How you work together and communicate are very important. Women can be assigned particular positions (such as marshalling the rear), or particular roles (such as a Surveillance Team who runs or cycles along the length of the march, conveying information as they go). You could use whistles and a code of sounds: two long blows could mean: "I need help from at least two women *now*."

Rehearsal   Take the time to actually walk the route or visit the location. Appraise how long the march may take, if your signals would be audible or if you have enough women. The starting and end points of a march can be trouble spots and must be well-covered. Figure out what you'd do if 500 more women than you'd expected show up.

Visibility   Women attending the event need to be able to identify you quickly and be informed of your plans and expectations. Wear brightly-coloured armbands, and distribute printed materials or make announcements at the beginning. You can make the time and place of the evaluation meeting know in these ways.

Children   They require a secure, open place in a march. The middle can be a good spot, or travelling in vehicles. If the route is long, a vehicle is a must.

First Aid   Several women skilled in first-aid and well-supplied first-aid kits are needed. Bulky supplies could be transported in the kid vehicle.

Police and Media   Since it is best to leave Safety Committee women undistracted, have other women assigned to handle the police and media.

Dealing with Harassment   It is important to develop and practice specific tactics. Swap stories about past events and imagine what *may* happen. What if several angry men push their way into the march? Or a man menaces women by driving too close? Or a woman bystander starts screaming obscenities or strikes someone? Do role-playing around these kinds of situations.

A strategy that is often effective is to isolate the source of trouble by visibly acting as a group. You can do this with other marshals or, if necessary, by calling on women in the event to help. If a man is harassing women, call together a number of women, link arms and surround him. One woman can call out directions, the circle can slowly move the man away and immobilize him until the march passes. If a lone woman from the event is verbally taking on a hostile bystander, invite women to stand with her, link arms and encourage her to rejoin the group.

Whatever you do, speak loudly so women will be clearly informed and know how to act together. Be explicit about what you want: "I need the help of you three women." And be specific about what should be done: "Let's link arms and move him over to the sidewalk. I'll do the talking."

What may be appropriate in one situation may be ineffective in another. An example is verbal self-defense. It can be a powerful tool to have 10 women firmly tell a man that his attitude stinks and you want him to leave *right now*. If that man is drunk or violent, talking may only increase the danger.

Attitude   While this is true for all women, it is especially important that the Safety Committee attend the event well-rested and alert; then you are more confident, responsive and visibly happy. It's best to forego that drink or toke. Trust your perceptions and hunches. And trust your judgements about how to act; after all, you *have* prepared together.

At the End   You may want to stay at the end points for some time after the event to be sure no-one is left to deal with a group of angry people who finally figured out that was indeed 500 lesbians! Make sure women know their way back.

Evaluation   Have an advertised, pre-arranged evaluation meeting at which you can hear your own and other women's comments and criticisms. Record what were effective and not-so-

Photo/ Cy-Thea Sand

effective tactics, and try to make this information available to future organizers.

Attending an Event

To ensure your personal, and the event's safety, keep the following points in mind:

* Pay attention to the Safety Committee's hand-outs and announcements. They have spent hours sorting these things out and their judgement bears respecting.

* Let the Committee know if you have skills or resources to offer. This could be anything from knowledge of first-aid or self-defense, to a vehicle.

* If you are bringing kids, discuss with them any safety plans before-hand. If they are young, it is wise to pin their names and phone numbers to their clothing in case you are separated.

While the above material relates mainly to public events like marches and rallies, we think that many of these principles and strategies are adaptable to social or private settings, such as dances or house parties. Being able to protect and defend ourselves makes us better able to realize our *right* to move freely and visibly in the world. The lessons of self-defense, non-violence and civil disobedience can serve as much as political organizing tools as they can as strategies for safety.

The above material thanks to Paula Clancy

Somewhere to Start

□ It is important to learn verbal and physical self-defense skills. Many community centres offer physical self-defense courses. Wen-Do is a method specifically designed for women (see *Resources* for addresses). Assertiveness training courses are often offered by women's groups, Y.W.C.A.'s, community centres, etc. Make sure children also learn self-defense skills.

An increased awareness of the possibility of assault is in itself a preventative measure. Don't fall for the myth that only straight women experience male violence.

□ Lesbians are often especially at risk when leaving lesbian social events, like dances, concerts and bars. Such events should have security women who stay near the doors and watch or accompany women to cars and busses. A good communication system for summoning reinforcements in case of trouble is essential.

□ Some cities have organized successfully against anti-gay violence. These public campaigns seem to grow out of especially bad periods of 'queer bashing', and involve speak-outs by members of the gay community, street patrols, publicity and often negotiations with the police. Gay groups in Toronto and Vancouver would be sources of information on organizing such campaigns. There are also Gay Liason police officers in some communities, and they may be useful in the case of a particularly bad outbreak of violence.

Photo/ Wendy L. Davis

□ Women providing services to victims of violence need to remember that not all the women will be heterosexual. If there are lesbians in your group, work out counselling methods that invite women to be open about their lesbianism without scaring them. If there are no lesbians in your group (why aren't there?), try to work with an outside lesbian group.

Any service organization in this field would benefit from a consciousness-raising workshop like *Stepping Out Of Line*. You don't want stray homophobic emotions to ruin your counselling.

□ Lesbian groups could work at checking out local transition houses, rape crisis centres and women against violence groups to make sure they are offering services that are accessible and useful to lesbians. It may very well be necessary to do basic consciousness-raising with staff and volunteers.

□ Lesbians can join with other women who are organizing to end violence against women. Does your area have a 24-hour crisis line or shelter? Are there on-going support groups for women who have been abused and assaulted? The Canadian Association of Sexual Assault Centres can provide information about how other women have organized their own communities.

□ Like all women, lesbians are often incest survivors, rape victims, battered wives. Talking with other women who have had similar experiences can be sanity saving. Support groups can often be found through rape crisis centres, social service agencies or feminist counselling networks. Try to find out if the group is operating from a feminist analysis of violence against women, and check out the support for lesbianism. If it doesn't feel right, ask the organization providing the service to set up a lesbian-only group.

□ Lesbians are not immune from manifestations of violence within ourselves and our relationships. We are still very closeted about the violence between and amongst us, often not wanting to either hear or talk about it. This has to change (see *Fighting Internalized Oppression* and *Lovers and Sexuality*).

*V*iolence against women includes physical harassment, psycho-logical abuse, battering, incest and sexual assault. Sexual assault is an act of domination, violence and aggression perpetrated through forced physical intimacy against a woman's will and without her consent. Sexual assault is the exploitation of a woman's body and is the logical extension of a sexist society which promotes violence against women through 'polarization of the sexes'. Sexual assault is encouraged by the political, economic and social structure of a society which views women as sex objects, as submissive, unthinking institutionalized nurturers and as the property of men. In a society which maintains inequalities between its male and female members, coercive sexuality and violence against women are reinforced.

— B.C.F.W. Policy Statement

Photo/Press Gang

Resources

Print

General

Fight Back: Feminist Resistance to Male Violence, ed. by Frederique Delacoste and Felice Newman (Minneapolis: Cleis Press, 1981)   Extensive anthology dealing with feminist responses to the range of violence against women: rape, battering, pornography, prisons, health-care, etc. Some lesbian content. Includes a directory of Canadian and U.S. organizations dealing with violence against women.

Women and Male Violence: The Visions and Struggles of the Battered Women's Movement, Susan Schecter (Boston: South End Press, 1982)   An "in-depth look at battering and the social movement against it." Contains information on violence against lesbians, lesbians in the shelter movement and their experiences of homophobia and heterosexism.

Reweaving the Web of Life: Feminism and Non-violence, ed. by Pam McAllister (Philadelphia: New Society Publishers, 1982)   Poems, essays, fiction, biography and analysis relating to feminism, the peace movement and non-violence.

Aegis: A Magazine on Ending Violence Against Women, Feminist Alliance Against Rape   "To aid the efforts of feminists working to end violence against women." Carries articles relevant to lesbians, such as homophobia in the anti-rape movement. Available from: Box 21033, Washington D.C. 20009.

Rape

Rape: The Price of Coercive Sexuality, Lorenne Clark and Debra Lewis (Toronto: The Women's Press, 1977)   The first Canadian study of rape with a theoretical feminist analysis of its social causes.

Against Our Will: Men, Women and Rape, Susan Brownmiller (New York: Bantam, 1975)   Popular history and analysis of rape from a feminist perspective.

The Politics of Rape: The Victim's Perspective, Diana E.H. Russell (New York: Stein and Day, 1974) Interviews with women who have been raped. Feminist perspective and analysis.

Against Rape: A Survival Manual for Women, Andra Medea and Kathleen Thompson (New York: Farrar, Straus and Giroux, 1974)   Subtitled "How to avoid entrapment and how to cope with rape physically and emotionally".

Battering

Battered and Blamed: A Report on Wife Assault From the Perspective of Battered Women, (Vancouver Women's Research Centre/Vancouver Transition House, 1980)   Besides letting battered women speak for themselves, this study analyzes the causes and effects of battering, and the role of transition houses. Includes a bibliography. Available from: Women's Research Centre, #201 - 517 E. Broadway, Vancouver, B.C.

Battered Wives, Del Martin (San Francisco: Glide Publications, 1976)

Getting Free: A Handbook for Women in Abusive Relationships, Ginny NiCarthy (Seattle: Seal Press, 1982)   "Self-help manual providing practical advice for overcoming fears, finding shelter, dealing with children and the batterer, for evaluating lawyers, doctors and counsellors, and for finding new friends and relationships". For women in abusive hetero-sexual relationships, but teaches useful skills relating to problem-solving and taking control of your life.

Incest

Voices in the Night: Women Speaking about Incest, ed. by Toni McNaron and Yarrow Morgan (Minneapolis: Cleis Press, 1984)   Stories and poems by women, some lesbians.

Daddy's Girl, Charlotte Vale Allen (Toronto: Bantam-Seal, 1980)   A women's account of her experience of father/daughter incest.

Kiss Daddy Goodnight: A Speakout On Incest, ed. by Louise Armstrong (New York: Pocket Books, 1978)

Pornography

Take Back The Night: Women on Pornography, ed. by Laura Lederer (New York: Bantam Books, 1980)   An extensive anthology.

Pornography: Men Possessing Women, Andrea Dworkin (New York: Perigee, 1981)   Analysis, including material on lesbians.

Film/Video

An extensive listing of audio-visual and print resources relating to violence against women was compiled by a Women Against Violence Against Women group in Vancouver and is available, along with some of the videos themselves, from:

Women in Focus Arts and Media Centre, 456 W. Broadway, Vancouver, B.C. V5Y 1R3 (604-872-2250)

There are a number of good films and videos produced by feminists on the subject of violence against women and self-defence. To find feminist producers and distributors in Canada and the U.S., see:

☐ *Finding Lesbian Resources*

Groups

Wen-Do is a method of self-defense specifically designed for and taught by women. It offers ways of dealing with physical, verbal and sexual assault. Besides teaching physical skills, Wen-Do emphasizes the importance of learning self-confidence, and courses include discussions relating to women's conditioning.

Wen-Do West, 2349 St. Catherines, Vancouver, B.C. V5T 3X8 (879-6390)

Wen-Do Prairie, 730 Alexander Ave., Winnipeg Man. R3N 1H9 (783-7889)

Wen-Do Central, #817 - 2 Carlton St., Toronto Ont. M5A 4A4 (977-7127)

Wen-Do Québec, C.P. 745, Succ. La Cité, Montréal P.Q. H2W 2P3 (523-6065)

To find your local rape crisis or sexual assault centre, consult the phone book.

The Canadian Association of Sexual Assault Centres (CASAC), c/o 77 E. 20th Ave., Vancouver B.C. A network of feminist organizations.

From Community to Movement

Organizing as lesbians to create changes in society that will benefit us isn't easy. Lesbian pride is not something any of us were born with.

But, as one woman said in a workshop, "You get to a point where the fear doesn't matter. You know you may *never* be acceptable to the majority of people in this culture. You have to come to terms with being a rebel and an outlaw and, after awhile, there is a kind of defiance and pride that exists with the fear. Sure, the fear is still there, but somehow you get beyond it. You stand up and act anyway, and when that happens, the feeling is almost like elation."

And we know more and more clearly that, once we begin, we *can* and we *are* creating real and visible change. There are thousands and thousands of lesbians across Canada and Québec — experienced, creative, energetic, committed and ready. *Let's move!*

When we are depressed and self-destructive, we are not doing anything to change the conditions of our own and other women's lives.

Fighting Internalized Oppression

I know violence from the bottom up. In some ways I am so comfortable with it, it scares me.

Beatings in my home were so common as to be a tradition and, although I was both angry at and terrified of my father, I reacted simply by participating in the constant vicious fighting that went on and by destroying things that were precious to me. This started long before my memory does.

I was probably 19 the first time I admitted — oh so tentatively — that maybe, *maybe* the punishment in our home was excessive. I was perhaps 21 when I was able to see, and confess, that I had been a battered child.

A new stigma, a new isolating factor — but with a new analysis. At last there was a chance to look at my own rage as not sick or inherent, and to look at the torture that seemed to trail me everywhere as not my fault.

At 13 I refused to submit to family and institutional (at that time, public school and Catholic Children's Aid) violence any longer, and fled the city. In every story I'd ever read, the tormented heroine was free once her physical chains were broken. But mine remained attached. My father was replaced by the men I met, and my own violence no longer had the safe and sanctified outlets it had had before. Suddenly I was a crazy 13 year old who trusted no one and hated deeply.

Pressures mounted and it became impossible for me to run away every time I was frightened or enraged. I found myself in an unknown and hostile town. At 16, I was trying to support myself and live with a sister

with whom I fought constantly, and trying to survive, without support, the loss of a lover. All this was, if not home, familiar. Depression and insomnia got worse and at any moment emotion threatened to erupt. My initial violence to myself at that point was to deny that emotion, as I had learned to, and seek succour in the form of sleeping pills.

The catch was that I got the benevolent guardianship of the psychiatric profession along with that attempt. And that is when the violence really began. Before psychiatry, my violence was limited to occasional physical outbursts — usually aimed at persons I considered threatening or provoking. Mostly, however, it manifested itself in gloomy depression and seething self-contempt and contempt for, and rebellion against, authority.

At the hospital, I learned new ways of being violent, and finally found a name for it — being crazy. I learned new and better reasons to hate myself. Previously I had thought that my father was fucked, that school and church were fucked, that police and social workers were fucked. Now I learned that it was me. *I* was neurotic. *I* was suicidal. *I* was unable to cope with normal society. *I* couldn't fit in. Though I screamed, "I don't want to adjust, I want to *change*", it was still *me* that needed changing.

I never believed anyone cared about me and I looked for ways to prove once and for all that they did not. I drank and picked fights. I drugged myself for years with anything I could get. I allowed myself to get into endless situations of danger because I was too frightened and too careless not to. I would, I believed, get what I deserved. Rape and other forms of violence seemed to seek me out.

I would occasionally desire something positive — schooling, or someone's friendship. And then, partly out of paralyzing fear and partly out of self-punishment, I would destroy my chances of getting it. Sometimes just by convincing myself it was unattainable. Often by actively throwing wrenches in.

One of the most effective weapons against myself was beating, often cruelly and relentlessly, the three beings in the world I could allow myself to trust completely. The fury would rise, the grief beside it. The utter, enveloping, incomprehensible and uncontrollable rage would move through me like a hot wind, and I would scream in despair and beat my pets and then I'd beat myself. I would cut my arms or write messages on my legs with razor blades *(I am not crazy)*.

Once I found myself striking my lover in anger and frustration. She didn't react. I pulled myself away from her in horror and collapsed, wailing, "I don't want to be like him." Daddy creeps his way back into my life. Or I'd go out and find a man who would beat me senseless with his uncaring and his penis, if not with his fists. And then I would tear myself apart for that as well.

Actually, my rage seldom spilled out onto others — physically. Once though, I destroyed the apartment I had taken so long to make lovely. Brimming with self-hate, I left the house with knife in hand. I had had enough. I wandered around the night city and hitchhiked. I waited for some man to do something, *anything*. I was going to kill him. Miraculously, no one said a word I could use as an excuse. Eventually I returned to my wrecked home and overdosed.

My few actual suicide attempts were the only truly kind things I did for myself during those times. It was as though everything was so wrong nothing could ever improve, and on two occasions I allowed myself the dignity of escape, of peace. The despair of those two failures was immense and more proof that, indeed, I could do nothing right, no matter how well planned and unflinchingly executed.

I fell in with a psychologist who had, quite by accident, retained some feeling despite his training. Of course, he was new at it. Alone, his friendship was enough to eventually convince me that there were some people I couldn't prove my ugliness to, and that gave me the chance to start pretending that I wasn't ugly. But it wouldn't have been enough to change it all.

Instead of cruising towards a new, if slightly delayed summit of frustration and despair, I took a vacation that has turned my life around. I returned to Vancouver and refused to go back home. At the insistent urging of a friend whom I suspected had finally cracked up and joined a bunch of weirdies, I went to a radical therapy workshop. And another one, and another one . . . and from there, I inched my way into feminism and the alternate community.

Anger, fear and violence are still very much part of my life. I haven't changed much — only learned some new tools and rerouted my rage. It irrigates my political work and affects others still, but now in a more positive form.

I can cry now, and the broken glass edge of despair is mostly memory. I have yet to be the brilliant, clean, constructive and cathartic fighter I aspire to be. Neither have all of my cohorts. I have punched out a window and slapped a face and turned my anger inwards 'til my stomach nearly bleeds, but each week I become better at moving it out, away from myself, not thrusting it in its twisted form onto others.

Still, it's damn effective in keeping me working, keeping me from giving in. Fighting to change, *change* and never relent.

— *B.C.*

I'*ve been drinking for 15 years. I started in order to be sophisticated* and sociable. I always liked the image of the melancholy, crazy, radical woman — it was romantic to be mad! As a teenager, I learned to chug-a-lug my father's booze after everyone had gone to bed. I would stand by the liquor cabinet, hold my nose and drink from the bottle, so that by the time I got to bed, I had that swimming feeling and I could sleep.

At 20 I was living alone in Toronto, 45 pounds overweight and spending a lot of time by myself. I discovered drinking alone. I would buy a case of 24 beer and order a pizza. I would get really sick, horrible hangovers, and that's when I began having blackouts and losing control. I always promised I would stop but never did. I liked the warmth of alcohol.

I was heterosexual at the time, and thought I was frigid because I didn't enjoy sex with men. I used alcohol to make it easier to sleep with them. When I began to have sex with women, I used alcohol to lessen my inhibitions. There was always a great deal of drinking in the lesbian community. Alcohol was an essential part of social life. When you arrived at a party, you would get a beer put in one hand, then a kiss hello. I drank and kept on drinking because I didn't have any self-confidence and didn't like myself.

It is very painful to remember what my life was like with alcohol because I realize now that I didn't have to do that to myself. I isolated myself for 15 years. I almost died. I destroyed relationships. I was constantly aware of the conflicts between my politics and my reality. I knew intellectually that alcohol wasn't healthy, but I couldn't integrate that understanding into my life.

After seven years of constant drinking, I was aware that this was physical self-abuse, that I had an illness. I rationalized my drinking by saying I drank because I didn't really care about myself, and nobody else cared about me anyway. It was a vicious circle because I wanted people to care. I was afraid that I could be wiped off the face of this earth and nobody would care. I was scared that my friends would let me die. All the while, I was organizing as a lesbian feminist and trying to pull together alternatives to beer drinking and bars, such as Women in Sobriety.

I did dangerous things when I was drunk. I was 20 the first time I got the dry heaves. At 22 I nearly fell in front of a subway coming from an office Christmas party. Somebody caught me as I fell and took me home. I was fired from my job after that party. Then came the loss of memory and people telling me of my drunken, outrageous behaviour. People would tell me that I had been violent and abusive. I scared myself, waking up in the hospital, arms restrained, tubes and IV's.

At one point, when my lover was dying from lung cancer, I freaked out. I had been drinking with two friends. They tell me that later that night, I was standing on the railing of a balcony of an apartment on the 35th floor, screaming, "Don't forget me." They tried unsuccessfully to get me down. I went absolutely crazy, and got physically violent with them. Finally they took me to the hospital. When I woke up, there was a roomful of people talking about putting me away. I ran away from the hospital to my friend's house but was so paranoid that I wouldn't let her into the house; I was convinced that she really didn't care about me anymore and that she had the police with her. I ranted and raved.

I used alcohol to make any difficult situation easier. I called my mother to end an 11 year silence, but before I could talk to her, I had to chug-a-lug a mickey of rum. As I was talking to her, I passed out and missed the train I was supposed to take to visit her. I didn't drink every day because I couldn't afford to, but magically there was always booze around and always money for more alcohol, even when there wasn't enough for rent and food.

I got drunk nearly every time I drank. I tried many times to control the drinking and after many disasters, I realized that I *couldn't* control it. One drink meant two meant three meant finding myself sick with a hangover the next day, not remembering what I had done or what had happened. I covered up my hangovers, telling people I was sick because I was overworked. I tried hard to appear 'normal'.

My coming to terms with being an alcoholic was a long process. Although drinking was common in the lesbian community, I was visible as an alcoholic. I decided to try A.A. for the first time mainly because someone else scared me: I did it so she wouldn't leave me. I was sober for nine months. Then one night at the Lesbian Coffeehouse I went to the fridge, said, "What the hell", and picked up a beer. Three women groaned. Later, we all went drinking and ended up being thrown out of the bar. I got beaten up somehow. I woke up in a strange apartment with several teeth loose, bruises all over my body, gravel in my scalp — and I had to face the community.

The remorse and anxiety attacks were indescribable — only another alcoholic could really understand what that horror is like. I had been so vocal about stopping my drinking. Everyone was aware of it, so it was especially hard when I ended my sobriety. After that, I tried everything. I humiliated myself, tried Anti-buse. I had reservations and complaints about A.A. I see now that I was not willing to face a sober life at that point. It took me three years to return to A.A.

One morning I was woken up by the sheriff. I was hung over and drenched in blood. I didn't know whether or not I had killed someone and if he was coming to take me away. At that point I knew I had to be prepared to accept the serious consequences of my drinking because I couldn't handle alcohol. I had to face the music and *stop* drinking.

Three days later, I crawled through the doors of A.A., this time for myself. I said, "I'm not going to drink anymore because I don't want to die." I wanted to be fully alive and have all my faculties. I no longer wanted the embarassment of facing my sisters. I wanted to get sober and stay sober. In despair and humiliation, I got on a train and exiled myself, not to return until I had got it all together. I had to leave all my friends who enabled me to drink because they continually rescued me. I needed the geographic distance and the pace of life in a new place. I drank for the first 23 days after leaving, then I joined A.A. here.

A.A. is people who know what it's like; people who understand what I need to protect my sobriety. They provide support. I have access to people all over the country, any time of the night or day, in any small town. They are people who know how hard it is not to take that one drink and people who can help me find other ways of coping when I'm in trouble. I am able to make a daily recommitment not to have a drink for this one day. I couldn't accept the idea of living the rest of my life without a drink, but I can face 24 hours at a time.

I have to be honest — it takes hard soul-searching to look at myself and my drinking. Depressive thinking is a luxury I can't afford. There are lesbian groups in A.A. I get tremendous support from them. I am learning about maturity; I missed growing up all those years I was drinking. I never learned how to love myself. While I may have criticisms of A.A., I realize that it's important to *get sober* first, then be critical.

I now like that I'm alive. It's amazing. I've gone from totally hating myself to really loving myself. I've learned how bad I was willing to feel and I'm not willing to feel that way again. I have to remain vigilant. I have to learn how to live sober, which means facing my emotions and learning that I can be sad, happy, frustrated and angry and handle it. I can't let myself get hungry, or lonely, or tired because it's irresponsible and dangerous for me. Sobriety is not happiness, but I'm learning to be content with it.

Since I've been sober, I was in a car accident, and my friend died of lung cancer. Both those times I chose not to take a drink when I could have had good excuses. So I know that I can live through catastrophes and survive. But I have to watch for the little things that build up. I am regaining a pride in myself. I am grateful that I have the benefit of a fantastic support system.

It's not an accident that I hated myself so intensely and became an alcoholic. I don't think it's a coincidence that I had revolutionary ideals and drank because of the pain of the real world. I know now that if I die as a result of this system, it won't be because I cooperated. I won't kill myself for them. It is a privilege to be active and to think clearly, to fight, to have an analysis of this system that helps us understand our pain. As women we need to be conscious of what we put into our bodies that prevents us from thinking and from being active.

I call on my addicted sisters to come out of the drug and alcohol closets and look at what causes us to blot out conscious existence. I am grateful to those who allowed me to keep coming back, to those who didn't write me off as simply a hopeless alcoholic, and to those who gave me the encouragement to fight my oppression.

And especially to the friend who said, "First the good news: I am your friend and I care about you. Now the bad news: I am leaving because I can't be around you when you drink."

— *Artemis*

*W*hen I used to think about "my violent lesbian relationship", part of my mind would start dishing out wise, calm sociological observations: I was young and inexperienced (no perspective); our class and family backgrounds were radically different (built-in conflict); we were an isolated lesbian couple (homophobia!), etc. Another part cowered in the background, yelling nasty, scary, disjointed *truths:* you're a first-class shit;

Graphic/ Claire Kujundzic

wait until she catches up to you: I'll *murder* her; o god do I *deserve* to recover?

But most of the time I felt incapable of analyzing or feeling the significance of that relationship and simply kept it filed under 'Absolutely Unbelievable.'

We beat each other up for about three of the four years of the relationship. I hadn't hit anyone before or since. I had never before engaged in verbal warfare or screaming matches or emotional blackmail. I had never watched so much day-time t.v. or lain catatonic on my bed for months or gone for weeks without speaking or for years without any friends. I still believe that we must have made the Violent Lesbian Relationships Top 100. It ended when I snuck out one afternoon with several suitcases, hid out briefly in a rooming-house and then fled the continent.

I took lots of fear and self-hatred with me — and

outright bewilderment. There was a huge gap between who I thought I was and what I had just done for four years. I could look minutely at her behaviour, how she had loved to play victim or lord it over me, and I found ways of explaining it in terms of her background — and how awful I was. But I couldn't, and seemed not to want to, face how I too had consented to being a victim, a prisoner, a bad woman.

With the help of a new city and friends, I've been able to shake much of that self-hatred and shame. I don't fully understand *why* I was so violent and immobile, but I've sorted out lots about my experience of anger and conflict and guilt. I'll never be that way again.

Those sociological explanations are also, I realize, the political heart of the matter. Violent lesbian relationships happen because of our family baggage, because we're alone and outcast, because we've bought into romantic garbage, because we're poor and under-employed and we drink and the world is hard-hearted. All of that is political.

— Nancy

One of the most powerful myths of this society is the belief in the separation between personal life and political activity. Interaction between people, family relationships, sexuality, emotional expression — all are considered private. We may be done in by politicians, work at rotten jobs and pay too much for our food, but our personal lives are *ours!*

This belief is destructive as well as untrue. Our private lives *are* shaped by society. We carry strong ideas about what 'proper behaviour' is: how women 'should' be, what love means, what sex means, how people communicate, how we get what we want...Our beliefs are rarely individual or unique; we have learned from our families, our schooling, our entire cultural conditioning. We were *taught* to be women — and in this society that means we were taught to be self-hating, insecure, fearful, emotionally dependent, sexually ignorant and politically powerless.

The false separation between personal and public causes us much pain. It is in our personal lives that we feel hurt, betrayed and out of control; we become destructive to ourselves and others. And it is all the worse because we believe firmly and consistently that failure is all our own fault. If we are unhappy, it is because we are not good enough, lucky enough, attractive enough, disciplined enough: *"I have sexual problems...my relationships always turn out bad...I have troubles with my family...I get depressed...my children are not turning out right. And it is all my fault."*

When we are depressed and self-destructive, we are not doing anything to change the conditions of our own and other women's lives. When we are so caught up in our individual problems that we cannot see past them, we are immobilized. When we believe that, "I am a failure", or "I can't cope with my life", we are thinking thoughts that have been planted and reinforced in us — ideas designed to keep us from examining why and how we find ourselves without power and choice.

We are the sum of our life experiences to date: the dynamics of our families, the realities of the class and race into which we were born. We have learned ways of surviving in the world that have worked for us. As

Photo/ Wendy L. Davis

the circumstances of our lives change, the ways of behaving and surviving that we have developed may no longer be the most useful ways for us to act.

Examining our feelings and behaviour and changing what is no longer useful is a natural process; it happens quicker and easier with the support of other people. It is a fine line between acknowledging and fighting back individually against all the ways we have been taught to keep ourselves down and accepting the myth that each of us can triumph alone and live a happy, complete life in an oppressive world.

Personally, we believe that the most useful approach for any woman trying to make her life better is feminism, both as an analytical framework *and* as an active movement for social change. As lesbians, we take care of ourselves in order to survive and resist the messages of self-hatred we've received. Our very existence as healthy, competent, energetic, happy lesbians is a statement of hope and victory.

> Not only do we suffer in response to the cultural standard of what and how a woman should be, but also, for many of us, our bodies are the places where the oppression and stress we confront as lesbians is manifested. Under stress? Hurting? Angry? We have not been taught many ways to deal with these feelings; so many of us deal with stress by internalizing it in our bodies, by holding tension in certain areas, by getting too little of the right kind of food and too much of the wrong kind, by not getting enough sleep or exercise and by not having avenues of expression open to us.
>
> We receive numerous messages in our lives not to love ourselves. As women, we are taught to always be taking care of others, nurturing others, healing others and letting our needs come second. As lesbians we have received another message: that we are sick and perverted for loving women. Yet the basis for wanting to take care of yourself begins with learning to love yourself. The romanticized idea of the 'Amazon' woman is overdone, but as women who love women, we have an incredible potential to love our woman selves and actualize our true strengths.
>
> During the process of bringing about change in our society, lesbians need to keep in mind that we've got to take care of, and bring about change in ourselves, our sisters, and our families — while at the same time confronting the larger issues that are making us sick. We need to develop the balance between being strong enough to fight social injustice and lesbian oppression, and gentle enough to nurture our bodies, our minds and each other.
> — *Lesbian Health Matters!*

Survival Tactics

Does this sound familiar?

7 a.m.	Rise from a deep sleep, rush through a shower, get the kids up, dressed, breakfast for the kids, maybe two cups of coffee for you, get the kids off to daycare.
9 a.m.	Traffic, driving...hit the office.
10 a.m.	Phones are ringing, people, emergency meetings, two more coffees.
1 p.m.	Time for a quick lunch on the run. Dessert with lots of sugar. Rush back to work.
5 p.m.	Drive across town to pick up the kids at daycare. Rush home to make dinner and arrange for a babysitter before a meeting.
7 p.m.	Off to a meeting which goes on until eleven. Lots of cigarettes. Friends in crisis want to talk afterwards.
11 p.m.	To the bar for a few drinks to unwind.
1 p.m.	To bed.
Next day	Repeat, except the shopping, the laundry, visiting friends, taking the kids out . . .

How many of us do something close to this routine every day? Many of us have full-time paying jobs and many of us do political work on top of that. We go to meeting after meeting, each one producing more work to take away and get done before the next meeting. There is so much to do to stop the injustice and discrimination in the world. We race against time doing our best to be effective and productive and create meaningful change. It all adds up to a great deal of intense stress in our lives.

One of the common responses to this mad rush against the forces out there is to put our feelings on hold so that we can carry on. As we take on more and more tasks, we forget to take the time to relax, be alone, take pleasure in the things and people around us. We've noticed that when a woman starts working too hard, or seriously commits herself to political work with all its additional responsibilities, she will likely come to a crisis point when she realizes she's taken on too much and faces burning out. There is panic in her voice, tears in her eyes. Everything looks bleak and hopeless.

The usual ways to try and cope are to smoke more cigarettes, drink more coffee and keep going. We smoke dope, drink alcohol to relax, and eat lots of sugar to get a quick high. Meanwhile our bodies are accumulating more tension and we wonder why we get sick so often.

Ulcers are becoming more common in younger women. Lung cancer (and we know that more women than ever are smoking) has surpassed breast cancer as the number one killer of women. High blood pressure, back pains, frequent headaches, constipation and low energy are all symptoms of stress. But don't be discouraged. There are ways to take better care of ourselves and to stop this slow death.

Time Control   Try to balance your time. If you have worked in meetings for three weekends in a row, take some time to do something for yourself. Take time to be alone, to be outside. Studies have shown that we need time to reflect on our experiences. Look around you and see how many people can no longer find joy in anything after long hauls of intense demanding work. One way to give yourself time to think about what's happening to you is to keep a journal.

Exercise   Do something physical. Ride a bicycle to work, run, swim, dance, play squash, do self-defence exercises, wrestle; do anything that will release physical tension, improve circulation, increase breathing.

Massage   Get and give massages. Feelings and tensions get stored in your body as muscle tension. Massage helps release this.

Relax   Learn a simple relaxation exercise. Do it every night for 15 minutes after work or before bed. It can be as simple as sitting in a comfortable chair in a quiet room, listening to your breathing, counting down from 10 and imagining yourself going deeper into relaxation. Pay attention to any parts of your body that still feel tight and slowly let them go. When you want to come back to a fully alert but relaxed state, tell yourself you will keep the feeling of being relaxed but will be more alert, and slowly count to 10. Being relaxed doesn't mean being asleep. Relaxed means having your muscles in a state of equilibrium without one part being more tense than another.

Eat   Pay attention to what you eat and how you eat. Tensions makes it difficult for food to be digested as the enzymes which break down food in your system are not secreted in adequate quantities, and gas and constipation result. Low enzyme production leads to inadequate absorption of vitamins and minerals, even if we are eating a healthy diet.

Most of us don't eat well; we eat overcooked, overprocessed food loaded with chemical additives and preservatives — food which is low in vitamins and minerals. Even fresh raw vegetables from the market have taken days to get there, resulting in loss of vitamins.

What is the big deal about vitamins and minerals? Coffee, cigarettes and alcohol all deplete our body reserves of vitamins and minerals. So does stress. Some vitamin supplements can help in combatting stress. The B-complex vitamins are essential for the normal functioning of the nervous system. Brewer's yeast is a fairly inexpensive way of getting B vitamins. Getting enough vitamin C is important as it is not stored in the body and is destroyed by smoking, pollution and stress.

Try to eat real food — fruit, vegetables, grains, beans, yoghurt; avoid processed foods, meat, pop, and coffee.

Connections are now being made between our emotional and physical feelings and what we eat. Alcoholism, tiredness and headaches have been linked to hypoglycemia. Schizophrenia has been helped by massive doses of vitamin B. Food allergies, which affect our moods, are more common than had been believed.

Sleep   Watch your sleep patterns. Try to figure out how much sleep you need to get to feel good the next day. Have you noticed confusion after periods of not sleeping enough? Everyone has different needs for sleep.

Isolation   Don't let yourself get isolated. Just as we all need time to reflect and think, we also all need social contact. Talking about things really does help. Talk to your friends. Join or form a group to talk to other women to get support and validation.

Almost all jobs are stressful; so is life in the city with noise, pollution and the fast pace. Political work has its added stresses. We are in a constant state of anger at seeing women who are battered by individuals and society. We are always fighting hard to make a difference in other women's lives. We are often emotionally drained from giving support, comfort and counsel to other women. The battle seems never-ending; the political work is never done. If we are to survive the struggle and continue making a difference, we must find ways of taking care of ourselves and our co-workers and friends. Mental and physical health are one, and health is power.

— Krin and Annette

Feelings

Our society sends out contradictory messages about emotions. We are told, on the one hand, that feelings are unimportant and useless; that it is logical thought that really matters. On the other hand, we are taught that feelings are all-powerful, that we are at the mercy of our uncontrollable emotions, that we can't possibly understand our own or another person's emotions.

For centuries, women have been characterized as being 'too' emotional. Lesbians are seen as somehow possessing the emotional attributes assigned to both men and women in this culture. We are — mythologically-speaking — cold, hard, dominating, cool and tough (read male) and also hysterical, possessive, jealous, frustrated, bitter and unhappy (read female).

It is no wonder that a certain amount of confusion exists within most of us when we try to think about what our emotions are, what they mean and how much credence to give them in our lives.

Generally speaking, women are socialized to be more conscious of, and comfortable in, expressing emotions than men. Feminists tend to see male social conditioning — the teaching of male children to repress and deny emotions — as a major factor in adult men's ability to drop bombs, rape, and live in and create an inhuman world.

All of us feel. If our feelings are not recognized and validated we may take convoluted paths to express ourselves. We may deny that we feel anything, or deny that we feel certain emotions like anger or pain. We may take out our emotions on others in our lives: men batter, women hit children; we make ourselves sick, we drink.

There are cultural prohibitions against expressing powerful emotions, especially for women who are supposed to always be 'nice'. But it's important to our survival that we keep up with our feelings; they are real, and come from our actual experiences in the world, past and present. It's important to release feelings; talking, crying, hitting (objects, not people!). Recognizing and releasing emotions allows us to understand what is happening for us, to figure out what is right or wrong in our lives, to start thinking about what to do about it all.

Mystical therapy concepts aside, dealing with emotions — ours or someone else's — is basically just common sense. It is especially important that lesbians, who are silenced in many ways and in many situations, have places where it is safe to feel and express out loud *our* emotional realities.

— *Sarah*

Talking about our lives, our problems, our confusion and our feelings to sympathetic listeners is a useful tactic for getting through life sanely and safely. Some of us are lucky enough to have friendships where this kind of emotional process-sharing happens naturally and some of us see therapists.

All of us could probably use ideas and techniques to create more safe talking places in our lives. Two approaches that we find helpful are peer counselling and support groups.

Peer Counselling

The basic premise of this type of counselling is that each of us knows, or can know, what we are feeling, and what we need to do for ourselves to make positive changes in our lives. We need a structure to enable us to listen to ourselves, to pay attention to ourselves and feel supported. Peer counselling is just that: a structured time set up on a consistent basis between you and a peer. The key word here is *peer:* it is important that the person you select is someone you consider an equal, someone who shares a similar life experience and perspective — and who you trust.

Choose a friend who can get together with you regularly, once a week or every couple of weeks. Arrange to use each other's home, if that is possible. Take an equal amount of time to talk to each other, since you want to ensure a truly equal relationship. If one person consistently gives more time and attention to the other than she is getting back, she risks building up resentment.

Have on hand some kleenex, a towel (for wringing or squeezing), cushions to sit on or pound, and possibly something for hitting the cushions or the floor (a tennis racket or a baseball bat). There are some things to keep in mind before and as you talk to each other. We tend to block anger by tensing our lower backs. Try to discover a way of moving which involves the whole back, getting the energy flowing from the small of the back, right through the shoulders and neck (another place we block the expressions of anger) and out through the arms and hands. In order to facilitate the expression of emotion in a peer counselling session, it is often useful to do a few stretching and bending exercises to open up these parts of your body.

When you meet, decide how much time you each will take and who is going to talk first. Begin by sitting in a comfortable position where you can make physical contact and look at each other in the eyes. Some people like to hold hands.

For the Talker   To begin with, just talk about what you are aware of. Pay attention to what is going on in your body and in your emotions. If you notice yourself holding your breath, pause, breathe deeply and describe what you feel.

If you are preoccupied with a particular problem, talk about it and pay attention to the emotional charge that comes up as you do this: "I notice I felt angry as I said that." "I feel really sad when I talk about how she . . ." In this way the emotional aspect is always included as you talk through your problem.

For the listener   The most important instruction to the listener in peer counselling is simply this: be quiet and just listen. Refrain from giving advice, analyzing or interpreting. You don't have to be a good counsellor. Just listen with your whole attention. Some other things you can do as a listener are:

Remind your friend to breathe deeply.

Ask her, "What's happening for you now?" or "What emotions are you feeling right now?"

It is sometimes helpful to point out what the person is doing physically, e.g. "I notice you shake your head when you say that." If she is clenching or wringing her hands, you could suggest wringing a towel.

She decides whether to accept or reject your suggestions. It is her responsibility.

Leave five minutes at the end of each person's time for her to do some self-validation. This means telling something she likes about herself and what she's doing with her life right now. You could end the session with a hug or some other form of physical reassurance.

— adapted from the Canadian Association of Sexual Assault Centres Newsletter

Support Groups

In the broadest sense, a support group is any collection of lesbians who come together to explore something they have in common: race, class, disability, mothering, coming-out, sexuality, occupation, etc. We use the term "self-help support group" to describe a structured group process used by women who want to figure out the emotions and experiences of an area of their life they feel is painful or problematic. These areas could involve alcohol, surviving incest, or violence in ourselves or our relationships. Often, the group's focus serves as a springboard for wide-ranging explorations of our feelings and lives.

Along with peer counselling, self-help support groups challenge the assumption that only professionals and experts — therapists, shrinks or counsellors — can guide us through personal pain to personal growth. The group has no leader, and operates from the premise that each woman is there to help *herself* and that *she* determines how the group can help her. Self-definition is a central concept.

Starting Up   An interested woman could start a group by advertising in the local lesbian, feminist or gay publications, or at places that lesbians frequent. A comfortable, safe and private meeting place is required; someone's home is probably best. Between five and seven women is the right size.

Understandings and Commitments   At the first gathering, it is important that women discuss their expectations and together work out how the group will function. A general discussion of the concepts of self-help, non-judgemental listening (see *Peer Counselling)* and the need for group democracy should happen.

All women in the group have to make specific commitments to each other. A committment to confidentiality is needed; this could mean not repeating information learned in the group, or never telling the names of the other women in the group, or not even disclosing that the group exists. Regular attendance is important and women should agree to inform the group if they'll be absent. Members make a

commitment not to use drugs or alcohol before or during meetings. Women agree to take personal responsibility for ensuring the group is as democratic as possible by: not letting anyone dominate discussions; speaking up if something 'feels wrong'; not assuming that other women are ok without asking out-loud. Women exchange a phone list and agree to be accessible to each other between meetings. Finally, women should agree to distinguish between their personal friendship circles and the function of the group (though friendships can arise).

The Meeting   Meetings must have enough structure so that each women's needs can be met, yet be loose enough to allow for the unexpected.

A timekeeper is needed. Her role is to call for rounds, tell women when their time is up, make sure kleenex and pillows are on hand and generally keep track of things.

Start with a brief round where women can say anything about their current emotional or physical state that might affect their participation that evening. Then, allot equal amounts of time to each woman to talk, without interruption, about her feelings, experiences or ways of coping. Other women can ask questions to help clarify what she's saying.

Exploring a particular topic each week is a good way to focus thoughts. If a good feminist book on the general subject exists, it could be used to provide inspiration. Topics like self-esteem, guilt, anger, power or sexuality could be used in many groups!

After everyone has spoken, have a short open discussion and then another round to see how each woman is doing. Choose the topic and timekeeper for the next meeting. A comforting and supportive way to finish off is to hold hands in silence for a minute or two.

When trust within the group has built up over a period of time, some relaxation of the structure becomes possible. Sometimes the group may spend a meeting focussing on one woman's experiences. Dynamics can occur within the group that mirror the problems in women's lives and time can be devoted to understanding those.

Evaluation Every two or three months an evaluation is needed. Women can restate their expectations, and the group's effectiveness and need to continue should be examined. Women will need the group or be able to attend it for differing lengths of time. If some are ready to leave, a decision should be made either to carry on as is, invite new members or dissolve. It is important not to let the group just wither away.

I found being part of a self-help support group beneficial in itself. I saw how other women coped with

their lives and their problems. That helped me draw parallels with my own life and gave me some perspective. In the group, you really have to practice your listening and communication skills, and that serves you well in all areas of your life.

Of course, the experience of being in the group is highly charged and there is the potential for hard emotional times. You are in an unfacilitated therapeutic setting, and it's essential to feel trusting of the other women. So everyone really has to take responsibility for making the group safe, caring and democratic.

— Nancy

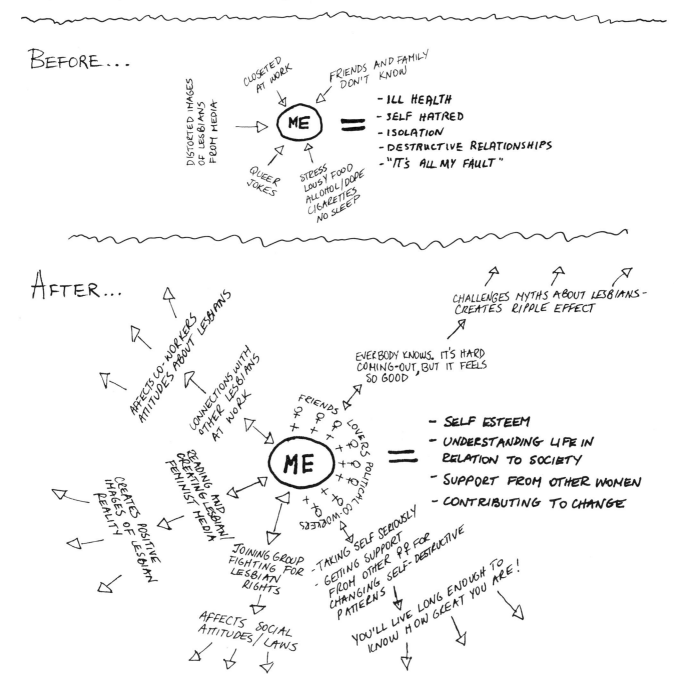

Somewhere to Start

☐ In some ways, our lives as women and lesbians can be thought of as life-long battles against the self-hatred our culture encourages us to feel. It is essential that we constantly remind ourselves to resist these destructive messages and behaviour.

☐ It is important to cultivate self-esteem and to get as healthy as you can. This section provides information on nutrition, stress management and emotional process. Use these ideas or read and research other techniques for achieving the same ends — or invent your own.

☐ Exchange with other women what you've learned about stopping self-destructive patterns. Being emotionally vulnerable is hard for most of us, but sharing feelings, contradictions, pain and confusion with other lesbians really does help.

Read, think and talk about how we've been socialized, how little affirmation there is of the reality of our lives. Together we *can* create friendship circles, political groups and communities where love and respect flourish.

Photo/ Dorothy Elias

*W*hen I look at my friends, I think
we are all getting stronger and
wiser and clearer and finer. Every one of us. We can all do things that would have been impossible for us five years ago. And we have all had, as they say, hard lives — politics, betrayals, disastrous relationships, poverty, children, pain, illness, stress. Some of us have been beaten up for being lesbians and some of us have been arrested and some of us have lost our children. Many of us see therapists and we still get depressed. But still, we are braver and stronger.

Sometimes late at night when I'm almost asleep, I think about life and journeys and wholeness and women, and I think maybe in this time, in this culture, living as a lesbian is the fastest, clearest way for a woman to know who she is, to get enough nurturing

and respect and loving to actually begin to live as a whole person. We all got so crippled by being brought up as a woman in this society. Our images of ourselves are so distorted and flawed and small.

Each of us has to somehow, some way throw out the lies about what being a 'woman' means, the lies about what being a 'lesbian' means — and fashion ourself and our life out of knowing nothing. We have nothing but ourselves to count on and maybe if we're really lucky and work really hard, some friends and lovers will be there to hold us when we cry. And that's a good start.

Ourselves. Our strengths. Our lovings. Our grievings. Our work. That's enough to take us somewhere. That's more — much more — than most women in this society have.

— Nym

Resources

Lesbian Health Matters! Mary O'Donnell et al (Santa Cruz Women's Health Collective) Based on a lesbian feminist perspective, this book is factual, wide-ranging and trustworthy. Deals with lesbian self-image, stress and the effects on our total health of living in an oppressive society. Available from: 250 Locust St., Santa Cruz CA 95060

Out from Under: Sober Dykes and Our Friends, ed. by Jean Swallow (San Francisco: Spinsters, Ink, 1983) Lesbians recovering from alcoholism and drug abuse share their process, analysis and visions. A clear and powerful statement of survival and hope. Has a fairly extensive bibliography.

In Our Own Hands: A Women's Book of Self-Help Therapy, Sheila Ernst and Lucy Goodison (Los Angeles: J.P. Tarcher Inc., 1981) Examines various therapy models: psychodrama, bodywork, gestalt, fantasies and meditation.

Includes a description of starting and maintaining a self-help group.

Our Bodies, Our Selves, The Boston Women's Health Book Collective (New York: Simon and Shuster, 1976)   The original and still the most comprehensive perspective on women's physical and psychological health. Has lesbian content.

Helping Ourselves: A Handbook for Women Starting Groups, Women's Counselling Referral and Education Centre (*WREC*) (Toronto: 1983)   "An easy-to-use practical book for women who want to share and solve problems with other women." WREC provides alternative mental health services to women. Available from: 348 College St., Toronto Ont. M5T 1S4

Getting Free: A Handbook for Women in Abusive Relationships, Ginny NiCarthy (Seattle: Seal Press, 1982)   For women in abusive heterosexual relationships, but teaches useful skills relating to problem-solving and taking control of your life.

Getting Clear: Bodywork for Women, Anne Kent Rush (New York: Random House, 1973)   "A book about female energy and how to use it". A classic, and not homophobic.

Solving Women's Problems, Hogie Wykoff (New York: Grove Press, 1977)   A radical therapy perspective on personal and social change. Practical and useful.

"I Thought People Like That Killed Themselves": Lesbians, Gay Men and Suicide, Eric Rofes (San Francisco: Grey Fox Press, 1983)   "The high risk of suicide among lesbians and gay men has long been neglected and misunderstood. Rofes presents a much needed, well-written and documented book that explodes the myth that homosexuality per se is self-destructive." — Del Martin and Phyllis Lyon.

Feminism as Therapy, Anica Vesel Mander and Anne Kent Rush (New York: Random House, 1974)   A basic overview.

The Radical Therapist, ed. by Jerome Agel (New York: Ballantine, 1971)   An anthology of writings from the radical therapy publication *Rough Times.* A number of articles relate to women and women's liberation.

Shadow on a Tightrope: Writings by Women on Fat Oppression, ed. by Lisa Schoenfielder and Barb Wieser (Iowa City: Aunt Lute Book, 1983)   "...articles, personal stories, poems by fat women about their lives and the fat-hating society in which they live." A feminist analysis with lesbian content. Available from P.O. Box 2723, Iowa City, IA 52244

The Obsession: Reflections on the Tyranny of Slenderness, Kim Chernin (New York: Harper Colophon, 1982)   Essays, feminist and somewhat literary.

Fat Liberator Publications, P.O. Box 342, New Haven CT   They produce and distribute materials relevant to the fat liberation movement.

Diaspora Press, P.O. Box 272, Langlois OR 97450   They produce fat liberation materials for lesbians only, including a calendar, *Images of Our Flesh.*

Some of the above Resources thanks to Bonnie Ramsay.

Groups

Alcoholics Anonymous (AA) is listed in your local phone book. In many cities there are gay AA groups and sometimes lesbian AA groups. For a complete international listing of gay/lesbian AA groups and information about starting such a group, write to the *International Advisory Council,* P.O. Box 492, Village Stn., New York NY 10014

Most cities have self-help or facilitated groups for lesbians dealing with problem areas in their lives. To find the local lesbian or gay group that can put you in touch with this informal network, see:

☐ *Finding Lesbian Resources*

See also Resources in:
☐ *Psychiatry and Therapy*
☐ *Violence*
☐ *Lovers and Sexuality*

I was tired of not knowing any lesbians who lived near me out in the Fraser Valley. Why didn't someone do something about that? This thought was immediately followed by the realization that I was the somebody...

Creating Communities

A woman spoke at the B.C. Federation of Women Convention. She was from Fort St. James or Hundred Mile or Quesnel or some little town up north. She was BCFW Regional Representative that year. She spoke about her year. About the trouble the local women's group got from the town when they put up International Women's Day posters with information about lesbian rights on them. And the struggles within the group about it. And about her being the only lesbian in the group. And the group falling apart. And the day-to-day struggle with the cold and the snow and the roads to get anywhere to do anything. And her partner, her friend, her lover — the only other lesbian she knew for 500 miles in any direction — being killed in a car accident.

She said she was ok now, though. She said it had been hard and that she was still a bit shaky. She wanted us to know that it wasn't easy being a feminist and a lesbian and trying to change the world in Fort St. James or Quesnel or Hundred Mile. She cried a bit when she was telling us. We cried too, listening. All 300 of us with our multiple relationships and our feminist therapists and our support groups and our lesbian political action groups and our telephones and our neighbours and our friends and our community. We all cried.

She went back home.

Maybe next year we can think of something a bit more useful than crying.

— *Nym*

I went to a conference on Women in Agriculture last fall in Oregon. I went because I am a farmer and a woman and wanted to meet and talk with other women interested in the kind of things I was. I also went because I am a lesbian and I was feeling very lonely and very crazy. I had country friends who weren't lesbians and city friends who were lesbians but I didn't have any friends who understood everything that was important to me.

There weren't any workshops listed about lesbianism at the conference. I knew 3 of the 200 women there. I tried to strike up conversations but I didn't quite know how to casually bring up lesbianism in the middle of fruit trees and produce marketing. The conference went from Friday to Sunday. By Saturday night I was feeling even more lonely and crazy than I had before coming. But, later that evening there was time for unstructured discussion groups and some brave woman had posted a notice that there would be a discussion of lesbians in the country in room 228. So I went.

There were about five other women in the room. We smiled tentatively at each other and found chairs. The door opened and another five women came in . . . and another three . . . and another ten. More and more and more women came into the room — each wearing the same tentative smile. By the time there were 50 women in the room, I was in tears. We went around the circle talking about where we lived and how our lives were. Almost everyone said how wonderful it was to be in this room with other country lesbians. Almost everyone said how they had kept looking around the conference and wondering . . .

We decided to create a Lesbians in Agriculture network, publish a regular newsletter and have weekend gatherings on different women's farms during the year. Many of us lived hundreds of miles apart and many of us would be going home to isolation and pretending, and our constant balancing act between loving the farming and needing some friends. But not quite the same as before. My *Lesbians in Agriculture* newsletter came in the mail yesterday. And we're planning a B.C. Rural Lesbian week on our farm this summer. And I know that there are at least 50 women scattered about the Pacific Northwest who do understand and who do think it's worth it.

— Nym

*T*his is a glimmer of a history of one community, Vancouver. I have decided to divide the lesbians of the 60's into three groups just as a way of organizing this, even though I know that we are not that easily divided and that many women might resent the way I label the groups. The three groups are: bar dykes, professional women who are lesbians, and heterosexual lesbians (I put myself in this last category).

The first woman I talked to was a bar dyke and here is a bit of her story.

In the 60's, the lesbian network operating in Vancouver was mostly around booze. There was the Montreal Club, the Vanport, the 725 Club and the New Fountain. These places were mostly situated around Main and Hastings, and mostly working class gays and lesbians went there, as well as the lesbians who had dropped out of society. There was a lot of serious role-playing and very little tolerance for those women who could not decide whether they were butch or femme. Bi-sexuality was a no-no.

There was harassment by the police, especially of minors. The women who played the butch role could be and were arrested for cross-dressing. These women had their own code of behaviour. Monogamy was in. The double standard that existed in heterosexual relationships existed for them as well — femme woman could not play around or even dance with another butch, but the butch could. The women who were butch could not show their feelings or get emotional support from each other. The women in the femme role could be emotional and were allowed to support each other.

The woman I talked to said that most butches, including herself, really wanted to be men. It was acceptable in her group for the butch to beat up on her lover if she felt so inclined.

They had an informal network that enabled them to get jobs. They supported each other against outsiders and knew that the cops were their enemies.

The second group was professional women who were lesbians. They met in small numbers at each other's houses. Their lives and styles of dress were not blatant and they only talked about their sexual choices to a few friends, some of whom were heterosexual. Some of these women did not think of themselves as lesbians or gay — they just happened to be in love with a particular woman. Their identity was their occupation, not their sexuality. They led relatively quiet lives.

The third group was the heterosexual lesbian. These are women like myself who either knew they were lesbians from an early age but never acted on it and after many years of celibacy ended up married or women who never even let themselves know that they were attracted to women. So in the 60's this group was living a heterosexual existence.

So we had our bar dyke, blatant in behaviour and dress; the professional women, living their quiet lives; a large proportion of us hiding behind the institution of heterosexuality; and a few, very few, women active in the homosexual rights movement.

Now for the 70's . . . in 1971, women from the Women's Caucus, the Women's Liberation Group and the Voice of Women were organizing the Indochinese Women's Conference. While organizing this conference, lesbian women decided that they had to start talking about the politics of lesbianism. They met with a great deal of resistance when they tried to make this issue part of the conference.

This conference seemed to be the first sign of lesbians in Vancouver emerging as political beings organizing around their own oppression. There were over 50 lesbians at the conference — a lot of them from the United States. While the conference was going on, most of the lesbians stayed at two houses. As one woman said, "All I remember was wall-to-wall lesbians."

Some of the lesbians who had come from the States were wearing buttons that said "Lesbianism is Revolutionary." One woman who was not a lesbian at the time remembers thinking that it was weird that a woman would wear that button and also be wearing a skirt.

After the Indochinese conference, political lesbianism became visible. In 1972 a Women's Place was created — an old house made into a space organized by women for women. A few lesbians took over the top floor for a Lesbian Resource Centre. Soon after, the Lesbian Drop-In started at the Women's Bookstore. Later, there were complaints that this drop-in was too political and so a second drop-in was started for lesbians who were not interested in politics.

In 1976, policy on lesbian rights was passed unanimously at the B.C. Federation of Women convention. Sounds good — passed unanimously. The truth is that a long hard struggle preceded the vote and quite a number of women quit the B.C.F.W. over the issue.

There were talks given on lesbianism at colleges, universities and a few schools. The B.C.F.W. Rights of Lesbians Subcommittee began giving workshops on lesbianism and how it fit into feminism. The sound of lesbian music drifted in from across the border and we now had Lavender Jane loving women and Meg Christian and her gym teacher. Later came the Lesbian Information Line (LIL), and the Lesbian Show on Co-op Radio, and the Over Forty Lesbian Drop-In, and the Younger Lesbians, and the Lesbian Mothers' Groups, and Lesbian and Feminist Mothers Political Action Group, and the Lesbian Defense Fund.

We started using the word "lesbian" when we applied for a liquor licence or rented a hall. We applied for grants to straight organizations like Secretary of State and the Human Rights Commission. We postered in libraries, welfare offices and colleges. We went on TV. We made videos and films. We did a lot. But we have a lot more to do.

Before the 70's, individual lesbians fought the police. They defied society with their manner of dress and their unacceptable behaviour. Nobody wanted them. They were like crabgrass coming through the sidewalks. Society had no use for them. They got stepped on — but they kept coming.

In the 70's we saw the different action groups forming and, like the individual lesbians who went before us, we were not wanted.

But whether they want us or not, we are here to stay. Proud of ourselves as lesbians. Proud of ourselves as women who choose to love women.

— Dorrie

Isolation — not knowing or being friends with other lesbians — is often a source of pain in our lives. Having contact with other lesbians is crucial, and lesbians have always found ways to create communities: loose networks of women related by friendship, shared social spaces like bars or clubs, mutual interests and activities — or simply by geographic location. We learn alot about what it means to be a lesbian from the lesbians we know. Our communities shape our self-definition.

Although it is most certainly a myth that all lesbians live in large cities, it is unfortunately true that the most easy-to-find lesbian communities exist in urban areas. Since the early 70's, there has been a blossoming of cultural, educational, service and political options for women, straight and lesbian. In some cities, you can socialize with other lesbians, have your car repaired by women, receive health care and emotional support in crisis from feminist and lesbian sources, live in a women's housing co-op or a lesbian collective house, participate in sports on a lesbian team, get cultural stimulation from feminist musicians, artists, dancers, listen to lesbian radio shows. . .sometimes even earn your living working cooperatively with other women.

The existence of such communities has been of immense benefit to many, many lesbians who might otherwise have been isolated from each other. For many lesbians who have come-out in the past few years, being part of a community *is* what being a lesbian is all about.

But whether we're talking about a large city or a small town, our communities do not just happen. They exist because women *organized* them.

*T*his is a story of how lesbians in one rural community began to organize. In 1981, the Canadian Lesbian Conference was held in Vancouver, B.C. I had been asked to co-chair a workshop on Rural Lesbians. Over 30 women from various communities in Canada came to the workshop. We discussed many things, one of the most important being our isolation as lesbians. We talked about how very difficult it was to meet each other, and what we could do to begin to end our isolation. This was especially relevant for me because there were women from at least three B.C. rural communities at the workshop, and none of us knew each other. It was interesting, exciting, challenging, stimulating and, as these things do, it ended and we all went home.

About two months later, I became increasingly aware that all of my friends lived in Vancouver. I was tired of not knowing any lesbians who lived near me out in the Fraser Valley. Why didn't somebody do something about that? This thought was immediately followed by the realization that *I* was the somebody, and if I wanted something done about my isolation, I was going to have to make the time, get busy and do it. But what? How to find and connect with other lesbians in such a straight, rural community?

I felt very awkward. I had never done any concrete organizing before and I had no contact with anyone else who had tried to reach lesbians in a small community. There wasn't a women's centre to use as a starting point. The only way I could think of to break the silence was to put an ad in the 'Coming Events' section of the local newspaper and hope for some response.

The ad said "RURAL LESBIAN PICNIC" followed by the date and a contact number: "Saturday, August 15th, Mission. 826-9922 for further information." I

delivered it to the papers in four local communities and they all accepted the ad with no questions or hesitation. So I waited to see what would happen, and I didn't have to wait long!

The morning after the paper with the ad appeared, I was informed by my boss that the mill where I had been employed for five years was 'cutting back' and no longer needed my services. It had nothing to do with the ad, of course, merely an unfortunate coincidence. I suppose it was also an unfortunate coincidence when they changed their minds and hired someone else to replace me almost immediately. And my phone began to ring. In the week before the day of the picnic, over 35 women called. I was simply astonished. In the end, only 3 of my friends came to the picnic. But still, all those women had called.

My next idea was to put another ad in two local papers advertising a Thursday Night Lesbian Drop-In in Mission. I again put in my phone number with no address. And again the phone rang and rang. And, to my amazement, six women came to the first Drop-In. So we decided to continue having the Drop-In every second Thursday night in my home. More and more women began to attend, and even more called for information.

The Lesbian Drop-In in Mission has been going for nearly a year now. In that time, almost 100 women have called to talk with me and get more information. Many of the callers are afraid to identify themselves, afraid of what would happen to them if they became visible as lesbians in such a small town. But, over 30 women have come to meet other lesbians at the Drop-In. There is a core group of 15 women who come fairly regularly, and several more who 'drop-in'

occasionally. Every lesbian who has seen the ad in the paper feels a little less alone! Whether or not she picks up the phone and dials the number, or even steps foot in the Drop-In, she knows that there are others.

None of this has come easily or without conflict. Both local papers have printed a number of Letters to the Editor in response to our little ad. The letters range from absurd to abusive. The papers have also printed, unedited, two letters from us. There have been phone calls ranging from teenagers gigling, silence, religious tirades and verbal abuse. Those are hard to cope with. For awhile, I was so tense about potentially angry calls that every time the phone rang, I got knots in my stomach and would want to throw up. Fortunately, that was balanced by the calls from women who said how excited they were to finally realize that they were not the only lesbians in the Fraser Valley.

I think we have been very lucky. I took an enormous risk by giving out my address to any woman who called and said she was interested in coming to the Drop-In. I worried that someone would give the address to a group of angry men who would show up on my doorstep Thursday night ready to run the lesbians out of town. I decided, though, that I wanted to make it as easy as possible for women to come out of their homes and begin to see and talk with other lesbians. I didn't want to grill them on the phone or to set up a strict criteria about who could come to the Drop-In. I figured we could deal with any problems as they came up. So far, only women who were serious about the Drop-In have come, and we have not been 'set up'.

Most of the women who come to the Drop-In are

afraid of being found out, but they come anyway. and they come again, often bringing friends. Each woman who comes contributes some money to pay for coffee and the cost of running the ad in the paper. Most of the women are not political, although some identify as feminist. We choose topics to discuss, including politics, what is feminism, coming out, telling your family, living as a lesbian farmer, dealing with relationships, children, jobs.

To my delight, the Drop-In took on the project of planning a Workshop on Lesbianism for the public, which was held on March 27th, 1982, a national Lesbian Awareness Day. Some of us went out postering to advertise the workshop, others passed out leaflets, some helped with the phone and advertising costs. We advertised in two local papers, and waited to see who would attend our Community Forum on Lesbianism. It seemed like an important project, given the emotional response manifested in the letters to the Editor every single week.

We organized the workshop as a panel presentation at the local Community College. Five lesbians spoke on topics that included a history of the Mission Lesbian Drop-In and the community forum, living as lesbians, the myths about lesbians and our reality, lesbians and the church, lesbian mothers and community responsibility. About 20 people attended, and we have been asked to plan more public information sessions for various groups in the future.

Unfortunately, the hostile elements of the community did not attend the forum. This gave us no opportunity to reach them to answer some of their fears and to provide them with correct information on lesbianism. I guess we'll have to keep up with the Letters to the Editor. I am ambivalent, at this point, as to whether or not it is possible to do more than reach people who are already inclined to support lesbians. The others who react hysterically seem to have completely closed minds.

I still think that providing accurate, factual information about lesbians, even to a few supportive people, can have potentially far-reaching effects. They can use that information in areas they work in, with people they know, people we would not otherwise reach. The circle widens, and people are less likely to make negative comments about lesbians when they know their friends will call them on their homophobia.

Bit by bit, one step at a time, lesbians in the Fraser Valley are building a support system, social network, a community for ourselves. And we are making an impact on the larger community — with one tiny ad in the back of the Classified section. Not one week goes by in the Fraser Valley where the word lesbian does not come up in the papers. I can bet that most major papers in the country don't mention lesbian nearly that often. We have broken the silence, and made ourselves visible. People may not like it, but everyone knows we exist, right here — not just in the big city. That is information I wish I had had when I was growing up and wondering about my life choices.

I am moving to the interior of B.C. this summer, and already arrangements have been made to keep the Drop-In going without me. The women who attend want it to be a weekly event. The ad will continue. New projects will be taken on. New ways will be figured out to connect with other Rural Lesbians to pass on what we have learned and to learn from the experiences of others. New women will come. New stories will be heard. New problems we will have to find ways to solve together. And each of us separately, and this new 'us' together, will continue to grow, to change and to carry on. We will never again be completely alone.

— Yvonne

Organizing a Lesbian Conference

One of the most effective ways of making connection with other lesbians is to have a widely-publicized weekend gathering. Lesbians have organized festivals, workshops, film festivals, seminars, and conferences. Such events are often powerful demonstrations of the strength and diversity of our communities. They can also be the birthplace of numerous new lesbian groups — not to mention new friendships.

The idea of organizing a festival or conference can seem totally overwhelming, especially if you are sitting there all alone, thinking about it. Take it step-by-step and not only will you organize a successful event, but you'll be in good enough shape to enjoy it yourself!

Figure out what you want   Make a list of your personal goals relating to the organizing and the event. Maybe you want to work with other lesbians. Perhaps you want to make some friends; or meet enough lesbians to form some sort of ongoing group; or bridge some of the gaps between lesbians in your area. Maybe you want to start a newsletter or find another lesbian who works in the same field as you. And perhaps you just want to sit in the same room with a hundred other lesbians, trade stories and feel the relief of seeing that there are *lots* of you after all. Write all your goals down. You may not achieve them all, but it is useful to have them in mind.

Find lesbians to work with you It is infinitely preferable to find *many* other lesbians to work with you, but a group of three can accomplish an amazing amount. If you approach women to help organize the project and they say no, make sure you ask, "Would you be able to do anything closer to the time of the event? Could you do some specific short-term work at the conference?" Keep lists of women who say they will help later.

If one of your goals is to have a wide range of lesbians come to the event, it is extremely useful to have lesbians from different social and political groupings in the organizing group. They will already have contacts within their friendship circles and will be in a better position to encourage their friends to come. Often we will take the risk of going to a lesbian event because our friends are going or because we know one of the women who organized it.

Have an exciting first meeting Tape big sheets of paper up on the wall; then all the women can let their imaginations and magic markers run wild answering questions like: What do you want to happen at the event? Who do you want to come? How do you want to feel?

Don't worry about practicality at this point. As well as giving you all ideas for the event, this brain-storming will help you get to know each other. Women who share in the work of envisioning an event and then making their vision real will stick with the work. It's when a woman finds herself working on something that isn't really her idea and doesn't really meet any of her immediate needs that she is likely to withdraw.

Organize your organizing group Make decisions about how often you meet and where. Do you want more women to join you? How will you get them involved? How will you keep track of your decisions? Will you take minutes at each meeting and put them in a binder for group reference? What will you do if you disagree with each other as you almost inevitably will? What are your experiences in groups that worked well? That worked poorly? How can you share the responsibility, the work and the power fairly? What do you want to learn from the process of working together on this event?

If the group has a vision of what the event will be like and what your goals are in making it happen, decisions made along the way can be evaluated against that shared goal. A level of tolerance for differing viewpoints is helpful as is an ability to compromise.

Decisions often have to be made quite quickly. Tell yourselves that you may and probably will make mistakes, that this is a learning process for all of you, that no one knows how to do a perfect job organizing something. Having women leave the organizing group because of unresolved conflict or because they feel unheard and powerless is perhaps a greater evil than a less-than-perfect event. (See *Notes to Facilitators* for more on effectively structuring meetings and keeping working groups functioning.)

Get the work done This is one way of organizing to get work done fairly efficiently. Make a list of what tasks need to be done. Most events would include: the programme, childcare, access for disabled women, food, dance or social, location, publicity, fundraising, finances and security. A small group of women form a committee or work group to accomplish one task. Meetings of the whole group for co-ordination, information-sharing and major decision-making are held once a month or every two weeks as the event draws near. The work groups meet and work in between.

The ideal organizing group would have enough women that each worked only on one task. If this is not possible, then clump different tasks together and have each work group be responsible for two or three tasks. If a woman works on more than one work group she can end up going to an awful lot of meetings and get very tired.

Think about money Probably you don't have any — and you'll need it. In larger communities, the first task of the group might well be to organize a fundraising social event. Ask a financially solvent lesbian or two to give the group a donation or at least a no-interest loan of a couple of hundred dollars. Keep your organizing and event costs as low as possible. Try to find someone to donate space instead of renting. See if any group members have access to photocopiers, typewriters, paper or other resources you will need.

What will you charge women to come to the event? Will you have a sliding scale to reflect our different financial positions? Can women with no money come? In your advertising solicit donations. Ask lesbian and gay groups in your province for donations. They probably don't have any money either, but a city group has access to more lesbians and can raise $100 easier than you can.

Pick a date Decide when your event will be held. Base your decision on how long it will take to organize. Probably longer than you think — at least 6 months for a major festival or conference and preferably 10 months. When is a good time for women in your area to attend? When is travel possible? Impossible? When are women most busy? Is good weather necessary?

Pick a location What kind of facilities do you need? How many women might come? Will you need many rooms? One large room? Keep in mind issues of accessibility for disabled women, childcare needs, kitchen facilities, proximity to public transit, etc. If a perfect solution to the location question comes to you, good. Otherwise leave it for a month or so while everyone thinks, or have a couple of women research location possibilities. It is really quite important to have a definite confirmed location at least three months before the event so you can do adequate advertising.

Planning the Programme   Decide what you want to have happen within the time frame of the event. Make a rough agenda. Don't forget that you want women to enjoy this weekend. Plan for it. Don't schedule things for an early morning if you are planning a late social event the night before. You want to provide women with a sense of accomplishment and participation.

Remember that some of the most exciting and productive connections at lesbian gatherings happen in unstructured time.

A successful event offers:

*Opportunities for each woman to speak and be heard (such as small groups, rounds, unstructured social time).

*A chance to feel connected to a large number of other lesbians (in plenaries, cultural performances, dances, singing together, rallies).

*A chance to meet new friends (small groups, working together on shared work shifts, activities like playing baseball).

*Ways of learning more about other lesbians (workshops about the realities of our lives, structures which encourage respect and listening rather than criticism and argument).

*Experiences which increase lesbians' sense of self-worth (cultural celebrations, success stories of organizing, strategies for increased connection and effective social change, having a good time at the event and liking the other lesbians there, etc., etc.).

Unless your organizing group has a good representation of mothers, lesbians of colour, working class lesbians and lesbians with disabilities you can be pretty sure that you will organize an event that is inaccessible to many women. If you're in this situation, make a better event by asking lesbians who experience additional kinds of oppression how the event could be open to and useful to them. Listen and then do what you've been asked to do.

Be inventive! Be creative! Be bold! How they organize a conference in Toronto may be totally inappropriate in northern British Columbia.

Think about safety and confidentiality   Lesbians, for very good reasons, are often fearful of attending events where they may be identified publicly as lesbians. How will you protect women's anonymity?

LESBIANS, HOMOSEXUAL WOMEN, DYKES, GAY WOMEN—ALL WOMEN LOVING WOMEN

1983 B.C. REGIONAL LESBIAN CONFERENCE
COME ENJOY A WEEKEND OF WORKSHOPS, DANCING, MEETING, SHARING, EATING, ORGANIZING, RELAXING AND MUCH MORE

WORKSHOPS AND SUPPORT GROUPS INCLUDE:		OTHER EVENTS INCLUDE:
—organizing together	—tolerance in the lesbian community	—cabaret
—coming out or not	—classism	—dance
—racism	—rural lesbians	—pride parade
	—third world lesbians	—art show
	—lesbian mothers	—sport:
	. . . and more	—pool tournament

TOP QUALITY CHILDCARE INCLUDING OUTINGS WORKSHOPS, FILMS, CRAFTS AND MUCH MORE . . .

MAY 20th to 23rd
TROUT LAKE COMMUNITY CENTRE
3350 VICTORIA DRIVE, VANCOUVER
WHEELCHAIR ACCESSIBLE / SIGN LANGUAGE
ATTENDANTS 876-0225 / INTERPRETED

Poster/Alison Kase

Do you want press coverage? By gay and feminist media only? By straight media? How will you advertise the event? In a rural area where gossip is a favourite community pastime, the safest way to organize a lesbian event might be to hold it at someone's house or land, have absolutely no media attending and advertise using a box number as your return address.

It is the responsibility of the security work group to ensure the on-site physical safety of the women and children present at the event. Some basics to consider are: will security women watch entrances to events to make sure only women come in? How will you communicate with each other? How will your security women be trained? Do you have a commitment to non-violence? Under what circumstances do you call the police? Have you made sure that all women at the event know about the security plans? Can your security women be identified by armbands? Have you set up adequate first-aid provisions? (Also see *Violence*)

Enjoy the process of working   Have short efficient meetings and make time for socializing afterwards. Organizing anything is a lot of hard work. Exhaustion is common and tempers can fray. Kindness and consideration of each other's needs and moods is important. The overall feeling of working together will never be uninterrupted bliss. But if the majority of you aren't feeling excited, productive and at least sporadically joyful, take time to ask each other what you aren't getting from the work and what you could do about it.

Some common causes of despair and disillusionment are:

* Trying to do more work than is humanly possible and feeling isolated and guilty.

* Having a strong disagreement with a specific decision or a general direction of the group and either not talking about it directly or feeling that you are not listened to when you try to talk.

* Feeling that the work you are doing is unseen and unappreciated.

* Feeling that a small group within the larger group is controlling the decision-making and you have no way to confront it.

* Feeling that you have conflicts in communication and style with one or several group members and no way to ask for help in resolving that conflict.

* Feeling that your work in the group is complicated by your emotional history with one or more members — current lovers, old lovers, etc., etc.

Do a dress rehearsal   Use big sheets of paper again and have the whole group imagine in detail what is going to be done when and by whom. Try to think of all the possible problems that might arise. What if only 20 women come? What if 200 women come and

We think that a successful conference should leave women with a taste for more: more contact with more lesbians; an increased commitment to offer time, money and skills to lesbian projects; excitement and belief that if we plan carefully we can all get more of what we need to survive. A good conference would leave us with an increased awareness of the position of lesbians in this society and a feeling of respect for the unique struggles of each of us. Lesbians would leave a great conference knowing that we can create at least some places where we can be real, where we can be valued, where we can be whole.

there isn't enough food? What if there are hostile men outside of the dance? What if a woman gets emotionally overwhelmed during a workshop? Who do you know is coming? What are their expectations?

Enjoy the event   The organizing group might like to get together for celebration and hysteria immediately afterwards.

Have an evaluation meeting   Get together within two weeks to compare your goals with what actually happened. Success could be measured by: the number of women who came, the bringing together of groups of lesbians who ordinarily don't communicate, the formation of ongoing groups or projects, the emotional tone of respect and celebration during the weekend, or the mere fact that you did it! You pulled it off!

Lesbian communities are crucial to our survival. They can also be stressful, divided and intolerant. Our perspective — coming from a primarily feminist-identified community in Vancouver — is limited, but we think it is relevant to many lesbian communities.

For many of us, coming-out and starting our 'new lives' as lesbians involves looking for models. We want to know the 'rules' of being a lesbian. We want some sense of what we can expect of our lives, of what our friends and lovers will expect of us. We are not overly tolerant of each other's differences. We forget our pasts. We have such a sense of urgency to create the future that we are impatient and sometimes cruel. We make mistakes. We don't know how to integrate our sexuality and our friendships, our politics and our

personal lives. We don't know how to deal with conflicts and differences, how to most effectively create change.

Although we reject society's view of lesbians, we tend to create definitions of our own that are equally restrictive and generally as untrue for the majority of lesbians. Our communities mirror the oppressive realities of the larger society. They remain, in large part, white and middle-class. These are the women who are visible, these are the values, attitudes and privileges assumed to be universal. We have been conditioned to be racist, to hold on tight to our class privileges, to not take into serious consideration women with physical or mental disabilities. Our communities are alien and irrelevant to many lesbians.

Guilt and polarization are not productive in building healthy lesbian communities. But refusing to look at the very real differences in options available to us due to this society's racism and class structure — and they're intrinsically linked — is guaranteed to perpetuate oppression. Our goal must be to learn, and then to act *on what we've discovered.*

Racism

We live in a society built on racist ideologies and practices; women of colour have amply documented the racism that permeates the women's movement and white lesbian communities. All of us would do well to read books by and about women of colour and third world women.

Lesbians of colour have found that getting together with other lesbians of colour is essential. Political and support groups, social networks and formalized caucuses within political organizations are all necessary for emotional support, affirming a shared reality and achieving political goals. They're also useful for demanding changes from white women.

If you are white, get together with other white women to talk about how you have internalized racist ideology. What did you learn about people of colour: Black people? Native people? Oriental people? Asian people? What messages did you get from your families? What are your experiences? How does racism operate in the world? in your life? at your workplace? your social circles? your political groups?

What can you do? Do you challenge racist remarks and jokes immediately? Do you know what groups are fighting racism in your area and are you supporting them? Are there organized groups of lesbians of colour in your area, and have you asked for their criticisms of the lesbian community? Are the connections between sexism, racism and homophobia made clear in your group's writings and presentations? Are you assuming that your materials reflect an anti-racist perspective without checking it out?

Classism

We have all been taught to blur class distinctions, to think that any individual who tries hard enough can make it and anyone who hasn't 'made it' just isn't trying. Myths which deny class damage us, and the realities of both our class backgrounds and present class identification affect us deeply. All of us can participate in consciousness-raising about class.

As working-class lesbians we've found it necessary to identify publicly as working-class in order to confront stereotypes and escape invisibility. Forming connections with other lesbians who also identify as working-class — either in formal or informal caucuses within political groups and in friendship circles — has been crucial.

Get together with several women and commit yourselves to a process of study — with lots of emotional moments. Talk about your lives. Each woman can trace her family history, including the racial background, education, occupation and life circumstances of family members. Recall the myths you learned growing up: what are poor people like? why are people poor? what are middle-class 'values'? what is the 'right' way to live? How do you live now? What access do you have to education, jobs and money? What are the differences among you?

Study the issue of class within your political groups: examine your own life situations, exchange relevant books and articles and start incorporating a class analysis into your work. Make sure this analysis is reflected in your literature and presentations.

Other tensions and conflict occurring within lesbian communities are outgrowths of our internalized oppression as women and as lesbians in this culture. As women, we are not very practiced at being powerful. We are unskilled at equal relationships; we haven't been brought up to work together. Often we are much better at nurturing others than at getting what we need for ourselves. Feminist beliefs give us a whole new set of ethics and values to try and live up to

— and more ammunition for berating ourselves and each other when we fail.

For many of us, it has been a relatively easy slide from heterosexuality to becoming a feminist and identifying as a lesbian — all within the protection of fairly supportive circles. Many of us have never come-out to anyone but our friends, lesbian co-workers and sympathetic feminists. We only know lesbianism from

Photo/ Sarah Davidson

within the safety of the women's community. And we never plan to go beyond that.

That often keeps us sheltered from the reality of thousands of other women who call themselves dykes, gay women or lesbians, and for whom that is both their identification and place of fighting back. Not many lesbians have the protection of the women's movement. The relative safety of the feminist community gives us the luxury of being intolerant, of looking at the lesbian with make-up and skirt and saying, "You don't belong here." Or saying to another lesbian, "You're still living with your husband and male children; leave them and then you'll be welcome here." Or thinking, "They're not feminists; why bother talking to them?" We make few opportunities for *all* lesbians to tell their stories, to have a place to receive the emotional support and intellectual understanding we all need.

We have to get serious about creating communities that offer something real for every lesbian.

Being tolerant of the differences amongst us does not mean a passive acceptance of them. They *do* matter: often they are based on differences in class, race, social status, age, physical or mental abilities — differences based on power and privilege. We must find constructive ways of eliminating inequalities, but there's not much hope of doing so if we aren't even speaking to one other! We have so much work to do to change the prevailing attitude towards homosexuals and lesbians as being perverts — sick people who need to be cured, saved, locked up, treated, a social disease to be prevented — that we need all lesbians, working from wherever they may be.

Somewhere to Start

☐ Find other lesbians! It may take a visit to a city, attendance at a meeting of the gay group in the next town, a letter to a women's or gay newspaper — but it's really important to at least make contact with other lesbians in your area. You can then create ways to connect with and support each other.

☐ Once you're in contact with even one or two other lesbians, an effective way of getting together is to have a once-a-month potluck supper and evening. The event can rotate around different women's homes and be as low-key or as intensive as the group wishes. Women can take turns planning the evening: discussions, films, videos, strategy sessions on custody or job protection are all possibilities. Contact the women's bookstore nearest you and arrange to get books, magazines and records on lesbianism and feminism to sell on consignment at these gatherings.

It may take a while before women start coming in droves to your monthly events, but eventually more will appear. You could list yourself as a group with a contact address and phone number in women's and gay publications, even in community service directories. (Think before you start publicizing your address and phone number; especially in small towns, you may want to pick up mail and messages care of another group).

☐ Once you have an on-going group, even if it's a small one, you could begin to plan some actions. Set up a newsletter, a women's concert, a dance, a drop-in at the local community college. Send speakers to community or church groups (in other towns, if necessary). Organize a weekend workshop to teach and learn skills for dealing with stress and isolation, to discuss ways of helping each other with the problems of your lives.

☐ Vital communities are built by making events, groups and resources available to a large variety of women. The planning for all lesbian and feminist events, be they meetings, conferences, rallies, dances or concerts should routinely take into account the following matters — and routinely invite feedback. *Quality childcare* is needed as a means of allowing parenting women and their children to fully participate. *Wheelchair accessiblity* is essential, as is transportation to and from events for women in wheelchairs. The needs of women with hearing impairments can be addressed by ensuring that events are *signed*. Considerations should be given to women's *allergies,* such as cigarette smoke.

☐ The advertising for our events and services should clearly state that *all* women or *all* lesbians are welcome, if this is the case. Information about the availability of childcare or wheelchair accessibility, for instance, should be given and a telephone number listed where further details can be sought.

☐ A varied selection of non-alcoholic beverages must be provided at our events. Going one step further, holding a chemical and alcohol-free event, such as a dance or conference, is a way of including women who will not attend if alcohol is present, as well as giving us all a chance to enjoy ourselves sober.

☐ Part of making a community accessible is making it easy to find. Printed materials that advertise lesbian, feminist and gay events and services should be distributed not only to obvious places like bookstores and bars, but as widely as possible. Community centres, libraries, schools, shopping centre notice boards, laundromats, community health or legal clinics and recreation facilities are all appropriate postering and pamphletting targets. Notices of our community events can also be sent in to newspaper 'Community Calendars' or classifieds, and to television and radio stations for community announcements.

Even government and non-government social service agencies should be informed that there is, for instance, a drop-in for young lesbians so that they can pass this information along.

☐ You or your group could take on the project of compiling and distributing a list of existing resources for lesbians. Such a list could include all lesbian, gay and feminist groups, as well as information about other progressive networks: food and housing co-ops, childcare groups, etc.

☐ Producing and distributing posters, articles and leaflets in different languages (or several together) is an effective way to contact many women. Similarly, simultaneous translation and/or multi-lingual programmes and events enable more of us to attend and make our voices heard.

☐ The words we use to advertise our events or to communicate our message in informational pamphlets or newspapers should be carefully considered in order to avoid speaking 'in code'. A rousing incitement to 'Smash The Patriarchy' might get interpreted as a violent dislike of a certain china pattern. Also, we don't all identify with the same words and images. Not every woman who loves women thinks of herself as a 'lesbian' — there are plenty of dykes and gay women, too. Visual materials should represent our many ages, races and physical make-ups.

☐ Having places for lesbians to gather is really important. A drop-in only requires a room and a bit of advertising to start, and can offer vital ongoing contact and support. A social and cultural space other than the bars is also a boon to our communities: a weekly/monthly coffee-house in loaned or rented space can provide us with the nourishment of music, films, art displays, speakers, theatre, as well as a central depot for loading and unloading information about our lives and work.

Resources

Sunday's Women: A Report on Lesbian Life Today, Sasha Gregory Lewis (Boston: Beacon Press, 1979) An interesting, but limited, sociological study.

Lesbian Connection: For, By and About Lesbians, Ambitious Amazons, Helen Diner Memorial Women's Center, P.O. Box 811, East Lansing MI 48823 Published about six times a year, this newsletter contains piles of information submitted by its readers about their lesbian communities and events. Mainly U.S., but some Canadian. Includes lists of "Contact Dykes" in rural and urban areas.

Children and Feminism, Lesbian and Feminist Mothers Political Action Group (Vancouver: 1982) An in-depth discussion of integrating children and mothers into our communities, as well as an invaluable guide to organizing childcare at events. Available from LAFMPAG, P.O. Box 65804, Stn. F, Vancouver B.C.

Our Own: Newsletter of the Older Women's Network, P.O. Box 6647, Santa Barbara CA 95054

The following are useful resources for fighting racism and classism in our communities.

This Bridge Called My Back: Writings by Radical Women of Colour, ed. by Cherríe Moraga and Gloria Anzaldúa (Watertown: Persephone Press, 1981) "An uncompromised definition of feminism by women of colour in the United States." Documents the analytical and lived links between racism, sexism, heterosexism and classism, and looks at the racism and elitism of our communities. Passionate, powerful, invaluable. (Available from Kitchen Table Press.)

Top Ranking: Racism and Classism in the Lesbian Community, Joan Gibbs and Sara Bennett (Brooklyn: February 3rd Press, 1980) Articles by Black and white lesbians describing and analyzing the existence of and struggles against race and class oppression in prisons, lesbian and women's communities and society in general. Available from 306 Lafayette Ave., Brooklyn NY 11238

Las Mujeres: Conversations from a Hispanic Community, ed. by Nan Elsasser et al (Old Westbury: The Feminist Press, 1980) An oral history of four generations of Hispanic women of New Mexico, including the story of a lesbian.

Nice Jewish Girls: A Lesbian Anthology, ed. by Evelyn Torton Beck (Watertown: Persephone Press, 1982) Wide-ranging and passionate exploration of being Jewish and lesbian. Examines anti-semitism in the lesbian feminist community. Essential reading.

Black Lesbian in White America, Anita Cornwall (Tallahassee: Naiad Press, 1983) Writings by a Black activist about her experiences in the civil rights, feminist and lesbian movements.

Black Lesbians: An Annotated Bibliography, J.R. Roberts (Tallahassee: Naiad Press, 1981) A comprehensive guide to materials by and about Black lesbians in the U.S., from an ancient legend of Black Amazons in present-day California to contemporary activism in the Black and Third World gay rights movement. A rich book.

All the Women are White, All the Blacks are Men, But Some of Us are Brave: Black Women's Studies, ed. by Gloria T. Hull et al (Old Westbury: The Feminist Press, 1982) An extensive anthology with sections on Black feminism and lesbianism. Includes an article that offers guidelines for conducting consciousness-raising sessions for women's groups working on racism — their own and the movement's.

"Racism is the Issue" *Heresies* #15 (Fall, 1982) A powerful collection that addresses racism (mainly in the U.S.) through poetry, analysis, history, journal excerpts and art. Available from 225 Lafayette St., New York NY 10012

No Turning Back: Lesbian and Gay Liberation for the 80's, by Gerre Goodman et al (Philadelphia: New Society Publishers, 1983) A book that addresses a broad range of issues, including classism in lesbian and gay communities and movements, and racism (advice by white people for white people). Available from 4722 Baltimore Ave., Philadelphia PA 19143

Azalea P.O. Box 200, Cooper Stn. New York NY 10276 A magazine by and about Third World lesbians.

The Other Black Woman: An International Magazine for Women, Suite D43, #72 - 15 41st Ave., Jackson Heights, New York NY A Black lesbian quarterly.

Subscribing to lesbian and feminist publications is the best way to learn about the experiences, successes and failures of other lesbian communities. For lists of these publications, and groups, see:

☐ *Finding Lesbian Resources*

See also Resources in:

☐ *How Do You Know?*
☐ *Fighting Internalized Oppression*

Photo/ Nicky Hood

At the age of 18, the ideas of feminism offered me a way to make sense of the world, a place to stand, an explanation.

Seeing Our Lives Politically

How often have you heard lesbians talk as though there were two kinds of lesbians, political and non-political — as though those were genetic categories? You either are, or you're not.

How often have you heard lesbians who identify as political, perhaps as feminists or as gay activists, lament the apolitical nature of other lesbians? "Oh, I have nothing in common with those women — all they care about is drinking and dancing. They have no political sense at all."

How often have you heard lesbians who are trying to get into political activity for the first time, or even in a new city, tell stories of feeling totally out of it, of not understanding what women are talking about, of feeling put down, not listened to, ignored?

How often have you heard lesbians say that political activists are all arrogant, that they see themselves as better than other lesbians? That they're critical and prudish and generally bad news?

Being, or not being, 'political' is clearly an area of emotion and conflict for us as lesbians. This is reflected by the many prejudices in our communities — and society at large — against seeing our lives politically.

What *is* this thing called political activism? For us, political activity is anything we do to make our own lives, our society and our world more fair, healthy and free. It means working — and fighting — to end the inequalities and dangers that we face. It means figuring out together what kind of world we want and what we can do to make it happen. Political activism can take any number of routes. It could be working to

influence present political structures, or setting up organizations to provide services that wouldn't otherwise exist, or doing educational or cultural work that enabled more people to understand how society functions. It could mean participating in a unionizing drive or joining a tenant's association. It could mean doing civil disobedience at a nuclear power station or boycotting a store with racist hiring practices.

Many lesbians *are* committed to a broad range of political activity, but it is still a small percentage. Given the disadvantages we face as women and lesbians in this society and the obvious need for our political involvement, why aren't there even more of us?

Lots of reasons. Not many of us were born into political activism! This society aggressively promotes our passive acceptance of the status quo and trains us *not* to think about the conditions of our lives. Most people are not encouraged to believe that we actually have any power to change things. We are supposed to be obedient, unthinking, uncomplaining, hard-working consumers. Period.

We are taught a version of history that places generals, presidents, prime ministers and kings at the centre, a history of events that just 'happen' as one great man after another wends his way through life. Changes are made by special individuals who did great things somewhere else, not by people like us — not by ordinary women or a tiny collective of lesbians.

Many of us are members of racial and ethnic groups that have been systematically denied basic political and human rights.

It's also true that, to most Canadians, politics means

the Liberals and the Conservatives and maybe the N.D.P., and none of that has much to do with real life or real people.

There are numerous other common beliefs about politics: it's sordid, messy, full of compromise and corruption, abuses of power and smokey back rooms. No one of integrity or ideals would go near it.

Lesbians are not immune from this sense of powerlessness and this belief in the irrelevance of traditional politics to our lives. We are also not immune from the reality that women in general have only legally been able to participate in federal electoral politics in Canada since 1919. Women are still not elected to provincial and federal legislatures in proportion to our numbers. At too many levels we still live in a society that sees politics – any politics – as men's work. And power – any power – as unsuitable for a woman.

On top of all that, most lesbians work outside the home and, like most women, usually in low-paying and exhausting jobs. One-third of us are raising children. There just isn't much time or energy left over.

It's also true that many of us have bought into one or an assortment of the myths about lesbianism that discourage us from looking at our lives politically. Some examples of this would be, "Lesbianism is a purely private activity," or "It's wrong to be a lesbian but we just can't help ourselves," or "It's perfectly natural to be a dyke and so what if some people have problems – I certainly don't."

We are additionally, and most effectively, stopped from being politicaly active by our belief that our personal safety as lesbians lies in being invisible. We know that being identified as a lesbian can lead to harassment, loss of jobs and children – and violence. We know that it really isn't safe for us to speak out. The extent of the oppression we live with can be measured, to a very large degree, by our difficulty in organizing politically *as lesbians*.

It is next to impossible to organize as a lesbian without being out. Political organizing implies public activity. Many of us are out within our lesbian communities, but there is a big difference between being out to 50 or even 500 other lesbians and being out to a heterosexual, homophobic world. Many of us can't be that public, many of us won't, certainly most of us aren't. Too many of us come up with all sorts of convoluted explanations of why we can't, or won't, or don't work publicly as lesbians because is it just too difficult and maybe too embarrassing to say we don't because we're scared. Being that out could cause us a lot of trouble.

Another force that specifically stops lesbians from becoming politically active is the disapproval within our lesbian communities. We are not always encouraging of each other's attempts to work for change: "Oh don't tell me you're one of those *boring* political women"..."Politics is so undignified"..."My life is just fine. Nobody hassles me about being gay. If you go around looking for trouble, you get it..."

It's as though if the majority of an oppressed group *knows* that the only safe way to survive is to hide, then they will try to tone down those members of the group who advocate increased visibility. It seems that the level of community disapproval of overt lesbian political activity has been increasing as the economy worsens and the prevailing political climate becomes more right-wing.

So lesbian activists fight against a homophobic society, often without alot of support from other lesbians. *Why bother?* Given the level of societal discouragement of any political activity and the specific fear that lesbians face in identifying publicly as lesbians, it seems amazing that *any* lesbians are politically active at all.

That there are so many of us active in movements for social change and that we have built a consciousness of and movement for lesbian liberation speaks of our individual and collective courage, of our unwillingness to any longer pay the price of invisibility.

We begin to think politically because it becomes important for us to make sense of our entire lives, of the world we see around us. We being to act politically because we want to change what we see.

I have difficulty tracing the sources of my political passion. It seems absolutely inconceivable to me to be any other way. My parents were Communists – disillusioned, timid and completely politically inactive – but nonetheless I was brought up believing that Right and Wrong existed and that crossing a picket line was a mortal sin. I didn't actually believe that social change was *possible* – after all, my parents had certainly tried and failed – but I knew my duty.

At the age of 18, the ideas of feminism offered me a way to make sense of the world, a place to stand, an explanation. I am not and have never been uncritical of the women's movement. Our attempts to translate feminist ideas into the world are all too imperfect. But still, when I hear lesbians sneer at feminism as irrelevant and reactionary and prudish, my temper flares. I mean, I was 19 before I knew that clitorises *existed* – and I learned that from reading Anne Koedt's "The Myth of the Vaginal Orgasm." And by no means least, the women's movement was where I met other lesbians. I have much to be grateful for.

I came to lesbian activism out of youth and naivete. I came out within 'alternative' circles and didn't experience much difficulty. Not really knowing about homophobia or prejudice or fear, I blithely proclaimed my newfound lesbian consciousness at my local women's group and announced that I wanted to start a Lesbian Resource Centre.

Eight months later I slunk out of that town. Being nothing if not stubborn, I spent the next years organizing within the women's movement as a lesbian.

During the past ten years of feminist and lesbian activism I have become much more optimistic about the possibilities of social change. I have seen the results of my work in women's lives, in writings, in organizations. I know that I was part of groups of lesbians, who created powerful, exciting, meaningful changes. I continue to do political work because I love it. I like trying to think of new ways to work together. I like having conversations about the world we want to live in. I like feeling as though I can measure my life against the progress we make.

And I love the women. I love mouthy, exciting, visionary, smart, hard-working, contradictory political women.

— *Nym*

Many of us were inspired to become politically active by the lesbians we met who were activists. Lesbians who were enthusiastic about their beliefs, who worked hard to integrate their ideas into their personal lives, who wanted to listen to our stories and who could give us new ways of understanding our

The pink triangle was used to identify the thousands of gay people who died in concentration camps in Nazi Germany.

dilemmas, our histories. Maybe someone who said, "Why don't you come to the group tonight and tell your story"..."Why not come to the drop-in and meet another carpenter?"..."Can you help us put together this pamphlet?"

Many of the stories about how we got interested in politics start, "Well I met this woman..." We know a truly outstanding energetic woman who got into feminism and lesbian activism because she met a woman with "these wonderful eyes" at the bar one night. Overwhelmed by passion, she followed the woman to her next meeting and has been going non-stop ever since. Lust is definitely a factor in the lesbian politicizing process.

I remember the first International Women's Day Celebration I attended at the New School in Vancouver. I went because my lover was going, but I knew I was not like any of those politicos — the group that didn't care how they dressed, the ones who were always going to meetings, the women who talked about theory and practice...

I stopped at the door of the workshop on lesbian feminism. There was a young woman speaking, about my age. She waved her arms around, like I did when speaking of something I cared a great deal about. But she was talking about politics — how could anyone care about ideas? She was speaking about the connection between loving other women and feminist analysis. Over my head — must be one of those academic types from some privileged upper middle-class family in some big city...She certainly seemed to be having a good time talking about that analysis of hers...But I bet she didn't know a thing about being in a bar, or having a good time.

Then she switched from the political stuff to telling women a bit about her own life. I was stunned. She grew up poor (like me), she came from Manitoba (like me), she had fallen passionately in love with a woman and then figured out that maybe she was a lesbian (like me), she had a long history of identifying as a heterosexual (like me) and she had a sense of humour (like me) and really wanted to live in a country (like me) and, and, and...I was so surprised to discover a perfectly ordinary woman (like me) who had managed to find something powerful and sustaining and reassuring in these ideas called feminism. I actually walked into the room, sat down and eventually asked about the group she belonged to.

I mean, what was there to lose? Women like that obviously had found something that made them happier and stronger — and if it could make sense to a woman who was like me, then it surely could be good for me.

— *Yvette*

For some of us, we were angry enough about an event that affected us that we did something about it. Maybe it was being sick and tired of being the only lesbian at work that prompted us to seek out a support group for lesbian office workers. Or it was having to deal with a husband threatening to sue for custody that made us pick up the phone and call the Lesbian Mother's group. Becoming politically active usually begins with self-interest: "I am willing to do this because I want something to change — for *my* benefit!"

When I was 12 years old I really wanted to change the world. I do political work because it's a shitty world and I don't like it. My whole analysis comes from personal experience. I organize as a lesbian because that's where I feel oppression most keenly. I imagine that would be different if I was non-white or differently abled.

— Niamh

Without contact of some sort it is almost impossible to live as a happy, let alone politically active, lesbian. We all need places to go for affirmation, to check out our ideas, to get a sense that there are at least a few others who think, love, plan and dream like we do. Making sense of the world from our particular viewpoint as lesbians doesn't happen magically just because we've identified as lesbians. *Talking* together is perhaps the easiest starting point. Whether it be in the context of a weekly sports or social gathering or simply spending time with our lesbian friends, we can use these opportunities to talk about what is happening in our lives. What we read in the papers or see on t.v. or hear from the people at work and on the street can all be grist for the mill.

What is *our* perspective on a particular issue? Does it look this way to everyone? How would it look to a heterosexual woman? A gay man? A straight man? How is it different for a lesbian? How are our individual perspectives shaped by our class, our race, our age?

This is how a lesbian perspective on a particular event and on the existing social, political and economic realities gets developed. This is how we begin to see ourselves in the society around us. Conversations help shape our ideas and inspire us to *think* about the world and our place in it. So many of us hunger for that kind of contact with others: intimate and challenging, moving beyond superficial responses to a depth that truly reflects our realities. No one else can give us that. It is something we can and must do with each other.

I was attracted to political work mostly because of the intellectual stimulation. I wanted more contact with more lesbians. I wanted to know other lesbians who were willing to step out and act on problems.

— Karen

There is much we can do as individuals — and even more when we work together and take action side-by-side. A group offers more ideas, more emotional support and a place to come to when the going gets rough. Although it's not simple to make a committment to a group of women and to stick together through the hard times, we need each other to survive. We can become each other's families: sources of love, comfort, encouragement — even a kick in the ass when necessary. It is a *new* kind of family, our social and political groups. We invent as we go along.

There is a wide variety of groups ranging from the therapy model with a minimal political analysis or action to the strictly action-oriented group which takes little account of emotional process or internalized oppression. Most of these groups operate as collectives with all members having equal responsibliity and equal power in the decision-making process. Their functions can easily overlap and groups often use a mixture of these approaches.

What Kind of Group?

Consciousness Raising Groups (CR)   A group of women get together to discuss what it is like to be a women and a lesbian in a male supremacist society. Each woman talks about her feelings and experiences. The goal is to find common elements and try to make sense of them. CR groups invite a method of self-exploration that usually requires a great deal of emotional support amongst members. They often lead to political action. It is a highly recommended process for any women. A good description of how to set up and structure a CR group is in *The Joy of Lesbian Sex.*

Support Groups   A full description of support groups is in *Fighting Internalized Oppression.*

Problem-solving Groups   These groups are often based on the book *Solving Women's Problems* by Hogie Wyckoff which uses radical therapy (RT) principles. Normally led by a trained facilitator, the group focusses on making emotional connections between an oppressive society and how we act out oppression in our lives. Women make contracts to change. RT advocates becoming involved in organized political activity as part of solving problems.

Study Groups   Study groups are formed to read, talk and learn from each other and usually strive for an analytical understanding of women's lives. Often the group focusses on a particular topic, such as

Photo/ Dorothy Elias

imperialism or lesbian feminist theory. Reading a specific book and using it for information and inspiration is common. Study groups are a form of self-education and a means of developing theory.

Drop-In Groups   A consistent location and regular time are set for any women to 'drop-in' and talk and meet other women. Often there is a commonality of experience among those women invited. For example, a lesbian drop-in may be advertised for any lesbian in the area, or the local community centre may offer a single mother's drop-in while they provide child care. This gives women an opportunity to stop by and know that they will find other women who share a similar interest, orientation or oppression. There is no obligation to return — you can attend once or choose to come regularly.

Drop-ins are sometimes sponsored by another group. One of the lesbian drop-ins in Vancouver is sponsored by the Lesbian Information Line and is held

at the Women's Bookstore. Several women from L.I.L. make a commitment to attend the drop-in regularly, to open the door, make the coffee, provide some continuity to the group and facilitate discussions and provide resource information. A core group of women attend regularly with a number of others who come and go. The number can range from four to forty. Often there is a theme under discussion which the women choose at the end of the drop-in for the next week. There are opportunities for any woman coming to the drop-in to talk about what's going on in her life. Information about events and groups is made available.

The drop-in enables women to make contact with other lesbians in an informal, relaxed setting. Women come to find out what's happening, to make social connections and to hear stories of other lesbian's lives. Drop-ins can be a life-sustaining contact for lesbians. (For a blow-by-blow description of a drop-in, see *Creating Communities.)*

Action Groups   Action groups form to do something: provide some service, do public education, influence the political process...Some are ad-hoc groups formed for a specific short-term action, like organizing a lesbian and gay rights rally; some have a single issue as their focus, such as lobbying for the inclusion of sexual orientation protection in the provincial and federal Human Rights Codes. (For a detailed description of a particular action group, see *Organizing a Lesbian Conference* in *Creating Communities.)*

Most groups are started by one or two women who figured out what they wanted to do, and invited other women to join them. If there is no appropriate or just *no* lesbian group in your area, you and your friends — or you alone — will have to start one. No lesbian group existed before some woman got brave or serious or lonely or angry enough to start it! (For ideas on forming a collective, see *Notes to Facilitators.)*

It is so clear to me: being political is two things. It is having a feminist perspective that shapes everything I do and say — the lens that I use, like a pair of glasses, to see and focus what is around me — a way of perceiving the world that is never static, that always demands adjustment to be sharp and accurate.

And politics is about taking that view of the world into my life — working hard to have other women join me in the fight — knowing that women will not change unless they have real, practical and beneficial reasons for doing so. Knowing too that, unless a vast majority of women from everywhere in this society understand the basic feminist issues, we won't get very far.

— Yvette

Somewhere to Start

☐ The argument against political activism that we find the most difficult to understand is the notion that politics are boring, meaningless, unnecessary and will probably ruin your sex life. What can we say? There are thousands of people in Canada engaged in organized political activity whose primary focus is to make homosexuality a crime punishable by death or at least life imprisonment. They are extreme right-wing bigots and easy to laugh off as totally nutty — but they're serious, they're organized, they have money, they've already been successful in seriously curtailing the availability of abortion to women in Canada and Québec — and they pose a serious threat to the small gains in acceptance of lesbianism as a valid life choice that we've made. We really don't, for our very survival, have the option of political inactivity. We find politics, and lesbian politics in particular, fascinating — and our sex lives are more than fine, thank you.

☐ The more we publicly come out, the less people will be able to believe the myths about us. It's hard to hang onto the image of lesbians as violent, pitiful, perverted, man-hating monsters when there are numbers of visible, confident, *proud* lesbians. Or when it's your sister, your best friend or your colleague who's being talked about!

Are *you* out as a lesbian? Not, "Well, sure I'm out — look at the way I dress — they must know"... "I've brought only women home for the last four years, so my parents must be catching on"... "I never talk about men at work"... *Are you out?* Have you sat people down and said, directly and explicitly, "I am a lesbian. This is what it means to me. This is why it's important for you to know."

Yes, there are repercussions for being a lesbian but, far too often, far too many of us do not look at our personal and political situations and realize that we are in a good position to take some risks.

☐ Keep these questions in mind: how would this situation (social, workplace, political, any scene) be different if I were out as a lesbian? What if I were to say the same thing but begin with, "Being gay..." Or

if I were to try and educate these people about lesbianism and expect them to do something about our oppression?

Try practicing in the mirror or do role-playing with friends. Imagine the situation in which you're asked, for the hundredth time, "Have you found yourself a nice man yet, dear?" Think of yourself responding, "No, Aunt Denise, and I'm not looking. I'm a lesbian. Women have been my primary source of emotional and social contact for eight years and I intend to keep it that way. I'd be quite happy to talk about it, if you're interested..."

☐ Another way of making our presence as lesbians and feminists felt is to engage in a little direct action.

Distribute Pamphlets: Some lesbian/gay groups produce information pamphlets on homosexuality for the general public. Drop them off at libraries, community centres, clinics, your lunchroom at work or school, etc. You could also give them to your family and friends.

Stickers: "This Exploits Women", "A Lesbian Was Here"...Sticker these on top of pin-up calendars, sexist cartoons and photos on your office bulletin board and ads on buses.

Cartoons/Graphics: Fight back with gay and feminist cartoons on bulletin boards, in the union newsletter...

Posters: "A Woman Without a Man is Like a Fish Without a Bicycle." Images are powerful and uplifting: they warm our hearts and help confirm our view of the world. Post them in your workplace or on the street: for the quick good-stick method, use sweetened condensed milk (diluted with water) in a house plant sprayer and press down with a wet sponge.

Spray It...if you want to say it! Lacquer-based spray paint does a weather-proof job on sexist billboards and blank walls.

Pamphlets, stickers, posters and collections of feminist cartoons can often be found in women's and progressive bookstores (see *Finding Lesbian Resources*).

Resources

One of the central themes of this book is that it is to our benefit to view *all* aspects of our lives from a political perspective. The *Resources* listed throughout this book are a good beginning. We especially recommend:

☐ *Feminism as Framework*

I still believe we need alliances to fight a society and a government which perpetuate many forms of oppression.

Working in Progressive Movements

Lesbians working openly as lesbians within various progressive political movements often face similar problems: isolation, not being taken seriously, lesbianism being dismissed as a 'personal' and therefore unimportant issue, ridicule and harassment.

Most lesbians in progressive movements, including the feminist movement, aren't out — or are out within the group, but not publicly. It might 'damage' the cause. Sound familiar? Sound any different from the situations lesbians face at the workplace or on the streets or with our families? Homophobia runs as deep and strong in progressive circles as anywhere else and often feels worse, because surely people who are fighting for justice and freedom would understand...

What happens to lesbian activists working in progressive movements? What are our experiences? What have we found to be the most useful and effective approaches?

The Women's Movement

It seems such a long time ago now that I can hardly believe it all happened within a period of a few months. The Maple Ridge Women's Centre was renting office space from the local of a powerful union. One night we had a Pub Night. About 50 women and men attended, and feminist musicians played and sang. Some of the music was identified as 'lesbian' — some Chris Williamson and Meg Christian songs. Within a week, the Women's Centre had received an eviction notice from the union.

The local paper misprinted a distorted interview with a women from the Centre, and another woman met with the union president without our group's backing. No one knew what was going on. We had a very nasty Women's Centre meeting with innuendos and accusatons flying back and forth of "women necking", but no one in the group would openly confront anyone else.

We could not, and did not, unite to fight the eviction. Group morale and energy was really low.

There was definitely a sense of deserting the ship. We moved out and disbanded. There were all sorts of rumours going around town. Another woman and I set up a meeting with our local M.L.A. who told us he had received letters from women complaining about the "deviants". We were told about unspecified people in the community being very upset.

I finally went to see the union president who said we had been evicted because "we didn't take care of the place", there were "dogs allowed in the centre" and that the space was going to be rented to a more "worthwhile community group." When I pressed for more information, he admitted that he was in full agreement with his wife who said that "the women's movement would lose a lot of momentum and frighten off women if it allowed lesbianism to be associated with it."

The main result of all of this was that since that time — four years ago now — there has been no public feminist activity in Maple Ridge. From this experience I learned to never start a service group without politicizing and educating about a broad spectrum of feminist issues, including a woman's right to choose lesbianism. In the Women's Centre, women were still straightening out their personal lives. We were so innocent. We had nowhere near enough political sophistication. We should have known the issue would come up. Every women's group should know how to fight this kind of attack.

— *Johanna*

A few years back, Derry McDonnell, editor of the "Monday Magazine" in Victoria, published an editorial piece in which he stated that the reason the Victoria Rape/Assault Centre would not receive funding from the Intermunicipal Council was because of the "undenied presence of a certain number of lesbian activists . . . within the centre." He intimated that we were counselling rape survivors to become lesbians and that we only wanted to gain access to schools to "preach the gospel of lesbianism to our female youth." Lastly, he said that our supposedly muddled financial statements were due to the disruptive influence of these radical lesbian feminists.

Within our collective, this incident motivated us to formulate our stand on lesbian rights. We had agreed, as members of the B.C. Federation of Women, to support that organization's policy on lesbian rights, but all that had not meant much to the members of the collective who were not lesbians. Now it mattered alot. We affirmed the right of members of our collective to counsel rape survivors, to speak in schools, to keep financial records. We do not ask women who join the collective what their sexual preference is, nor do we do 'lesbian' counselling. We agreed that all of us are subject to the 'slander' of being called lesbians whether we are or not, simply because we are feminists and a threat to the male order. For us, lesbian rights are intimately linked with feminist analysis and practise.

I also want to articulate my own thoughts and feelings about the *Monday Magazine* harassment. When the editorial was printed, I had only been out as a lesbian for a few months. I had been a feminist for a long time, and always felt strong and upfront about my politics. When I acknowledged to myself and others that I was a lesbian, I suddenly felt vulnerable. I realized that I could be outspoken as a feminist because I had the respectability and legal sanction of being heterosexual. The patriarchy had been able to call me names and harass me, but now they could put me in jail or revoke my landed immigrant status because I gave my love, support and energy to women.

So when I sat in the office alone and read the man's rantings, I was very frightened. A very few years ago I would have been indignant. Now I was scared. I could not and would not deny that, yes, there are lesbians within our collective. But I could not go to him and say, "Listen, it's me you're talking about, and I don't like it."

I'm feeling stronger as time goes on about being an open lesbian, but I know I still have a long way to go. The *Monday Magazine* incident was a good lesson for me about the attacks that we face for our choice to be sexual with and love women. I want the personal courage to call turkeys like Derry McDonnell on their misogynist, homophobic accusations.

— *Cory*

I discovered feminism and lesbianism at the same time. I was 19 and it was the early 70's. Five days after I first made love with a woman, I was helping to disrupt a big feminist conference to demand support for lesbian rights. I was not particularly politically astute, or committed; it was just the spirit of the times. Lesbians loved women and went to meetings.

For years I worked as a feminist and as a lesbian in the women's movement, struggling to have lesbianism validated. The most blatant homophobic reactions I have ever experienced were from other feminists. My most painful personal struggles for self-worth and acceptance were within the women's movement.

— *Nym*

The women's liberation movement has been accused of being 'a bunch of lesbians' from the very beginning. In speaking out against the confined role of all women, feminists have been punished and ridiculed with one of the worst epithets available for women: lezzie, dyke. The cultural message has been very clear: "Step out of line, you get called a dyke — and that'll scare you enough to teach you to stay in your place."

In a sense, the women's movement has been forced to come to terms with the issue of lesbianism by these outside attacks, aided by the fact that many of the movement's most visible fighters are indeed lesbians. In the late 60's and early 70's, the 'lesbian issue' was in the foreground of the movement's internal struggles. Many feminists, some of whom were lesbians, believed that the women's movement's public support of so contentious an issue as lesbian rights would discredit the entire movement and prevent progress on other crucial issues to women, such as reproductive rights, childcare, access to the workforce and participation in society's decision-making processes.

Others believed lesbianism to be simply a matter of selecting women as sexual partners and therefore something to be accepted and dealt with on a personal level. It wasn't seen as really relevant to feminist struggles in any analytical or organizational sense. Although there were a few lesbians in the women's liberation movement, the majority of women were heterosexual, and lesbian-baiting or focussing on it as an issue was seen as a red-herring.

Many other feminists — again, some lesbians, some not — believed that a refusal to publicly support lesbian rights was completely antithetical to such basic feminist premises as the right of all women to control our own bodies, define our own sexuality and live as autonomous and independent persons. They believed that the women's movement was refusing to take a public stand on lesbianism out of fear and homophobia.

Out of this whole debate and process of disagreement came important theoretical work on the relationship between lesbianism and feminism, as well as most feminist groups taking positions supportive of lesbian rights. The women's movement is generally a tolerant and supportive atmosphere in which lesbians can work. But the struggle for recognition and increased understanding is ongoing.

Within the women's movement, acceptance of lesbians and support for lesbian rights is primarily an acceptance of individual lesbians on a personal basis or an acceptance of those lesbians within the group. It is a positive development that so many women have worked through their conditioned responses, fears and anxieties about lesbianism and are now personally comfortable with lesbians. The next steps are to insure that there is a solid *political* understanding of the relationship of lesbianism to women's liberation, and to pass on to others the awareness that lesbianism is a valid life choice for *any* woman. It is not only the responsibility of lesbians to fight for lesbian rights; it is the responsibility of every feminist. Lesbian oppression affects all women.

As right-wing forces gather strength, the women's liberation movement is under increasing attack. Homosexuality is a major rallying point for 'Moral Majority' organizations and public support for lesbianism becomes increasingly risky. Many women's groups are facing a choice: to try and play it safe on such touchy subjects as homosexuality and abortion and hope that the good work they are doing in other areas will compensate for what we all know is a failure of conscience; or to continue speaking out and acting — and face such repercussions as loss of funding, malicious publicity and possibly more direct attacks, such as break-ins or fire-bombings.

---

*T*he myth that lesbians are not 'real women' underlies the ideas about lesbianism that exist in this culture. It is the source of most other myths about lesbians, the source of the women's movement inability to see lesbian oppression as connected to all women's oppression and the source of most lesbians' unwillingness to connect our struggle for freedom to that of every woman.

When we have done workshops with lesbians, a recurrent anxiety surrounds what is perceived as a polarization between 'feminist' lesbians and 'ordinary' lesbians. This anxiety is expressed in many ways: as intolerance of differences, as criticisms of social and sexual behaviour, as discomfort. Taken to a very individual level, a common pattern seems to be that lesbians who have come-out within the context of the women's movement — usually out of a heterosexual background — take some years coming to terms with a small niggling question of whether or not they are 'real' lesbians. Lesbians who came to identify as lesbians without the support of a feminist community, without an analysis of lesbianism in political terms, usually alone and usually quite young, tend to carry a small niggling question about being 'real women.'

Two sides of the same cultural myth, and a polarization that makes it extremely difficult to see the commonalities and connections.

— *Nym and Yvette*

Caucuses

You are a lesbian and member of a feminist organization which is working on one area of importance to women: health, rape, class, legal matters, self-defense, abortion, publishing, children, education, employment. . . There is no stated policy supporting the rights of lesbians and the lesbians in the group are individually tolerated. You want the group to develop a political understanding of the oppression of lesbians and incorporate that into its policy; then you want the group to use the policy to stand publicly in support of lesbian rights. How do you begin?

Start with yourself   Sit down and figure out what you want the group to do about lesbian oppression. Do you want them to donate money to an upcoming lesbian conference? Do you want to make a speech at a Gay Rights Rally and do it in the group's name? Do you want to publicly protest the firing of a lesbian child-care worker?

Why do you believe this is a relevant issue for the group? Take the time to think through your responses and write them down. This will provide you with some of the analytical connections between your group's work and the fight to end lesbian oppression.

Besides doing this theoretical work, you will need to prepare for the long, emotional process of consciousness-raising...

Join with other lesbians   Discuss your ideas with other lesbians in the group. Get together *as lesbians.* Talk about your experiences as lesbians both in the world and in the group. This information should be kept confidential unless women are ready to speak out.

This kind of grouping is the beginning of a caucus. As with any new entity, you need to define how to work together. Will you meet regularly? How do you plan to make decisions? How will you disagree? How do you see your relationship to the larger group? What kind of projects/goals do you want to take on? Is there a commitment to stay together? How will you support each other?

You will need to explore certain issues relating to strategy. For instance, assess the membership of the larger group. What are their various life situations and experiences? What is the general political perspective of the group? How much analysis has been done? How much education needs to be done, both amongst yourselves and in the larger group? What are the steps the caucus must take to realize its goals? How do proposals get passed by the larger group? These sorts of questions need not necessarily be tackled at your first meeting, but you must eventually sort out how your work as a caucus will fit into the overall goals and practices of the organization.

Once you have established your identity as a caucus and agreed upon some initial working proposals...

Introduce the caucus to the group   In order to give your coming-together and work a political context, define yourselves as a lesbian caucus. Inform everyone that this caucus is not a splinter group set up to fragment the organization. Reassure them that the purpose of a caucus is to bring together individuals who are united by a specific oppression, an additional layer of discrimination over and above our common oppression as women. In a caucus, women identify and articulate that specific oppression, and define the links between it and the position of the women in the larger group. Living as a lesbian in the world brings with it very distinct experiences which heterosexual women never face. This is why the caucus would only include lesbians. It will provide emotional and intellectual support as women begin to place their common experiences in a political context, rather than keeping it on a personal, individual level. And the caucus will initiate policy changes, do educational work among the general membership and develop action plans that further the group's overall purpose.

> *The consequences of being a lesbian in this society are quite severe. The consequences of associating with, or supporting lesbians are also severe. But it is our belief that turning on each other, denying and betraying, blaming and fighting, hiding and lying, will be much more destructive to the women's movement and to our goal of a society in which all women are free.*
>
> *– The Lesbian Caucus of the*
> *B.C. Federation of Women, 1976*

You can use the example of women's caucuses in unions to give a framework for your decision to form a lesbian caucus.

After describing the caucus and its function, outline your proposals; they will be very general at this point. Make a commitment that the caucus will report regularly to the group and seek its approval for any work it undertakes. Remind women that, as part of the larger group, the caucus is working within the established decisions of the group and no action will occur without the whole group being thoroughly informed and in agreement. Fear and suspicion are greatly reduced when women know that decisions affecting them will not be made without them. Ask that the caucus be recognized as an 'official' part of the organization, and invite other lesbians in the group to its next meeting.

Running into resistance   After the discussion in the larger group, you will have a sense of any potential trouble spots. If the group — or parts of it — are resistant to the idea of a lesbian caucus or disagree with the working proposals, or if there are obvious homophobic reactions, don't be surprised. Ask women what they need in order to make a positive decision about your work. Ask for time to supply them with more information. Strategically, it is crucial to recognize that along with fighting for specific demands, you are educating individual women about lesbianism. 'Winning by any tactic' is *not* an appropriate goal. You are engaged in a process with women who you believe can change. Your role is to be a catalyst in transforming attitudes and behaviour.

You will not achieve your goal if you fight for immediate approval of a proposal and the group is fragmented, if half the membership resigns or if they throw you out for being so disruptive. Fighting for the right of a lesbian caucus to exist as a *political* entity within your organization may be your first 'action.'

Educate!   At some level, we *all* still carry myths about lesbianism, and women's reactions of fear, hostility — and sometimes curiosity — are reflections of this. If a structure is not set up to work through these emotional responses, you will nevertheless have to deal with them when they surface, usually inappropriately during heated discussion of your proposal. The *Stepping Out of Line* workshop has proved to be an effective part of such a structure. The caucus may wish to facilitate the workshop, or ask for outside facilitators so they may participate more fully.

As a caucus, you can write for the group's newsletter, distribute articles as part of the caucus report and loan out books. Let women know that they can approach you to discuss their ideas and feelings. Be prepared to expose your personal life — and be prepared for the occasional hostile reaction. It may seem that you are going over the same information again and again and that the same arguments repeatedly surface — but do it. Caucus members should be sure to keep in touch with one another, both to evaluate this educational work and to provide emotional support.

Moving forward   Once the caucus has thoroughly developed an action plan or proposal, write it up and take it to the group. Provide an ideological framework for your work and ask that this analysis be incorporated into the group's policy and basis of unity. This prevents the specific action from being seen as a one-shot deal.

Give women lots of time to study the proposal, to take it away and return with their questions and suggestions for changes. After all, you are trying to get agreement from as many women as possible, not just a majority vote that may yield approval of the proposal, but not long-term committed support.

Once the plan has been approved and acted upon, do an evaluation. How did what happened compare with your original objectives? What did you learn? Carry out this evaluation within the caucus and the larger group.

The group now has some practical experience both with a caucus 'in action' and with taking a stand on lesbian rights. This will make it that much easier for the caucus to take it's next step in ensuring that a lesbian feminist perspective is integrated into all areas of the group's theory and practice.

What We Can Do . . .

A newspaper or newsletter group . . . could solicit lesbian-related materials on a regular basis and/or put together a special issue on lesbianism.

A health group. . . can include lesbian health issues in a workshop series and make sure this information is also available in written form.

A rape crisis centre. . . could initiate a workshop on violence against women for the local lesbian drop-in or gay group.

A printing or publishing group. . . could design and distribute a poster or publish a book or pamphlet on lesbianism.

A women's centre or Status of Women group. . . could stock books on lesbianism in their library and publicize that they are available.

Any group. . . could offer space, money and any other resource to help in the formation and maintenance of lesbian groups.

Public Speaking Tips

It can be difficult for feminists to easily and confidently respond to questions about lesbianism during speaking engagements or interviews. Far too often our answers will either ignore, deny or side-step the issue.

Feminists are questioned about lesbianism because it is such a powerful symbol of women's deviation from the traditional female role. Here are some useful responses:

"We support the right of any woman to choose whatever lifestyle and choice of sexual partners she finds most satisfying to her."

"This is a women's group and we exist in order to offer support to all women and to fight for the liberation of all women. Many women are indeed lesbians, and we certainly support the right of a woman to select lesbianism as a valid life-choice. The

Photo/ Sarah Davidson

major focus of our work is, however, rape prevention (publishing, self-defense instruction)..."

"*As a member of the B.C. Federation of Women, we support policy on lesbian rights which states, 'The B.C. Federation of Women... fully affirms lesbianism as one of a variety of strong and free life choices for women, and recognizes that the struggle for acceptance of lesbianism as a valid lifestyle is the struggle for the right of any woman to define her own life.' The B.C.F.W. is made up of 50 feminist organizations which also support this policy.*"

If you are accused of being 'a bunch of lesbians', or hassled by someone in an audience, a good response can be:

"*Since you are so interested in the topic of lesbianism — which we are not here to discuss tonight — I would be happy to recommend several excellent books on the subject and refer you to a lesbian organization for more information. You could consider having a speaker from the Rights of Lesbians Collective come in for your next event.*"

"*Yes, there certainly are lesbians among us, as there are among you. We fully support the right of any woman to a choice of lesbianism. For information, please speak with me afterwards.*"

"*You seem to be bringing up the accusations of*

lesbianism in order to silence us and avoid dealing with the issues we are raising. I would like to continue."

We recommend responding to questions about whether or not you personally are a lesbian by either saying yes or no, but never by denying your lesbianism if you identify as such. The point is to look for the ways to connect feminist action with lesbianism and loving women. Say something like:

"*Are you asking me if I fight for women's rights because I love women? As a feminist of course I respect, admire and love women. I work on this issue because of my commitment to make this a better world for all women. I am very serious about this commitment.*"

Providing audiences with written materials they can take away is a positive way of dealing with a touchy subject. A short, factual brochure on lesbianism or a printed statement about your group and its position on various topics, including lesbianism, could be handed out.

All women in the group should be familiar with the hand-outs and have discussed beforehand how to handle accusations or questions about lesbians. It's great if everyone is prepared to respond in a similar manner. It's *crucial* for *all* women in the group to be prepared to speak positively about a woman's choice to be a lesbian.

The Gay Movement

Many lesbian activists work with gay men in fighting to end the discrimination faced by all gay people in this society. For women wanting to work openly and specifically as lesbians, the gay movement seems a logical choice. Outside the largest urban centres, there's no other choice. Social circles, support networks and communities are built by gay women and men together, and the political organizations which form reflect this shared base.

Just as lesbians in the women's movement have to almost continually educate other women about heterosexism and homophobia, lesbians working in the gay movement have to confront sexism and misogyny. It is an uphill battle and generally waged more successfully if lesbians within a mixed gay group have either a formal or informal caucus structure. The caucus provides a place to check out perceptions, work on strategies, settle differences and give and get emotional and political support.

> We have come to see that homophobia and gay oppression, even for men, are based on sexism and the institutional power of male supremacy. Gay men have some male privilege in society, particularly if they remain closeted or out-woman-hate heterosexual men...
>
> Gay men face a choice! They can accept society's offer of short-term benefits, or they can challenge the patriarchal basis of those very privileges and work for the long-term elimination of the entire system of sexual oppression.
> — Charlotte Bunch
> *Our Right to Love*

In many gay organizations, women and men have agreed to structural experiments that equalize the decision-making power. For example, half of decision-making committees *must* be women, or women have 50% of the voting power regardless of their actual numbers in the group.

The ideas of the gay movement — or at least of the majority of men in the gay movement — don't represent a vision of the kind of world we personally are working towards. However, many lesbians are not merely critical of the misogyny of the gay movement, but see *no* value in doing that political work. We consider that attitude short-sighted. Lesbian activists should consider the gay movement in the same way we look at any progressive movement. That is, our involvement within that movement is essentially an exercise in coalition politics. We do not trust that our needs, visions, perspectives or priorities will necessarily be reflected in the policies and actions of the movement. We create support systems to ensure our personal survival, and we work to influence the movement as a whole according to our vision and analysis.

Lesbians in general have benefitted from the slight shift in public acceptance of the 'gay life-style' since the late sixties. That change in attitude has happened primarily because of the work of the gay movement. The women in that movement have fought for years — for all of us — with tenacity and courage and very little credit. It's time to stop sniping and start learning.

---

*W*hen I first came out I was involved with a woman who was doing a lot of political things. I remember saying to her, "I don't know how you can do it. I just can't see myself making that kind of commitment to a movement."

She said, "Well, not everyone can do it. But those of us who can, have to for those who can't."

Now I find myself in that same position. I don't like rallies or crowds or bars so I started out doing very quiet kinds of work, like driving the getaway car for women postering. I happened to be at the Co-op Radio studio the first time the *Coming-Out Show* was aired. I wasn't working on the show — just sitting around being intimidated. I didn't have any idea what I could do until someone asked me to do some reporting and I quite got into it. After I had been involved with the show for a while I realized that radio is a really good forum for exposing what's happening. And there's an awful lot more happening that anyone knows about!

I got quite inspired and enthused, but I still wasn't using my name. It was partly a closet and partly not wanting my personality to be in the spotlight. I use my name on the air now, but I'm still not comfortable tap-dancing in the limelight. I've interviewed a lot of gay celebrities and I've been generally unimpressed. It's the day-to-day stuff that I think is really important and that excites me.

The *Coming-Out Show* began as the only place where you could say you were gay on the air. It started with more men than women, but very soon lots of women with a strong feminist commitment began working on it. It became apparent after a while that there was a need for a separate lesbian show and many of the women left the *Coming-Out* Show to form the *Lesbian Show*. I chose to stay with the *Coming-Out Show* and have worked on the show for two and a half years now.

Most publicity about the gay movement deals only with men and I think that's dishonest. It's important that lesbians are clearly visible within the gay movement. Society at large lumps lesbians in with gay men whether we like it or not. If we're not in there painting a strong and clear picture of ourselves we will continue to be invisible and anything known about us will be distorted.

It takes a strong feminist commitment to continue to work with gay men. Although both the feminist movement and the gay movement aim towards eliminating sexist stereotypes of people, the gay movement doesn't always focus on sexism as an issue. When I've felt burnt out and depressed by the whole thing I usually get sympathy from other women. I've been told that the only reason the men on the show work with women is because they think it's politically correct. Maybe that's true, but whether the men are working with the women because they want to and out of a commitment to a feminist perspective, or whether it's just because they think they ought to doesn't really matter. Political and philosophical understanding will grow out of an intellectual choice.

The feminist movement has created a space where women can grow and define themselves and become strong individuals. That is essential. But as I see it, the feminist movement is too self-contained. It feeds internally. The gay movement has more of a focus on outreach into society at large. I see changes in society as being so badly needed that we can't ignore them, and the gay movement is aggressively trying to make changes. I want to work towards changing people's attitudes and the gay movement feels like the place I can do that best.

— Jackie

Other Movements

Many lesbians work politically in trade unions, anti-racist groups, political parties, community organizations, the peace movement, as environmental activists, as socialists, as anarchists... There is probably no group in Canada or Québec working for social change that doesn't have lesbian members. More and more of us are coming-out within these progressive movements and demanding, agitating and organizing for a recognition of lesbian oppression as one of the social evils our movement opposes. So far, our experiences have similarities, regardless of the particular movement. There are too few stories of successful educational campaigns to draw iron-clad conclusions, but it does seem as though there are some common and crucial elements.

It is a mistake to assume that because a group holds a progressive or even radical analysis of society that it will necessarily be supportive of lesbianism. Homophobia is an emotional disease caught in childhood and difficult, although not impossible, to cure. People's reactions are irrational and highly-charged. Attempting to deal on an intellectual level alone is rarely enough. When you start organizing openly as a lesbian, know that what you are taking on is a lengthy process of consciousness-raising. In a mixed group you are confronting not merely homophobia, but thousands of years of heterosexual male conditioning which sees women — all women, any woman — as existing primarily to be sexually available to men. The arguments you'll get will be entirely more sophisticated — probably to do with the triviality of personal concerns, the importance of the 'real' revolution, the awful consequences to the credibility of the group. But you can hear and see and feel the fear and hostility.

*A*s both a feminist and a lesbian, my experience as an active member of a large Canadian Labour Congress affiliated union has been that of treading a fine line between all that I am and stand for and the compromise demanded of me just to survive in such an environment.

In many ways, it is easier to build supportive networks around the issue of feminism and women's rights in a union than it is to directly confront and organize around lesbianism. The women's movement has developed concrete strategies to deal with women's issues. As lesbians we have yet to develop strategies to deal effectively with the issue of sexual orientation within trade unions. There are women's committees which function as ad-hoc advocacy groups within the union structure. Women have begun to articulate their needs in terms of contract clauses which promote and

Photo/ Dorrie Brannock

protect women's rights. But the presence of an active women's committee within a union does not mean that the issue of lesbian rights or sexual orientation will be dealt with automatically.

Both my strategies for progress and my understanding of these issues stem from my experience as a worker in a variety of different occupations, all of which can be characterized as within the female job ghetto. I have been a clerk in a grocery store and drug store, cashier in a large chain, a biller and coder. In all these jobs my co-workers have been almost entirely female and only the last was unionized. Except for the last two jobs, I would have been fired immediately had I come out as a lesbian.

I became involved in the union when I and another woman were hired to work in the newly mechanized section of a large company. Most of the workers were female, young and naively anti-union. We looked around and saw no union presence on the floors where we worked — no shop stewards, nothing. So we started with health and safety issues, wrote articles for the union newsletter, and got the union to do a three-year study on health hazards from noise and video display terminals. Almost immediately we saw that what we needed was a woman's caucus and when we started talking about it, several women got involved immediately.

Working-class women have no access to power. Through a union, women can create self-determination in some areas of our lives, and that is very exciting. As women workers, we have a responsibility to try to take back as much control over our own lives as possible. Fighting for our issues is one way of doing that.

Once the women's caucus was established, we had to tread a very fine line between supporting the union and working with integrity in not allowing the union to dictate to us what our issues were or what our strategies would be in supporting women.

For instance, the union was very worried that in cases of sexual harassment we would support the woman being harassed by directly confronting the man on the floor of the workplace. The union thought that this kind of action would divide the workers. In fact, direct confrontation is a very effective strategy. We saw it as our only option when a woman was being harassed day after day and had no recourse except a complicated internal grievance procedure that would take six months and result in the man perhaps being reprimanded. More likely, the woman would not be believed because the definitions of sexual harassment are at best ambiguous.

I found that it was to my benefit to be as open about my lesbianism as I could. As an active shop steward, when management approached me on any issue, my sexual orientation was out in the open. I wasn't hiding, I wasn't fearful of the consequences of being found out. It also made my life much easier emotionally — I wasn't playing a game. By my being out, sexual orientation was talked about openly instead of being dealt with through rumours. I know I was in the unique situation of being able to count on union support even though we didn't have a contract clause covering sexual orientation.

The major problem I found as a lesbian trying to be active in my union was that people were fearful that my interests would not include anything but sexual orientation clauses and lesbians being harassed or fired, that I wouldn't address women's or union issues in general. Anyone who steps out and says we should fight for specific issues gets accused of splitting the union. My major strategy was to make sure that it was clear that I was fighting for women's and union concerns and not just for what could be seen as self-motivated causes.

Much of the work we did around sexual orientation was in changing consciousness. Sometimes I felt isolated, but I know the work that I did in my local has affected every union involved in the Canadian Labour Congress. The important part for me was not to become ghettoized, that I not get typecast because of my sexual orientation. It is in my interest that all women participate in the unions. I am a trade unionist. I was willing to be a spokesperson on that issue but I didn't want to be credible on that issue only.

Tolerance for each other is very necessary. Because I was being careful about not being typecast, I took the stance that my lesbianism was just a natural part of my existence both inside and outside the union. I was willing to speak about my fight for sexual orientation clauses, but I made a point of being just as knowledgeable and just as articulate on the issue of maternity leave. I think that is the responsibility of every lesbian within a trade union setting. Our interests lie with *all* women, not simply with other lesbians.

— *Jesse*

I came out when I was a member of a revolutionary organization. My coming-out was, on the one hand, very easy because of the strength of feminism. I believe that at this time, because of the women's movement, coming-out becomes an act of self-definition and autonomy as well as support and love for other women. On the other hand, my coming-out was very difficult because of the friction within a left organization that had no analysis of lesbian oppression. There was an ongoing debate around the role of feminism but, as in most left organizations, lesbian and gay struggles were not addressed.

Women in the organization were radicalizing around feminism. There was a women's caucus. Reactions to my coming-out varied. Some women said, "Well, that's great, that's how you are solving your problems with men." They couldn't see that defining myself as a lesbian involved a political struggle; they saw it as a personal solution, an escape. Others were really supportive.

You join a left organization because it's a way of struggling against oppression in the world. By joining you are already isolating yourself from the mainstream. Coming-out compounds that isolation because you are then isolated from your brothers and sisters inside the organization too. I had been part of a large current in the leadership of the organization. Coming-out put me in a minority position which I shared with some women who were pushing for a stronger feminist analysis and perspective, as well as some gay men who had not only been radicalized by being gay, but believed that gay male liberation could only be effective if it were built on an anti-misogynist analysis. We were fighting for discussion to take place around lesbian and gay oppression.

When the organization was created, one of the agreements was that there would be full and open discussion of lesbian and gay oppression and that a full position would be developed. Three years later the debate still hadn't happened. We had tremendous differences within the organization. Viewpoints ranged from whether this was an important issue at all to seeing it as pivotal to women's liberation and the revolutionary process. Some people refused to accept a position that homosexuality was as 'natural' as heterosexuality.

Some of us fought for three years: we had organized as a formal group in the organization, developed incredible theory, and worked from that theory. We got no validation for that work from the leadership. On top of that, the organization started making changes in its theories and practices around women, questioning its longstanding support for a broad autonomous women's movement and decreasing its work amongst women.

We found ourselves losing confidence in the leadership. It was really hard for me to see a future in the organization, and I began to question my relationship to that leadership. The struggle was making me physically ill. By the time I left, I was feeling disillusioned and smashed. I had believed very strongly in the organization; I had gotten a lot out of it. I felt betrayed.

The left is very male-dominated and often there is a strong male hierarchy. My coming-out meant a social rupture with men in the leadership; my insistence on an anti-patriarchal perspective resulted in a related political break with them. Our current was perceived

Lesbian/Gay Women Against the Budget

Too many people still believe lies about lesbian/gay women. Actually, women who love women are your friends, family and colleagues. We live full, productive lives, work in every conceivable job, and belong to all ethnic, religious and political communities. We make up 10% of the female population and we've been working hard to end the discrimination we experience. The Socreds think we **deserve** discrimination.

* Labour Minister McClelland has labelled lesbian rights "frivolous." He has refused to include protection against discrimination on the basis of sexual orientation in the new Human Rights Act (Bill 27). The removal of the "no dismissal without reasonable cause" section of the act means that we have lost the one legal avenue open to us to fight discrimination in housing and employment. Our chance of unjustly losing our children in custody cases is greatly increased.
* The Residential Tenancy Act (Bill 5) allows landlords to raise rents and evict without cause. Lesbians will end up paying higher and higher rents or being evicted by prejudiced landlords.
* The Medical Services Act (Bill 24) would give the government access to doctors' confidential medical files. This could lead to identification of women who are gay — and more discrimination. The government has recently promised to amend this legislation, however, at this time, our concern remains.
* Cuts in social services and education affect us as single mothers, consumers and workers. All women in B.C. are losing essential services like the child paternity support program, emergency services, family support services, and many more.
* Bills 2 and 3 mean that being a lesbian could be an adequate reason for being fired, not hired, or passed over for promotion.

This government is trying to roll back the clock in B.C. Lesbian/gay women join the Solidarity Coalition in saying "NO!" We will not live in fear. Together we will create a British Columbia where diversity among people is respected and ALL citizens have rights.

What you can do

* Call and write your member of the Legislature in Victoria.
* Support the rights of lesbian/gay women in your community group, organization, church, union, etc.
* Invite speakers from Lesbians Against the Budget to talk to your group.
* Join in Solidarity actions in your community.

July 7, 1983: the government of B.C. brought in a budget accompanied by 27 pieces of repressive legislation relating to housing, human rights, employment, etc. A massive province-wide protest movement — the Solidarity Coalition — *quickly developed.* Lesbians Against the Budget *sent voting delegates to the coalition Steering Committees, worked with gay men in the* Gay/Lesbian Caucus *and functioned as an official subcommittee of* Women Against the Budget. LAB *did educational outreach to lesbian communities and other groups within the coalition, maintained a high media profile, marched and picketed. This is* LAB's *information leaflet.*

as a threat to traditional patriarchal ideas about the separation of 'personal' struggles from 'political' ones and to established ways of operating inside the group. This mirrored ways in which open lesbians are threatening to bourgeois society: we demonstrate that women are capable of living, relating and creating intellectually, independent of men and male authority.

While our organization certainly internalized some of the homophobia of this society, I don't think that left and mixed organizations are inherently incapable of fighting in lesbians' interests. I still believe that we need such alliances to fight a society and a government which perpetuate many forms of oppression. I continue to believe that we need a socialist and a feminist revolution. When there are huge feminist and lesbian and gay movements, organizations will be forced to respond to our struggle in part because many of their own members will demand it.

Lesbians will want to participate in creating and pushing for broader struggle and organizations; after all, we are also workers, women, Québécoises — as well as lesbians. We may decide to join a left group as an organized current and press for a better understanding of our struggle. There are ways of organizing, like ensuring that lesbians can caucus within a group and that women are strongly represented in leadership. But we must always maintain our autonomous organizations as well as make alliances. We must have the final say in defining our needs and our goals.

My priority now is to build the feminist movement and to start working around lesbian liberation. Right now I see no organization in Canada which is even close to having an adequate analysis or practice around women's and lesbians' oppression and liberation.

I do think it's essential that the lesbian movement has a materialist analysis: that it understands that lesbian oppression is rooted in the patriarchal family, that the family is essential to economic class relationships and essential to capitalism. The only way to create the conditions where women can change that relationship is for us to have state power: to have the power to socialize domestic labour and to completely break down the existing division of labour between women and men. I think it's important to reach the majority of lesbians who are working class and to use organizations like trade unions to start to construct an active lesbian movement.

Because we have created an open lesbian community, it has become both a strength and a weakness. It's safe and open and supportive so we don't have to mention lesbianism or integrate it into our work. Women don't work around the issue of lesbianism because it is so linked to their personal everyday lives, because women don't analyze lesbianism within a broader perspective. Women have put a great deal of energy into creating acceptance for lesbianism within the women's movement. Now we need an outward struggle to take on things like sexual orientation protection clauses in union contracts as well as general feminist demands that start breaking down gender roles.

A community can be really powerful. What we need to do is take that power and that support and move out — or the community can become an end in itself. We can become isolated and crushed. I think it is really important that those of us who have political skills move out where it is really dangerous and start doing mass organizing around lesbian and feminist issues.

I'm getting scared. Our enemies, like the Ku Klux Klan and the Right to Life, are very organized and public and have a lot of money. We need to fight them right now. We need to build a mutually supportive relationship with other groups under attack — women needing abortions, East Indians, unionists — while creating a public presence for ourselves as lesbians. We need to convince other groups to support us as we support them. I believe we *can* do this.

— Sara

Somewhere to Start

☐ Make sure you have a system of political and personal support. Try to establish contact with other lesbians in your group. Outside the women's movement, other women who are feminist or open to feminist ideas are the logical people with whom to start your educational work. Gay men can be valuable allies. Based on who is around and receptive, you could go on to form a lesbian (or women's or lesbian/gay) caucus as described earlier in this section.

☐ It is equally important to seek out lesbian activists in other progressive movements, to exchange organizing strategies and to relieve our shared sense of isolation. Advertise in the local feminist newspaper or in your organization's newsletter. Arrange for a lesbian meeting at the conferences or gatherings you attend. At lesbian conferences, meet with other lesbians working openly in political groups. Ideally, create some sort of ongoing activist support group or network. There really are lots of us and we quite desperately need to find each other.

☐ Choose a specific demand to organize around. Passing a policy resolution, donating money, issuing a support statement, signing a petition – these kinds of demands can supply you with a visible reason for doing educational and consciousness-raising work on lesbianism. You will have to bear in mind that your *basic* goal is to change people's attitudes and get long-term, reliable supporters, not merely to manipulate the passage of a resolution.

☐ Distribute literature, write letters and articles for your newsletter, arrange/offer workshops and seminars and loan out books on lesbianism. Writing provides a way to make the intellectual and analytical arguments about how the political philosophy of the organization connects to lesbian rights.

☐ Talk about your life. You'll end up answering questions, going for coffee and talking, talking, talking – often about your personal life. The more people in the organization see and know you as a real individual, the less they will be able to hang on to the myths that "all lesbians are..." Invite people for dinner. If you have a willing lover and/or friends, introduce them. Expose people to as many lesbians as possible. It can all be quite emotionally draining.

☐ Stay involved with a lesbian community. It may be your only source of validation when the going gets rough. Even if you don't get much support for your political work, at least it's ok to be a lesbian.

☐ Decide early on what 'winning' means. Are you prepared to leave the organization if you're not supported as a lesbian? What changes do you want before you could stay? How long are you willing to work at this? (Once you become identified as a lesbian activist, you'll never get to stop – be forewarned.)

If your experiences within a political movement are, over a period of time, completely invalidating your reality as a lesbian, if you are compromising beyond your ability to bear it, if you are thoroughly miserable, depressed, ill – *get out*. You can take a break and go back with renewed vigor, or you can find or create meaningful political work that does not destroy you as a lesbian.

☐ Don't be too hard on yourself. Being courageous and clear and out every minute of every day is humanly impossible. We do the best we can as often as we can – and it's better than doing nothing. If you think of yourself as committed lifelong to a movement for social change, then remember that you have many more years to influence that movement. What you

don't do today, you can do next year. Changing attitudes is a slow process. Don't kill yourself with overwork and stress and malnutrition and drinking and cigarettes and 18 hour meetings. If you die, get very sick or totally burn out, it is going to affect the world less than if you can keep going for another 50 years.

☐ You will have to remind yourself and the other lesbians around that the work you are doing *will* make a difference. At the very least you have exposed more people to new information, to a new set of analytical tools. You will have undoubtedly provided validation for other lesbians within the organization – and probably inspired at least one other woman to begin looking at what her love for women might mean.

☐ The first thing any progressive organization can do is *not assume all women are heterosexual.* Do this both in the context of the work that's done and within the group itself. Bearing in mind that heterosexism is often subtly expressed, reflect the reality that many women are lesbians in all written and visual materials. For instance, a group fighting violence against women should be sure to include violence against lesbians in its pamphlets or posters; an anti-poverty organization should acknowledge that not all welfare mothers are heterosexual.

☐ A progressive group can incorporate an understanding of lesbian oppression and its relationship to women's liberation the way it would any political concept: by exploring personal experiences, reading books, inviting speakers, attending workshops, etc. Arranging a *Stepping Out of Line* workshop would be an excellent starting point.

☐ Invite lesbians to join the group and/or use its services. Since lesbianism is socially invisible and lesbians hide their identity for fear of real repercussions, it may be necessary to *actively* solicit participation. Make a point of distributing materials to places where lesbians hang out and specifically say, "Lesbians Welcome."

☐ The lesbians in the group may want to caucus as a means of supporting each other and developing proposals for how the whole group can best meet the needs of lesbians and fight for lesbian rights. Encourage the formation of such a caucus – but don't leave it to the lesbians in the group to always initiate support for lesbian issues.

☐ Formalize any ties the group has with lesbian organizations. So often connections are made on a personal basis and when individuals leave, all the work

Photo/ Dorothy Elias

goes too. Ensure continuity by keeping records of meetings and agreements. Similarly, if the group develops a policy/action plan on lesbianism, make sure it is written down and passed along to — and discussed by — all new members.

☐ In any relevant printed materials, workshops and lectures the group prepares, include lesbian oppression and its connection to the oppression of all women. Take the group's banner regularly to appropriate lesbian events and demonstrations. Ask lesbian groups what kind of tangible support they could use: space for drop-ins or meetings, use of office equipment, donations of money or skills, etc. Encourage other groups to take public stands on lesbian issues. In any coalition, provincial or national organization lobby for support of lesbian rights.

Each individual in the organization can take on talking to their friends, parents, children and co-workers about the realities of lesbianism and lesbian oppression.

Resources

Still Ain't Satisfied: Canadian Feminism Today, ed. by Maureen FitzGerald et al (Toronto: The Women's Press, 1982)   An anthology surveying contemporary issues in the Canadian women's movement, including lesbianism.

Black Lesbian in White America, Anita Cornwall (Talla-hassee: Naiad, 1983)   Writings by a Black activist on her experiences in the civil rights, feminist and lesbian movements.

Lesbianism and the Women's Movement, ed. by Nancy Myron and Charlotte Bunch (Baltimore: Diana Press, 1975) The first articulation of a specifically lesbian perspective on feminism.

Sappho was a Right-on Woman: A Liberated View of Lesbianism, Sidney Abbott and Barbara Love (New York: Stein and Day, 1973)   Interesting account of struggles in

U.S. east coast women's movement in the late 60's and the early 70's around lesbianism.

Building Feminist Theory: Essays from Quest, (New York: Longmans's, 1981)

This Bridge Called My Back: Writings by Radical Women of Colour, ed. by Cherríe Moraga and Gloria Anzaldúa (Watertown: Persephone Press, 1981)   An uncompromising definition of feminism by women of colour.(Now available from Kitchen Table Press)

Right Wing Women, Andrea Dworkin (New York: Wideview/Perigee, 1983)   Fascinating, original writings by a radical feminist that address, among other things, the connections between anti-feminist, racist and homophobic currents in right-wing movements in the U.S. A 'know your enemies' book.

Women and Male Violence: The Visions and Struggles of the Battered Women's Movement, ed. by Susan Schecter (Boston: South End Press, 1982) An "indepth look at battering and the social movement against it." Includes information on lesbians in the shelter movement and their encounters with homophobia and heterosexism there.

It Could Happen to You...An Account of the Gay Civil Rights Campaign in Eugene, Oregon, The Gay Writers Group (Boston: Alyson, 1983) An account of the 1978 repeal of the gay right's amendment to the city charter, and analysis of the local gay and lesbian organizations and struggles.

"Lesbians and the Gay Movement" by Barbara Gittings and Kay Tobin, in *Our Right to Love: A Lesbian Resource Book,* ed. by Ginny Vida (Englewood Cliffs: Prentice-Hall, 1978) An historical overview based on the authors' years of personal experience.

Flaunting It! A Decade of Gay Journalism from The Body Politic, ed. by Ed Jackson and Stan Persky (Vancouver/ Toronto: New Star/Pink Triangle, 1982) Wide-ranging anthology of Canadian lesbian and gay writers. The editors have tried to ensure equal representation by women and there are several interesting personal and analytical perspectives on the political relationship between lesbians and gay men.

No Turning Back: Lesbian and Gay Liberation for the 80's, by Gerre Goodman et al (Philadelphia: New Society Publishers, 1983) "This book is for lesbians, gay men and our allies." An ambitious anthology that tackles a range of issues, including relations between gay men and lesbians, and the gay liberation and women's movements. Available from 4722 Baltimore Ave., Philadelphia PA 19143

Coming Out: Homosexual Politics in Britian from the 19th Century to the Present, Jeffrey Weeks (London: Quartet Books, 1977) A history of the attitudes and organized activities of lesbians and gay men. Includes materials on the gay movement and the left, and relations between lesbian and gay male organizations.

Come Together: The Years of Gay Liberation 1970-73, ed. by Aubrey Walter (London: Gay Men's Press, 1980) Articles from the newspaper of the English Gay Liberation Front. Mainly gay men, but some lesbian content and some examination of the relation between lesbians and gay men.

Out of the Closets: Voice of Gay Liberation, ed. by Karla Jay and Allan Young, (New York: Douglas Books, 1973) An anthology of personal stories.

Gay American History: Lesbians and Gay Men in the U.S.A., Jonathan Katz (New York: Avon 1978) An extensive documentary history, including a huge bibliography.

Gay/Lesbian Almanac, Jonathan Katz (New York: Harper and Row, 1983)

The Early Homosexual Rights Movement, John Lauresten and David Thorstad (Albion: Times Change Press) An historical account.

Homosexuality and Liberation: Elements of a Gay Critique, Mario Mielo (London: Gay Men's Press)

Pink Triangles: Radical Perspectives on Gay Liberation, ed. by Pam Mitchell (Boston: Alyson, 1980) Written by activists involved with left politics in general, gay and lesbian liberation in particular, these essays also deal with issues between lesbians and gay men.

"Lesbians and Gays in the Union Movement" by Susan Genge, in *Union Sisters,* ed. by Linda Briskin and Linda Yanz (Toronto: The Women's Press, 1983)

Homosexuality: Power and Politics, The Gay Left Collective (London: Allison and Busby, 1980) Articles from the English socialist newspaper, *Gay Left.*

Gay Left: A Gay Socialist Journal, 38 Chalcot Rd., London NW1, England Produced by an all male collective, this magazine does have some lesbian and feminist content. Distributed in North America by Carrier Pigeon, Rm. 309, 75 Kneeland St., Boston MA 02111

The Lavender and Red Book: A Gay Liberation Socialist Anthology, The Lavender and Red Union (Los Angeles: Lavender and Red Union, 1976)

"Towards a Marxist Theory of Gay Liberation", in *Capitalism and the Family,* by David Fernbach (San Francisco: Agenda Publishing, 1976)

Capitalism, the Family and Everyday Life, Eli Zaretsky (San Francisco: Agenda Publishing, 1976)

Feminism and Marxism: A Place to Begin, Way to Go, Dorothy E. Smith (Vancouver: New Star, 1977)

Marxism and Feminism Charnie Guettel (Toronto: Women's Press, 1974)

Feminism and Materialism: Women and the Modes of Production, ed. by Annette Kuhn and Ann Marie Wolpe (London: Routledge and Kegan Paul, 1978)

Beyond the Fragments: Feminism and the Making of Socialism, ed. by Sheila Rowbotham et al (London: Merlin Press, 1970)

Capitalist Patriarchy and the Case for Socialist Feminism, ed. by Zillah R. Eisenstein (New York: Monthly Review, 1979)

Thanks to Sara Diamond for some of these resources.

See also:

☐ *Feminism as Framework*
☐ *Work*

*There is a strong tradition of lesbian organizing in Canada
and Québec. . . The question now is, what do we want to do?*

Building
a Lesbian Movement

*T*he National Lesbian Conference
was held in Vancouver in 1981. It
was amazing and inspiring . . . 500 lesbians talking,
working, playing together. And marching through the
streets of Vancouver. The conference organizers had
scheduled a Lesbian Pride March for Saturday late
afternoon, starting at the courthouse steps and
marching right through the downtown area and the
West End to the community centre where the evening
dance was to be held. All day Saturday you could hear
women at the conference asking, "Are you going to
the march?" "Well, I haven't decided yet; it's so
public."

I decided to go; I was nervous about it. I had never
been on a lesbian march before, and it was an illegal
one — we didn't have a permit. There weren't all that
many women massing at Robson Square as the time
drew near to begin, and I became more scared.

So there I was, sitting on the steps of the courthouse
at Robson Square waiting for the march to start, and
suddenly it all seemed so familiar. Except for the fear,
that is. There was my friend Ellen on the steps with
the megaphone yelling about childcare and telling the
kids to go the car *right now,* just like she has done at
nearly every demonstration I have been to in the past
10 years. And there was Elf trying to get someone to
hold up the other end of the B.C. Federation of
Women's banner, just like always.

And there were my friends and others: the women I
always see at International Women's Day Parades, and
rallies for abortion rights, and El Salvador and Anti-
nuke Day. We had our banners, our megaphones, our
armbands, our marshals and our songsheets, and it
was like every Vancouver march I have ever been on,
except this time — for the very first time — we were all
there as lesbians, for lesbians.

It was a great, exhilarating, wonderful march,
linking arms and singing and chanting and smiling.
The rush of joyous energy was probably in exact
proportion to the terror I had felt. There was no
trouble on the march. We didn't obey the traffic lights,
stopped lots of traffic and waved back at the people
cheering us on from the sidewalk and smiling at us
from their windows. It was altogether wonderful.

— Nym

Lesbian communities are absolutely necessary to our
survival. We need places to come and be real, to know
there are others close by who see the world as we do,
to let down our guard, to rest, to not be so afraid and
alone — to just be. We need mirrors of our realities
and of ourselves.

But communities do not try to actively reach out
and educate the rest of society about the experience of
living as an oppressed people. Communities are not
out to transform the world. Political movements *are* —
and therefore are essential for our continued existence.

Some of us are relative newcomers to our lesbian
identities and some of us live in areas where a lesbian
community still barely exists. Others of us have lived
for years in lesbian and women's communities. What
most of us share is uncertainty about how to take the
step beyond developing and maintaining a community
to building a movement.

There is a myth that organizing as lesbians on lesbian issues requires 'special' strategies, that it is so difficult and overwhelming that only really politically sophisticated activists would even consider taking it on. Organizing as lesbians is no more difficult than organizing around anything else and in fact is such an untouched field that almost any tactic brings results. Lesbianism is more emotionally loaded than some other issues, but abortion and rape were virtually unmentionable words when feminists first began talking about them. There was a time when it was inconceivable to build a political analysis and a movement on such 'personal' issues as sex roles or women's work.

If we are serious about our intent to change social and political conditions for all lesbians, then we must begin to think of ourselves in those terms — as lesbian organizers deliberately working to create a movement to *profoundly* affect this society.

We've had a lot of arguments over the years with political people about lesbian activism. Is forming a lesbian group separatist? Is organizing as lesbians divisive to the women's movement? Why do we need to form lesbian groups? Should lesbians work in the gay rights movement or the women's movement? Is there a need for an autonomous lesbian movement? What should such a movement do?

The emotional heat of these discussions has centred often around the question of separatism. Is organizing specifically as lesbians separatist? Separatism is seen as divisive, politically naive, and destructive. Where did the term 'separatist' come from and how did it become so emotionally loaded?

The concept of lesbian separatism was first articulated in the early 70's by a lesbian feminist group in Washington, D.C. called the Furies Collective. The Furies advocated the withdrawal of lesbians from participation in the women's movement (or other movements) except as autonomous lesbian groups. By doing this, we as lesbians would be able to define for ourselves the reality of lesbian oppression, articulate our needs and visions and prevent ourselves from being silenced by the heterosexism which prevailed everywhere, even among our feminist sisters. We could create for ourselves a lesbian consciousness and a lesbian political voice which would be clear, loud and truthful. Our political strategy would be to work only with other lesbians or only from a position of strength as a lesbian group in a coalition with other groups.

The concept of lesbian separatism inspired excellent theoretical work on the role of the institution of heterosexuality in maintaining all women's oppression, and contributed to the creation of a vigorous lesbian identity within the women's movement. The term lesbian separatism though, has taken on many additional meanings. In the U.S., a version of lesbian separatism developed which considered separatism as an end in itself rather than a strategy. The analytical basis of this 'cultural separatism' has not been so clearly defined, but an underlying belief is that lesbians, by virtue of *being* lesbians, are different from other women. As a strategy for the creation of a different world, these lesbian separatists advocate withdrawing from interaction or work with anyone other than lesbians. Rather than attempting to influence or fight within existing movements for social change, the creation of our own spaces, networks, services and support systems will enable us to survive within the patriarchy and will ultimately, through the withdrawal of women's energies from the male-defined world, cause its downfall.

Some of the more contentious beliefs of this current of lesbian separatism are that lesbians should not work with heterosexual women, or with men at all. Some separatists believe that women and lesbians are oppressed by the amount of futile energy which is put into raising children, especially male children who will grow up to become oppressive men. They are therefore critical of lesbians raising male children and object to the presence of male children at women-only events. Separatists often argue that men and women are "different species" and that violence and insensitivity are biologically inherent in the male and that sensitivity, nurturance and reverence for life are inherent in women. There are clearly major differences in both theory and practice between women who believe in lesbian separatism as a political strategy and women who believe that lesbian separatism as a lifestyle — cultural separatism — is in itself a political strategy.

Cultural separatism in its more extreme versions has not been a major ideological force in lesbian organizing in Canada and Québec. The *fear* of separatism or the fear of being *labelled* a separatist has been much more of a reality. The word separatist, bearing its full emotional weight, has too often been used to describe *any* lesbian-only organizing. Within both feminist and gay movement circles, there seems to be a very real fear that lesbians organizing as lesbians is destructive or somehow dangerous. Feminist arguments usually include, "Lesbianism is only relevant to a small minority of women." Or, "Lesbianism isn't a political issue, so how can you organize on it?" Or, "If all the lesbians started working on lesbianism, they'd stop working on other (more timely and important) issues." The impact of this kind of debate is generally to immobilize lesbians who might otherwise be active.

Despite the many factors which prevent large numbers of us from working together as lesbians, there is a strong tradition of lesbian organizing in

Photo/ Nicky Hood

Canada and Québec. Usually a lesbian group forms in an urban area to provide specific services, such as information phone lines, drop-ins and social and cultural activities. The group may have come out of an existing mixed gay organization (particularly in the Maritimes and the Prairies) or out of the women's movement (as in Vancouver, Toronto and Montreal). Its focus may not be explicitly political, but the group often ends up being the lesbian presence or representing a lesbian viewpoint within the formal or informal structures of both the women's and gay movements in their area. Sometimes lesbian groups form in order to represent a lesbian viewpoint within an existing political organization; the Rights of Lesbians Subcommittee of the B.C. Federation of Women is an example. In the 80's, lesbian groups are forming for the explicit purpose of doing public political activity, such as Lesbians Against the Right, in Toronto.

At any rate, the very existence of an openly lesbian group, however innocuous its purpose, usually causes enough public reaction that the group is forced into political analysis and activity out of sheer self-defense. Connections are formed or strengthened with gay and feminist groups in the region. This combines with the fact that a visible lesbian community tends to strengthen individual lesbians who then begin to take risks in their workplaces and the organizations they belong to, knowing there are other lesbians to whom they can look for support.

Ten years of gay and feminist activism and ten years of lesbian organizing in Canada and Québec have built large lesbian communities in all urban — and many rural — areas. There are strong informal links between those communities. There is a fair level of positive lesbian information in women's movement publications — and in gay movement publications. We have had a series of highly successful National Lesbian Conferences, from the first in Ottawa, 1976 to the most recent in Vancouver, 1981, with 500 lesbians attending and 300 of us taking to the streets for a Lesbian Pride March. We have many lesbians working within women's groups. We have many lesbians working with gay men in gay rights organizations. We are beginning to have lesbians openly working in gay and/or women's caucuses within unions, churches, political movements...We have, in total, *thousands* of lesbians with well-developed informal communications systems and a fairly strong sense of network and community. The question now is, *What do we want to do?*

Shall we continue to focus on the difficulties of organizing as lesbians? Shall we foster the divisions among us? Shall we argue interminably about whether it's 'better' to work with gay men or straight women? Shall we continue to rank each other on the basis of political correctness? Shall we demand feminist identification as a pre-requisite to organizing as lesbians? Or, in the latest turn-around of 'more radical than thou', shall we denounce feminism as the primary agent of our repression as lesbians, denying our identity and connection as women?

Or shall we begin the work of building a movement of lesbians? A movement of all the different kinds of lesbians we are, a movement based on the commonalities of our experience of living as lesbians in the world and a high level of tolerance for our differences. Can we take our long tradition of survival against high odds, our talents for helping each other survive, our gifts for creating warm loving circles of friends, of giving each other respect and validation as lesbians — and use those skills in our political work? Can we envision our lesbian movement not as a traditional formal organization but much more as a sense of identification, source of information, of access to other lesbians, of political and emotional and practical support?

Can we feminists see ourselves as a caucus *within* that movement? Can we understand that lesbians are already everywhere and make it a goal of our movement that none of us are working anywhere *alone?* We will, of course, continue to work in the women's movement for we are, after all, women; but at the same time, we will create bonds with other lesbians to figure out strategies for incorporating a lesbian feminist perspective into the work of our feminist group. So that maybe none of us would ever again have to be quiet about our lesbianism? So that lesbianism would become more and more a real choice for more women? That, of course we have common cause with gay men in fighting the homophobia of a society which oppresses us both. But we could do that work not as isolated lesbians but with the backing and ideas of other lesbians who have experience with that kind of coalition politics.

And why should one or two lesbians fight a lonely and difficult battle against discrimination in their workplace when there are other lesbians in other areas who have been through that battle and know what works well? Can we use every scrap of responsibility and creativity and imagination we've got to find each other, listen to each other, respect each other and move to make changes? In a hundred ways, in a thousand ways, in as many ways as there are lesbians?

*I*n B.C. we've started a new provincial lesbian network. It's quite unstructured and women from all over B.C. are involved. It's about half lesbians who have had some experience in feminist or lesbian groups before and half who haven't. Almost everyone said very strongly that they didn't want to be part of another organization that was all boring meetings and debate and nothing getting done and everyone feeling bad. We decided that what we wanted was an organization that would increase our strength as individual lesbians regardless of where we lived, what we did, or what political beliefs we held. We figured that we wanted to create visible lesbian communities everywhere in B.C. — not just in the big cities — because too many of us were going mad from the isolation and the invalidation and the struggle. And that doing the

organizing work of creating such communities meant taking quite enormous personal risks and that none of us were particularly willing to take those risks without a pretty tangible support system.

So we are working on projects like: publicizing the existing lesbian and gay groups in the province, raising money through dances in cities where there is a large lesbian community and using that money to support lesbian groups and events in small towns and rural areas, facilitating tours by lesbian musicians, printing a newsletter of resources, events, contact groups and individuals, printing pamphlets for doing public education work which any lesbian can use as she chooses, holding regional and provincial gatherings. We made a commitment to have money and women available to any lesbian who is facing any kind of personal attack for her activism.

We share a lot of pain when we meet and it's too soon to say whether or not our ideas will really work over the years, but the feeling at our gatherings is quite amazing and quite wonderful. Hardened cynical old activists get all teary-eyed. And renewed.

— Nym

Photo/ Wendy L. Davis
Lesbian Liberation: You Won't Get It Under Capitalism

Know Your Enemies...

Vancouver, 1981: An unidentified group — most likely members of the Klu Klux Klan or the 'Moral Majority' — leafletted an entire suburb door-to-door with hate literature about homosexuals. The leaflet advocated that homosexuality be made a criminal offense and that the death penalty be reinstated to rid the world of gay and lesbian people. The leaflet was also racist and anti-Semitic.

It's frightening. *They are very serious.* And we were not right there, following or preceding them with accurate, positive information about our lives. We did not host neighbourhood seminars so that people could come and see a cross-section of homosexuals, ask some questions and dismiss the hate literature as lies.

The information in the leaflet, however horrible and extreme it may be, remains in the minds of many people as the only explicit material they have ever read on the subject. While they may not believe it, it works to create a climate where they are suspicious of homosexuality. So when they hear about gay men being beaten up or lesbians having their children taken away, those occurences seem mild in comparison to the gas chamber.

ATTENTION

Vancouver is a city that we are proud to live in. ARE YOU aware that our city is about to be ruined by a menance of frightening propotions?

Vancouver has become known as a "Gay Haven" and is now attracting homosexuals from all across Canada. Only five years ago Vancouver had a gay population of 50,000. TODAY there are between 100,000 to 200,000 Gays in Metro Vancouver. There are well over one million homosexuals in Canada. If many of these move to Vancouver, it is easy to see that our city could one day be dominated by homosexuals.
Will Vancouver become San Fransisco North?
Let's look at the TRUE FACTS about homosexuality:
Many people think that you can always tell when a person is a homosexual. This is simply NOT TRUE. The obvious homosexuals, the fairy and butch types make up only 20% of the total homosexual population.

Many are still in the closet. Many homosexuals are married or have dates as a cover. These homosexuals are very careful to hide their homosexuality from other people. You pass many homosexuals on the streets each day without realizing it. Some of your friends, relatives and co-workers are secretely homosexual.
Is it possible to cure or change a homosexual?
It is impossible to cure or change a real homosexual. Once a homosexual, always a homosexual. This has been proven by countless studies which have had little success in trying to change homosexuals.

Why is homosexuality DANGEROUS?
Homosexuality is dangerous. Homosexuality can spread. A person can be converted to homosexuality at any time. YOU could become homosexual tomorrow if there is a homosexual around you, or if you have a homosexual relative. Thus homosexuality could end the existence of the human race. Homosexuality is like a contagous disease that must be wiped out. There is only one solution.
Homosexuals must be killed. Otherwise they will overrun the world. These Queers must be stopped.
Homosexuality is an abomination against God. Homosexuals, directly or indirectly are responsible for all the major problems in the world today. Now these queers are abducting our children. These queers are seducing, raping and killing our children. YOUR son or daughter could be next. NOW is the time to stop these sick perverts. You must protect your children against these queers who want to take over. What can you do? Lobby your MP for laws making homosexuality illegal. Lobby to have the death penalty returned for any person convicted of being a homosexual.
Meanwhile, if you see a queer on the street and there are no witnesses around, beat that queer so that he will never walk again. The Nazis knew what to do with queers. God is on our side. Remember, the only good queer is a dead queer.
It is bad enough that we must put up with alot of Asians, Blacks, Jews and other filth. Must we also tolerate Faggots?
WATCH FOR MORE NEWS FROM THE CITIZENS ' FOR MORAL VALUES

Citizens Majority for Moral Values International 1st Van. Newsletter

One day there will be a better world where the Bible will be the Law.

Phone the right-wing groups in your area and ask them to send you information on homosexuality and women's liberation. Read their stuff and discuss its ramifications with women around you. Looking at it will give you some idea of the fear many people have of gay people and women's liberation. It is essentially a fear of the destruction of the traditional female role — service and maintenance of men and children — and with it, marriage and the nuclear family.

The right-wing takes this threat quite seriously. Far too often, lesbians don't. Most of us aren't out to deliberately smash the state, destroy the nuclear family or abolish heterosexuality as an institution. We simply want to love other women and create our lives with them. We don't take our individual actions, multiply that by hundreds of thousands of women and examine the results.

We *are* in a position to radically alter the fabric of this society and *they* know it! Once we know it, the better able we will be to knowingly make those changes and handle the repercussions. What happens when we don't take the time to find out what people are saying about us and to figure out why? We are left isolated, without any clear analytical response, stuck in a reactionary position with few defenses, dealing only on a personal level. We are unable to respond effectively to the real threats being thrown at us, and we lack the strong backing of other progressive groups.

If only because there exist fairly persistent — and often viciously hateful — campaigns against our right, our ability and our willingness to love other women — *that* constitutes sufficient grounds for building a powerful, autonomous lesbian movement.

Somewhere to Start

☐ Think big. Think long-term. Think step-by-step. What could we accomplish in five years? Ten years? Twenty years? Positive articles about lesbianism regularly in major papers? Sexual orientation protection in every human rights code? Good movies and books about lesbians? Active lesbian caucuses in every feminist group, every trade union, every political organization? Lesbian mothers consistently winning custody cases? Lesbian centres in every community? Thousands and thousands of women coming out? Strong Canadian and Québecoise representation in the international lesbian movement? Actual literal changes — in our lifetimes? We're all planning to be lesbians for a long time — can we begin to see our political commitments in the same time-frame?

☐ Begin from where we are. Already, most of us have lesbian friendship and social circles and many of us are involved in political groups. These are the starting points, this is where we can locate our individual and collective efforts to end lesbian invisibility and to ensure that no lesbian has to act alone.

☐ Communication is essential. Contact between groups in a common area can be maintained through newsletters, regional coalitions, annual conferences — even informal social occasions. Inter-regional communication is also vital. We can make use of existing Québecoise and Canadian newsletters, *Lesbian/Lesbienne* and *Amazones d'Hier, Lesbiennes d'Aujourd'hui* and *The Grapevine*. Feminist, gay and progressive print and other media can also be used.

☐ Structuring our groups and networks in such a way that they are self-sustaining is important. The money needed to do our work should come from ourselves and our communities. On-going, long-term organizing will be most effective if our groups are accessible to the majority of lesbians who have full-time commitments to jobs and to children.

☐ Encourage tolerance and respect for differences in ourselves, our friends, our lesbian groups and our communities. Thouands and thousands of lesbians working together — even if we disagree with each other on many things — can accomplish a lot more than ten lesbians who agree on everything (if we could even find ten...). We need to listen to each other with our hearts as well as our brains and *believe* in our strength, our love and our movement.

---

*Y*ou are sitting on a grassy slope, watching the crowd gather. Thousands of people are coming, moved to act by anger and commitment and effective organizing.

Linda was fired from her job six months ago by a reactionary school board for the 'crime' of openly discussing lesbianism and homosexuality with her teenage students. The firing itself had been fairly routine. More and more women and men were losing their jobs for daring to speak out on issues that mattered. Linda had been teaching in a rural community which was perhaps less progressive than some others; but still, speaking out on lesbianism had seemed such a minor thing to do. After all, this was 1998 and positive public response to homosexuality was increasing. In many circles, it was alright for young people to experiment with their sexuality: boys with boys, girls with other girls, as well as the standard girl-boy pairing. What had been so terrible about Linda's position?

Well, she was not only visible as a lesbian, she was promoting homosexuality and lesbianism as healthy, positive life-choices for her students. She was not content for lesbianism to be merely tolerated. She believed that being a lesbian was incredibly powerful for her and wanted young women to see it was a real option for themselves, not just something to play with.

After the firing there had been a series of meetings with the school board, lots of local and provincial media, support from activist groups. Linda decided to stay in town. She dealt with the harassing calls, the taunts and jeers on the street. Maybe there hadn't been enough of us with her. Half the town came to that last schoolboard meeting, clearly divided on homosexuality being advocated in their school.

Some of Linda's friends had gone to the bar with her afterwards to further discuss strategies. But she had left the tavern alone, followed by a gang of men. They attacked her outside her home, savagely beating her with pipes and clubs. Who knows if they meant to kill her, but by the time she was found and taken to hospital...

You wonder why it always seems to take a tragedy to get people to come together?

There are lots of banners here: the Teacher's Federation with its women's, gay and lesbian caucuses clearly visible; dozens of unions, gay liberation groups, at least 15 lesbian organizations, Native women's groups, the Y.W.C.A., the Welfare Rights Coalition, the Union of Unemployed Workers, the Coalition to Fight Racism, Dykes on Bikes, women you know from the bars, feminist groups, the Young People's Association, child-care organizations, disabled women's groups... on and on and on as the banners unfurled. You were pleased: this massive demonstration was one in a series of protests held across the province and the last big push needed to get that Human Rights legislation passed. After 10 years of hard struggle, this would be the last province to pass the "no discrimination on the basis of sexual orientation" bill. The federal level would be next...

There are at least 50,000 people — a good sized turnout for this issue. Lesbianism and homosexuality were still controversial in some political circles, and the reactionary forces were not at all pleased that lesbians and homosexuals were no longer isolated or politically invisible. Rallies and protests certainly had gotten bigger over the last 20 years as the work of grass-roots consciousness-raising began to take effect. People were seeing the commonalities between seemingly separate struggles, and there were hundreds of new faces at each public event. It leaves a good taste in your mouth to see so many young people here. This is, after all, one of the reasons for the protest — the right of young people to have access to varying information in their places of learning.

You notice the police beginning to surround the demonstration: cops on motorcycles, the dogs, the riot gear, the plainclothes cops with their video cameras in the crowd — even a helicopter hovering overhead. There had been a time when we used to get government permission and police escorts for our demonstrations, as though we needed protection from the public. We were so careful not to step on anyone's toes. But when we began to organize with the goal of radically altering the system, our outlook — and experiences — changed. Governments had ordered police to harass us, to beat us, to make our rallies chaotic, to infiltrate our groups, to censor any positive press. It became apparent to many of us that the state and its forces were not there to protect us or serve *our* interests. They wanted us marginal, ignorant, living in our ghettos, feeding the machinery of a society which needed to keep us second-class citizens, without any real power. And real power was what we were after — fundamental change in those areas where we experienced the most pain: sexism, class oppression, racism, homophobia, capitalism, the destruction of the air and the earth, the threat of war.

The rally is underway. The Wen-Do women and security committee have formed a circle between the crowd and the cops. You marvel at the support here for a woman's right to choose lesbianism. It hasn't come easily! This was the first time you know of that lesbians had reached out for such public and political support and gotten it. The benefits of 20 years of focussed organizing, of bitter struggles with feminists, with gay liberationists, trade unionists, socialists, let alone the battles with those who had very little political awareness — all those years were finally beginning to pay off. The dream of a large, powerful, *democratic* Common Front was slowly coming true.

It's almost embarrassing to remember what you were like 20 years ago. You had fallen head over heels in love with a woman at 19. Up until then you had assumed you would end up like everybody else, heterosexual and married, your youthful period of travelling, questioning, searching out new ideas only a phase. Loving a woman had been a major turning point; it meant leaving behind layers of self-hate and learning to love yourself.

How you had resisted feminism! You knew it would mean coming to see the world through new eyes, never being able to go back — and it meant work. But the women around you loved you and helped you shape a solid feminist analysis that had been your mainstay through all these years.

Your vision had been pretty short-sighted though, like that of the whole movement. You had spent 10 years being active as a feminist in many organizations; there were so many injustices to protest, so many meetings to attend. You often read of revolutions in other countries, but it was difficult to see how any of that could apply to this context. You had really believed, secretly, that other women — smarter and more committed — would soon emerge to lead the movement. You would just have to follow, your participation would have no real impact, liberation would somehow just happen around you, not *because* of you, and in 20 years at the most you could get on with living in freedom. How idealistic!

One day you woke up and you were 30. You had basically been doing the same thing for 10 years and the world hadn't changed all that much. Why is it that we so easily lose sight of our vision when the struggle is hard? There had been many splits in the women's movement — not just serious disagreements, but horrible, dangerous divisions.

Feminists were involved in bitter fights, often publicly. There had been harm done not only to our public image and credibility, but to individuals. Our belief that it was possible to love women, to work together, to be respected and cared for, to disagree while staying united had been shaken. And not believing that change was possible seriously affected the movement. We stopped taking risks, stopped searching for more successful ways of organizing. We didn't know how to learn from our differences.

The public image of women's liberation was as a movement made up of lesbians only. Lesbians believed it to be a group for reformist heterosexual women. Poor women and women of colour saw it as a movement of white, middle class professionals. You hadn't seen many new faces coming to feminism during that time. Nobody came, and nobody seemed to care. Only the panti-hose ads on t.v. ever mentioned the word 'revolution' anymore!

Fueled by your resentment at the divisiveness of the lesbian community, you had unexpectedly gone on a tirade at a regional lesbian conference years ago. You think awhile, remembering the circle of tense faces in the workshop on "Communities." You could see yourself standing, speaking louder and louder, passionately waving your arms, tears in your eyes.

"I am so angry at every lesbian in the women's movement who denies that it's important to be working *as* a lesbian and *for* lesbianism.

"Angry at the feminists and lesbians who discuss the merits of lesbian organizing without every having done any.

"Furious that feminist ideology has been trivialized into rules of etiquette.

"Angry at the lack of visibility of lesbians within the women's movement.

"Angry that so many lesbians talk about lesbianism being such a positive life choice, yet never publicly identify as lesbians so other women hear about it.

"Angry at those lesbians who don't actively promote lesbianism; who assume that heterosexuality is a normal way for the majority of women to live.

"Angry at lesbians who have the luxury of being apolitical.

"So angry that we don't aggressively bring feminism to lesbians.

"Angry that every lesbian doesn't automatically consider taking politics into the world at every conceivable opportunity.

"And very, very sad that although we say lesbianism is about loving women, we sit back and act helpless while lesbians die of booze and despair."

You had been so dissatisfied then; you recognize it now as a time of profound change. You took that anger and with the help of other women, turned it into a political direction that had lasted 15 years.

There had been that scary, exciting night at someone's home when a number of you had committed yourselves to finding a way to unite lesbians, to creating a movement of *all* lesbians, a network that could provide the support and analysis needed to change attitudes, to make clear the connections with all kinds of political struggles. It had seemed a far-fetched and monumental task.

Together, you had re-established the regular lesbian drop-in and phone-line. Those services provided much needed support to the hundreds of women who came or called over the years. You facilitated consciousness-

raising sessions and encouraged the groups to do direct actions: it made no sense to give lesbians information they had no way of testing! Other lesbian feminists you knew started coming-out groups. All in all, you figured there were at least 5,000 more raging lesbian feminists across the country in the last 10 years as a result of your work and that of other groups active in similar grass-roots organizing.

Over the years, lesbians had come together regularly in small groups, locally and regionally. Debates and discussions everywhere focussed on lesbian perspectives on world situations, on current political and popular writings and the day-to-day realities of our lives. Lesbians began listening more carefully to each other, asking for information: "What has it been like for you to live as a lesbian in a small northern town?" "How do you manage to feed and clothe 3 children on that salary?" Those were the first steps toward making our community a more viable place to live. Slowly we started to see just how much richness and diversity and skill there was among us.

Sculpture/ Persimmon Blackbridge

The dream of a Lesbian Network came true in '88 at the Canadian and Québec lesbian conference in Winnipeg. You were thrilled to see such support for an organization that would be open to any woman anywhere who called herself a lesbian! The aims of the network were really general those first years, a necessary step in promoting a postive, varied image of lesbians organizing together. The goals had included: "Supplying accurate information on lesbianism... working to change attitudes and end homophobia and sexism...providing emotional, political and financial support to lesbians and lesbian groups across the country..." Your personal goal during that time had been to encourage every single lesbian you came into contact with to *do* something to make the world a better place.

Being politically active as lesbians — for lesbians — became increasingly widespread. The debate then entered the arena of coalition politics. How do lesbians make the links with other groups? How to develop a broad political analysis that would connect all our seemingly separate struggles? How to work with men and women who were often perceived as oppressors? What did lesbianism have to do with gay liberation, feminism, socialism, anti-racism, anti-nuke work?

Lots of clapping and cheering below, and your attention is drawn back to the rally and the speaker, a woman in a bright red jumper with greying hair and flashing eyes. Anne! Your heart warms as you think of your friendship with her, a love that has lasted for 20 years, changing and ripening as you work side by side, sharing the sweetness of sexual intimacy. You've managed to maintain an openness that permits you both to come to each other with new learning, joys, problems, new loves. The children in your life are biologically hers and they help bond you and the other woman who has made a long-term commitment to them. She is one of the women who will grow old beside you.

She talks of turning to one another for protection and inspiration. She asks people in the crowd to walk up to someone they don't yet know, "Shake their hand, find out why they came, ask what they intend to do to prevent this kind of senseless violence that brought us here today from happening again...go on, do it!"

She continues as people begin to move about, "We must learn to turn *to* each other when we are in trouble. It's too easy to turn *against* each other instead, too easy to blame our troubles on someone we don't know. Linda was murdered by the oppressor's biggest weapon — bigotry. We must be vigilant about not letting hatred eat away at us."

You grin, liking the intensity in her voice.

"There are 50,000 of us here right now. What if, for the next rally, each of you would take personal responsibility for bringing someone new? That would mean 100,000 of us standing here, ready to show the police, the government — the people who would kill lesbians — that we are many and *we will not be silent.* And when we start to yell and move and act, they will know we mean it!"

There would be a one hour special on lesbianism aired tomorrow on national television. The Feminist Media collective had lobbied hard to get access to prime-time. Millions of people would get some accurate, positive information on women loving women. The Human Rights Legislation would be the next victory — a small one, and certainly not the end. That much women had learned from the struggle for women's suffrage: the right to vote had not meant freedom. But each step did serve to change attitudes, to create a climate where it became unacceptable for the majority of people to see lesbians and homosexuals as less than fully human. This kind of visibility made it possible to encourage huge numbers of people to ask *why* about those areas of their lives that seemed out of their control, to share with them ideas that could enable them to see their lives in political terms. Once the Human Rights Legislation was through, there would be another short-term goal, something concrete to organize around. But for tonight you could rest easy.

You throw back your head and look at the blue sky through a golden tree. It's really fall — so soon! You kick your way through piles of crisp leaves. The day will come, you know it, when peace will be the norm, when women will be free, and when lesbians will be proudly accepted. You believe that with an intensity that races in your veins and a passion that sustains you like oxygen. That is the fire that gives you the courage to face tomorrow's struggles, and those that will surely come with the morning after that and the one after that.

There will be no 'after the revolution' — *this is it!*

— *Yvette*

Finding Lesbian Resources

Information about lesbianism and contact with other lesbians are crucial to our survival. Getting that information and making those contacts can be hard if you don't know where or how to look. What we have compiled here are some general guidelines for how to locate materials and groups.

Lesbian groups often change addresses so, rather than attempt a comprehensive and soon out-of-date list, we've concentrated on what to read and where to write/phone/go to discover what is happening in different regions. We've also given sources for the books, audio-visuals and periodicals recommended throughout the book.

Look in the phone book Try the white pages under "Lesbian", "Gay" and "Women." Also look under the name of the town/city: the *Vancouver Gay Community Centre* is listed under "Vancouver." Phone the crisis line (often listed at the front of the phone book) and ask for information on lesbian and gay resources. If there are none, phone any and all women's movement groups. Try rape crisis centres, women's centres, Status of Women groups, etc. They may not know, but sooner or later you'll get a lesbian who works in one of the groups and hopefully she'll know. You don't have to give your name to any of these people and they're all quite used to getting phone calls. Just say, "I'm new in town and I'm trying to find other lesbians/gay women. Can you tell me of any groups, drop-ins, clubs, bars, newspapers...?"

Subscribe to newspapers Phone calls don't work in most small towns and rural areas — yet. Subscribe to a variety of feminist and gay periodicals. They are the best sources of information on existing groups and upcoming events.

Bookstores Write to feminist and gay bookstores and ask for their catalogues. Order books by and about lesbians directly from them. Check out your local public library, too. Lesbian, gay and progressive librarians have gotten some amazing collections into some unlikely places.

Canada and Québec

Lesbian/Gay Publications

Subscribing to both a national gay publication and a local or regional paper is the most effective way of finding out what groups exist in your area and of getting news of upcoming conferences and cultural events. Most gay publications will be mailed out in non-identifiable wrappings; they can also be picked up directly at feminist, gay and progressive bookstores.

Some of the following publications reflect a primarily gay male perspective; see also *Feminist Publications* below. A number of gay groups put out local newsletters which are not listed here.

Lesbian/Lesbienne, P.O. Box 70, Stn. F, Toronto Ont. M4Y 2L4 A quarterly newsletter containing lists of lesbian events and groups across Canada and Québec.

Amazonnes d'hier, Lesbiennes d'aujourd'hui, C.P. 1721, Succ. La Cité, Montréal, P.Q. H2W 2R7 Une revue pour lesbiennes seulement, d'une perspective de lesbienne radicale.

Grapevine: Newsletter of the Lesbian Mothers' Defense Fund, P.O. Box 38, Stn. E, Toronto Ont. M6H 4E1 Reports on the activities of Canadian L.M.D.F. groups, Canadian and international legal disputes involving lesbian mothers and movement news.

The Open Door: Rural Lesbians Newsletter, Northern Lesbian Collective, R.R. #2, P.O. Box 50, Usk Store B.C. V8G 3Z9 "...provides us with an opportunity to celebrate our survival as lesbians living in a rural/northern environment."

Flagrant, The Vancouver Island Lesbian Newsletter Collective, P.O. Box 651, Stn. E, Victoria B.C.

B.C. Provincial Lesbian Connection Newsletter, P.O. Box 33537, Stn. D, Vancouver B.C. "A forum of news and ideas by, for and about lesbians with a specific focus on B.C. and the Yukon."

Voices: A Lesbian Survival Manual, c/o I. Andrews, RR #2, Kenora Ont. P9N 3W8 Focusses on the concerns of lesbians living in rural northern Ontario.

The Body Politic: A Magazine for Gay Liberation, P.O. Box 7289, Stn. A, Toronto, Ont. M5W 1X9 *The Body Politic* primarily reflects a gay male perspective, but it carries a comprehensive and up-to-date list of lesbian and gay groups in Canada and Québec, as well as bi-national and international news.

Rites: For Gay & Lesbian Liberation, P.O. Box 65, Stn. F, Toronto Ont. M4Y 2L4 A newspaper with bi-national and international coverage and a commitment to equal lesbian participation.

Angles, P.O. Box 2259, Vancouver B.C. V5B 3W2 "Vancouver's community newspaper for gays and lesbians." Carries a comprehensive list of B.C. resources.

Fine Print, P.O. Box 3822, Stn. D, Edmonton Alta. T5L 2K0 "A newspaper for and by the gay community."

GO Info, P.O. Box 2919, Stn. D, Ottawa Ont. K1P 5W9

Le Berdache, C.P. 36, Succ. 6, Montréal P.Q. H2L 4J7 La journal de *l'Association pour les droits des lesbiennes et gais du Québec.*

Feminist Publications

The following are feminist publications which often — and in some cases, *always* — carry material and information with lesbian content.

Kinesis, c/o Vancouver Status of Women, 400a 5th Ave. W., Vancouver B.C. V5Y 1Y8 "News about women that's not in the dailies."

Room of One's Own: A Feminist Journal of Literature and Criticism, P.O. Box 46160, Stn. G, Vancouver B.C. V6R 4G5 A quarterly.

Images: The Kootenay Women's Newspaper, P.O. Box 736, Nelson B.C. V1L 5R4 Carries rural lesbian information.

Herizons: The Manitoba Women's Newspaper, P.O. Box 551, Winnipeg Man. R3C 2J3

Northern Woman Journal, 316 Bay St., Thunder Bay Ont.

P7B 1S1 A bi-monthly feminist newspaper with some lesbian content, serving the women of northern Ontario.

Hysteria, P.O. Box 2481, Stn. B, Kitchener Ont. M2H 6M3

Broadside: A Feminist Review, P.O. Box 294, Stn. P, Toronto Ont. M5S 2T1

Canadian Women's Studies/Les cahiers de la femme, Founders College, York University, 4700 Keele St., Downsview Ont. M3J 1P3 An academic journal.

Fireweed, P.O. Box 279, Stn. B, Toronto Ont. M5T 2W2 A literary quarterly; #13 was a special lesbian issue.

Resources for Feminist Research/Documentation sur la recherche féministe, Dept. of Sociology, O.I.S.E., 252 Bloor St. W., Toronto Ont. M5S 1V6 An academic journal with bi-national and international resource lists; vol. 12 #1 was the *Lesbian Issue;* it can be ordered separately.

Entr'elles: revue féministe de l'Outaouais, C.P. 1398, Succ. B, Hull P.Q. J8H 3Y1

Communiqu'elles, 3585, rue St.-Urbain, Montréal P.Q. H2X 2N6

La vie en rose, 3963, rue St.-Denis, Montréal, P.Q. H2W 2M4

Atlantis: A Women's Studies Journal, Mt. St. Vincent University, Halifax, N.S. B3M 2J6

Common Ground: A Journal for Island Women, 81 Prince St., Charlottetown, P.E.I. C1A 4R3

Bookstores

The following are feminist and gay bookstores which carry a good selection of lesbian titles and often tapes, records, newspapers, posters, stickers, etc. Progressive bookstores have been listed for areas where no feminist or gay bookstores exist. Most bookstores supply catalogues on request and will fill mail orders — even for books they don't normally stock.

Feminist, gay and progressive bookstores often function informally as 'community centres'. They are usually friendly places, with up-to-date notice boards for news of local events, groups, meetings, places to live, services available... They're a good place to start. They're also good places to support. If you have a choice between buying from one of these stores or from a chain, walk that extra block.

British Columbia
Everywoman's Books, 641 Johnson St., Victoria V8W 1M7 (604-388-9411)

Ariel Books, 2766 W. 4th, Vancouver (604-733-3511)

Vancouver Women's Bookstore, 315 Cambie St., Vancouver V6B 2N4 (604-684-0523)

Little Sisters Book and Art Emporium, 1221 Thurlow St., Vancouver V6E 1X4 (604-669-1753)

Alberta
Common Woman, 8208 104 St., Edmonton T6E 4L6 (403-432-9344)

City Limits, 503 22nd Ave. S.W., Calgary (403-290-1889)

Saskatchewan
Tumbleweed Books, 2210 Albert St., Regina (306-586-4452)

Onion Books Cooperative, 650 Broadway, Saskatoon (306-665-7611)

Manitoba

Liberation Books, 160 Spence, Winnipeg (204-774-0637)

Ontario

Toronto Women's Bookstore, 73 Harbord St., Toronto (416-922-8744)

Glad Day Book Shop, 648a Yonge St., Toronto M4Y 2A6 (416-961-4161)

Ottawa Women's Bookstore/Libraire des femmes d'Ottawa, 380 Elgin St., Ottawa (613-230-1156)

Québec

Libraire l'Androgyne, 2nd floor, 3642, boul. St.-Laurent, Montréal H2X 2V4 (514-842-4765)

Maritimes

Red Herring Coop Books, 1652 Barrington St., Halifax N.S. (902-422-5087)

Publishers

The following are feminist publishers in Canada and Québec; they all have catalogues and will do mail orders.

Press Gang Publishers, 603 Powell St., Vancouver B.C. V6A 1H2 (604-253-2537)

The Women's Press, 16 Baldwin St., Toronto Ont. M5T 1L2 (416-598-0082)

Les editions de la pleine lune, C.P. 14, Succ. G, Montréal P.Q. H2W 2M9

Editions de remue-menage, C.P. 607, Succ. C, Montréal P.Q. H2L 4L5

Les editions communiqu'elles, 3585, rue St.-Urbain, Montréal, P.Q. H2X 5J2

The following have published books of interest to feminist and lesbian readers; they also do mail orders.

New Star Books, 2504 York Ave., Vancouver B.C. V6K 1E3

Talon Books, #201-1019 E. Cordova, Vancouver, B.C. V6A 1M8

Pink Triangle Press, P.O. Box 639, Stn. A, Toronto Ont. M5W 1G2

Eden Press, Suite 12-254 Victoria Ave., Montréal P.Q. H3Z 2M6

Radio

The Lesbian Show, CFRO 102.7 FM Vancouver Co-op Radio (604-684-8494)   Thurs. 8:30 p.m. A collection of tapes of past shows is available; write to 337 Carrall St., Vancouver B.C. V6B 2J4

The Coming-Out Show, CFRO 102.7 FM (see above) Thurs. 7:30 p.m. "A newsmagazine by and for gays and lesbians."

Soundwomen, CKLN 88.1 FM c/o Ryerson Polytechnical Institute, Toronto, Ont.   Sun. 11:30 a.m. Lesbian and feminist music, community news, announcements.

Leaping Lesbians, CKMS 94.5 FM (105.7 cable) Kitchener/ Waterloo, Ont. (519-744-4863)   Thurs. 6-8:00 p.m.

Gay News and Views, CKMS 94.5 FM (105.7 cable) Kitchener/Waterloo Ont. (519-886-CKMS)   Tues. 6-8:00 p.m.

Parallèles lesbiennes et gaies, CIBL 104.5 mf Montréal P.Q. (514-526-1489)   Lundi 19h30

Gaies-riez-roses, CION 103.7 mf Radio Grand-Portage, Rivière-du-Loup, P.Q.   Un dimanche sur deux 17h.

L'Heure gaie, CKRL 89.1 mf, Cité Universitaire, Québec P.Q.   Jeudi 19h.

Television

Pacific Wave (formerly Gayblevision), Cable 10, Vancouver B.C. (604-689-5661)

Coming-Out, Cable 13W, Winnipeg, Man. (204-269-8678) Thurs. 11 p.m. Produced by the *Winnipeg Gay Media Collective,* Box 27, UMSU, University of Manitoba, R3T 2N2

Film, Video and Other Media

Women in Focus Arts and Media Centre, #204 - 456 W. Broadway, Vancouver B.C. V5Y 1R3 (604-872-2250) Since 1974, *Women in Focus* has been a national and international distributor and producer of feminist film and video. They also have gallery and performance space. A number of the productions they carry have lesbian content; contact them for rental and catalogue information.

Video Inn (Satellite Video Exchange Society), 261 Powell St., Vancouver B.C. V6A 1G3 (604-688-4336)   They have a library of over 1200 tapes by Québecois, Canadian and international producers, some of specific interest to lesbians and feminists.

Womanspirit Art Gallery and Resource Centre, 359 Dundas St., London Ont. N6B 1V5 (519-432-2826)   Among other things, they publish *Spirale: A Women's Art and Culture Quarterly.*

Branching Out: Lesbian Cultural Resource Centre, 2 Bloor St. W., Toronto and P.O. Box 141 Stn. A, Toronto M4W 3E7

DEC Films (Development Education Centre), 427 Bloor St. W., Toronto Ont. M5W 1X7 (416-964-6901)   *DEC* is a distributor of films and videos relating to many progressive issues.

New Cinema, Unit 1, 75 Horner Ave., Toronto Ont. M8Z 4X5 (416-251-3728)   Among other productions, they distribute *The Word Is Out.*

Canadian Filmakers Distribution Centre, 525 W. Pender St., Vancouver B.C. V6B 1V5 (604-732-9396) or Suite 403, 144 Front St. W., Toronto Ont. M5J 1G2 (416-593-1808)

Vidéo Amazone, B.P. 429, Succ. Stn. Victoria, Montréal P.Q. H3Z 2V8 (514-489-8392)   Producers and distributors of the video *Amazones d'hier, Lesbiennes d'aujourd'hui (Amazons Then, Lesbians Now).* For women only. Available in both French and English.

Video femmes, 10 McMahon, Québec P.Q. G1R 3S1 (418-692-3090)   A production and distribution centre for videos by women.

Powerhouse Gallery, 3738, St.-Dominque, Montréal P.Q. H2X 2X8 (514-844-3489)   A feminist art centre.

National Film Board of Canada (consult the phonebook for regional addresses)   They distribute and produce hundreds of films, some of specific interest to lesbians and feminists.

Records and Tapes

These small, independent companies will fill mail orders.

Lucy Records, P.O. Box 67, Saturna Island B.C. V0N 2Y0
Producer and distributor of Ferron.

Mother of Pearl Records, Woodmore Man. R0A 2M0
Producer and distributor of Heather Bishop.

Lesbian/Gay Contact Groups

The following groups are not, happily, the only lesbian and
gay groups in Canada and Québec. There are *hundreds*
more. Listed here are groups that have an ongoing existence
and tend to function as information sources about other
local/regional activities, actions and facilities. The provincial
organizations would be able to refer you to groups in your
location. Information phone lines could tell you about
dances, political and support groups and rallies; they also
often do counselling, etc.

The Body Politic (see *Lesbian/Gay Publications* above)
regularly carries a comprehensive list of most groups in
Canada and Québec.

Lesbian Mothers'Defense Fund, P.O. Box 38, Stn. E,
Toronto Ont. M6H 4E1 (416-465-6822) This group
has been able to help several lesbian mothers with
custody disputes; they have also acted as a contact
point and support system for lesbian mothers. Their
newsletter, *Grapevine,* is a networking tool for lesbian
mothers across the country. There are also active
groups in Calgary, #124-320 5th Ave. S.E., Calgary
Alta. T2G 0E5 (403-264-6328) and in Montréal, C.P.
222, suc. de Lorimier, Montréal P.Q. H2H 2N6
(514-524-1040)

British Columbia

*B.C. Federation of Women Rights of Lesbians Subcom-
mittee,* P.O. Box 24687 Stn. C, Vancouver V5T 4E6

Rural Lesbian Association, P.O. Box 1242, Vernon B.C.
V1T 6N6 A support network for B.C. lesbians living
outside urban areas. Among other things, it has a lending
library of lesbian books.

A Provincial Connection, P.O. Box 33537, Stn. D,
Vancouver B.C. The B.C. provincial lesbian organization
working to encourage the growth of lesbian communities
throughout the province, to share skills and resources, and
to end isolation.

Kamloops
Thompson Area Gay Group, P.O. Box 3343, V2C 6B9
Regular meetings and socials for lesbians and gay men.

Kelowna
Okanagan Gay Organization, P.O. Box 1165, Stn. A
V1Y 7P8 (contact phone: 604-763-9191)

Port Hardy
*North Island Gay and Lesbian Support and Information
Group (NIGLSIG),* P.O. Box 1404, V0N 2P0 For gay
people of north Vancouver Island.

Prince Rupert
Gay People of Prince Rupert, P.O. Box 881, V8J 3Y1
(604-624-4982)

Revelstoke
Lothlorien, P.O. Box 8557, Sub. #1, V0E 3G0

Terrace
Northern Lesbians, P.O. Box 250, R.R. #2, Usk Store,
V8G 3Z9

Vancouver
Lesbian Information Line (LIL), (604-734-1016) Thurs. and
Sun. 7-10:00 p.m.; recorded message at other times. Their
mailing address is 1501 W. Broadway, V6J 1W6

*SEARCH (Society for Education, Action, Research and
Counselling in Homosexuality),* P.O. Box 48903, Bentall
Centre, V7X 1A8 (604-689-1039) Phone line every day
7-10:00 p.m. for information and counselling; recorded
message at other times.

Young Lesbian Drop-In, 1349 Burrard St. Sat. 3-4:00 p.m.

Vancouver Gay Community Centre, P.O. Box 2259,
V6B 3W2 (604-684-6869)

Victoria
Feminist Lesbian Action Group (FLAG), P.O. Box 1604,
Stn. E, V8W 2X7

Womyn's Coffee House, 1923 Fernwood Every Wed. night.

West Kootenays
West Kootenays Gays and Lesbians, P.O. Box 642, Nelson
V1L 4K5 (contact phone: 604-352-3504 Their activities
include holding social events and producing a newsletter.

Alberta

Alberta Lesbian and Gay Rights Association (ALGRA),
P.O. Box 1852, Edmonton Alta. T5J 2P2

Lesbian Outreach and Support Team, P.O. Box 6093, Stn.
A, Calgary, Alta. Based in Calgary, this group has an
outreach programme for lesbians in small communities.

Calgary
Lesbian Information Line, (403-265-9548) Tues. and Fri.
from 8-10:00 p.m. plus a 24-hr. answering service. One of
the projects of the *Womyn's Collective* which also sponsors
dances, a lesbian drop-in, etc. Their address is the Old Y,
Rm. 314-223 12 Ave. S.W.

Gay Information and Resources Calgary, P.O. Box 2715,
Stn. M, T2P 3C3 and Rms. 317-323 at the Old Y
(403-234-8973) Information and counselling 7-10:00 p.m.
Mon.-Fri.

Edmonton
Womonspace, #7 - 8406 104 St. T6E 4G2 (403-433-3559 or
488-2290) A social and recreational group for lesbians.

Every Woman's Place, 9926 112 St. (403-433-3559)

Red Deer
Gay Association of Red Deer, P.O. Box 356, T4N 5E9

Saskatchewan

Prince Albert
Prince Albert Gay Community Centre, P.O. Box 1893,
S6V 6J9 and #1 - 24 10th St. E. (306-922-4650) There is

a phone line Wed. and Thurs. 8-10:00 p.m. and socials Fri. and Sat. nights.

Regina
Lesbian Association of Southern Saskatchewan, P.O. Box 4033 (306-522-4522 and 352-8397)

Regina Women's Community and Rape Crisis Centre, #219 - 1810 Smith St., S4P 2N3 (306-522-2777 and 352-7688)

Saskatoon
Gayline, (306-665-9129) Mon. to Thurs. 7:30 - 10:30 p.m. One of the projects of *Gay and Lesbian Support Services,* #217 - 116 3rd Ave. S. Counselling and support groups are also available.

Manitoba

Manitoba Gay Coalition, P.O. Box 27, UMSU, University of Manitoba, Winnipeg R3T 2N2 (202-269-8678)

Thompson
Gay Friends of Thompson, P.O. Box 157, R8N 1N2 (204-677-5833) Tues. and Thurs. 8-10:00 p.m.

Winnipeg
Lesbian Line, (204-774-0007) Thurs. 7:30-10:00 p.m.

Gay Community Centre, 277 Sherbrooke St. (204-786-1236) Open daily from 5:50 p.m. (Sun 1:00 p.m.) Includes a cafe for lesbians and gay men.

Ontario

Coalition for Gay Rights in Ontario, P.O. Box 822, Stn. A, Toronto M5W 1G3 (416-533-6824)

Guelph
Guelph Gay Equality, P.O. Box 773, N1H 6L8 (519-836-4550) Organizes activities for the gay and lesbian community and offers information and counselling via the phone line.

Hamilton
Gayline Hamilton, (416-523-7055) Wed. to Sun. 7-11 p.m. Provides peer counselling and information about other Hamilton groups, including the *Gay Women's Collective* which meets every 2nd Monday. P.O. Box 44, Stn. B, L8L 7T5

Gay Community Centre, #207 - 41 King William St. (416-523-7055)

Kitchener/Waterloo
Lesbian Organization of Kitchener (LOOK), P.O. Box 2422, Stn. B, Kitchener N2H 6M3 (519-744-4863). They produce the radio show *Leaping Lesbians* and have a womyn's coffeehouse the 1st Thurs. of the month.

London
Gayline, (519-433-3551) Mon. and Thurs. 7-10:00 p.m. for information and peer counselling; a recorded message at other times.

Mississauga/Brampton
Gayline West, (416-453-GGCO) They provide peer counselling.

Niagara Region
Gayline, (416-354-3173)

North Bay
Gay Fellowship of North Bay, P.O. Box 665, Callendar P0H 1H0 For gay men and lesbians.

Ottawa/Hull
Gays of Ottawa/Gaies de l'Outaouais, 175 Lisgar St. and P.O. Box 2919, Stn. D, K1P 5W9 The *GO Centre* is open weeknights 7:30-10:30 p.m. *GO* also operates a *Gayline* (613-238-1717) for referrals, information and peer counselling, a *Gay Youth/Jeunesse Gai(e) Drop-In* Wed. 8:00 p.m. and a *Lesbian Drop-In* Thurs. 8:00 p.m.

Women's Centre/Centre des femmes, Rm. 211-D, University Centre, 85 Hastey (613-231-6853)

Peterborough
Gays and Lesbians of Trent and Peterborough, 262 Rubidge St., K9J 3P2 (705-742-6229) Drop-in and phone line Tues to Thurs. 7:30-10:30 p.m.

Thunder Bay
Gays of Thunder Bay, P.O. Box 2155, P7B 5E8 (807-345-8011) Phone line Wed. and Fri. 7:30-9:30 p.m.; recorded message at other times.

Northern Women's Centre, 316 Bay St., P7B 1S1 (807-345-7802)

Toronto
Lesbian Phoneline (416-960-3249) Tues. 7:30-10:30; recorded message at other times.

Lesbian and Gay Youth Toronto, 730 Bathurst St., M5S 2R4 They have a phone line (416-533-2867) Mon., Wed. Fri. and Sat. 7-10:30 p.m.

Gaycare Toronto, 519 Church St. They have a drop-in Thurs. 7-10:00 p.m., free counselling and a phone line (416-243-5494) 7-11:00 p.m. every night.

530-GAYS A recorded message for young lesbians and gays.

Windsor
Gay/Lesbian Information Line (519-973-4951) P.O. Box 7002, Sandwich Postal Stn., M9C 3Y6

Québec

Association pour les droits des gais et lesbiennes du Québec (ADGLQ) 263 est, rue St.-Catherine (514-843-8671)

Association gaie de l'ouest Québecois (AGOQ) C.P. 1215, Succ. B, Hull J8X 3X7 (819-778-1737)

Hull-Ottawa
Telegai (613-238-1717)

Montréal
Lesbiennes à l'écoute (514-843-5661) Mercredi, jeudi, vendredi et samedi de 19h à 23h.

Gayline (514-931-5330) Thurs. and Sat. 7-11:00 p.m., for women.

Gay Info., (514-932-2395) Le jeudi et samedi de 19h à 22h30.

Centre d'information et de reference des femmes, 3585, St.-urbain, H2X 2N6 (514-842-4780)

Québec
Centre homophile d'aide et de libération (CHAL) 175, prince-Edouard, G3R 4M8 (418-623-4997)

Témiscouata
Gay Phoneline (207-498-6556)

New Brunswick

Northern Lambda Nord, P.O. Box 990, Caribou, Maine 04736 (207-498-6556)   This group serves both western New Brunswick and northern Maine.

Fredericton
Fredericton Lesbians and Gays, P.O. Box 1556, Stn. A, E3B 5G2 (506-457-2156)

Moncton
Gaies et lesbiennes de Moncton, C.P. 7102, Riverview

St. John
Lesbian and Gay Organization - Saint John (LAGO-SJ), P.O. Box 6494, Stn. A E2L 4R9

Nova Scotia

Halifax
Gayline, (902-429-6969)   Thurs. to Sat. 7-10:00 p.m. for counselling, information and referrals. A project of *Gay Alliance for Equality,* P.O. Box 3611, Halifax South Stn. B3J 3K6

Lesbian Drop-In, 1225 Barrington St. (902-429-4063)   Every 2nd and 4th Friday of the month. Music, relaxation, conversation.

Newfoundland

Gay Association of Newfoundland, P.O. Box 1364, Stn. C, St. John's Nfld. A1L 5N5   They provide a range of support for gay people in Newfoundland: counselling, dances, discussion groups and a newsletter.

Feminist Groups

Feminist groups are often a source of support for lesbians. There are hundreds of groups, and many different ways of finding them: the phone book, social service agencies, community centres, library notice boards, women's and progressive bookstores, etc.

The federal government publishes a list of women's groups — including some lesbian groups — in Canada and Québec. The groups are listed by region; you can have your group included by sending in the information. Copies can be ordered from:

Listing of Women's Groups, Women's Programme, Secretary of State, Ottawa Ont. K1A 0M5

United States

Publications

The following are lesbian or feminist or lesbian feminist newspapers and journals from the United States. Without a doubt, this is an incomplete list: our publications come and go at such a marvellous rate.

A couple of annual directories of women's publications and other media can be found in the *Resources* of *The Media* section. Also, *Our Right to Love* offers a comprehensive list of lesbian and gay rags.

Azalea: Magazine by Third World Lesbians, P.O. Box 200, Cooper Stn., New York NY 10276   Literary, lesbians of colour.

Big Mama Rag, 1724 Gaylord St., Denver CO 80206   A feminist newsjournal with local, U.S. and international coverage. Very thorough, lots of material of interest to lesbian feminists.

Common Lives, Lesbian Lives, P.O. Box 1553, Iowa City IA 52244   Writings by lesbians.

Conditions, P.O. Box 56, Van Brunt Stn., New York NY 11215   Literary, with an emphasis on lesbian work.

Feminary, P.O. Box 954, Chapel Hill NC 27514   "A feminist journal of the south" with a lesbian feminist perspective.

Focus, 1151 Massachusetts Ave., Cambridge MA 02138   A literary journal for lesbians; it's been around a long time.

Heresies, P.O. Box 766, Canal St. Stn., New York NY 10013   "A feminist publication on art and politics."

Lesbian Connection, P.O. Box 811, East Lansing MI 48823   "A national newsletter full of information about lesbian events and issues, addresses of Contact Dykes throughout the U.S. and Canada.

Lesbian Contradiction, 1007 N. 47th, Seattle WA 98103   "A journal of irreverent feminism."

The Lesbian Insider/Insighter/Inciter, P.O. Box 7038, Powderhorn Stn., Minneapolis MN 55407   Offers good coverage of lesbian issues and culture.

Lesbian Herstory Archives Newsletter, P.O. Box 1258, New York NY 10116   Carries bibliographies, research queries, new discoveries.

Lesbian Voices, P.O. Box 2066, San Jose CA 95109   Literary journal.

Off Our Backs, #212 - 1841 Columbia Rd. NW, Washington D.C. 20009   Comprehensive feminist monthly concerned with local, U.S. and international news, with coverage of lesbian issues.

Sinister Wisdom, P.O. Box 660, Amherst MA 01004   "A lesbian/feminist journal of art, language and politics."

SisterSource, P.O. Box 14070, Chicago IL 60614   A lesbian feminist newspaper of the midwest.

The Wishing Well, P.O. Box 117, Novato CA 94948   "National magazine featuring self-descriptions (by code numbers) of gay women wishing to safely write/meet one another." Longstanding and reputable.

Publishers

The following are lesbian, feminist and/or gay publishers in the United States. They will send catalogues on request and do mail orders.

Naiad Press, P.O. Box 10543, Tallahassee FL 32302   Major publisher of lesbian works: fiction, bibliographies, non-fiction, reprints.

Kitchen Table: Women of Color Press, P.O. Box 2753, New York NY 10185   Works by and about women of colour.

Persephone Press...unfortunately no longer exists. Some of their titles are being reprinted or distributed by other publishers. Consult your local bookstore.

Alyson Publications, P.O. Box 2783, Boston MA 02208 Publishes work for lesbians and gay men.

Spinsters, Ink, #8 - 233 Dolores St., San Francisco CA 94103 Fiction and non-fiction with a feminist perspective, often lesbian.

Seal Press, 312 S. Washington, Seattle WA 98104   A feminist publisher of fiction and non-fiction.

The Crossing Press, Trumansburg, New York 14886

The Feminist Press, Box 334, Old Westbury NY 11568 Publishes works for women and children, often of an educational nature. Not specifically lesbian.

Womyn's Braille Press, P.O. Box 8475, Minneapolis MN 55408 They produce feminist and lesbian books and periodicals on tape.

Cleis Press, P.O. Box 8933, Pittsburgh PA 15221   A feminist/lesbian publishing company.

Frog in the Well Press, 430 Oakdale Rd., East Palo Alto CA 94303   Lesbian works, fiction and non-fiction.

Metis Press, P.O. Box 25187, Chicago IL 60625   Works for lesbian feminist readers and their children.

Diaspora Distribution, P.O. Box 272, Langlois OR 97450 Distributes self-published works by lesbians.

Records and Tapes

The following do retail and mail-order distribution of lesbian and feminist musicians' recordings; *Ladyslipper,* in particular, distributes the music of hundreds of women. Write to them for catalogues.

Ladyslipper, #82 FP, P.O. Box 3124, Durham NC 27705

Olivia Records, 4400 Market St., Oakland CA 94608

Redwood Records, 476 MacArthur Blvd., Oakland CA 94609

Radical Rose Recordings, P.O. Box 8122, Minneapolis MN 55408

Film, Video and Slide Shows

The following produce and/or distribute audio-visual materials of interest to lesbians and feminists. See also *Resources* in *The Media.*

Iris Films, P.O. Box 5353, Berkeley CA 94705

Multi-Media Resource Center, 1525 Franklin St., San Francisco CA 94109

Serious Business Company, 1145 Mandana Blvd., Oakland CA 94610

Women Make Movies Film Library, 257 W. 19th St., New York NY 10011

Women's Interart Center, 549 W. 52nd St., New York NY 10019

Women's Educational Media, 47 Cherry St. Somerville MA 02144

Jump Cut: A Review of Contemporary Cinema 24/25 (Mar. 1981)   This issue carried a special section on lesbians and film and an extensive list of producers and distributors. Available from P.O. Box 865, Berkeley CA 94701

Contact Groups

There are hundreds and hundreds of lesbian and gay organizations in the United States — we're not even going to try to list them.

Feminist, lesbian and gay newspapers usually carry current information about groups, events and projects, so getting a copy of your local/regional publication is a good starting point. The following are some other useful resources.

The National Gay Task Force, 80 5th Ave., New York, NY 10011   They can be contacted directly for lists of groups in specific regions.

Our Right to Love: A Lesbian Resource Book, ed. by Ginny Vida (Englewood Cliffs: Prentice-Hall, 1978)   This book has an excellent list of groups. Although somewhat out-of-date by now, it is so comprehensive that you will certainly find some group to get in touch with!

Gayellow Pages, Renaissance House, P.O. Box 292, Village Stn., New York 10014   Lists of gay and lesbian resources in the U.S. and some international.

International

The following are feminist publishers in England:

Sheba Feminist Publishers, 488 Kingsland Rd., London E8

Virago Press, 41 William 1V St., London WC2

The Women's Press, 124 Shoreditch High St., London E1 6JE

The following are sources of information about lesbian groups, publications and activities throughout the world:

International Lesbian Information Secretariat, NVIH-COC, Frederiksplein 14, 1017 XM, Amsterdam, Netherlands   Telephone: 234596/231192

International Lesbian Information Service, The Cheap Stencil Service, PL45, 00251, Helsinki, 25, Finland   This group puts out a newsletter.

International Gay Association, Secretariat c/o *CHLR,* Box 931 Dublin 4, Ireland

Connections, Issue 3: Global Lesbianism, 4228 Telegraph Ave., Oakland, CA 94609   Contains lists of groups, publications and contacts for lesbians in many third world countries.

LISTEN (Lesbian International Satellite Tribadic Energy Network), #15 - 192 Spring St., New York NY 10012   Their intention is to create an international lesbian communication and solidarity network.

PRESS GANG is a feminist organization consisting of a publishing collective and a printing collective. Our books and posters may be ordered directly from: Press Gang Publishers, 603 Powell St., Vancouver B.C. V6A 1H2

Daughters of Copper Woman, by Anne Cameron. Stories of the spiritual and social power of the native women of Vancouver Island.   *$7.95 paper*

Falling From Grace, by Elly Van de Walle. Poems about the experience of breast cancer and mastectomy.   *$5.95 paper.*

An Account to Settle: The Story of the United Bank Workers (SORWUC), by Jackie Ainsworth et al. In which bank workers organize a union in the banks.   *$3.25 paper.*

The Anti-Psychiatry Bibliography and Resource Guide, by K. Portland Frank. Examines the oppression of people by the psychiatric establishment.   *$4.50 paper, $12.50 cloth.*

Jody Said, by Beth Jankola. A collection of poems.   *$2.95 paper.*

Women's Labour History in British Columbia: A Bibliography 1930-48, by Sara Diamond. *$5.00 paper.*

For Children:

The Day the Fairies Went on Strike, by Linda Briskin and Maureen FitzGerald, illus. by Barbara Eidlitz.   *$4.95 paper.*

Muktu: The Backward Muskox, by Heather Kellerhals-Stewart, illus. by Karen Muntean, *$2.95 paper.*